"Unputdownable! Regina Scott has outdone herself with this, the third of the American Wonders stories. With characters as multifaceted as a diamond, vivid descriptions of western Washington's majestic scenery, and a plot with more twists and turns than the path up Mount Rainier, *A View Most Glorious* is historical romance at its best. I highly recommend it."

Amanda Cabot, bestselling author of *Dreams Rekindled*

"*A View Most Glorious* is, indeed, glorious! I thoroughly enjoyed Regina Scott's well-researched story that takes you into the troubled city of Tacoma, Washington. It's 1893, and spunky suffragette Coraline must climb a mountain to strike a blow for suffrage and help gain women the right to vote. But suffrage isn't the only reason to climb an imposing Mount Rainier. What awaits her if she fails is far more treacherous. Desperate to succeed, she must put her hope in a man who appears as rugged and wild as the mountain she's to climb. But her guide Nathan Hardee is so much more . . . This adventure-filled tale with its wonderful characters will have you holding your breath as Coraline faces more opposition than what the mountain can throw at her. And with so much at stake, she can't afford to lose."

Kit Morgan, *USA Today* bestselling author

A VIEW
MOST GLORIOUS

Books by Regina Scott

AMERICAN WONDERS COLLECTION #3

A VIEW MOST GLORIOUS

{{ }}

REGINA SCOTT

Revell

a division of Baker Publishing Group
Grand Rapids, Michigan

© 2021 by Regina Lundgren

Published by Revell
a division of Baker Publishing Group
PO Box 6287, Grand Rapids, MI 49516-6287
www.revellbooks.com

Printed in the United States of America

Library of Congress Cataloging-in-Publication Data
Names: Scott, Regina, 1959– author.
Title: A view most glorious / Regina Scott.
Description: Grand Rapids, Michigan : Revell, a division of Baker Publishing
    Group, [2021] | Series: American wonders collection ; #3
Identifiers: LCCN 2021006658 | ISBN 9780800736415 (paperback) | ISBN
    9780800740542 (casebound) | ISBN 9781493431793 (ebook)
Subjects: GSAFD: Love stories. | Historical fiction.
Classification: LCC PS3619.C683 V54 2021 | DDC 813/.6—dc23
LC record available at https://lccn.loc.gov/2021006658

Baker Publishing Group publications use paper produced from sustainable forestry practices and post-consumer waste whenever possible.

21   22   23   24   25   26   27   7   6   5   4   3   2   1

To my team—Emily, Rachel, Kristin M, Kristin K, Brianne, and Karen—thank you for all you did to see this book through. To Glen Storbeck, Pierce County Library historical research librarian extraordinaire, for getting excited about my urgent queries and finding me answers. To my father, who first shared with me the wonders of God's creation. And to our heavenly Father, who created all the views most glorious for his children to enjoy.

1

She was causing a stir.

Wouldn't be the first time. Coraline Baxter was used to heads turning, eyes widening when she walked in a room. It happened at the society balls her mother insisted she attend, where she was expected to be the best dressed, the most polished. It had happened at the Puget Sound University, where she had been one of a few women. It happened when she arrived at the bank, where she was the only female accountant.

So it shouldn't surprise her that it was happening at Shem's Dockside Saloon, which likely hadn't seen many women and certainly not ladies accompanied by a father.

Stepfather, something corrected her. Beside her, Stephen Winston blinked blue eyes wreathed in wrinkles he'd earned by peering at ledgers all day. His gloved hand gripped the gold head of his ebony walking stick as he glanced around the dimly lit eatery. The occupants likely hadn't seen many gentlemen of his caliber either. His tailored coat, satin-striped

9

waistcoat, and gold watch hanging by a thick chain proclaimed him a man of means.

Means seemed hard to come by for most of the men in the room. The rough plank floors, open beams, and unplastered walls spoke of toil, hardship, and the camaraderie of men with pride in their own worth. Still, it was little more than a shanty perched over Puget Sound, and it was hard to smell the brine over the smoke in the air.

She tried not to wrinkle her nose. Winston didn't bother to hide his dislike. His lips were slightly curled under his trim white mustache. And he was staring.

They were staring back.

Dozens of them. Each cap or hat covered hair that peeked out below as if it were none too sure of its surroundings. Wool sweaters were rolled up at the sleeves to display arms that had labored for long hours. Gazes sized her up, showed interest or suspicion. Her mother had taught her to dress for the part she would play in any situation, but she hadn't realized the gray taffeta overcoat that was cut to show the lace at her throat and sleeves would look so out of place here. Then again, she'd never visited a saloon before and had no plans to repeat the experience.

Conversation dwindled, stopped. Someone shoved back a chair with a screech of wood on wood.

"Do you see him?" Cora hissed.

Winston started to shake his head no, then stiffened. "There. That table near the wall. That may be young Nathan."

Nathan Hardee was no longer the youth her stepfather had remembered. That much was clear. He was facing away from them. Shoulders in a dark wool coat stretched wider than the back of the wood chair on which he sat. Lamplight picked out gold in the wavy brown hair that spilled nearly to those shoulders. Winston hurried forward, and she followed, careful to keep any part of her coat from touching the sawdust-covered floor, scarred tables, or a patron. Still they watched her.

Let them look. She had more important things to concern her.

An older man about her stepfather's age and with hair as white rose from the table as they approached. He was a little taller than Winston, but narrower, and his face was carved in lines and hollows, as if life had worn him thin.

"Mr. Winston?" he asked, brown eyes darting from her stepfather to her and back again.

"Yes," Winston acknowledged. "You must be Waldo Vance."

Around them, voices rose, glasses clinked. One of the gang had recognized them. They were accepted.

For now.

Vance nodded to her stepfather. "That's right. This is Nathan Hardee. I believe you knew his father."

Hardee showed not the least welcome as he swiveled in his chair just enough to meet her stepfather's gaze. The son of a prominent family, Winston had said. She'd met dozens over the years. He didn't resemble any of them.

Society men strived for the same golden tan on their skin, but his was likely more the result of his work guiding people into the wilderness than the time he'd spent at lawn tennis. Society men often wore beards and mustaches, some quite prominent, but his was just thick enough to hide behind. Society men had the same assessing look, but few had so dark a green to their eyes, like the cool shadows of a forest. Society men dressed in plaid coats during the day or deepest black at night, not brown wool and poorly spun cotton. When she approached, society men bowed and flattered. He had to notice her standing at Winston's side, yet he didn't rise as propriety demanded.

"Afraid you've wasted your time," he said in a deep voice that reverberated inside her. "I'm not looking to act as a guide."

He hadn't even given her a chance to explain or make an offer. Frustration pushed the words out of her mouth.

"A shame. We pay handsomely, and there's not many who can say that right now."

His gaze drifted over her. "I hear you can't pay either."

Winston's ivory cheeks flushed crimson. "Now, see here," he blustered. "You have no call to impugn my reputation. I am the director of the Puget Sound Bank of Commerce. We may have been overly generous in these trying times, but we are as secure as the mountain itself."

"A mountain I won't help you climb," Hardee said, turning to face the wall again as if that would be enough to dismiss them.

There had to be something she could say to persuade him. Money didn't seem to matter—oddly enough. Neither did prestige. And forget the need to posture and prove himself a gentleman. Her cause probably wouldn't sway him either. Too few men in the city could be bothered to support women's suffrage. How could she get through to a man who apparently needed nothing?

"This is not what we were promised," her stepfather fumed. "I wrote you specifically, Mr. Vance. I understood you had the authority to arrange matters."

Vance shrugged. "You can lead a horse to water . . ."

"But apparently you can't make him drink," Cora concluded. "Unless it's the questionable drink of this fine establishment." She turned to her stepfather. "We might as well go. We have no need to link ourselves with wastrels."

Hardee rose. Goodness, how he rose. He dwarfed her stepfather and Vance. He likely dwarfed every man in the room. The top of her head reached only to the broad bone of his chest.

"Just because I won't do your bidding," he said, gazing down at her, "doesn't make me a wastrel."

"But it does make you a fool," Cora said, grasping any opening he would give her. "Lumber barons are digging ditches to keep a roof over their heads; shipping heiresses are cleaning toilets to make ends meet. We're offering good money, just to guide us up Mount Rainier."

"Why," he asked, eyes narrowing, "would a woman like you want to climb Mount Rainier? I won't risk my life on a whim."

She raised her chin and met his assessing stare with one of her own. Fear and anger and frustration fought for supremacy. A whim, he called it. Striking a blow for suffrage, returning the right to vote to the women of Washington State—a whim. Refusing the advances of a tyrant—a whim. Securing her future, making herself beholden to no man—a whim.

"I don't need to justify my reasons to anyone," she told him. "I'm offering generous pay for your skills. We need a guide to see me safely to the summit and back to Longmire's Medical Springs. Are you that man?"

He didn't answer, gaze on hers as if he could see inside her for the truth. She'd been in society too long not to know how to hide her secrets. If sweet looks didn't suffice, bravado generally did.

"He is," the older man insisted, head bobbing. "No one knows the mountain better than Nathan Hardee. He's guided business leaders and government agents up that mountain. You couldn't be in better hands."

As if he disagreed, Hardee flexed the fingers of his large hands, hands business leaders and government agents trusted. Did that mean she could trust them? Did that mean she could trust him?

He didn't trust her.

"Not interested," he said, and he returned to his seat once more.

-------- H—H --------

He couldn't state it more baldly. He wasn't taking a spoiled, high-society sweetheart into the wild. He still couldn't believe Waldo had suggested it.

"Just hear them out," his mentor had urged as they'd ridden into Tacoma with the pack mules for supplies. "This is a good opportunity. Enough to allow us to buy lumber and nails to add another room before winter."

The amount of money Stephen Winston had offered was indeed a pretty price, if it was real. The Panic had robbed families of their homes, men and women of their dignity. The financial turmoil could well force him and Waldo back into the society Nathan abhorred if he didn't accept work.

But not this work. It smelled of nonsense. How did he know she wouldn't cry complaint the moment things became difficult—and they would become difficult—then refuse to pay him? He'd had one or two society members attempt to treat him that way. They thought he was still one of them. What did he need with money?

He hadn't been one of them for years, and God willing, he would never be one of them again.

Besides, how did he know the banker and his daughter even had money to pay? The fellow wasn't the only one in Tacoma with the threat of ruin hanging over his head.

Men reacted badly to ruin. Look at his father. Look at himself.

The beauty beside him tugged at her father's sleeve. "Come, Winston. We are wasting our time. Surely we can do better."

Waldo glanced at him and jerked his head toward the pair. That was Nathan's cue to placate, apologize. Most men probably begged her pardon when they refused her. And they likely refused her rarely. That pale hair piled up on the top of her head with curls teasing her fair cheeks. Those big blue eyes. The figure outlined in the wasp-waist coat. She probably crooked her finger and they all came running.

Not him. He'd left behind society's rules for the glory of God's creation. Playing proper hadn't changed the fact that his father was gone, along with the bulk of the fortune he'd amassed selling land in the burgeoning city. Nathan knew what it meant to fall from grace.

"Go out to the carriage, dearest," the banker told her. "I have a few words I'd like to say to Mr. Hardee, and I'd prefer not to say them in front of a lady."

Her brows went up, as if she were surprised by his forcefulness, but she nodded. The banker watched her traipse out of the saloon.

So did every other man in the room.

"Save your breath," Nathan told the fellow. "Nothing you say will change my mind."

All the bluster went out of him, and he plopped down in

the chair Waldo had vacated. Waldo pulled up another to join them.

"Forgive the subterfuge, Mr. Hardee," Winston said, face sagging as if he had wearied himself with all the posturing. "What I said to Coraline is only true. While I have no intention of remonstrating, I simply didn't want her to hear me beg."

Again Waldo glanced Nathan's way. Nathan ignored him to focus on the banker. "Why would a man like you need to beg? Is there something more at stake in this climb?"

"Entirely too much," he admitted with a sigh. "Coraline is a member of the Tacoma Women's Suffrage Association. The ladies have asked her to climb the mountain to raise awareness and support of their cause."

Nathan snorted. "There are far safer ways to gather support and other women more experienced at climbing."

"True," Winston allowed. "I gather the idea was that if Coraline could manage it, then any woman could manage it."

"And if any woman can climb the mountain, then why not give them the vote?" Waldo concluded. "Makes sense to me."

"I'm all for every person having the vote," Nathan told them both. "I'm still not convinced Miss Winston must climb the mountain."

"Miss Baxter," the banker corrected him. "I am Coraline's second stepfather."

So her mother was on her third husband? That was a wretched thing to have in common. Nathan's mother had been through two other men since his father had died as well.

"Miss Baxter, then," Nathan said. "Climbing Mount Rainier is a grueling feat. I won't subject an untried climber to it."

"But you must." He leaned closer, blue eyes imploring.

"I may not have been there at Coraline's birth, but I am her father in every sense of the word, and I want her to be happy. My wife believes the only way for a woman to be happy is to marry well. If Coraline doesn't reach the summit, she has promised her mother she will return and marry the man of her mother's choosing." He lay his hand on Nathan's arm. "Please, my boy, help me save my daughter from an unhappy future."

He could see the fellow's point. The men Nathan's mother had married hadn't made her particularly happy, from what he'd heard. Other women in society seemed more resigned than pleased with their marriages. Good for Miss Baxter for trying to break the mold.

But to risk her life?

He pulled back his arm. "I'll think on it."

The banker beamed. "That's all I can ask. I will hope for good news soon." He rose, nodded to Waldo, and headed for the door.

Nathan raised his empty glass to order another sarsaparilla.

"Stuff and nonsense," Waldo spat out.

"I agree," Nathan said.

Waldo scowled at him. "I was talking about you."

"I warned you not to get your hopes up," Nathan reminded him. "It's hard enough climbing the mountain with an experienced group of hikers. She wouldn't last past Longmire's."

"Seems to me she has more grit than that," Waldo grumbled as the barkeep brought them two more of the earthy drinks. He nodded to the man. "Sorry for the bother, Shem. You got any stew on?"

"Soup only," Shem Holland answered, setting a heavy

glass down with a grimace nearly swallowed by his thick brown beard. "Vegetable."

"We'll take two bowls," Nathan said.

Shem hitched up trousers that bagged at his waist. "You mind if I see the money first? Whole lot of folks mistake me for the poor farm these days."

Nathan pulled out a dollar and tossed it on the table. The metal gleamed on the dark wood. Shem's eyes gleamed nearly as brightly.

"Coming right up," he said, scooping the coin into the palm of his hand.

"Be careful showing silver like that," Waldo fussed as the proprietor hurried away. "Some men would do most anything for money these days." He glanced left and right before muttering, "Except climb Mount Rainier."

"It's a fool's errand," Nathan insisted, leaning back in his chair.

"Says you. You took her in dislike afore she ever opened her mouth. I saw it."

Nathan shrugged. "I've met enough like her."

Waldo shook his head. "No, you ain't. I'll have you know that little girl graduated from the Puget Sound University, one of the first women to do it."

That was impressive. He knew how rigorous college studies could be. As the son of a prominent businessman, he'd graduated from the State University in Seattle. But that had been eight long years ago. Life had changed. He'd changed.

"She rides too," Waldo continued, as if warming to his theme. "Real good, I hear. And she's a gem at lawn tennis."

Nathan eyed him. "Do you even know what lawn tennis is?"

Waldo pouted. "No, but it sounded hard."

"Miss Baxter is obviously a paragon," Nathan said. "But that doesn't mean I have to take her up the mountain."

Shem hustled back with a tray, setting it down in front of them with a flourish. The battered bottom of the tin bowl was evident through the clear liquid, and Nathan could count the pieces of carrot and celery clinging desperately to the sides. The soup was accompanied by two thin slices of bread.

"How about some butter?" Waldo asked as Shem straightened.

"'Fraid not," he said. "Had to sell the cow."

"Maybe you should have cooked the cow," Waldo said, poking his spoon at the vegetables.

"I'm just doing what I can to stay open," Shem said.

Waldo pointed his spoon at the barkeep. "You saw Miss Baxter. You think she can climb a mountain?"

Shem grinned. "She's got pluck. Rumor has it even Cash Kincaid is sniffing at her heels, but she'll have none of it."

"Good for her," Waldo cheered.

She had sense and courage, then. Kincaid was ruthless, his tactics just short of illegal. If he was the man her mother intended for Miss Baxter, Nathan couldn't think of a better fellow to receive a setdown. He only wished he could be the one to give it to him.

He pushed back his chair. "Finish my soup, Waldo. I have something I need to do."

Waldo frowned. "Now? I thought we weren't starting home until tomorrow. We have to pick up the supplies."

"We may have to delay a day or two," Nathan told him. "It all depends on how long it takes Miss Baxter to feel ready to climb a mountain."

2

Though she was curious about what her kindhearted step-father had said to Mr. Hardee, Cora decided not to press Winston as he joined her in the carriage.

"He still refused, I take it," she said instead.

"For the moment," Winston said, settling in his seat across from her.

"Alternatives?" she asked as the carriage started for home. Out on the gray waters of Commencement Bay, a white-sided steamship blew a blast as it headed for South America or Asia.

Winston shifted on the brown, padded leather bench, mouth tight below his mustache. "A few—a very few, mind you—other guides were recommended to me, but I am uncertain of their characters, particularly when it comes to escorting the fairer sex under such circumstances."

The fairer sex. It wouldn't be the first time someone had tried to minimize her capabilities because she was female. This idea that women were somehow less was what prevented them from winning the vote as well.

"I don't need a guide to coddle me," she informed him as the carriage turned onto Tenth Street, away from the warehouses and into the multistoried buildings that made up the heart of the city. "Just one who knows his way around the mountain."

Winston glanced out the window to where the snowcapped peak dominated the skyline to the southeast. So close, as if she could walk to the base in no more than an hour when in truth it was sixty-some miles away by wagon road and trail.

"Are you certain this is prudent, dearest?" he murmured, brow puckering. "Nathan seems certain you could be harmed. Perhaps some other lady more experienced could climb."

She'd made the same argument when her friend Mimi Carruthers and the other members of the Tacoma Women's Suffrage Association had asked her to consider the matter. It was a tremendous honor. She gave Winston the answer they'd given her.

"Miss Fuller has already climbed it once. Doing so again would hardly make as much impact as if a lady of some social standing did it for the first time."

"Judge Wickersham's wife, then," Winston said. "No one could assail her standing in society or her success at climbing."

"Mrs. Wickersham is not a great supporter of our efforts," Cora reminded him. "Like those in the Seattle Women's Suffrage Association, she feels we are best served by focusing on domesticity rather than demonstration."

He looked at her hopefully. Like her mother, Winston couldn't accustom himself to the fact that she wasn't afraid to demonstrate.

"It must be me," Cora told him. "And you heard Mother. It's climb or marry. I prefer to climb."

Winston sighed. "I simply cannot like the risk."

Cora smiled at him. "Funny. You're usually the one to encourage me to take risks with the bank's money."

He returned her smile. "And I have acknowledged that you have a better eye for sizing up proposals than I ever had. But this is something else entirely." His gloved hands folded over each other on the head of his walking stick. "It was one thing for you to attend college and enter the workforce. The right people will appreciate and commend you for it. This venture could well cost you your life."

A chill went through her, even though the day was warming. "Surely not. Many people have attempted the summit in recent years. Mr. Van Trump has gone five times."

"And more have turned back from weather, exhaustion, or the inability to find a safe route," Winston insisted. "I want better for you."

"So do I," Cora promised him as the carriage turned onto C Street and paralleled the trolley tracks. "But we both know Mother has set her sights on Mr. Kincaid. Find me a guide."

He nodded. "I'll see what I can do, but I will hope young Nathan changes his mind. At least he was one of us."

He began to sound like her mother. Cora arched her brows. "I saw very little evidence that Mr. Hardee ever spent time in good society."

"His conversation certainly didn't betray the fact," Winston allowed, "and his manners were not what I had expected, but make no mistake. The name Hardee commanded a great deal of respect in the area when you were a girl. His late father amassed a fortune selling real estate when the Northern Pacific first arrived."

Cora made a face. "And his son prefers to live like a fur trapper in the wilderness?"

"It was a sudden change in circumstance." Winston tugged

at his red-speckled tie as if the blue silk had tightened around his neck. "The poor fellow was found dead at his desk. Gunshot wound to the temple."

Cora shuddered. "How awful. What of his mother?"

"She soon remarried. You recall Mrs. Quinton?"

"She's Mr. Hardee's mother?" The interconnections in the small community still surprised her on occasion. Mrs. Quinton was a social hostess as well regarded as Cora's mother. Hardee had fallen indeed if he was no longer associated with her. Was it a willful choice or something in his character that made him unwelcome in society? Perhaps it was a good thing they must seek another guide.

The carriage rumbled to a stop under the porte cochère at the side of the house, and Winston climbed out to assist her in alighting. She couldn't help glancing up at the fine home her stepfather had built for her mother. Tall fluted columns held up the overhanging roof of the carriageway, while pedimented windows looked out on the street and gardens behind. The white siding, crenelated white trim, and fan window over the door and into the servants' quarters at the top of the house added an elegance few could achieve. It was her mother's pride and joy.

The wood-paneled side entryway opened to grand stairs down to the ballroom below and a corridor to the rest of the house. Lily, the ladies' maid she shared with her mother, came to take her coat even as Winston went ahead of her toward his study at the back of the house.

"Where is my mother at the moment?" Cora asked the little dark-haired maid as they continued to the main entry hall, paneled in white with tall ceilings.

"In the drawing room, miss," Lily answered, draping the

fabric over her lean arm. "Answering invitations that arrived this morning."

Good. Her mother generally received a number of invitations a day—to charity events, to balls, to evenings at the theatre. Too often they included requests for Cora's company. Tonight, in fact, they were scheduled to attend a concert at the Tacoma Theatre. If her mother was occupied answering the requests, Cora had every opportunity to escape to her room to determine her next steps if Winston could not find them a guide. Perhaps Mimi knew someone.

But Cora had only set her foot on the polished oak stair when her mother's call came.

"Coraline? Will you attend me, please?"

The last word was used only for propriety's sake. There was no question Cora would obey the summons. Pasting on a smile, she stepped down and went to join her mother.

The family parlor was everything a lady of fashion could want, from the creamy walls covered in gilt-framed landscapes to the marble-tiled hearth to the emerald velvet horsehair sofa and matching chairs. The impeccable furnishings were merely more evidence as to why the woman now known as Mrs. Stephen Winston was highly regarded among those in society, or at least such society as the City of Destiny offered.

City of Destiny. What a nickname to bequeath the pioneer metropolis of fifty-two thousand people. But the Northern Pacific Railroad loved slogans. The catchy phrases fit so well on the marketing tracts they distributed by the thousands and the advertisements they placed in every major newspaper coast to coast, encouraging people to visit, via rail, of course.

Would anyone heed them in the midst of the Panic?

She shook off the dark cloud that threatened and approached her mother, who was seated at the walnut secretary near the eastern window. The frilly white curtains behind her framed her blond majesty. She offered Cora a polite smile that did not quite reach her pale blue eyes as she slipped her pen into the gilded holder.

"Judge Wickersham's wife requested our assistance in gathering blankets and clothing for the poor farm. It seems they've been overrun. I thought we'd ask Mrs. Carruthers and Mimi to join us."

Thirty years and thousands of miles could not erase the sophisticated tone that had helped make her mother the toast of Philadelphia. But at least this was one request Cora had no trouble accepting. "Certainly, Mother. When I return from the mountain."

Her mother's pleasant look did not waver in the slightest. "Then you were able to come to an agreement with this Mr. Hardee."

"He declined to be employed," Cora said, wandering closer to the hearth, bare now before autumn arrived. "But Winston assures me we have options."

Her mother smoothed her silvery gray silk skirts, setting the tassels along the hem to fluttering. "Of course you have options. Any number of gentlemen would be delighted for you to show the least interest. Mr. Kincaid is particularly attentive."

Cora grimaced at the familiar refrain. "I have no need of a husband, Mother. I am gainfully employed."

For a brief moment, her mother's face tightened, making her look far older than the few gray hairs in that elegant blond coiffure would attest. "You will be glad for a clever husband like Mr. Kincaid if these financial difficulties continue. I don't know where we'd be now if not for dear Mr. Winston."

That was true enough. Cora barely remembered her father, who had abandoned them when she was six, though she could not forget the rumors others had been certain her mother needed to know. Run off with the parlor maid and a sizable amount of his employer's money, it was whispered. At least her mother had been notified of his death a year later. Too bad her choice of second husband had been worse. Cora still remembered the stench of alcohol when he'd leaned too close. After her father and her first stepfather had died, she and her mother had been evicted from their home. They had only survived because of her mother's ability to secure a new husband.

"Winston is a paragon," Cora agreed. "But we both know how easily marriages can go awry. I prefer to look after myself."

Her mother set the pen more securely in its filigreed holder. "At least tell me you've decided against this foolhardy attempt to climb the mountain. It isn't seemly, Coraline. I raised you to be a lady."

A lady beholden to the men around her. No, thank you. "Ladies climb mountains, Mother. Look at Miss Fuller."

Her mother lifted a delicate brow. "Miss Fuller writes well enough in her father's newspaper, but she is hardly the model I wish for my daughter. And neither are these suffragettes."

Another common argument. "Mimi is a suffragette," Cora pointed out.

"A fact her poor mother laments every time I see her. The entire cause is spurious. Women have no need to vote. We influence politics and society through our husbands." Her look softened. "With your beauty and intelligence, Coraline, you could marry a railroad executive, a senator, a governor! Think of the power you would wield then."

Cora glanced around at the marble hearth and the Oriental carpet. "I don't mind a smaller sphere, Mother, so long as it's my own."

"And you can achieve that sphere by marrying well," her mother insisted.

"Which I will achieve by using my skills and wits," Cora argued. "I don't need a man, any man, to plan my future."

A noise at the door made her turn. Darcy, the downstairs housemaid, bobbed a curtsy, her black skirts pooling. "Begging your pardon, Mrs. Winston, Miss Cora. There's a fellow here to see you about climbing the mountain."

———— {{ }} ————

Nathan cooled his heels on the doorstep of one of the nicest houses on the street. It hadn't been difficult to get directions to the banker's home, and he hadn't been surprised to find it nestled along C Street, among others of its kind, with its back looking out over the bay and the mountain beyond. They were all showy places dripping multicolored bric-a-brac and boasting ballrooms, more than one parlor, and quarters for servants. He'd spent much of his youth living in such a house. He didn't miss it.

But it felt odd not to be invited inside. Once no door had been closed to him. Men had wanted to befriend him, to do him favors. Young ladies had vied for his attentions. All that had vanished overnight when his father had died and the amount of his debt had become known.

At least now when someone attempted to strike up an

acquaintance, he could be sure it had little to do with the size of his bank account or the reputation of his parents. Though there were still a few who thought he could be used . . .

The paneled front door opened, and the brown-haired maid peeked out as if suspecting he'd run off after her initial refusal to allow him inside.

"Mr. Hardee," she said, nose up as if she objected to the very smell of him, "Miss Baxter and her mother will see you now."

He nodded and followed her into the house. Even the entry hall was grand, with tall walls and a crystal chandelier lit by electricity. The stairs to the upper regions were so polished he could almost see his reflection in them as the maid led him past to the first door on the left, stepped aside, and motioned him to enter the parlor. The room was crowded with fine furnishings, including side tables covered by lace-edged doilies and vases filled with the kinds of flowers ladies paid to have grown for them. They still paled beside the beauty standing near the white marble hearth.

"Mr. Hardee," Miss Baxter said, smile guarded. "What a surprise. May I introduce you to my mother, Mrs. Winston?"

He inclined his head to the regal beauty sitting as tall and straight as a fir in the chair beside the walnut secretary. It was clear where Miss Baxter got her looks. "Ma'am."

"Mr. Hardee." Even the two words seemed more than she wanted to give him.

"Do I take it you've changed your mind about guiding us up the mountain?" her daughter asked.

Before he could respond, her mother tutted. "You must forgive her, Mr. Hardee. My daughter tends to focus on her goals to the exclusion of all else. Would you care for refreshment? I suppose tea or lemonade would not be of interest, but I believe our groundskeeper may have some beer."

Miss Baxter said nothing, but her face turned an unbecoming shade of red.

"Lemonade would be welcome," he assured her mother.

Her mother looked to the doorway, where he realized the maid waited. She hurried off now.

"Please, won't you sit down, Mr. Hardee?" Mrs. Winston asked. "You might find the chair by the window the most comfortable for you."

The chair in question was polished wood and least likely to be stained by what she must imagine dusted his trousers.

Miss Baxter didn't argue with her mother's choice, though she seated herself on the chair's twin on the other side of the window from him.

"You didn't answer my question," she pointed out. "Are you willing to guide us up the mountain?"

"I'm considering it," Nathan said, taking a seat.

She cocked her head, and sunlight glinted on the light blond hair piled up on top. "What made you change your mind?"

He wasn't about to go into his feelings toward Cash Kincaid. "Perhaps I simply like aiding a lady in her cause."

"How very heroic of you," her mother said, though the words hardly sounded like praise.

Miss Baxter's eyes, as blue as the waters of Puget Sound and as deep, narrowed as she straightened. "Then you champion women's suffrage, Mr. Hardee?"

"I do," he admitted. "Not that my opinion is of any account."

"A good many businessmen feel differently," her mother

said. "Why else did the amendment to the state constitution fail four years ago?"

"Because those businessmen feared we'd vote to prohibit the sale of alcohol," Miss Baxter said. "Any man with any sense would see the value of having engaged citizens of both genders."

"I fear this is what you will have to listen to all the way to the mountain, Mr. Hardee," her mother said with a shake of her head. "I'm not sure the pay is worth your time."

Her mother probably thought paying meant her daughter could abuse him as she liked. He knew the game. He wasn't willing to play it. "I will earn my fee honestly, should Miss Baxter and I reach an agreement."

Miss Baxter nodded, smile hovering.

"I hope such an agreement will not be necessary," her mother put in with a finality that belied argument. "You must dissuade my daughter from this reckless course of action, sir."

Nathan leaned back in the chair, at least as far as the stiff wood would allow. "It doesn't have to be reckless. There are precautions that can be taken—the right shoes, the best equipment, a guide who knows the route and can read the mountain."

Miss Baxter's brows went up. "Read the mountain?"

"Rainier is a grand lady," he explained. "Sometimes she turns shy and hides behind a veil of clouds. Sometimes she turns melancholy and cries great tears of rain and snow. And sometimes she gets downright perturbed and hurls rocks or great chunks of a glacier at you. You have to be ever vigilant to please her."

"Like some other ladies I know," Miss Baxter said with a glance to her mother.

"How very poetic," Mrs. Winston said. "But I fear your descriptions only raise my concerns further."

"Always sorry to concern you, Mother," Miss Baxter said before turning again to Nathan. "But I'm ready to climb that mountain. When can we leave?"

Nathan held up his hand. "I share your mother's concerns, Miss Baxter. An unseasoned climber endangers not only herself but those around her. Before I guide you up on Rainier, I'll need to know that you have what it takes and that you have a good idea what you're up against."

Something sparked in her eyes, like electrical lines crossing and just as dangerous. "What do you mean, sir?"

Nathan ticked off the items on his fingers. "First, stamina. It's a long, steep climb at altitude that can challenge lungs and heart. Second, determination. You never know when things can go from bad to worse. Running away isn't always an option. And third, obedience. Once we leave the city, everything changes—what, where, and when we eat; where we rest; how far we travel and in what direction. I need to know you'll do as I say, without question. It might make the difference between living and dying, for both of us."

Her mouth worked, as if she couldn't decide which of his demands to argue with first. When she finally spoke, the words came out nearly as clipped as her mother's.

"You'll find I have plenty of stamina and determination, Mr. Hardee. But I can assure you that I have never been good at obeying. You'll simply have to accustom yourself to the fact."

3

There, she'd said it. He might as well know from the beginning that she didn't intend to jump at his least command. The only person who held such a place in her life was her mother. From love and respect.

And necessity.

He dropped his large hands. "Then I'm afraid I can't help you, Miss Baxter."

The words were like an arrow. She refused to duck or worse, beg for mercy. "Can't or won't?" she challenged. "Since I'll be paying for your time, I see no reason why I shouldn't be making the decisions."

"I fear she has only grown more headstrong over the years," her mother put in. "I have surrendered all hope of ever changing her."

If only that were true!

Darcy returned then with a silver tray holding three crystal glasses and a matching pitcher of lemonade, drops glistening on the sides. She set the tray down on the table closest to Cora's mother.

"Thank you, Darcy," she said. "I'll pour. You may go, but stay close in case Mr. Hardee requires his hat."

Very likely he hadn't left a hat with the maid when he'd arrived. Very likely he didn't own the sort of hat gentlemen wore about town, derbies or top hats. She could see him with a wool cap pulled down over that unruly brown hair or something made from an animal skin, with the tail dangling to his broad shoulders.

Her mother graciously poured the lemonade, and he rose to accept his glass and bring Cora hers. For a moment, their fingers brushed, and something more than the cool of the glass tingled up her arm. She pulled back so hastily a few drops sloshed out to land on her skirts. She shifted to hide the telltale marks.

Mr. Hardee returned to his seat and took a cautious sip, as if her mother had offered him hemlock.

"Very nice," he said after swallowing. "Thank you."

"You are very welcome," her mother said. "I am glad you and Coraline were able to agree this was a poor decision from the beginning. When will you be leaving town?"

He glanced at Cora. Waiting. Wondering. Giving her a chance to change her mind.

Few other guides, Winston had said. And none of them so well suited as this man, despite his possible estrangement from his mother. It was possible she wouldn't reach the top without him. Shouldn't she try to bridge the gap?

She set her glass on the nearest doily. "We could still reach an agreement, Mr. Hardee. I would prefer to pay someone I can trust."

"And I'd prefer to guide someone who trusts me," he replied. "But that trust means you'd have to accept my word that a situation was dangerous. If I tell you to move or hold still, I'd need to know you'd listen."

"Certainly I'd listen," Cora told him. "But if I saw a better option, I'd tell you."

He blew out a breath. "Can't you accept that I might know best? You're hiring me to guide you. You must know you can't do this alone."

Which was such a shame! "I know," she assured him. "And I will accept your recommendations whenever possible. But you must accept that I know my capabilities. I make my own choices."

"It's an unbecoming trait," her mother said. "But she can be that stubborn."

She gritted her teeth to prevent an unkind retort from slipping out.

"I can work with stubborn," he said, deep voice a rumble that echoed inside her. "Just realize, Miss Baxter, that sometimes what I tell you isn't a recommendation. I'll try to be very clear on which is which."

Cora nodded, shoulders coming down. Perhaps he could be reasoned with, after all. "Then it seems we have an accord, sir. How would you like me to prove I have stamina and determination?"

His smile lifted, and she was certain birds sang in chorus outside the window. "I think we can safely say you're determined. Tomorrow, we can check on your stamina and Mr. Winston's."

"Tomorrow is entirely inconvenient," her mother said. "We have services in the morning, and nothing is open in the afternoon. Do you attend the Methodist, Lutheran, or Presbyterian church, Mr. Hardee?"

How easily she left out any other denomination. The City of Destiny boasted more than a dozen churches now, for many kinds of faith.

"None of them, ma'am," he answered. "There are few churches where I live, and none close enough to ride to on a Sunday. I generally have to worship in the fields. But I'd be delighted to join you tomorrow. We can check your husband's and daughter's stamina afterward."

Her mother smiled, but Cora felt her annoyance, as hot as if someone had lit the fire in the hearth on a muggy August day. Her mother could not be pleased at the idea of him attending services with them. What would her rivals think to see her with this rough fellow?

"How kind," her mother said. "But we wouldn't want to put you to any trouble."

"No trouble," he said. "I'd want to worship in any regard. Where would you like to meet and what time?"

"Near Wright Park and St. Helen's," Cora said, fighting a smile. "At half past ten."

He set down the glass and rose. "I'll see you then. Thank you again for the hospitality, Mrs. Winston."

She inclined her head. "You are welcome, Mr. Hardee."

"I'll see myself out." He strode for the hall.

Cora watched him go. Such confidence in that stride. They'd do well together on this venture.

"I cannot like this," her mother said. "His manners are lacking."

Cora turned to face her. "You didn't exactly welcome him."

Her mother's hand pressed against the lace at her throat. "I always welcome guests in a way most suited to their characters. But perhaps we should discuss your behavior."

Here it came. "I was sealing a bargain, Mother. Nothing more."

Her mother sniffed. "Is this what is expected of you at the bank? I will speak to Mr. Winston about the matter. Your behavior made you appear contrary and difficult. I am surprised the fellow agreed to escort you, but then, some people will do anything for money. Since you have nothing yet in writing, I suggest you let him know tomorrow that you've changed your mind."

"You promised to support me in this climb, Mother," Cora reminded her. "And I agreed to your stipulation about what happens should I fail. You cannot expect me to back out now."

"And you cannot expect me to say nothing as you endanger your life for some cause," her mother protested. "All I want is the best for you."

Cora sighed. "I know, Mother, but I wish we could agree that *best* does not mean marriage, particularly to a man like Cash Kincaid."

Her mother's lips thinned. "Must you be so difficult?"

She was being difficult? "Forgive me for distressing you, Mother, but I must do this."

Her mother let out a frustrated breath. "At least find a more suitable escort than Mr. Hardee."

Cora offered her a sugary smile and played the best card in her hand. "I would think you'd approve of Mr. Hardee, Mother. He's the son of Mrs. Quinton."

Her mother blinked. "What? That's impossible."

"I was as surprised as you are," Cora assured her. "But Winston insists he is one of us."

"Mr. Winston is rarely mistaken," her mother allowed.

"I will speak to him about that matter as well." Now her hand fluttered to her brow. "This heat is oppressive. I feel a headache coming."

Immediately, guilt walked up and sat heavily in Cora's lap. "That's a shame, Mother. Is there anything I can do?"

Her mother gave a martyred sigh. "No, no. I shall endure the concert this evening. We promised Mrs. Carruthers she and Mimi could join us. But very likely I will be too ill for services tomorrow."

Very likely. Little was more important to her mother than keeping up appearances, and Mr. Hardee did not fit the picture.

At times, neither did Cora.

She did her best that evening to bring credit to her mother by looking attentive and appreciative. That was her role at the theatre, to adorn her stepfather's box, one of the few that curved out from the wall along the left and right of the stage from the orchestra pit to the gallery at the rear. The Tacoma Theatre boasted the largest stage on the West Coast, bigger even than those in fabled San Francisco, with more than one thousand seats surrounding it. She could see most of them from her vantage point, and only a few were full. More signs of the Panic, perhaps?

Mimi's mother thought otherwise.

"Someone ought to tell this Master Polonius that August is entirely too warm for a concert," she said, waving her silk fan before her round face. Like Mimi, she'd worn her black hair piled up high and her puffed sleeves short, but still her skin looked redder than it should. Defying even the warm August night to defeat her, Cora's mother looked her usual cool self in cream-colored satin, with Winston in evening black beside her at the front of the box.

Mimi positioned her own lace-edged fan to cover her conversation as she leaned closer to Cora. "How go your plans for climbing the mountain?"

Ever since Cora had met the raven-haired, sable-eyed Mimi Carruthers at the Annie Wright Seminary, she had been drawn to her bubbly personality. Mimi thought fast, moved faster. She instantly banished melancholy, and no trial seemed too large to overcome when she was at Cora's side. She'd been the first to join the Tacoma Women's Suffrage Association, but Cora had gladly followed. Between the two of them, they'd wrestle back the vote, which the women of the state had had twice now before the Territorial Supreme Court had overturned the laws.

"We think we may have a guide," Cora murmured. "He'll be attending services with us tomorrow."

"Excellent." Mimi's dark eyes sparkled. "The feat will win us converts, Cora. I know it."

"Mimi," her friend's mother interrupted. "You seem to have attracted an admirer."

Cora glanced down into the seats near the stage, where other friends of theirs had gathered. Johnny Westacre, who'd been her partner for the last two years in lawn tennis, was staring up at their box, mouth open, as if in wonder at the sight of them. He bent in a bow that made his wavy black hair fall into his face. Mimi giggled.

"And why shouldn't he admire Mimi?" Cora asked. "She's in fine looks tonight. The green of that dress sets off her hair to perfection."

Mimi's mother smiled proudly while Mimi brushed the satin at her shoulder with her free hand.

"He could just as well be gaping at you," she pointed out

to Cora. "Though we may have to have words if you've set your cap for him."

"I haven't set my cap for anyone," Cora informed her archly as their mothers began discussing social obligations. "And I'm not sure Johnny's family would allow him to speak to me right now, in any event."

Mimi frowned. "Why?"

She could not tell her friend that the Westacres had applied for a loan, and she had refused it. What else could she have done? They'd offered no collateral, no specific plan for repayment. She'd suggested to Johnny's father ways to improve his application so that he might reapply. He'd been rather pointed in his refusal.

"Bank business," she merely said.

Mimi puffed out a sigh. "Not everyone appreciates that sort of thing the way you do. But I'm sure *he* does. If only we could turn him to our cause." She nodded to the box next to theirs.

Where Cash Kincaid now stood, tall and polished. Limelight glowed on his dusty blond hair, giving him a halo she knew he didn't deserve. Still, it wasn't hard to see why every unmarried lady in the area was keen to make his acquaintance. That square-jawed face and those classic features combined to resemble something that might be found on a Greek statue. So did his physique, outlined to perfection in his evening black.

He must have noticed her look, for he bowed in her direction. Mimi's elbow dug into her side, but Cora's mother spared her from a response.

"Good evening, Mr. Kincaid. Are you looking forward to Master Polonius's performance?"

"I am indeed," he said, voice hinting of an Irish accent. "Though I suspect I will find it difficult to keep my eyes on the stage when such beauty sits beside me."

Mimi giggled again and applied her fan to affect. Cora turned her gaze out over the theatre instead. Perhaps that's why she noticed other looks being directed their way.

In the gallery, in the less expensive seats near the rear wall, Nathan Hardee and his colleague, Mr. Vance, were watching. Neither had changed into evening clothes. The rough cotton and wool looked out of place among all the satin and gilt. Why was it so difficult to imagine them enjoying a concert?

And why was Mr. Hardee frowning at her? Was he already regretting his decision to help?

———— {{ }} ————

"I'm glad you agreed to help her," Waldo said, gaze on the gilt-edged, white-lacquered box that stuck out from the wall on their right.

Nathan was finding it hard not to look at Kincaid instead. Staring at the man who'd ruined his father was only slightly worse than gazing at Miss Baxter. In the carmine satin dress, gold fringe dripping from her shoulders, she shouted wealth and power. Small wonder Kincaid was lurking like a lion that had spotted its prey, his smile too oily, too ingratiating. The fellow was nearly tripping over himself to impress her.

"I haven't agreed yet," he cautioned Waldo as the lights began to dim. "I'm not sure she or her stepfather will be able to reach the top. I'm going to send them up Eleventh Street tomorrow."

"Oh, you *are* testing them." Waldo shook his head. "Teams

of horses struggle up that grade, even with empty wagons behind them."

Nathan tipped his head toward the stage and settled into his seat. With a huff, so did Waldo. The thick green curtain had parted to reveal their host for the evening, in a black tailcoat and a shirtfront so white it flashed in the light. Nathan nodded as the fellow rhapsodized about the noted violinist who was about to perform. Master Polonius was the very reason he'd bought the tickets instead of another few sacks of flour for the winter. He knew the feel of the wood under his fingers, the sound that vibrated against the bow and resonated inside him. Listening to a master of the craft always inspired.

But as the broad-chested violinist stepped into sight amid polite applause, Nathan's gaze was drawn once more to where Kincaid had greeted Miss Baxter moments ago. Though the entrepreneur had been all charm, the lady hadn't responded in kind. In fact, for a moment, the thoroughly controlled and collected Miss Baxter had lost her poise.

Nathan would be the first to name Kincaid for the snake he was. What had the fellow done that Miss Baxter saw beneath the façade when so few others ever had?

4

"You must speak to the commissioners of the Tacoma Theatre Company," Cora's mother told Winston as the carriage trundled for home. "Going to the theatre used to be so pleasant, surrounded by acquaintances, but apparently anyone can come through the doors these days."

Had her mother seen Mr. Hardee among the attendees? Cora couldn't begrudge him a seat. Master Polonius was a player of some depth, sharing classics from days of old and more recent popular tunes. When the lights had come up at the end of the performance, her gaze had been drawn in Mr. Hardee's direction. Such a look of satisfaction had sat on his face that she knew she wasn't the only one who would count the evening worth her time.

"Now, dearest," Winston said. "Some have had to forgo the delight of an evening at the theatre in these trying times. I'm sure the commissioners are grateful to fill as many seats as they can."

"Perhaps they should apply for a loan, then, instead of agreeing to house vagrants."

Cora bristled, but Winston merely patted her mother's

hand. "There, now. Let's speak of more pleasant things. I was glad to hear that Mr. Hardee agreed to guide us, after all."

Her mother did not look nearly so glad. "And I was surprised to hear he claimed to be related to Mrs. Quinton, of all people."

Winston's smile was sad. "A tragedy when a mother will not acknowledge her son. But rest assured, they are related. He is the child of her first marriage. He left town before you and I were wed and you were returned to your rightful place in society."

"And he will be joining us for services tomorrow," Cora felt compelled to remind them both.

Her mother heaved a sigh. "Is it too much to hope he might forget?"

He didn't. He was waiting at the appointed spot, near the base of the stone steps leading into the five-story tower that made up the entrance to the church when Cora accompanied Winston the next morning. As expected, her mother remained abed.

Mr. Hardee must own only one set of clothes or had brought the one set with him to the city, for he was still wearing the brown wool coat and trousers of yesterday, only more wrinkled, as if he'd slept in them. His hair, however, had been neatly combed and his beard freshly trimmed, if the paler line of skin around his mouth was any indication.

"Miss Baxter, Mr. Winston," he greeted with a nod.

"Mr. Hardee," Winston returned. "I understand you'll be joining us for services today."

"If I may," he said. "My partner sends his regrets. He's worshipping with other friends."

A shame Mother wasn't here to see such manners.

"Well, we are delighted to have you," Winston assured him. "The church was constructed after you left the city, but I think you'll find it suitably inspiring."

He started forward with Cora on his arm, and Hardee fell in behind.

The long oak pews stretched on either side of the central aisle, while tall windows let in light. She'd always liked how the eye was drawn to the gilded altar at the front and the ornate cross behind it. She nodded to this acquaintance, that family. From near the front on the right, Mimi shot her a smile. Then her brown eyes widened as she must have taken in Hardee just behind. It seemed others had noticed as well, for a murmur blew like a spring breeze through the congregation.

Generally she sat between her mother and Winston. Now Hardee took her mother's spot. His body shadowed the pew, and she felt each of his movements. As the accompanist took her place at the piano, he picked up the leather-bound hymnbook and held it open in his large hands for Cora. Being polite or attempting to rescue her?

Still, his warm bass paired quite nicely with her soprano. And he bowed his head more humbly than most men when the minister offered the opening prayer. He even remained focused during the sermon, which always seemed to run a little long to her mind. Surely Reverend Franklin could encourage charity without using an excess of adjectives.

Her guest didn't seem to have a problem with it. "A fine sermon," he told their elderly minister as they stopped to greet him on the way out the door.

"Mr. Hardee is visiting," Winston explained.

"Indeed," Reverend Franklin said before turning to Winston. "A disturbing rumor has reached my ears. Husted's

Grocers is about to declare bankruptcy, and this after we lost Prescott's and Dunlevy's."

"I'll see what I can do," Winston promised him.

Hardee glanced back at the building as he escorted Cora and Winston to where their carriage waited at the side of the church. Usually, more than a dozen coaches stood next to the planked sidewalk. Today theirs was one of four.

"Too many businesses rely on credit," he mused.

"And how are we to expand without it?" Winston countered, drawing himself up. "The astute use of credit positioned this city for greatness."

"And could bring it to its knees," Hardee pointed out.

Winston nodded. "You're right. You understand such matters all too well, I suspect."

Hardee directed his gaze toward the waters of the Sound, sparkling in the distance, and did not respond. Perhaps he did understand how society worked. Never open the door to your true thoughts or they'd be used against you.

They reached the carriage, and he paused to look her up and down. She matched him look for look.

"Thank you for allowing me to join you," he said. "We'll be practicing this afternoon at half past one. Change into whatever you intend to wear to climb the mountain and meet me at the corner of Eleventh Street South and Pacific then." He turned and headed downtown.

"Apparently we still need to discuss this concept of obedience," Cora told her stepfather, who chuckled.

------------ {{ }} ------------

He wasn't sure she'd show. He'd given her an order, after all, and she had never promised to comply. But he was glad to see the carriage coming down Pacific that afternoon, past the banks and shipping companies that lined the wide street. Her mother was right—few offices were open on a Sunday, and fewer carriages and wagons filled the road. The coachman had plenty of room to guide the horses to a stop at the corner as a church bell higher on the hill tolled half past.

He went to the door of the carriage to help her down and caught himself staring as she stepped onto the wooden planks of the sidewalk. "I told you to change into your climbing clothes."

She spread her navy skirts, setting the gold chains that decorated the top of the darts to flashing. "These are what I intend to wear to climb. Will they not do?"

"Not in the slightest," he told her. "The skirts are too narrow. You'll never jump a creek much less a crevasse. And the sleeves are too short. That lace from your elbows to your wrists might look pretty, but it will never protect you from the freezing temperatures at night."

She put her pert nose in the air. "I want to climb a mountain, not spend the night on it."

"You'll have to spend two nights or more on it to reach the summit," he explained. "This isn't a stroll through the arboretum at Wright Park, Miss Baxter."

She dropped her hands. "Very well. I'll find something that meets your requirements. Can I at least wear this for whatever test you had in mind today?"

Might as well. At least it would give him some idea as to her abilities.

"It will have to do," he said. He glanced into the carriage and met the eyes of a dark-haired woman. "Where's your stepfather?"

"Attending to my mother," she said, and something in the tone told him to leave the matter alone. "We will be in broad daylight. Lily will be watching. It's all perfectly aboveboard."

"As you wish." He took her shoulders and pivoted her to face up the hill. "Climb to the top."

She eyed the steep slope that few climbed if they could avoid it. "That's easy."

"In ten minutes."

She frowned at him. "Why does the time matter?"

"Because there are places along the route to the summit that must be crossed at a certain pace in a set time or the melting snow makes them treacherous. Ten minutes, Miss Baxter. Starting now."

She huffed at him, but she picked up her skirts and started climbing. Nathan followed.

She had a good pace and decent form, leaning into the climb and sweeping across the short plateaus where Eleventh Street crossed others. The curls below her upswept hair bobbed in the breeze, and he had to fist his hands not to reach out and touch one. At least the sidewalk was as sparsely populated as the street today. Every man still stopped to watch her pass, smiling and doffing his hat. Nathan tried not to scowl at them.

She had to pause and catch her breath twice, but she reached Yakima Avenue at the top of the hill with two minutes to spare.

"Satisfied?" she asked between gasps that set her bodice to quaking.

"Not quite," Nathan said, raising his gaze to her perspiration-lined face. "We'll try again tomorrow with a pack."

She drew herself up. "A pack? Why must I carry a pack? I am paying you to escort me, sir."

"And I'll need to carry my own pack," he told her. "I'll carry most of the food and equipment as well, but you'll carry some of the food, your clothes, and your bedding. Depending on how much you decide to take, the pack might weigh thirty to fifty pounds to start. Pack light, and it won't be too bad."

She brought a hand down to her skirts. "But apparently light won't do."

"I'll look over your clothes and see what can be done," he promised.

She shook her head. "Oh, Mother will love that." She narrowed her eyes. "Do you intend to check Winston's clothing too?"

"Anyone who's never been climbing before, yes."

That seemed to placate her. "Very well. I'll just wait for the coach to come get us."

"No," Nathan said. "No coach. We walk down."

She stepped away from him. "Why? I proved I could reach the top, and well within your time limit."

"You proved you could climb a sidewalk," he told her. "That doesn't mean you can climb a mountain. And even if you can, you have to climb down." He moved aside and bowed, hand spread wide. "Your carriage awaits, my lady."

She picked up her skirts once more and started down.

But at a fast clip she could not safely maintain. It was the same on the mountain. Exhilaration at reaching the summit made some reckless on the way down. He skirted around her, put himself in front of her, and slowed his pace.

"Isn't there somewhere else you'd rather be?" she demanded.

Nathan glanced back at her. As her gaze rose to meet his, defiant as always, she stumbled. He whirled as she pitched forward and caught her. Her form was soft, supple, warming him even from the quick touch. She blinked up at him as if just as arrested by the contact.

"Nowhere more important than here," he assured her. He set her on her feet again.

She brushed off her skirts as if almost falling had dirtied them, or maybe it was the proximity to his person that concerned her. Nathan took another step back just in case.

"Thank you," she said. "I'll be more careful."

"Wise choice, whether climbing up or down," Nathan acknowledged. He made himself turn and continue toward the street below. She did not stumble again, and he told himself to be glad for that. At length, they reached the carriage.

She eyed the hill as if she had found new respect for it. "A pack tomorrow, you say?"

He nodded. "After we take care of other matters. First, I'll assess your equipment and clothing, then we'll visit Dickson Brothers on Pacific to purchase what else you'll need. Ask your stepfather to draw some money for you."

She raised her chin. "I have no need to apply to Winston for funds. I have money of my own."

He glanced to where several men were lounging near the shipping offices, as if hoping for work to materialize even on a Sunday. "I wouldn't say that so loudly if I were you. With this many out of work and hungry, crime will be on the rise."

She paled. "Just know that I'll be ready to do what must be done."

He'd take her at her word, for now.

5

"A bath," Cora told Lily as they climbed down from the carriage. "As hot as you care to make it. I could soak for an hour."

"Yes, Miss Cora," the maid said as they entered the house. "I'll just ask Charlie to bring in the tub." She headed for the back of the house.

Cora started for her room, but Darcy caught her the moment she reached the main entry hall.

"Oh, Miss Cora, I'm so glad you're back. Your mother sent down her regrets, but Miss Carruthers insisted on waiting for you."

"I'll see her," Cora promised, turning for the drawing room.

Her friend was sitting by the window as if hoping to catch a glimpse of Cora the moment she arrived. Now she popped to her feet in a rustle of green-striped taffeta and darted to Cora's side. "There you are! I convinced Mother to let me come visit only to find you gone. I simply couldn't wait until tomorrow to hear all. That was your guide? Were you with him just now? And without a chaperone too, you daring girl!"

She took Mimi's hand and led her to the horsehair sofa. Mimi sank down beside her.

"His name is Nathan Hardee," Cora explained. "He was assessing my stamina for the climb just now, and I did have a chaperone. Lily was there the entire time."

"Oh." Mimi looked the slightest bit disappointed, pink lips pursing. Then she fluffed out her puffy green sleeves. "Well, you clearly passed his assessment. When do you leave?"

"We haven't decided. It appears I have equipment to purchase first, and I must find a different outfit."

Mimi eyed her up and down. "What's wrong with what you're wearing? I remember when you first showed it to me. I thought it the perfect outfit for an enterprising lady. And it would look very well for the photograph they are sure to want for the papers."

"Apparently it isn't warm enough for the climb," Cora told her. "He promised to look over my wardrobe so I can choose something more appropriate."

Mimi nudged her with her elbow. "You'll allow him in your room? Has your mother agreed to this?"

Cora sighed. "No, but I'll have to find a way to explain it to her. I certainly don't want to fail because of some absurd sense of propriety."

"You won't fail," Mimi predicted. "You've never failed at anything you've set your hand to. That's one of the reasons we asked you to represent us. Your success will be sure to turn heads."

"So long as it turns hearts to our cause as well," Cora agreed.

She chatted awhile longer with her friend, then bid her farewell in time to climb the stairs—which seemed inordinately higher than she remembered—for a nice long bath before dinner.

She leaned back against the copper sides of the bathing tub and closed her eyes, breathing in the heady steam scented with oil of roses even as she willed her sore muscles to relax. Who knew climbing that hill would be so difficult? Of course, climbing down had been more surprising. How easily those large hands had held her, keeping her safe.

Lest at any time thou dash thy foot against a stone.

She snapped open her eyes. How silly. The remembered verse had to do with the watch care of angels, and Nathan Hardee was certainly no heavenly guardian. Though he did appear to be doing a thorough job of taking care of her, despite her protests to the contrary.

Her mother consented to come down to dinner that night, though she wore her pink satin dressing gown with the enormous white ruffles at the wrists and hem. She was quiet and sighed a great deal as Darcy served the first course, a white soup. But the reprieve Cora had hoped for was all too short-lived.

"I cannot like how Mr. Hardee monopolizes your time," she said between sips of the savory soup. "You have social obligations to consider."

She had been dodging social obligations since starting college three years ago, but her mother continued to campaign.

"In truth, I should be at the bank tomorrow," Cora said with an apologetic look to Winston.

He dabbed soup from his mustache with a damask napkin before answering. "Not at all, dearest. I fully support your endeavor to climb the mountain. Though I'm sure you can spare your dear mother time for a ball or two with your friends."

Cora bent over her soup. "I'm not sure anyone should be hosting a ball when so many are struggling."

"Those who manage their money well are not struggling," her mother insisted. "Are we to be expected to forgo every pleasure because a few find themselves insolvent?"

"Hardly a few, my love," Winston said. "At services today, Reverend Franklin related more who have joined a long line of bankruptcies in recent months. Even the Washington National Bank of Tacoma will be closed. The stockholders voted to liquidate." His blue eyes looked a bit liquid themselves, as if he felt for the bank director.

"Please give me a full accounting, Mr. Winston," her mother said. "I must consider who to invite to the reception I am planning for September."

"Of course, dearest," Winston said dutifully.

Her mother patted his hand. "Tomorrow you can assist me with the guest list."

"Actually, Mr. Hardee would like a moment of Winston's time tomorrow," Cora said. "He'd like to test our ability to carry a pack up a hill."

Her mother drew herself up. "A pack! My husband and daughter are no common laborers. You have no reason to port a pack like some mule."

Had she sounded so haughty when she'd questioned Mr. Hardee earlier? In truth, she'd thought he might be throwing up barriers, as men tended to do whenever she attempted to access places they thought should be reserved for them alone. But he'd likely seen her as spoiled and willful. He was the expert on climbing, after all.

Shame washed over her, as cold as a wave on the Sound. She gave her mother the same answer he'd given her. "Everyone must carry a pack, Mother. It's too difficult to carry enough otherwise."

"Then take a packhorse," her mother said. "Or better yet, a wagon."

"I doubt either could make the ascent to the summit, dearest," Winston said with his usual gentle smile. "Now, let us talk no more of matters that distress you and enjoy this marvelous repast with which we have been blessed."

Her mother returned his smile then, but she was less forgiving when Hardee arrived at ten the next morning at the same time as Miss Fuller, who, like Cora, was a member of the Tacoma Women's Suffrage Association. Darcy came to fetch Cora when her mother refused to see them.

"They can both be obliged to wait," her mother said when Cora went to appeal the decision. "Mr. Hardee's assumption that this is in any way a suitable time to call might be expected given his sojourn in the wilderness, but Miss Fuller is supposed to be a lady."

"Perhaps I'll just speak to them until you're ready," she said. She left her mother in Lily's capable hands and hurried for the parlor.

At least Darcy had had the foresight to allow them into the house. Cora would have been mortified to keep the first woman to have climbed Mount Rainier standing on the stoop.

Her muscles protested as she descended the stairs. Well, they would become accustomed to her new activities. She was always a little sore for a few days when lawn tennis commenced again each spring. Surely this was no different.

Darcy had placed the visitors in the formal parlor on the opposite side of the house. This room was stiffer, more ornate. Its intent was to impress, not to encourage lingering. Accordingly, most of the furnishings were of hardwood, polished to a high gloss. They teetered on the thick Persian carpet, its crimson and sapphire coloring matching the stripes on the heavy satin drapes over the window.

Mr. Hardee, still in the same outfit, stood near the carved wood hearth, his wavy hair visible in the gilt-edged mirror above. He dwarfed the dark-haired lady seated on the chair beside him. Fay Fuller had been a legend among the ladies of Tacoma since her historic climb three years ago. Her light brown curled bangs stuck out from under her flat-topped hat as if ready to explore the world. Her figure in the blue striped bodice and skirts was sturdy, as if she brooked no nonsense. Her dark eyes held an assessing gleam as she smiled up at Cora.

"Miss Fuller," she said, holding out her hand. "How nice of you to call."

The newspaper columnist shook her hand with a firm grip. "I just returned from the World's Fair to find Mimi's note waiting. I understand they've convinced you to climb the mountain."

"They did," Cora admitted, taking the chair closest to the lady. "Mr. Hardee has agreed to guide me and my stepfather."

Miss Fuller turned her smile up at him, and it seemed to warm. "You couldn't be in better hands."

Now, why did she have a sudden urge to tug the lady's hat down over her eyes?

"You're too kind," he said, inclining his head in Miss Fuller's direction. "I know you've recounted your climb in the newspapers and at speaking engagements around the area, but would you mind explaining the circumstances to Miss Baxter, so she understands what to expect?"

Miss Fuller nodded, gaze returning to Cora. "That's why I'm here. I must admit to some surprise, however, that you are so eager to climb, Miss Baxter. You are not, to my knowledge, a member of the Tacoma Alpine Club."

Cora must have looked confused, for he stepped closer to her as if in support. "Miss Fuller was one of the founding members of the club for climbing enthusiasts."

"Generally one climbs a few smaller peaks before attempting Tacoma," Miss Fuller added.

"So, you are of the camp that believes the mountain should be named after the city," Cora said.

"It is the native name for the mountain," she corrected her.

"Depends on which native you ask," Hardee put in with a smile.

This time Miss Fuller's look to him was more challenging. "Professor Plummer has the enthusiastic support of more than fifty prominent tribal members."

His smile broadened. "And I could give you fifty just as prominent members who claim otherwise."

Cora watched them, fascinated. How easily they argued on a controversial subject that had divided more than one household in the area. This sort of equality was the very reason she and Mimi were advocating for the vote.

"Be that as it may, sir," Miss Fuller said, chin coming up, "you cannot deny that reaching the summit is a challenge for even an experienced climber."

"It is a challenge," he acknowledged. "But more difficult for a woman, I think."

Cora stiffened. So did Miss Fuller.

"It is a matter of fitness and determination," she insisted. "The same rugged conditions—extreme temperatures, cutting wind—affect both male and female. The same unforgiving terrain must be crossed."

"The only difference, it seems," Cora said, "is that I must conquer it in skirts."

Miss Fuller positively glowered at Hardee. "What nonsense have you been telling her?" Before he could answer, she turned to Cora. "Not skirts, Miss Baxter. I advise bloomers."

Cora stared at her. "Bloomers! I was certain the photograph I saw in the newspapers after your climb showed you in skirts."

She rolled her eyes. "The photographer was very careful to give that appearance. To assuage the sensibilities of the public, he said. But if you look closely, you'll see bloomers at the bottom. Flannel, to be exact, with flannel combinations underneath. Anything less simply isn't safe for the maneuvering required."

"Having second thoughts, Miss Baxter?" Hardee asked.

Why was he intent on scaring her off? Didn't he want payment for his services? And oh, her mother! She'd have apoplexy at the idea of Cora wearing bloomers in public. Well, sacrifices must be made if they were to secure the vote. And she wasn't about to admit defeat and find herself engaged to the likes of Cash Kincaid.

"No, Mr. Hardee," she said. "Merely wondering where I might procure flannel bloomers in time to make the climb as we planned. What do you suggest, Miss Fuller?"

❈ ❈

Many women would have balked at Miss Fuller's description of the daunting circumstances, let alone the need to dress in something still considered scandalous. Miss Baxter had claimed she had determination. Nathan could not doubt she had it in abundance.

She questioned Miss Fuller further—about her route, advice on what to carry, and the time it had taken to make the ascent.

"Nearly twelve hours?" She shivered. "Then you must have spent the night."

"In an ice cave made by steam vents," she said. "Cooking on one side, freezing on the other. I cannot recommend it. I know others have managed to reach the top and back to one of the camps within a day. I will pray you have the same fortune."

"You have been so kind to allow me to quiz you like this," Miss Baxter said with a smile. "I wonder whether I might impose a moment longer."

Miss Fuller nodded. "I must meet my father for lunch, but I believe I can spend a little more time."

"Excellent," Miss Baxter said, rising. "I cannot be certain I can have bloomers sewn in time. Mr. Hardee said he would advise me on which dresses might suit, but I would greatly appreciate your thoughts on the matter, Miss Fuller. Would you be willing to assess my wardrobe?"

Miss Fuller stood. "Of course. Lead the way."

He wasn't sure he was invited, but he followed them from the room anyway.

The second story of the Winston mansion was as impressive as the first. Warm wood paneled the walls from the floor to about waist height, with wallpaper showing fanciful blue swirls on cream above. Here and there, oil paintings hung from rails along the ceiling. Brass sconces gleamed with electric lights.

Miss Baxter's room was at the front northwest corner. He couldn't seem to make himself step over the threshold. Everything was lacy and frilly and entirely feminine. Was it the deep pink of the coverings on the poster bed, or did he truly smell roses?

Miss Baxter went to the carved walnut wardrobe on the far wall and began to pull out things for Miss Fuller to inspect. He fought for breath. Had he ever been in a lady's bedchamber except his mother's? Certainly Annabelle had never allowed him past the first floor in all the times he'd called on her and her family. She'd been a stickler for propriety, his Annabelle.

His Annabelle. He snorted and quickly covered it with a cough. He'd been so impressed with the way she carried herself, the way she talked and laughed. But what he'd taken as perfection had been a slavish absorption with society's dictates. He would never forget the resigned look on her face when she'd handed him back his betrothal ring.

"You must see it is impossible, Mr. Hardee," she'd said, delicate chin quivering. "I cannot align myself where there are no expectations of a future." She'd dropped her dulcet voice as if even saying the next words would cause her to suffer. "To marry into a family with a suicide." She'd shuddered.

All he'd been able to see at the time was what he had lost— his father, his standing, his profession, his home, and the woman he'd thought to marry. Better to leave it all behind, go somewhere he might find peace.

"Coraline?"

He brought himself back to the moment to find Mrs. Winston beside him, eyes darting from him to Miss Fuller and back.

"I'm certain we have sufficient seating downstairs that you do not need to entertain in your bedchamber," she told her daughter.

Miss Baxter's smile was as polished as Annabelle's had ever been. "Mother, allow me to introduce Miss Fuller, the famed climber. And of course you remember Mr. Hardee. They were advising me on suitable clothing for our adventure."

"How very considerate," her mother said. "But you should not repay such generosity by making Miss Fuller take the place of your maid."

Once more, Miss Baxter's lovely face was reddening. Miss Fuller moved toward the door. "We are finished in any event. Miss Baxter, I hope I have been some use to you."

"Tremendously so," Miss Baxter assured her. "Allow me to walk you out. That way, I can play maid to you."

She sailed past her mother. With a quick smile, Miss Fuller followed.

Nathan inclined his head as he turned to do likewise. "Mrs. Winston."

Her gaze speared him in place. "I do not wish to find you on the chamber story again, Mr. Hardee. I hope I have made myself clear."

He topped her by a good foot, outweighed her in muscle, but he edged around her, feeling as trapped as if he'd stumbled upon a rattlesnake that had crossed the Cascades. "Ma'am."

He took the stairs down entirely too fast. Miss Baxter and Miss Fuller had just reached the front door.

"Miss Baxter, I wish you all the best," the reporter was saying. "I'll plan on interviewing you when you return triumphant."

"I'd like that," she assured the lady before opening the door for her. "The more publicity, the better."

As soon as Miss Fuller was down the steps, Miss Baxter turned to him. "Give me a few moments to make a list, and we can go shopping. I know just what I must put in this pack I'll be carrying."

6

Her mother balked at allowing Cora to use the carriage, until Cora reminded her that Winston would be participating in this shopping expedition. As it was, her mother still sent Lily with Cora again. The maid squeezed herself into a corner of the coach beside Cora and gazed at Hardee across from them as the carriage set off for the bank to retrieve Winston.

"I've never shopped at Dickson Brothers," Cora admitted as they left the grand houses on C Street and turned down the packed dirt road toward the business district on Pacific. "It seemed a gentleman's bastion."

"I suppose it is." Though the day was sunny, the shadowy interior darkened his face until it appeared carved from mahogany. "Though not from any animosity toward the ladies. Make no mistake, Miss Baxter. You are one of a rare few willing to make this journey."

"That will change in the coming years," Cora predicted, settling her striped skirts around her. "There is nothing a lady cannot do if she sets her mind to it. Or her legs. Suffrage is just the beginning."

He smiled, but it faded as he glanced out the window.

Cora peered out as well. They had been coming past the tall steeple of St. Luke's Episcopal Church and heading toward the grand stone façade of the Methodist church on the corner. A crowd had gathered near the steps and spilled out onto Pacific, men in rough coats like his. They seemed to be shoving each other, and their voices rose like the blast of a steam engine.

He rapped on the roof and called up to their coachman. "Turn down Seventh."

Either Oscar didn't hear him over the shouts of the crowd, or he waited for Cora's confirmation, because he kept driving. Now the voices turned sharp, hard, like hail pummeling the coach. Faces scowled in at her, red and puckered. Fists shook in warning.

Smack! The coach rocked with the impact.

Cora stiffened. "One of them threw a rock at us!"

Lily tugged her away from the window. "Don't show yourself, miss. You'll only make them madder."

Then they were past. The normal noises of the city returned: the rattle of wagons and vans, the mournful wail of a locomotive on the docks. She could almost believe the altercation was only her imagination.

Almost.

"Why would they protest against a church?" she asked, removing her arm from Lily's grip.

He squinted back the way they had come. "Too many have lost their jobs, and the charities run by the churches can't make up the difference. Those men had nowhere else to turn."

"I can understand that," Cora said as Lily shuddered beside her. "But they have no call to resort to violence."

"And you have horses, a carriage, and a coachman," he

countered. "Seeing all that can't be easy when you have no hope of a roof over your head or food in your belly tonight."

"It's a small step from here to there for some," Lily murmured, hugging herself.

The memories swarmed her, like rats chittering over a choice piece of refuse. She and her mother had come so close to penury, yet always her mother had found a man to support them. Was it so wrong to want to support herself?

Coming up on their left, the sight of the white stone prow of the Puget Sound Bank of Commerce fueled her resolve. Two stories tall with arched windows and gilt lettering on the black sign above, the bank looked as solid as the mountain itself. Patrons moved in and out through the brass-fronted doors on the corner with the usual decorum. As the carriage rolled to a stop, Hardee jumped down to help her alight. His hand swallowed hers to hold it cupped in strength.

She would not dwell on that.

She offered him a smile in thanks and went to collect Winston.

Just stepping into the carpeted lobby made breath easier. Something about a bank inspired confidence and optimism. People spoke in hushed voices, as if something important was about to happen. Cashiers in tall, gilded cages went about their duties with dignity and purpose. One of them, a Mr. Johnson, hurried around the end of the row to meet her.

"Miss Baxter, I'm so glad to see you," he said, completely ignoring Hardee at her side. "Mr. Busey asked about his proposal, and I didn't know what to tell him."

"If he asks again before I return," Cora answered, "assure him I intend to recommend it to the directors, but they may be more inclined to view it favorably if he offers collateral.

He recently built a fine house above the First Ward. That might do."

"Yes, Miss Baxter," he said. "Shall I fetch Mr. Winston for you?"

"Please."

He hurried off.

"Seems to be asking a lot to suggest a man risk his own home," Hardee rumbled beside her.

"It's a lot to expect a bank to risk its holdings on a new venture too," she countered. "We are not heartless, sir. Merely prudent."

"Could be one and the same."

Cora decided not to comment. She'd heard enough complaints from businessmen whose proposals she'd refused that a woman with a head for business must not have a heart for kindness. Rubbish.

Before the Panic, with Tacoma ever-growing, she'd had at least three investment proposals a day to review and determine whether to recommend to Winston and his board of directors for funding. She had had a hand in building the new hospital near Wright Park, the bridge to the tide flats, and three department stores.

Her stepfather came out of his office near hers just then, top hat on his head. Nodding to depositors, he set off toward her, walking stick swinging.

"Ready to purchase what we need for this trip?" she asked as he joined her.

Winston's smile remained, though his focus hopped about the bank lobby faster than a rabbit. "No trip. No, no. I won't be going anywhere except to escort my favorite daughter to view the mountain." He took Cora by the arm and led her out the door, steps faster than they'd been moments before. Hardee followed.

Cora eyed her stepfather as he handed her up into the coach. "Why so cautious?"

"Merely attempting to keep rumors of our solvency from circulating," he replied with a nod to their coachman before following her. Seeing Lily, he seated himself next to their guide. Between the two of them, they managed to make the bench seat look entirely too crowded.

"Mr. Hardee," Winston greeted him.

He inclined his head. "Mr. Winston. Thank you for joining us."

"I'm certain it will be worth my time," he assured him.

It was certainly worth her time, and not just because they were equipping themselves for the climb. She was itching to see how gentlemen shopped. Like many of the stores she favored, Dickson Brothers was housed in a redbrick building three stories tall. But it had jaunty flags flying from every corner and bunting draping the wide front windows, which displayed white-fronted gentlemen's shirts, shiny black shoes, and a considerable variety of hats.

Lily stayed in the coach with Oscar, their coachman, but Cora went inside with Winston and their guide. She was a little disappointed to find Dickson Brothers to be arranged like a typical store, with white-lettered signs hanging on gold chains from the high ceilings, pointing the way to various departments. Hosiery. Shoes. Haberdashery. Cologne. Cologne? She sniffed the air. The stores where she shopped generally smelled of exotic flowers or warm vanilla. Here the air was scented with leather and spices and the faint aroma of pipe smoke.

She spotted a few gentlemen being attended on either side

of the main aisle, which led toward wide stairs to the upper floors. Hardee made for a glass-fronted counter in the center of the space, where a fresh-faced clerk with pomaded auburn hair put on a beaming smile.

"Welcome to Dickson Brothers," he declared. "How may I be of assistance?"

Cora set her list on the counter in front of him. "We are outfitting an expedition to climb Mount Rainier. I've been assured Dickson Brothers is the place to shop."

He looked from her to Hardee to Winston, as if trying to determine which to thank for the honor. "Happy to be of assistance. Are both you gentlemen climbing?"

"And the lady," Hardee said, his deep voice booming in the quiet store.

Half a dozen eyes darted her way.

"In the name of women's suffrage," Cora said, loud enough to carry.

The clerk's reddish brows shot up, but he quickly schooled his face. "How nice. Well, you'll find all you need here. Climbing shoes, woolen blankets, blue eyeglasses."

"Blue eyeglasses?" Cora glanced to their guide.

He nodded. "They protect your eyes from the glare of sunlight on snowfields. Men have gone blind for a time without them."

"Two pair then," she told the clerk. "Unless Mr. Hardee needs one."

"I have everything I need," he said.

Somehow, she wasn't surprised.

The clerk seemed more than happy to dash all over the store and collect the items Cora had listed. Or perhaps he feared she'd say more about suffrage to the other customers.

Either way, the pile on the counter began to grow. Rubberized Army blankets, guaranteed not to rot or soak up rain. Thick woolen socks to ward off blisters. A cotton outing shirt for Winston. A brass-cased compass for her. And oversized canvas packs for them to carry it all in.

Hardee wandered off from time to time to return with other items she hadn't realized she'd need. One was a small steel trowel.

"I did not think to take geological specimens," she told him.

The clerk, who was tallying up their goods so far, began turning red.

"It's for burying waste," Hardee explained. That gleam in his eye challenged her to make a fuss. Her mother would have. His mother probably would have.

"And what about a canteen?" she asked the clerk instead.

Shoes proved to be the most difficult. Their clerk could only point her to the shoe department, where more men in tailored wool coats stood before a wall of small boxes set on polished wood shelves that reached to the ceiling. Every few feet, a hook held black laces, hanging in bunches like fresh-caught fish. The scent of leather was overpowering.

When Hardee explained their purpose, one of the clerks hurried to find shoes for Winston, offering two styles to consider, both thick leather with heavy soles in which metal caulks could be embedded. The other fellow studied Cora's laced-up gray tooled-leather boots for some time before climbing a ladder and bringing her a pair of brown shoes.

"Smallest pair I have, ma'am," he said with an apologetic smile, "and secondhand at that, outgrown by a lad whose father climbed on occasion."

Hardee nodded toward one of the wrought-iron benches

that sat opposite the mountain of shoeboxes. "Let's try them on. Too tight or too loose, and they could do more harm than good."

Cora went to sit and began loosening her laces. He brought her the climbing shoes and waited patiently as her stocking feet came free. Then he knelt in front of her.

Cora sucked in a breath as his hands cradled her foot, guiding it into the shoe. Who else had ever touched her feet? Even Lily merely held the shoes or boots and let Cora slide her feet inside. This touch was too intimate, too tender. She wanted to yank back her foot and push him away.

She bent. "I can handle this, sir."

He remained kneeling, watching, as she tried on the other shoe and then set about lacing them up. If he noticed her hands were shaking, he didn't comment.

"Stand," he ordered as she finished, and she was on her feet before she could think better of it. The shoes felt heavy and stiff, quite unlike the kid leather and satin she was used to wearing.

But she realized why he had remained on his knees. He poked here and prodded there, before having her walk from one side of the department to the other. A number of gentlemen seemed to have decided to purchase shoes today, for the long, narrow department was filling, and all gazes were on her. She kept her head high, her steps firm. As she came by a group, someone whistled.

"Gentlemen, please," one of the clerks begged.

"I hope you show this kind of support for women voting," Cora said.

Hardee stood and sent them a look, and they all found other ways to occupy their time.

"No pinch?" he asked as she returned to the bench.

"No," she said, sitting. "At least, no more than my other shoes."

He regarded her as she began removing the shoes. Odd that she was so breathless. Perhaps yesterday's climb was still affecting her.

"You don't need to climb a mountain in your other shoes," he pointed out.

"But I do need to play lawn tennis for hours and dance all night at a ball," she replied, lacing up her boots. "I haven't blistered yet."

"Well," he allowed, "I suppose that's something."

At last, he agreed they had all they needed. They returned to the front counter, and Cora opened her purse to pay. Their auburn-haired clerk once again looked from her to Winston, then slid the bill his direction.

Cora put a finger on it and pulled it closer to her. Glancing down, she frowned. "This can't be right."

He chuckled. "I know. It's a lot of money, but such things don't come cheap."

"I didn't imagine they did," Cora informed him. "But you stated the price before including them in the pile. I know the total. What you quoted is high by nearly five dollars."

He stood taller, face reddening again. "Now, see here. I added it up myself." He shoved the paper at Winston once more.

Out of the corners of her eyes, she saw Hardee fold his arms over his broad chest. Cora kept her gaze on the clerk as her stepfather added the sums. Sweat trickled down from his pomaded hair, shiny in the electric lights of the store.

"I'm afraid she's right, young man," Winston said, thick

finger pointing to the tally. "See here? You must have added her climbing shoes twice."

He snatched back the bill and scanned it again. "Easy thing to claim. I hear you own a bank and all."

"Yes, well, that does predispose me to add correctly," her stepfather allowed with a friendly smile.

"Fine. If you're wrong, it will come out of my pocket, but I'm sure five dollars is nothing to you."

"Five dollars isn't nothing to anyone these days," Hardee said, deep voice like distant thunder. "I suggest you apologize to Miss Baxter and Mr. Winston, or they may find another store that would appreciate their business."

The clerk's Adam's apple bobbed as he swallowed. "Yes, sir. My apologies, miss, Mr. Winston. I should have checked my sums."

Cora drew out the necessary funds. "Thank you for your assistance. We'll take the lot now, in the packs, if you please."

She turned to their guide to see that half-smile on his lips again. "I believe we intend to practice, sir. Shall we?"

-------- {{--}} --------

Nathan waited partway up the Eleventh Street hill as Miss Baxter and her stepfather climbed to the top. With the pack on her back, all he could see of the lady was the sway of her skirts, and he tried not to watch overly much.

Still, he couldn't help remembering how she'd dealt with the clerks at Dickson Brothers. The queen couldn't have been more commanding. And she was clever. He wasn't sure why that surprised him. She'd graduated college, after all. Then again, she wouldn't be the first to manage impressive feats more on her family's connections than her own talent.

They reached the top and started back toward him. Her posture was off. No doubt she'd leaned forward going up to compensate for the pack. She couldn't do that coming down without oversetting herself.

Of course, posture was relatively easy to correct. A shift of the pack contents, practice keeping shoulders over hips. He was more concerned about the older man. Winston's pace was slowing even downhill. The banker drew abreast of Nathan, and he held out his hand to stop them. "A moment, sir. I may have put the wrong contents in your pack." He eased it off the older man's frame, which trembled from his efforts.

Nathan slipped the pack onto his own shoulders. "Only right I carry it the rest of the way."

"Thank you," Winston acknowledged before starting down again.

Miss Baxter paused a moment. "I very much doubt you make mistakes like that, Mr. Hardee. So, I add my thanks as well." She continued down the hill.

Easy to thank him now, but he couldn't carry the man's pack on the mountain any more than he could carry hers. His thoughts chased him to the bottom.

"Miss Baxter," he said as Winston stood by the carriage, chest heaving and face sweating, "look through these packs. See if there's anything you can live without or if there's a way to better balance the load either between them or within them."

She raised finely arched brows as if surprised he'd entrust such a task to her, then bent over the packs at her feet.

Nathan drew the banker closer to the coach.

"I realize this is an unusual amount of effort," he said,

"but if you intend to climb Rainier, you'll be enduring this sort of thing for the better part of three days. More if the weather turns on us. Your health concerns me, sir. Perhaps you should wait at Longmire's."

The banker eyed him a moment, blue eyes bright in a face sagging with weariness. Then he shook his head. "I can't," he confessed. "Cora must have a chaperone."

Nathan knew society's rules. A lady couldn't be alone with a gentleman without a member of her family or an older woman chaperone present. Mrs. Winston was hardly climbing a mountain. And he doubted he could find another woman who could be ready to accomplish it on such short notice.

"Be that as it may," he said, "I don't know if you can reach the top."

Winston raised his head. "I must. I told you, I will not allow Coraline to be forced into marriage."

Nathan glanced to where Cora was digging through the backpacks. Her pale hair was beginning to slip from her pins, forming a silvery mass about her face. "And you simply can't put your foot down with your wife?"

"I believe you have met Mrs. Winston," he said. "She is not an easy woman to dissuade. Her unswerving determination is one of the qualities that drew me to her. I inherited my fortune, you see, and I'm not the sort of fellow to dine on ambition. I never thought to marry until Mrs. Winston showed interest. I knew immediately she would push me to new heights, and she has, while I provide her the security she desires. She believes a husband will provide Coraline with the same security."

The day felt colder, as if the alpine wind blew down from

the mountain even now. "I wouldn't want to trust my daughter's future to Cash Kincaid."

The banker's gaze kindled. "Then we understand each other. Cora must climb to secure her freedom. She needs our help. I am counting on you to see us safely to the top and back again. I don't expect you to disappoint us."

7

She'd done it. If she had somehow doubted, her neck and back would have reminded her she'd just carried a pack, thirty pounds by Hardee's estimation, up to the top of the Eleventh Street hill and back down again. Surprisingly, descending had been as difficult as climbing, but surely the pack would be a little lighter on the mountain. They would have eaten some of the food when they started down, after all.

Their guide didn't seem as thrilled by the accomplishment. As they rode home in the carriage, he kept studying Winston, head cocked and green eyes narrowed, as they discussed her stepfather's climbing apparel. She could imagine Hardee's thoughts. It took the entire trip back to the house for her stepfather's face to return to its usual color. Hardee had wondered whether she had what it took to climb a mountain. He must be wondering the same about Winston.

"What are our next steps, Mr. Hardee?" she asked as the carriage approached the house.

Before he could answer, Winston nodded toward the drive.

"Our discussion may have to wait, dearest. It seems Mr. Kincaid has come to call."

Now she could see the other carriage waiting on the drive, sides a lacquered green. How hard his coachman must work to keep the brass appointments gleaming despite the rain and mud.

"If you wish to clean up first, Coraline," Winston said as the coach came to a stop, "I will make your excuses."

"And I'll excuse myself now," Hardee said as he opened the door and hopped down. "To answer your question, Miss Baxter, we'll finish packing and go over the route tomorrow. Plan to leave midmorning the day after."

Air rushed into her lungs. He'd agreed. She was ready. She wanted to sing, to shout. She settled for a ladylike nod that would have pleased her mother. "Excellent. But by all means, stay a moment, Mr. Hardee. I'd like Mother to hear the news. And you can better answer any questions she might have."

As Winston handed her down, their guide hesitated. Why? Surely not vanity over how he was dressed. He hadn't seemed concerned about the picture he presented before, even at the theatre.

"Come along, my boy," Winston said, trotting past him.

Hardee waited only a moment more before joining Cora in following.

Her mother was entertaining their visitor. In the formal parlor, of course. The silver tea service glinted on one of the walnut side tables, and an assortment of little cakes sat on the violet-patterned bone china her mother had had imported from England.

Cash Kincaid rose as Cora entered, ever the gentleman in his buff tailored coat and heather plaid trousers.

"Miss Baxter," he said, inclining his head. "I was hoping if I imposed on your mother's excellent hospitality long enough, you'd return."

"Hosting you is never an imposition, Mr. Kincaid," her mother assured him with her most charming smile. "And see how eager Coraline is for your company? She didn't take time to change after her walk."

By the dampness under her arms and down her back, her exertions were likely evident. She'd hear about it later from her mother.

"I fear I didn't change either," Winston put in smoothly. "But allow me to introduce you to the son of an old friend of mine—Mr. Nathan Hardee."

Something flickered behind Kincaid's icy blue eyes, but his smile remained. "Hardee."

"Kincaid."

The single word was as sharp as a rifle shot. Cora glanced at their guide with a frown, but his gaze was on her mother's guest, as if he didn't trust what would happen if he looked away.

Kincaid turned to Cora. "Please, my dear. No need to remain standing. You look tired."

"I don't feel the least bit fatigued," Cora said, strolling over to the windows though her legs balked. "Mother, Mr. Hardee assures me I am ready to climb the mountain. We set out the day after tomorrow."

She thought her mother might protest, even with their visitor watching, but Kincaid spoke first. "I cannot say I'm surprised you'd attempt the climb; however, I am surprised by your choice of guide. The Hardee family is not known for its . . . reliability."

"If you expect me to stand here and pretend to be part of the wall like the maid, you better think again," Hardee said. "I've guided more than a dozen parties up the mountain in the last few years. Not one was lost."

Kincaid chuckled. "Oh, that's the measure of success, is it? No one died. I suppose that's something."

"It is something to me," her mother put in. "I would very much like dear Coraline to return unscathed." Now she eyed Hardee as if doubting him.

Kincaid stepped between Cora and the window. "My most fervent hope as well." He took her hand. "You must know you have no need to climb the mountain to impress me. One word from you, and I would make you my bride tomorrow. Today, if your mother would allow it."

"Don't be silly, Mr. Kincaid," her mother said with an airy laugh. "I'd need at least a month to plan a proper wedding."

Cora pulled away from him. "No need to trouble yourself, Mother. I won't be marrying Mr. Kincaid."

"Never say never, my dear," he teased her. "But if you are determined to climb, allow me to find you a guide who won't abandon you when things become difficult."

Hardee took a step closer, and heat radiated off him, as if Kincaid's words had kindled a fire in his chest.

"I grow weary of hearing you denigrate Mr. Hardee," Cora told the businessowner. "It shows a lack of both prudence and character."

"Coraline!" her mother scolded. "Really. I don't know how Mr. Kincaid abides your ungracious behavior. You may leave."

Was this how Hardee felt when her mother ordered him about? Cora kept her head high as she walked from the room.

In the entry hall, she paused to clutch the stair rail. It was firm and unyielding. What would her mother say if she found the power to wrench the thing down and hurl it across the room?

Probably remind her that ladies did not display such a lower-class appreciation of strength.

A smile tugged.

"Miss Baxter."

Turning, she found Hardee a few steps away. His face had settled into hard lines, but somehow she knew it wasn't because of anything she'd done.

"Thank you for standing up for me," he said. "Though I can fight my own battles."

"Of course you can," Cora agreed, dropping her hand. "I merely didn't see why Mr. Kincaid needed to start a battle to begin with."

He took a step closer, and darkness seemed to advance with him. "Given his barbed hints, I should tell you about my family."

She didn't want any more darkness, not now. Her heart already felt heavy. She waved a hand. "Your family circumstances are none of my affair."

He peered closer, as if he didn't believe her. "They are if they affect your trust in me. Kincaid sowed some seeds. I won't let the weeds grow between us. You have to believe in me or you won't follow my directions, and someone could get hurt."

To believe in him. He didn't know what he asked. People were unreliable—look at her mother, look at her father and first stepfather. Even Winston had flaws, refusing to stand up to her mother, for one. It was better, safer, to rely on her own abilities. That way, she would only be disappointed in herself.

"We are paying you to guide us up a mountain, Mr. Hardee," she said. "You have experience to commend you. I don't need to know more than that."

"Don't you?" He towered over her, and she raised her chin, refusing to back away. "Kincaid claims I'll abandon you because I abandoned my own family."

The words were like a slap. "You left Tacoma after your father's death. Winston told me."

"Did he tell you how my father died?"

Something must have showed on her face, for he nodded. "It seems he did. Like Kincaid, my father built a fortune on opportunities. But he made some poor choices and lost everything. Rather than face his creditors or even my mother and me, he took his own life."

Winston had said as much, but hearing it stated in such a hard, cold fashion raised the bile in her throat. "Oh, Nathan. I'm so sorry."

His green eyes blazed. "No more sorry than we were. My mother quickly found another man to marry. I chose a different path. Some saw it as a retreat, that I was running away from my problems as surely as my father had. I see it as moving toward a better, cleaner future. I'm beholden to no man, indebted to none. I have little to lose as I refuse to acquire more than I need. If some judge me for that, it's their concern, not mine."

How different. Every man she knew, even Winston, was always reaching for more. What would it be like to be content? To be sufficient?

"Thank you for telling me," she said. "You're right. At

some point I might have remembered Mr. Kincaid's poisoned words and wondered. Now I know the truth. I promise you, I will not allow it to slow me in achieving my goal."

———— {{ }} ————

The muscles in Nathan's back were like iron, as if he'd carried her pack twenty miles in a day. What, had he let Kincaid's jibes get to him, after all?

"There's more that you should know," he said. "My father may have been precariously perched, but the loss that pushed him over, that caused it all to crash, was a debt called in by Cash Kincaid."

She stared at him. "Well then. That only lowers my estimation of Mr. Kincaid further. If my climb makes him think about his behavior, so much the better. I will not let you down."

Amazing. She was climbing a mountain to win women the vote and safeguard her own future, but Nathan was the one she didn't want to disappoint.

"Until tomorrow, then, Miss Baxter," he said, giving her a bow. It was harder than usual to leave the house.

He had a few tasks yet to complete, but he could not forget her promise as he started away from the stretch of elegant mansions and fine carriages. His father and mother had always been focused on their own spheres—the world of expansive transactions and social superiority. He had not consciously thought of making them proud. They had pride enough. His mother still did. He tried to see her from time to time, and she generally refused. Silk-draped walls did not pair well with homespun. He was far more welcome among Waldo and his friends.

The old pioneer had arranged the supplies they needed but waited for delivery until Nathan could tell him Miss Baxter and her stepfather were ready to leave. He'd also picked up food for the trip and the climb. In the meantime, he and Nathan had been bunking in Shem's back room, with the horses and mules at the closest livery stable. He could hardly wait to let his friend know they would be leaving the day after tomorrow. Time to get home to their cabin, where no one judged him for what he wore or how he acted.

Where no blue-eyed beauty made him wonder what might have been had he stayed.

"Hardee! Nathan Hardee!"

Nathan turned at the call. A man was striding toward him. The brown beard could not disguise the round face or the grin it wore.

"Mr. Thackery," Nathan said with a nod.

Eugene Thackery raised his bushy brown brows until they nearly disappeared under his derby. "Why the formality? I'm delighted to see you."

He would be the first. Nathan had lost track of the number of so-called friends who had distanced themselves from him after his father's ruin.

"Then I'm glad to see you too," he said. It had been a long time since he'd engaged in the social niceties, but he remembered the routine. "How are your parents, your sister?"

"Well, thank you." His mouth remained open a moment as if he meant to ask after Nathan's family. Then he closed his lips and smiled.

Nathan could comment on the weather or the shocking price of vegetables. All seemed trite. He glanced over the fellow again. Well-cut wool coat and trousers in the narrow plaid that every businessman seemed to be wearing, if Kincaid and Winston were any indication. Perhaps more girth than the last time he'd seen him—a good cook? And a wife. Nathan nodded to his left hand, where a gold band gleamed. "Married, I see."

His smile widened. "Married, and never happier. I have been blessed with a son, and we have another child on the way."

His awe at the fact was evident by the lift of his chin and the sparkle in his gray eyes.

"Congratulations," Nathan said, and meant it.

"I was heading for a late lunch at the Union Club," Eugene said. "Join me. I'd like to hear what you've been doing."

Nathan cocked his head. "You sure about that?"

"Absolutely!" He sobered. "My father was ill at the time yours passed, so I couldn't break away to find you and extend my condolences. I heard you left town."

"I have a homestead out on the mountain road," Nathan said. "It suits me."

"It looks as if it does. Please. Be my guest. I'd like to hear all about it."

He ought to refuse. What good could come of it? Surely Eugene noticed the differences in their clothing and boots. Nathan would no longer be accepted as a man of his social class. Look at how Mrs. Winston treated him.

But it had been a long time since anyone like Eugene had cared to converse at any length. And he was hungry.

"Very well," Nathan said, and Eugene moved in beside him.

"It's a fine establishment," he said. "Built in the last few years. Good thing too. It's not as if many of us have money to spare to finance such an undertaking now."

"You're doing all right?" Nathan asked as they neared the white three-story building on the edge of the hill. "I seem to recall you were a major shareholder in the St. Paul and Tacoma Lumber Company."

"We get by," Eugene said. "We've had to cut back on hours here and there, but the country always needs lumber. Once things settle, I expect we'll be back to full strength and then some."

They all talked that way—the newspaper editors, Winston, Kincaid. This Panic was a minor matter, easily resolved. It hadn't been minor to the men crowding around the church this morning. He'd seldom seen such anger or despair.

None of that was evident at the Union Club. Gentlemen lounged before the twin bow windows on C Street, with a view toward the mansions their fortunes had built. Others strolled the covered deck at the back of the building, gazing down at the railroad and granaries that fueled the city's exports. At Eugene's request, the frock-coated doorman called a waiter in a long white apron to lead them to a table overlooking Commencement Bay. The linen tablecloth was nearly as snowy as the peak in the distance.

They ordered the special of the day—steamed clams still in their shells with crusty rolls and fresh-churned butter—and Eugene told him all about his wife, Amelia ("sweetest woman I ever met and to think she'd want to marry me"), and his little boy ("clever lad. He'll go far—you'll see"). Nathan dutifully asked after mutual friends and acquaintances and talked about his cabin and work. Eugene volunteered, gingerly, that Annabelle had married a lumber baron and moved to San Francisco. Odd that Nathan felt nothing at the news.

"So, you've climbed the mountain more than a dozen times," Eugene marveled. "That must be a record."

"I've only been to the summit twice," Nathan told him, pulling a clam from the shell with a silver fork. "The climbing party generally doesn't want someone else along to get the credit."

"Unfair," Eugene commiserated. "But it's seldom those who do the work that history remembers. When are you going again?"

"Next week, if the weather holds," Nathan said. "I leave the day after tomorrow with Miss Baxter and Mr. Winston of the Puget Sound Bank of Commerce."

Eugene leaned back on the padded seat, gray eyes widening. "So, she's really going to do it. Amelia was at the meeting when Miss Baxter was asked."

"Your wife is a suffragette, then," Nathan surmised.

"She is." Eugene's smile and tone attested to his pride in the fact. "She has high hopes this climb will wake people up, make them think. What chance do you give Miss Baxter of success?"

Originally, little. Now that he'd seen her determination and knew what was at stake for her personally?

"Eighty percent," he said, "and only because weather might hold her back."

Eugene grinned. "That's high praise." He regarded Nathan a moment, then lowered his fork with a chink of silver on china. "I know that look. Be careful, Nathan. More than one man has backed away, disappointed, from attempting to prove himself to Miss Coraline Baxter."

Nathan frowned. "I've no need to prove myself. I'm just doing what she paid me to do—lead her up a mountain."

"So long as she doesn't lead you down a primrose path. I tell you, Nathan, that cool beauty can go to a man's head. Look at Kincaid."

Nathan toyed with the next clam, twisting it around in the shell. "He claims he wants to marry her."

Eugene threw up a hand. "Half the bachelors in Tacoma want to marry her! She's refused any that have offered. Rumors were she was holding out for bigger game, but they don't come much bigger than Kincaid."

"Would you want your sister to marry Kincaid?" Nathan challenged.

Eugene shuddered. "No, thank you. As far as I can see, he's hoping marriage to her will allow him to wiggle more firmly into good society. I'll be cheering when Miss Baxter refuses him."

His hand fumbled in his coat a moment before producing his card. He leaned forward again to offer it to Nathan. "And I'll be cheering for you as well. If you ever want to leave your mountain hideaway, regain your place in society, let me know. I failed you when you most needed my friendship. I'd like the opportunity to be a better friend now."

Nathan took the card. "Thank you. I'll remember that."

But he doubted that anything could tempt him back.

8

Cora had another long soak in the tub that afternoon. It wasn't as if she was going to have the opportunity once they left Tacoma. And spending any time with Cash Kincaid always left her feeling as if she needed a bath.

She'd first become aware of him at the Puget Sound University. Hard to miss a man who offered the school a quarter of a million dollars to fund its growth. Every student had been invited to the ceremony recognizing the gift. He'd looked so humble at the podium beside the dean, acknowledging the praise heaped upon him with a self-deprecating smile. A businessman with philanthropic tendencies. Commendable.

"And this is Miss Baxter, one of our finest students," the dean had said as he'd introduced her at the reception afterward. "She is quite accomplished in the area of mathematics."

"Miss Baxter," Kincaid had said, smile brightening, as if someone had turned on the electricity. "A pleasure."

It had been a pleasure, at first. Over coffee at the café nearest the school and with the other students in her class, he'd been willing to share business practices, debate the merits of the gold standard, argue over the rates of lending. At moments, she thought he might be open to supporting women's suffrage. When he'd first called at the house, she'd expected more of the same, and a little thrill had gone through her that he would single her out. Perhaps she wouldn't have to work for Winston when she graduated. Perhaps she'd become an accountant for Kincaid Industries, guiding the company to greater glory.

Then he'd met her mother, and everything had changed. No longer was Cora someone to be mentored and encouraged. She was as her mother had always wanted her to be—the grand prize in a matrimonial race. A shame she had no interest in competing. Everything he'd said, everything he'd done, had been because he intended to have her.

And so she'd taken out pen and paper and reevaluated him as she would one of the proposals that crossed her desk to review at the bank. A few questions of his associates, asked with sufficient charm and interest, had gained her knowledge of business practices he would never have disclosed publicly. To his credit, he was handsome, he attempted to be polite, he had wealth, and he might be persuaded to support her cause. To his debit, he was manipulative, conniving, tight-fisted with his workers, callous to the needs of others, and occasionally cruel in exacting revenge for some slight.

Proposal denied. Not even worth further discussion. She'd filed her assessment in her desk.

And she'd refused to allow her mother to force her into marrying him. She would climb a mountain to keep her freedom.

Now everything for the trip lay on her bed for packing. Besides the things they had purchased from Dickson Brothers, another package had arrived that afternoon. Lily had brought up the parcel wrapped in brown paper.

"Miss Fuller brought it by," she said, offering it to Cora.

Cora hurried to untie the twine. Inside lay thick folds of gray-blue flannel. A white note fluttered out. Lily caught it, and they both bent their heads over it.

"A loan only," Cora read aloud. "Do them proud. It will be their second time at the summit."

Lily frowned, but Cora shook out the folds.

Her maid goggled. "Are those bloomers?"

"And a coat to cover them," Cora acknowledged, turning from side to side to see how they draped. "We'll likely have to find a way to cinch in the waist. But I am indebted to Miss Fuller for thinking of me."

"Your mother won't allow it," Lily predicted, taking a step back as if she thought the flannel might bite.

Cora lowered the fabric, stomach knotting. "You're right. We can't tell her."

Lily's lips compressed, but she shook her head. "We can't lie to the mistress."

"I won't lie," Cora promised. "But these are important, Lily. Wearing them might be the only way I make it safely to the top of Rainier. Please, say nothing."

Lily had nodded, and now the precious bloomers and coat were neatly refolded on the covers, waiting their turn to go into the pack at the foot of the bed.

She was out of the bath and standing as Lily laced her into her satin-covered stays when there was a knock at the door. Before she could dart to the bed and hide the bloomers, her mother swept in.

"I am pleased to see you remember some of your manners,"

she announced as she glanced at the dinner dress draped over the chair.

Cora edged away from the bed, anything to keep her mother's gaze from going in that direction. "I am not a savage, Mother."

"I will have to accept your word on that," she said. "I was quite distressed by your reception of Mr. Kincaid this afternoon. We do not treat guests with such contempt."

Only those who did not live up to her mother's standards, but Cora decided not to say that aloud. "I cannot like him, Mother. I wish you would accept that."

Her mother moved to the dressing table and rearranged the tortoiseshell brush and comb in front of the mirror. Could she see the bloomers in the reflection? Cora could scarcely breathe.

"I grant you his wealth is newly acquired," her mother said, "but most men here could say the same."

"It isn't his wealth that concerns me, but his attitude." She winced as Lily tugged the strings tighter. "I have heard stories that he takes opportunities which prove the ruin of others."

Her mother glanced in the mirror, and Cora froze. So did Lily.

But her mother merely patted a strand of silvery blond hair back into her coiffure before straightening to look at Cora. "It is unbecoming for a lady to discuss a gentleman's financial dealings. I blame that college of yours for putting such ideas in your head. When I agreed to allow you to attend, I had hopes you would meet a nice young man you could admire."

Her mother had hoped for a match. It took money to send a son, or daughter, to college, therefore the graduates must come from a certain social class. But Cora hadn't attended to find a wealthy husband. She'd wanted qualifications no business could deny. A college degree put her head and shoulders above most male accountants in the city.

She'd still had to accept a position at Winston's bank. A lady accountant, it seemed, made too many men nervous. Even Cash Kincaid. Funny how the only one she felt comfortable being herself around was Nathan Hardee.

"Which of your dinner dresses will you be taking on this trip?" her mother asked, moving toward the wardrobe.

At least she could no longer see the bed. Cora shook her head at Lily, then edged to the bloomers and tipped them down into the pack. "I won't need dinner dresses, Mother. The only place I'll be dining is around a campfire."

"Nonsense," her mother said, opening the carved walnut doors and perusing the offerings as if she hadn't helped pick out each herself. "Surely there are hotels with dining rooms along the way. They will expect you to change out of your travel dirt. And, at the very least, you must have one for the send-off party at Lake Park."

Cora straightened. "Mr. Hardee hasn't mentioned a send-off party."

Her mother drew out Cora's sea-green silk gown and studied it as if determined to find flaws in it too. "Of course he hasn't mentioned it. I didn't consult him in the matter. Miss Carruthers has done excellent work in making the arrangements for me. I believe there will be a considerable escort."

Cora stared at her. "Mother, what have you done?"

"Merely ensured your social standing, dear," her mother said. "Pack the lavender silk." She replaced the green gown, shut the wardrobe, and sailed for the door. "See you at dinner."

———— {{ }} ————

Her mother had not been willing to offer more details over dinner, but Cora learned the full of it the next morning when Mimi came to call.

"As soon as your mother approached me, I knew her vision would fit perfectly with our plans," her friend assured her as they strolled the gardens behind the house. All the homes along this part of C Street backed up to Cliff Avenue and had rear lawns looking out over Commencement Bay. Her mother had taken some trouble to plant roses, lilacs, and hawthorns, giving the space the look of an English garden.

"I suppose it will give us added publicity," Cora allowed, skirts brushing the grass as they approached the two-story carriage house at the back of the garden.

Mimi adjusted her green velvet hat against the brine-tinged breeze as if she feared for the pheasant feather adorning the crown. "Indeed. If we show how many people support you, others will be sure to rally to our side."

There was that. Mimi may not have become an accountant, but she knew how to calculate.

"Very well," Cora allowed. "But only to Lake Park. It would be unfair to Mr. Hardee and our friends if they went farther."

Mimi nodded. "Certainly. They can return home after the dance."

"Dance!" Cora cried so loudly one of the horses neighed in answer from its stall in the carriage house.

"Dance," Mimi insisted. "So pack something pretty. I've arranged to split the proceeds with the hotel, so we will raise money for our activities at the same time. Many will be staying the night at Lake Park to send you off in the morning in style."

It was nearly as impossible to argue with her friend as it was with her mother. "Mr. Hardee isn't going to like it," Cora predicted.

Mimi tossed her head, making her hat slip on her upswept raven hair. "Mr. Hardee will simply have to accustom himself to it."

And Cora would have to be the one to explain it to him when he called tomorrow.

———— {{ }} ————

Nathan stood looking up at the grand house on Tacoma Avenue. Three stories edged in bric-a-brac, at least eight bedrooms, all but one of them as empty as the owner's heart. Why was he here?

"Sorry, sir," the older maid said when she answered his knock. "Madam has gone out, and we're not sure when she might return. If you'd like to leave a card?"

He hadn't carried a calling card in years. It wasn't as if he had many neighbors to call upon or time for such things. And most of the people homesteading in the Succotash Valley would likely have laughed at such an affectation.

"No, thank you," he said before turning to go.

"I'll be sure to tell her you came by," the maid called after him.

Not that that would make any difference.

He paused on the sidewalk, feeling as adrift as the clouds crossing above him. No. He would not succumb to the melancholy that had driven him out of the city at his father's death. He'd felt adrift then too, watching doors closing and nothing opening.

"We must go on with our lives," his mother had said,

twisting a silk handkerchief around her fingers as they rested in the lap of her mourning gown. "Mr. Porter of the Northern Pacific has let me know he holds me in the highest regard. As soon as appropriate, we will wed."

He'd gaped at her. "Wed? You're marrying again?"

"Yes," she'd snapped. "And it isn't as if I have a choice. Your father left me nothing, and you . . ."

"Have nothing to offer either," he'd finished for her. "Thank you for the reminder, Mother."

"You're young," she'd retorted, spine stiffening. "You'll have opportunities. It's different for women."

Somehow, he thought Cora would have found another path.

He shook his head as he started for the banker's home. She hadn't given him permission to use her first name. Likely, she never would, him being the paid help, after all. But his mind refused to think of her any other way now.

The maid let him into the house with no questions this time, to the fancy parlor he'd seen when he'd come with Miss Fuller. He knew the practice. Family and close friends were invited into the family parlor deeper in the house. It had been an accident that he'd been allowed there when he'd first called. Of course, either parlor was better than waiting on the porch.

He made sure to take a seat on one of the hard-backed chairs near the window, nonetheless. By the way Cora was eyeing his coat, she'd realized he'd only brought the one with him. Not that he needed all that many where he lived.

Her mother insisted on joining them, gowned in mint green with roses embroidered on the long bodice, and this time she did not offer refreshments.

"I'd hoped to see your pack," he told Cora.

She shifted on the hard seat near his, her gaze sweeping the flowered carpet. Not humility, not this woman. What was she trying to hide? Had she changed her mind?

Disappointment nipped at him. Likely only regret for the lost wages.

"I will bring it down shortly," she promised, "but we must discuss something else first. I have been informed that we will have an escort when we leave tomorrow."

"Escort." The word hung in the air as tangibly as the scent of her mother's perfume.

"An accompaniment, if you will," she hurried to assure him. "And only to the hotel at Lake Park. Were we planning on staying there?"

He nodded slowly, trying to imagine what sort of escort she'd planned. The militia lining the street on horseback, sabers crossed overhead? Tacoma's own brass band marching beside them, playing them out of the city? "How many people are joining this accompaniment?"

Again she shifted, as if the chair had grown hot. "I'm not entirely sure. A dozen, perhaps?"

Her mother tutted from her perch on a tufted chair across the room. "You have many more admirers than that, Cora-line. I would expect no less than forty. Miss Carruthers tells me every room at Lake Park will be filled for the dance."

Words failed him a moment. "Dance."

Cora surged up from her seat and set about pacing the room, her skirts swinging as if even the geometric pattern on the edges longed to escape. "Yes, a dance. To raise money for our cause. I'm sure it will be delightful. Let's discuss the rest of the trip. I believe you were going to share the route."

He was still trying to accustom himself to the fact that there'd be a dance. Was this a game to her, after all?

"I'd planned to stay at a friend's farm the second night," he said, leaning back on the chair and stopping at the warning creak. "My cabin in the Succotash Valley the third, then Longmire's Springs before we start climbing. For the climb itself, the first night at Camp of the Clouds in Paradise Park and Camp Muir at about the nine-thousand-foot level the next two nights. Then return to Paradise Park and reverse order on the way back."

Cora paused to aim a frown his way. "So long?"

He crossed his arms over his chest, recognized the defensive gesture, and forced his hands to fall to his sides. "It might be possible to go faster. But I'd like to give you and your stepfather as much time as possible to prepare yourselves to climb. You've done well in town, but climbing at altitude can sap the breath and hinder the heart. Best to get used to it gradually."

"The timetable is unacceptable, as are the locations," Mrs. Winston declared. "Mr. Winston cannot possibly be away from his bank so long. And surely there are more suitable lodgings. I understood Mount Tacoma was an important attraction to visitors."

"It is," Nathan agreed as Cora resumed her pacing. "But no hotels have yet been built on its slopes. You'll have to accept my word for that."

Her mother regarded him. "You disappoint me, Mr. Hardee. From what Mr. Winston told me of your background, I had expected a gentleman who recognized the finer points of good society."

"I recognize them, ma'am," he said. "I just don't see the need for them in this case."

Her mother lifted her chin. "I can see you are determined to be unreasonable. I shall accompany you to Longmire's Springs."

Cora jerked to a stop. "But Mother . . ."

Her mother held up a hand. "I see it as necessary, Coraline. None of you with the possible exception of Mr. Winston have any sense of decorum. I will have Lily pack my trunk."

Cora opened her mouth as if to protest, then shut it again and cast him a look.

Cora, asking for his assistance? Pigs must be soaring over the house this very minute.

"If you insist on coming, you can't bring a trunk," he told her mother. "The mules can't handle one."

"Then I suggest," her mother clipped out, "that you bring a wagon or better yet a carriage."

She had no concept. "Not possible. The roads between here and there aren't ready to accommodate a carriage. You'd break an axel on the first stretch of corduroy."

Her blue eyes narrowed until he could feel the chill from across the room. "You must think me a fool, Mr. Hardee. I know no roads are made of fabric."

He did think her a fool, but not for mistaking the word. "Corduroy roads are made by embedding logs into the mud, ma'am. It keeps the dirt from washing away in the rain. They make for bumpy, hard riding. Carriages can't handle the constant strain. Neither can most wagons. We'll be riding horses and stringing mules. And the weight of the packs has already been accounted for. If you want to come along, you'll ride a horse and carry a pack like your daughter."

Cora's face broke into a grin that tugged him closer. The brief glimpse disappeared as she schooled her face and looked to her mother. "You see, Mother? It simply isn't possible for you to join us."

Her mother rose, and he stood as propriety demanded. Her gaze traveled up to his face, and her lips compressed as if she found the very height of him insulting. "I will speak to Mr. Winston. He will have something to say in the matter. You may go, Mr. Hardee."

He looked to her daughter. "After I've approved Miss Baxter's pack."

"It's all right, Mother," she said in a rush, turning for the door. "It will only take a moment."

Mrs. Winston accompanied her out of the room.

Nathan sank onto the chair. Winston had said his wife wasn't easily swayed. The banker had better be persuasive this time, because Cora's mother would never tolerate the trip from Tacoma to Longmire's Springs.

And having her along would be a constant trial to his patience, and Cora's determination to reach the summit.

9

Mimi's send-off rivaled the one President Harrison had been given when he'd visited the city two years ago. Carriages lined C Street in both directions, some bearing banners reading "Votes for Women." Ladies waved handkerchiefs out the windows. Gentlemen on fine mounts rode back and forth, greeting friends and acquaintances. And a group of older ladies gathered under the trees along the plank sidewalk, looking about in surprise, as if they wondered when the circus elephants would arrive.

"I believe they wish to support suffrage, dearest," Winston explained when Cora's mother questioned him. "I suspect they must keep to the shadows because their husbands wouldn't approve."

Cora would have liked to encourage them, but she had enough on her hands keeping her mother from the packs that lay waiting in the shade of the porte cochère. As it was, her mother kept ordering Lily to fetch something else to add to the pile: a lace-edged petticoat, a feathered hat, a gilt-edged hand mirror, and Cora's jewel case.

"Take them all back," Cora told the maid. "I don't need them, and there isn't room if I did."

"I know, miss." Lily glanced toward her mother. "But maybe you could tell her that."

It wasn't as if she could tell her mother anything. Neither could Winston. He had been unable to dissuade her from coming with them. In fact, her mother had insisted on riding in the carriage to Lake Park, her saddle horse and his tied behind. The yellow-sided coach also crowded the porte cochère, trunk and hatboxes stacked on top. Charlie, their man-of-all-work, was bringing Cora's horse, Blaze, from the stables, her red leather sidesaddle in place and a red, white, and blue satin banner stretched over the back of the palomino proclaiming Cora's support for women's suffrage. When Nathan and Mr. Vance arrived with the mules, they had to thread their way onto the drive.

And when had she started thinking of him as Nathan?

The heat in her cheeks told her she was blushing as she went with Winston to greet them.

"Well met, my boy, Mr. Vance," her stepfather heralded. "We seem to have a few more things that require accommodation. I don't suppose you have room in the packs."

"No," Nathan said from his saddle on a chestnut mare. "The loads are balanced. I explained that to your wife yesterday. And neither the carriage nor what's on top can be taken beyond Lake Park."

Her mother must have heard, for she raised her voice where she stood beside the carriage. "You must tell him to do as we want, Mr. Winston. We are the ones hiring him."

"And we are the ones who must listen," Cora suggested. "Mr. Hardee understands such things."

"You put a great deal of stock in his opinions," her mother complained, flicking a speck of dust off the shoulder of her sky-blue coat so that the lace at her wrists fluttered.

"Why yes, Mother, I do," Cora agreed, "seeing as how I am putting my life in his hands." She turned to Nathan. "Would you care to inspect my pack, Mr. Hardee? I'd like your concurrence that it is appropriately balanced and carries the necessary items."

He swung down and followed her to where Charlie had strapped the pack behind her saddle.

"I'm terribly sorry about all this," she said, taking the gelding's reins in one hand and stroking the white flash down his nose, for which he'd been named. "I tried to convince her to stay home, but she would have none of it."

"She'll give up once she sees the road down to the Mashel River," he predicted, loosening the strings at the top of the pack and peering inside.

"I wouldn't count on that."

He chuckled as he moved this and that aside as if weighing each item. Then he straightened. "The right things, well balanced. Nice work, Miss Baxter."

Warmth rose inside her once more. "I learned from the best, sir."

He inclined his head.

Charlie stood waiting to help her mount. He bent with interlaced fingers.

Before she could raise her foot, Nathan's hands spanned her waist. She sucked in a breath, and he tossed her up into the sidesaddle.

Swallowing, she hurriedly settled herself, draping the navy riding habit about her limbs.

"Ready?" he asked, green eyes as deep as the forest they would soon enter.

Cora nodded, then found her voice. "Ready."

He glanced to Oscar on the top of the coach. "Follow us out of the city."

Her pulse was galloping, faster than Blaze could go. It must have been the excitement. This was it. She was heading for the mountain, and glory.

As soon as Nathan had remounted, he and Mr. Vance set off from the drive, each holding the rope attached to a well-laden mule. Cora followed. The carriage rumbled behind them.

A shout went up. It was joined by a dozen others. The women under the trees waved at her, faces hopeful. Mimi's clear alto started the song.

> Daughters of freedom arise in your might!
> March to the watchwords Justice and Right!
> Why will ye slumber? Wake, o wake!
> Lo! On your legions light doth break!

A chorus rang out over the sound of tack, the rattle of carriage wheels, and the drum of hooves.

> Sunder the fetters "custom" hath made!
> Come from the valley, hill, and glade!

It was amazing, unthinkable, stupendous. She was causing a stir of the very best kind. She kept her head high as they rode along C Street and down to Pacific. Businessmen came out of the banks and waved their hands over their heads.

Lady shoppers and the clerks who attended them crowded the windows. Other wagons and carriages stopped in the street to watch them pass.

Things settled a little as they turned right at Nineteenth, rode up to Jefferson, and followed the steel tracks of the Tacoma and Lake Park Railway past the wooden steeple of Our Lady of the Holy Rosary. Some of the gentlemen had started the chorus of "The Boy I Love Is Up in the Gallery," and the ladies in the carriages were laughing as they all thundered over the bridge spanning the gulley beyond the church. The road widened on the other side.

"You're too slow, Miss Baxter!" Johnny Westacre shouted as he galloped around her.

"And I've always considered you too fast," Cora flung after her friend with a laugh.

A moment more, and the other carriages, including her mother's, followed him.

"Race you to Lake Park!" Mimi cried with a wave.

Tempting, but Blaze would have to go far the next few days. No sense tiring him.

Cora cantered up beside Nathan, sweeping away dust with her free hand.

"You're not going to join them?" he asked.

There was no surprise in the tone, only curiosity.

"Not now," Cora said. "And I apologize again for all the fuss. High spirits. And my mother has always preferred to lead."

"She'll have to learn to follow once we leave Lake Park," he said as the cavalcade disappeared among a copse of fir.

Cora sighed. "We can always hope."

With her parade gone ahead, quiet settled over her. They

were up on a plateau that stretched into the distance. On every side, fields of golden wheat lapped up against towers of dusky green hops under a heavy gray sky. Here and there a log cabin, barn, or clapboard house spoke of families and progress. Men and women out toiling glanced up as they passed.

The blast of a horn broke the silence. Nathan and Mr. Vance pulled the mules to the side of the road and Cora came in behind them as the steam engine chugged past, yellow sides gleaming. Only a few riders gazed out from seats in the car behind.

"Where are they going?" Cora asked as the dust settled.

"Fern Hill, perhaps," Nathan said as he and his partner urged the mules forward once more. "It has a community with a school and a church. It's too late in the day to start for Lake Park."

She came alongside him and Mr. Vance again. "I suppose I should have known that. We get proposals from the outskirts of the city on occasion—farmers wanting to buy more land or new equipment, merchants hoping to expand their locations. There's talk of extending the Tacoma and Lake Park Railway out to the mountain."

Nathan glanced at her. "You get involved in such matters?"

"If someone asks the Puget Sound Bank of Commerce for money, I do," Cora assured him. "When there's just discussion over dinner or at parties, providing my input becomes trickier. Some men don't like women to have opinions."

He snorted. "Idiots."

She eyed him. "You surprise me, sir. You certainly haven't been shy about countering my opinions about this venture."

"You're entitled to any opinion you like," he said. "But there are opinions, and there are facts. One can be argued; the other can't."

"A bit limited, but in general I agree. Unfortunately, I've found any number of people only too happy to argue against facts, especially the fact that women are in every way capable of voting."

He nodded thoughtfully. "So have I."

"Why, Mr. Hardee, did we just come to a consensus?" she asked with a laugh.

He smiled. "Stranger things have happened, Miss Baxter. Though I doubt we'll ever reach such an accord with your mother."

"What will you do if she insists on bringing the carriage?" she asked.

"Steal the horses."

She stared at him. That face was firm, unyielding, yet there was a twinkle in his green eyes.

Cora laughed. "You're teasing me. Seriously, sir, we must have a plan. If the way is as difficult as you say, we can't let her delay us."

"That eager to climb?" Mr. Vance asked.

"That determined, Mr. Vance," she answered. "Make no mistake. I love my mother dearly, and I do all I can to respect her wishes. But I will climb that mountain, whether she likes it or not."

Easy to say when they'd left the city only moments before. She had no idea what lay ahead. And neither did her mother.

At least she rode well. Waldo had said as much, and Nathan could see it in Cora's upright posture, her ease on the tooled leather sidesaddle, and the way she held the reins.

"Fine horse," Nathan commented.

She brushed down the silky mane. "Blaze is a thoroughbred, through and through. And what of yours?"

He gave the mare's reddish-brown shoulder a rub. "Honoré was bred by a friend of mine, a sturdy horse for hard work."

As if she disagreed, Honoré tossed her head.

"Mine's named Bud," Waldo put in. "Short for Buddy. And this here's Sparky." He nodded back toward the pack mule. "Nathan's towing Quack."

Her brows went up, and she twisted as far as the sidesaddle would allow to glance at the piebald mule behind Nathan. "Quack?"

"His bray is shorter and deeper than most mules," Nathan explained. "Waldo thinks he sounds like a duck."

Waldo nodded as she faced front again. "Like a mallard in flight. You wait."

"I look forward to hearing Quack give voice," she assured him. "Excuse me. I should make sure they all kept moving to Lake Park. For all I know, Mother decided to turn west to Fort Steilacoom instead or Mimi accosted some farmer to convince him to champion women's rights."

She urged her horse into a gallop, the banner flapping against his side.

"Who's going to win in the fight between her and her mother, do you think?" Waldo asked, watching her.

"Normally, I'd say Miss Baxter," Nathan told him. "But she hesitates to take her mother on directly."

Waldo shook himself. "Who wouldn't? Step one foot out of line, and you're in for a tongue lashing. Well, if the mother insists on coming, I say we charge extra. We agreed to take Miss Baxter and her stepfather, not that lot."

"That lot will leave after tonight," Nathan promised. "And her mother won't last. If the road doesn't deter her, our friend Henry's place will."

Waldo laughed. "Can't see her sleeping in a barn, that's for sure. And somehow, I don't think she's partial to folks like him."

———— {{ }} ————

They reached the Lake Park Hotel in time for dinner. The three-story clapboard structure, its front facing the lake, sat on a rise surrounded by grassy prairie. Below, ringed by firs, Spanaway Lake sparkled like a diamond in an iron setting, its breeze-rippled waters reflecting the white-capped mountain in the distance.

Cora was waiting for them in the lobby. Though the space boasted wood-paneled walls and several plush red-velvet chairs, her riding habit looked right at home. "Mother left the carriage at the livery stable beyond the hotel," she reported.

Nathan nodded. "We saw it when we stabled the mules. That's where we'll be sleeping tonight."

She frowned. "Surely that's not necessary. I know the rooms are full, but someone can share so you and Mr. Vance can get a good night's sleep."

Nice of her to think of them.

Waldo hitched up his trousers. "The supplies we need for the next month are in those packs, miss. I don't intend to let them out of my sight for more than a meal or two. Speaking of which." He inhaled deeply, gaze darting toward the entrance to the dining room at the left of the lobby. "That's roast beef."

"And duck and lamb," she added. "I already checked the menu. You go ahead. I have to change before I join Mother and Winston."

With a grin to Nathan, he trotted for the dining room.

"You look fine to me," Nathan said.

She smiled. "Why, Mr. Hardee, how you do go on. You could turn a lady's head with such praise."

He nodded to the men lounging by the clerk's station. They were all watching her. "You've already turned heads. But I expect that's nothing new."

The prettiest pink, like the first anemones poking out of the snow, bloomed in her cheeks. "Now look, you've put me to the blush."

How could he not look, like every other man in the place? He knew what they were thinking. A wife like her was why half the men in the area built farmsteads, broke their backs sawing timber, or bent over desks all day. Coming home to her would make any work worthwhile.

He reined in his thoughts. A wife? Employment? Where had those thoughts come from? He'd turned his back on all that. He belonged to no one. That's how he preferred it. And no amount of time spent in Coraline Baxter's company was going to change that.

Especially the dance that night.

All her entourage joined her in the ballroom behind the hotel. Well, ballroom might have been too kind a word, for all the hotel insisted on using it. The walls were unplastered, the ceilings low, and the space dimly lit by oil lamps suspended on brass chains. But the plank floor was well polished, and the fiddler and pianist who took up their positions at the head of the room knew how to play. According to the sign in the lobby, they staged a dance every Friday and Saturday evening during the summer months.

And more than the guests came. At two bits, most anyone could pay the price of admission. The fine silk gowns of the ladies who had accompanied Cora brushed up against the cotton dresses of the local ladies as they waited along the walls for a gentleman to request a dance. The black suits and white shirtfronts of the gentlemen from Tacoma were a stark contrast to the red flannel and blue denim of the farmers from around the area.

And then there was Cora.

Gowned in purple silk, she spun around the dance floor, skirts belling. Each time she smiled, he wanted to smile back. Each time she laughed, something rose up inside him to answer. She was light, she was joy. She coaxed hope out of hiding.

And that was dangerous. His father's death, the reactions of so-called friends, had taught him to limit hope and dreams to something smaller, easily attainable, within his control.

So, he watched from a distance. The music swelled around him, punctuated by laughter and snatches of conversation. Perfumes mingled into a heady scent.

"You concerned about that wall?" Waldo asked, joining him.

Nathan glanced back at the rough wood. "Not particularly. Should I be?"

"Not that I know of. I just couldn't think of another

reason you thought you had to hold it up." He rubbed his hands together. "Plenty of lovely ladies to choose from. Let's dance."

"Go right ahead," Nathan said. "Enjoy yourself."

Waldo narrowed his eyes at him. "You got something against fun all of a sudden?"

"No. I'm having a fine night."

Waldo nodded slowly. "Yeah, I can tell. Suit yourself." He strutted away.

Nathan glanced around, and the hairs on the back of his neck went up. Cash Kincaid was bowing over Cora's hand while her mother simpered at him. When had he arrived? Didn't matter. Nathan pushed off the wall.

"One dance," Kincaid was crooning as Nathan reached them. "What's the harm?"

"I have already refused once, Mr. Kincaid," Cora said, voice firm. "Please don't pursue the matter. I'd hate to embarrass us both."

Kincaid's face tightened. By the wrinkle on Cora's nose, so had his grip on her fingers.

Nathan reached in and removed Kincaid's hand. "I'm afraid I can't allow Miss Baxter to dance any more tonight. She needs to be rested so she can climb the mountain."

Mrs. Winston's eyes were as blue as glacier ice and just as sharp, but Cora moved closer to Nathan.

"Quite right, sir," she said. "I wouldn't want to ruin my chances with a hasty misstep now."

"I thought, Mr. Hardee," her mother said, each word clipped, "that you wanted my daughter to practice."

"Climbing, ma'am, not dancing. Best to sit out. Won't you join me, Miss Baxter?"

"I'd be delighted," she said, putting her hand on his offered arm.

Nathan could feel Kincaid simmering as they turned away. He made a show of strolling slowly over to the nearest bench and handing her down as if she were made of fine crystal.

"Thank you," she murmured as he sat beside her. "Mother would have insisted that I dance with him."

"No always works for me," he suggested, putting his back once more to the wall.

She sighed. "It works for most people. Just not my mother and, I fear, Mr. Kincaid. So, I thank you again."

"Maybe you shouldn't," he said. "I told him the truth. You still have a mountain to climb."

"I know." The simple words were built on the determination he had come to expect.

And respect.

She had to climb a mountain, but why did he feel as if he were the one struggling up the slopes for the sky?

10

They left Lake Park the next morning, without the carriage. Cora had attempted to reason with her mother again, but Nathan won the day.

"I sent your coachman back on the streetcar," he said when he found them still arguing in the hotel lobby after breakfast. "You want to take your coach, you'll have to drive it yourself."

"You are impossible," her mother fumed. "Winston, discharge this man, immediately."

"Now, dearest," her stepfather said with an apologetic look to Nathan, "Mr. Hardee is the best, and I would not entrust your life or Coraline's to less."

Her stepfather managed to convince her to retire to her room to change into her riding habit. He went with her as if to make sure she did so.

"At least you didn't have to steal the horses," Cora teased Nathan, swishing her navy habit across the plank floor.

He nodded but turned away to speak to the clerk.

Cora frowned after him. Last evening at the dance, when

112

they'd sat out a moment, she'd felt . . . something. She knew that appreciative look in his green eyes, that tilt of his mouth. It was almost as if they were becoming friends.

But he'd turned away, as if her company could not satisfy now. She was aware of a distinct lowering of her spirits.

"There you are," Mimi called, sweeping into the room in cerulean silk and turning all heads in the process. She came to give Cora a hug. "Everyone else may protest to rise so early, but I will wave to you until you fade in the distance. And when you return, we will crow your triumph."

"We will," Cora promised. "And thank you."

"What are friends for?" Mimi smiled as she pulled back. "Now, go. Finish your preparations."

Waldo, as Mr. Vance had insisted she call him, was at the livery stable ahead of her, saddling the horses. Nathan was strapping the packs into place. Cora tried not to notice the muscles that bunched his coat as he worked. She patted Blaze, then hefted the saddle off the side wall and set it in place on the gelding's golden back. Turning, she found Nathan watching her.

"Don't you have someone who does that for you?" he asked.

She bent to cinch the saddle in place. "Oscar, our coachman, or Charlie, our man-of-all-work, will do it if I ask. But I believe if you own a horse, you should know how to take care of it." She straightened to look for the bridle and reins.

He handed them to her. "Very wise."

She wasn't sure why his compliment delighted her. She'd never sought approval and was used to it being withheld. But she couldn't deny it felt rather pleasant.

Her mother and Winston joined them a good half hour

later in front of the hotel. By then, Mimi had collected a cadre of gentlemen who appeared to want to know all about her, and only a few looked dismayed that she had turned the conversation to the subject of women's rights. Nathan and Waldo had everything else ready, including her mother's saddle horse, Duchess. Winston assisted her mother in mounting. Nathan approached Cora.

"Your hand, sir?" she asked, lifting one booted foot.

In answer, he grasped her waist and lifted her into place again.

She would not react. She would not react.

A shame she could not convince her pulse.

"Thank you," she said with all the cool politeness her mother had taught her.

From the steps of the hotel, Mimi applauded.

As if Nathan knew what Cora was feeling, he smiled. Every pretense fell away, and she smiled back.

"You're welcome," he said, large hand resting on the banner over Blaze's side. "It will be a long ride today. I'll do what I can to make it easier, on all of us."

He turned away, and she drew in a breath, gathered her reins, and directed Blaze forward.

They rode past the hotel, and Mimi waved her hands and cheered. Cora waved back. Then she turned her gaze toward the south.

As if determined to hide from her, the mountain was missing from the southeastern horizon. A cool mist hung in the air, dampening her cheeks. Waldo took the lead, with her mother and Winston behind. That left Cora to ride beside Nathan.

She'd ridden with gentlemen before, even Cash Kincaid

before she'd taken his measure. She couldn't remember noticing how easily they held the reins, how well they sat in the saddle. She certainly had never wished they might ride a little closer, so she might see the depths of their eyes or bask in the glow of their smile. What was wrong with her?

She forced her gaze forward. They were following a wide wagon road across a prairie that seemed to go on for miles in all directions. As when they'd traveled into Lake Park, clapboard houses, some two stories tall, stood among fields fenced in stands of fir.

Cora recognized the waving grain surrounding them. "That's wheat, and the taller stalks are corn."

"The staples to feed a family and the city," Nathan agreed. He nodded to a wall of evergreens that was growing closer in the distance. "Farther on it will be logging. A growing city needs lumber too."

Even years after the fire that had destroyed much of downtown Tacoma. Aside from the new city hall and some of the establishments in the business district, many of Tacoma's buildings were still made of wood.

The trees crept closer on the west, then on the east, as the road gently rose. After climbing a steeper hill, they rode down into a draw and crossed a creek that was more mud than water. Her hair, heavy with the damp, sagged under her riding hat. Mist glistened on the red leather of the saddle.

On the other side of the creek, the winding trail led up over hills, higher and higher, until she and Nathan broke out onto a broad prairie. The mist had risen with the land. The sky was blue, endless. And to the southeast . . .

Cora reined in and stared. White, rugged, massive, Rainier stood in majesty.

"The lady is expecting you to call, it seems," Nathan said, riding past. "Best not to keep her waiting."

Still feeling humbled, Cora urged Blaze forward once more.

They soon reached the forest again. Tall fir and cedar shadowed the road, as if they traveled through the tunnel Mr. Hill had bored through the Cascades to bring the Great Northern Railroad to Seattle. The way was just wide enough to go two abreast. Cora rode next to Nathan. The forest crowded close, sheltering them from the sun. Dusky-leaved rhododendron, feathery fern, and spiky salal covered the ground beneath the towering evergreens. The only break in the canopy came where giants had toppled. Mushrooms dined on their corpses.

"What made you come this way when you left Tacoma?" Cora asked as they cantered through the ale-brown waters of a creek. "You had so many choices—south to Olympia, north to Seattle, across the Sound to Port Townsend, east to the coal fields or all the way to New York, for that matter."

He kept his gaze trained on the trail ahead. "I just walked south until I ran out of road."

Walked? He hadn't even had a horse? "And that's when you met Waldo?"

He nodded. "He'd lost his wife and son, so he needed someone to look out for him."

She tried to imagine wandering away from the city into the unknown. "But to come so far. What did you hope to find?"

Her surprise must have been evident in her voice, for he drew himself up.

"Myself, Miss Baxter."

He clucked to his horse and rode ahead of her. As the

path narrowed further, she could not safely pace him again for some time.

They crossed marshland, the mud sucking at their horses' hooves, then around clear blue lakes. She smiled as they clomped across the first stretch of corduroy, but when she glanced back, her mother avoided her gaze. That won a laugh from her. Facing forward, she caught sight of the mountain again before they plunged back into forest.

The land was gradually rising once more, but she had not realized how high they had climbed until they came out of the trees and a valley spread before them, seamed by streams. Here and there, a homestead stood, like an island in a sea of green.

They stopped to rest the horses and eat a little. Fleecy clouds danced across the blue sky. Birds called from the wood. As her mother nibbled on the hardtack and cheese Waldo offered, Cora went to join Nathan where he stood looking out over the way ahead. He didn't acknowledge her presence, and she could see nothing in that wide valley that would require such concentration.

She puffed out a sigh. "Have I offended you, sir?"

He turned from the view, face committing to nothing. "No, Miss Baxter."

She shook her head. "Then why the sudden standoffishness?"

He raised a brow. "I didn't think it was all that sudden."

Was that a sparkle returning to his eyes? Better. "Oh, you have your moments, I'll grant you that. But I thought we were becoming friends. I hope nothing my mother said jeopardized that."

"It wasn't your mother," he said. He paused a moment, as if considering his next words. Then he met her gaze.

"Take a good look at me, Miss Baxter. Are you sure friendship is wise?"

She put her hands on her hips and made a show of looking him up and down. That height was less obvious here, where treetops caught in the clouds. But there was no denying the muscle and sinew, grit and determination.

Once more she felt . . . something. A frisson, a fizz, like she'd taken a sip of ginger beer on a hot day.

"I see nothing to concern me," she told him. "Your conversation is informative and engaging. Your character seems sound."

He leaned closer, until he blotted out the view and even the light. Perhaps she should be afraid, but she had the odd notion that this was where he belonged, filling her senses, her world.

"And what if it's all pretend?" he murmured. "What if I'm a hardened mercenary out to steal you blind?"

Though her pulse kicked up a notch, she spread her hands. "You picked a poor place to do it. We left the silver and my jewels at home."

He straightened with a chuckle. "My career as a thief is ruined."

"I guess you'll have to lead me up that mountain, after all."

She could have climbed to the stars on the back of that smile.

He broke her gaze to nod toward the others. "The ride down into the valley is one of the steepest we'll descend. I'll have Waldo and the mules go first, your mother and Winston behind. You'll ride right ahead of me."

So he'd be watching over her? Her pulse seemed to like that idea, for it gave another little skip.

"That sounds like a wise plan," she said. "And thank you for your patience with my mother. I know it's not easy."

He glanced to where her mother was scolding Waldo for failing to bring along napkins. "She uses propriety like a shield against anything new or different. I understand. My mother was the same way."

She still struggled to see the resemblance between the mountain man before her and the prosperous doyen who led society alongside her mother. "Do you see her often?"

"No," he said, and he did not meet her eyes. "My mother doesn't like reminders of unpleasant things."

And he was the unpleasant thing? How horrid. As frustrated as she often was with her mother, she respected what her mother had done to survive and protect herself and Cora. And she was thankful her own choices, however different, had not split them apart, yet.

Would a friendship with him prove the final divide between her and her mother?

———— ⟨⟨ ⟩⟩ ————

Nathan watched Cora ahead of him as they started down into the Ohop Valley. At the front of the column, Waldo eased the pack mules down the slope. Mr. and Mrs. Winston seemed to have no trouble following, picking their way along the rutted trail. The tree-covered hillside gradually grew, like a wall, on their right, even as the sheer drop to their left gradually shrank. He should remain focused, but other thoughts intruded.

Friends, she'd said.

The idea beckoned to him. He'd lost so many friends over the years. Even the few who had been steadfast through his father's death had fallen away when Nathan had forsaken the city for the wild. Annabelle, who'd claimed to love him beyond distraction, hadn't been willing to associate with him. Why did Cora want to befriend him now?

Once, friendships had been based on what he had to offer: connection, advancement, advice on investment through his father. He'd associated with men who could offer something in return. Now his friendships were built on something deeper: support in good times and bad, appreciation of each other's character and goals. Faith in a loving, merciful God.

Was any of that possible between him and Cora?

It took a good hour to work themselves safely down to the valley, another to follow the base of the hill to the west across marshy fields. So, it was late afternoon when they rode onto Henry's farm.

Nathan had always admired the place above the junction of the Mashel and Nisqually Rivers, where fields of wheat and oats surrounded a cozy log house and barn. Horses grazed on some of the fields, raising their heads to eye him and the others. Honoré picked up the pace and whickered a greeting. One of Henry's sons, Thomas, was fixing a fence and lifted a hand in welcome.

"Why are we stopping?" Mrs. Winston demanded as Nathan reined in beside Waldo and the mules near the cedar shake outbuilding used to dry fish. "I do not see a hotel."

"No hotel," Nathan said, swinging down from the saddle. "We'll be sleeping in the barn."

Cora pressed a hand to her lips, but her mother stared at him.

"Nonsense." She turned to her husband. "Winston—pay

the occupant of that house. I will require my own bed, freshly made. And a bathing tub with plenty of hot water."

The green-painted front door banged open, and a gang of youngsters poured out onto the wide porch and down into the yard, shouting greetings and questions. Their grandfather ambled out behind them. He was a small man, not much taller than Cora, with a lined face that spoke of age. That age was belied by the twinkle in his dark eyes as he sighted Nathan. Though he wore the trousers, striped shirt, and gray wool waistcoat of a gentleman, the band in his jaunty broad-brimmed hat was woven of bright colors.

"Nathan Hardee," he greeted in English perfected by decades of straddling two cultures. "You bring me guests."

"I do," Nathan said, striding forward to meet the famous guide and shake his hand. "This is Mr. Winston, his wife, and their daughter, Miss Baxter." He turned to the others. "Meet So-to-lick, also known as Indian Henry."

Mrs. Winston's face was the same shade of red Cora turned when she was angry or embarrassed. "Sir," she managed.

Her husband had already dismounted. Now he came forward and extended his hand as well. "A pleasure, sir. Your name is legendary."

Henry shook hands. "Then my story will live beyond me. A man cannot ask for more than that. Come. You are welcome."

Mrs. Winston suffered one of the older children to lead her and her horse toward the barn.

Cora slid down from the sidesaddle and took her reins in hand. "Thank you for allowing us to stay the night, sir."

"Henry," he corrected her with a smile. "And you must tell me why you came all this way to see me."

She glanced quickly at Nathan. "Mr. Hardee is going to guide me to the top of the mountain."

His dark eyes lit. "Ah, you will climb it like my good friend Miss Fuller."

"Exactly like Miss Fuller," Cora agreed. "I hold her in the highest esteem."

"She is a good woman," he said. "Now, go. Settle your horse. We will eat together soon and talk more."

She followed Waldo and her family toward the barn.

"So, you will marry her?" Henry asked, watching them.

Nathan started. "No."

He pursed his lips. "Why not? She is passable. She speaks well. Her dress and her horse say she has money. You could use money."

Nathan smothered a laugh. "Miss Baxter is a fine woman. I'm not interested in marriage."

Now he frowned. "You have land and a good reputation. Do you not want sons and daughters to carry on your story?"

Like a storm, longing rushed at him. As an only child, how often had he dreamed of having a brother or sister at his side? He could imagine children of his own, running about the yard outside his cabin, splashing in the shallow waters of the lake behind it, peppering him with questions as he and their mother taught them all they'd learned about God's marvelous creation.

A mother with pale hair and big blue eyes, who thought she could climb a mountain.

He blinked away the vision to find his host regarding him with a smile as broad as the mountain itself.

"Right now," Nathan said, "I just want to get Miss Baxter and her father up Rainier and back safely."

He nodded. "Good. She will see your strength, your skill. And she will feel herself beholden to you. *Then* you ask her to marry you."

"Then I take my well-earned pay and go my own way," Nathan insisted, but the older man was already heading toward a rock-lined pit, where his grandchildren were piling wood.

Nathan blew out a breath. Henry had chosen to live in two worlds. He honored his native traditions, but he worshipped a Christian God. He hunted wild goat on the mountain slopes, where his wife, daughters-in-law, and granddaughters picked berries with baskets they had woven themselves, yet they spent most of the year raising horses, wheat, oats, and vegetables. His sons, Wickersham and Thomas, bore both a Boston, as Henry called English, and native name. He welcomed all, was respected by all.

Why did Nathan find it impossible to imagine straddling the gap between Cora and the world he had once known, and the man he had become?

11

Her mother remained prickly, but Cora had never had so fine an evening. Henry and his wife, Sally; their sons, Wickersham and Thomas, and their wives; and all the children joined them for roast venison over the campfire, the first corn of the season, and fresh-baked cornbread with butter and blueberry preserves. They regaled her with stories of others who had braved the slopes: how James Longmire had discovered the hot springs that healed and the funny beard on Philemon Van Trump, the first "Boston" man to reach the summit.

"And now you will climb it," Sally said with a shake of her head that set her long black hair to waving. "Like Miss Fuller. Maybe I should climb it too."

"No," Henry said, giving her a squeeze where she sat next to him on a rough wood bench. He scooted closer, until his brown trousers brushed her dusky red skirts. "I am an old man now. I need my wife near me."

She gave him a playful shove. "Not so near. Not until you jump in the creek."

Her family laughed.

"You will have trouble climbing," Thomas told them. Like his father, he was short and stocky, with the same gentle smile. "The snows have just departed."

Wickersham nodded. He was taller than the rest of his family, and his nose was sharper. "Summer comes late to the mountain this year."

"And what do you all say about the name?" Cora asked as the stars began to wink overhead. "Many in the city favor Tacoma, despite what the Board of Geographic Names said. I understand it is a native word."

Wickersham and Thomas started laughing.

Henry shrugged. "I know many words like it, in several languages."

"But do you prefer Rainier or Tacoma?" she tried again.

"I am certain you are putting Mr. Henry and his sons in a difficult position, dear," her mother said. "You cannot ask them to choose a side on so controversial an issue."

"Why not?" Sally asked. "Many ask Henry to speak on many issues."

"Thank you for considering my position, Mrs. Winston," Henry said. "But to answer your question, Miss Baxter, I, like many I know, call it the mountain. That is enough."

Waldo rose from beside Nathan. "I should check on the horses. Miss Baxter, why don't you come over here and sit? Less smoke on this side of the fire."

Nathan frowned after him as he strolled toward the barn. Sally nudged her husband and sidled closer once more.

But Waldo's point was well taken. Much more time in the drifting smoke, even the little the hot fire put out, and her hair would smell of it. She gathered her skirts and moved to sit on the stump Waldo had vacated.

"Tired?" Nathan asked as she settled herself and the others began talking of work they must do the next day.

"Not at all," she assured him, stretching hands to the warmth. "I could stay in such company all night."

"Not much longer," he said. "We have a long ride ahead of us to reach my cabin tomorrow."

Thomas, who was sitting closest to her, nodded. "You will like my friend Nathan's house. It is small now, but he will add rooms soon."

"That's the idea," Nathan agreed, lifting his cup of tea in salute.

Her mother, on Nathan's other side with Winston, spoke up again. "I do hope you have more suitable arrangements there."

"You, Mr. Winston, and Miss Baxter may have the beds, ma'am," he answered. "Mr. Vance and I will sleep on the porch."

"That hardly seems fair," Cora protested.

"Coraline, you must not deprive Mr. Hardee of the opportunity to act like a gentleman," her mother ordered.

Or deprive her mother of a bed, it seemed.

As if she thought Cora might persuade Nathan otherwise, her mother rose and shook out her skirts. "Come, dear. We must leave the gentlemen to their discussions."

If they had been in the dining room at home, that would have been the cue for all the women to follow her mother to the formal parlor for tea and genteel conversation while the men enjoyed brandy and cigars and talked business and politics. Somehow, she didn't think Henry and his family followed such customs. Indeed, the women showed no interest in joining her mother. They were cuddled up against their husbands and children, ready for the next story to be shared.

How pleasant that must be. So comfortable in each other's company they could sit together, touching, sharing, learning. Her world felt as stiff as corset stays and as binding.

But she knew her duty. She climbed to her feet. "Yes, Mother. Good night, all. Thank you for a glorious evening."

A dozen voices called good night. The deepest and warmest came from Nathan. She wrapped the sound around her like a blanket as they started for the barn.

"There is no need for effusion," her mother said. "You might find it more efficacious to speak sparingly to such people and to use simple words."

Cora had to grit her teeth a moment before responding. "Henry and his family speak perfect English, Mother. I doubt any of them had any trouble deciphering my intentions, or yours."

"I'm simply grateful it is only one night," her mother replied as they entered the cavernous building. Someone had lit a lantern that brightened the space, but the sides and roof still disappeared beyond its glow. She could hear the horses shifting as they settled in their stalls. The air was thick and musty. Her mother wrinkled her nose as if she opposed even the earthy smell.

Waldo was coming down the center aisle between the stalls, another lantern in hand. "Everything fine here. You need any help climbing to the loft?"

Her mother glanced up. "The loft?"

"That's where the clean hay will be," he advised. "Didn't think you'd want to sleep down here in the dirt."

Her mother dropped her gaze to the packed earth floor—

where bits of straw, grass, fern, and other materials clung together—and shuddered. Then she raised her chin and glanced around the barn.

"There," she said, pointing to a wagon parked at the edge of the light. "I will sleep in the wagon. Please remove all items from the bed and gather my things."

Waldo put a hand to the back of his neck and studied the crates and barrels crowding the bed of the wagon. Cora took pity on him.

"The loft will be fine, Mother. It will be far more private than down here, where anyone might come in at any time. And the hay will be more comfortable than a wagon bed. You go up first, and I'll follow with our blankets."

Her mother's lips were a tight line, but she marched herself to the wooden ladder, gathered her skirts with one hand, and began climbing.

"Have someone bring up my valise as well," she instructed Cora. "I must change for the night."

Waldo shook his head as she disappeared into the loft. "She can change into nightclothes if she wants, but I'd sleep in my clothes if I were you. Nights can get cold the closer you get to the mountain. Best to wear as many layers as possible."

"Thank you, Waldo," Cora said. She headed for the packs, where they lay near the stalls.

"Coraline!"

Her mother's scream had Cora and Waldo running for the ladder. The older man reached it first and scrambled up. Cora had to go more carefully with her skirts. When she came out at the top, she found her mother trembling in a vast bowl of hay.

"Something moved," she said, voice shaking. "I saw it."

"Probably mice," Waldo explained. "We're not the only ones seeking a warm, soft bed."

"I can't . . . I won't . . ." Her mother drew in a deep breath and gathered her dignity. "Mr. Vance, surely there are other accommodations."

"I suspect you could sleep in the house, ma'am, but you'd likely be sharing a bed with Henry's granddaughters. I understand they're staying the night too. And, of course, I'm not sure you could persuade the little boys to sleep elsewhere."

Her mother closed her eyes, as if the choice were too dear.

"I'll stay up, Mother," Cora said. "Keep the mice away from you."

She sighed as she opened her eyes. "That is very kind of you, dear, even if I wouldn't be in this predicament except for my love for you. No, you need your sleep as well. I should be the one to stay awake. You may go, Mr. Vance."

He shifted on the hay. "I'll bring up the bedding. But I'm sleeping up here too, ma'am."

She turned her back on him.

He moved closer to Cora, the hay rustling under him. "If you come partway down the ladder, miss, I'll bring over the bedding. But I won't touch her things."

"The bedding would be very helpful," Cora assured him.

Winston climbed the ladder just as she had finished spreading the blankets—one over a pile of hay, one ready to curl up in. He waded to their sides.

"What's this I hear about you refusing to sleep, my love?" he asked her mother, who had remained standing.

"There are vermin in this barn, Mr. Winston," she informed him. "I would not sleep a wink knowing I might be

129

accosted at any moment. I will remain vigilant and alert you and Cora should I see one approach."

Cora had a vision of her mother crowing like a rooster every few hours. She caught Winston's eye, and he straightened his spine.

"I cannot allow such a sacrifice. You will sleep between me and Coraline. We will shield you."

"Mr. Winston," her mother protested. "That is entirely too intimate. What will our daughter think of such behavior?"

"I think Winston is very clever and very dear," Cora said, coming to kiss her stepfather on the cheek. "Now, please, Mother, come to bed. We'll all need our rest if we're to continue the journey tomorrow."

———— {{ }} ————

Cora, her mother, and her stepfather were huddled together when Nathan climbed to the loft an hour later. Someone was already snoring.

"What do you bet it's the mother?" Waldo asked, stretching out on the other side of the loft with Nathan.

"I don't care if it's all three of them," Nathan said, lying back on the soft hay. He tugged his wool blanket closer. "I need my sleep, and so do you."

A grunt was his only answer. He was drifting off to sleep when Waldo spoke again.

"Henry says you're thinking about marrying her."

That woke him up. "Henry is wrong. I'm just the guide, the hired help."

"You could be more," Waldo mused. "You were once."

"That was years ago. You know I have no interest in going back to that life."

"Sure. We have it good out by the lake." The hay whispered as Waldo must have turned. "But a wife, children. I want that happiness for you."

The blanket was like lead over him. "I know you miss yours, Waldo, and I'm sorry for your loss. But you of all people know the dangers of living as we do."

"I know the dangers of living alone too," he retorted. "If you hadn't happened upon me after that falling tree near took my leg off, you can't make me believe I would have survived. The good Lord put you right where I needed you most."

"Where we needed each other," Nathan amended. "And I will be forever grateful for your friendship. I wouldn't have made it the first year without your guidance. Now, get some sleep. We have a long way to go tomorrow, and based on today, I'm guessing a dozen complaints a mile."

———— ⁂ ————

He woke as dawn's fingers reached through the gaps between the logs to caress the hay and those sleeping on it. Rising quietly, he slipped his blanket over his shoulder and moved toward the ladder. Someone snorted in a dream. Definitely the mother. He grinned as he glanced that way.

Cora lay on her side, golden lashes fanning her cheeks, knees curled up. Her mother had all but torn the blanket from her. Even as he watched, she gave a little shiver and hugged her knees tighter. He didn't stop to think. He waded to her side and draped his blanket over her slender form. She sighed and burrowed deeper into the warmth. A smile lifted her pink lips. Bet they were a lot softer than that blanket.

He turned away and forced himself to the ladder.

On the floor, he retrieved the worn book from his pack, gave Honoré some more oats, then headed out into the light.

Pearly beams slanted through the trees on the hillside and sent shadows fleeing across the fields. The cool, crisp air brushed his cheeks as he approached the firepit. Beyond the trees around the edge of the yard, the Mashel River rushed on its way down the valley. Closer to hand, Henry's spring gurgled a greeting. In a few moments, Henry and his family would wake to go about their day. This was the only moment he'd have to himself until after the sun set again.

He laid the book down on a stump, bent to rekindle the fire from last night, and added two more logs. As the blaze crackled and warmth spread, he opened his Bible.

Bless the Lord, O my soul, and all that is within me, bless his holy name.

Yes, there was always reason to praise him. That clear blue sky, the soft breeze that brought the scent of ripening wheat. The mist yesterday that had wet every surface, giving all of creation a drink. The breath in his lungs. The strength in his body.

Purpose. Hope.

Peace.

Thank you.

At the sound of footsteps, he turned his gaze toward the barn. Cora was moving in his direction. Her navy riding skirts were rumpled and speckled with hay. More hay stuck out of her hair. She smiled at him as if she didn't notice. Or didn't care.

"Good morning, Nathan. May I call you Nathan? It seems unreasonably formal to use our last names when we'll be spending so much time together."

He slipped his Bible down beside his leg. "I thought your mother preferred unreasonable formality."

She tossed her head, and some of the hay fluttered to the ground. "I am not my mother."

That was clear enough. He'd admired how easily she'd conversed with Henry and his family last night. She'd been alert, engaged, and interested, while her mother had sat straight and mostly silent, as if resenting having to deal with people she chose to see as different.

"You can call me Nathan," he allowed. "But I'll only call you Cora when your mother isn't around."

"Coward," she teased.

"Survivor," he countered. "I value my head, and your mother is too good at taking it off."

She sank onto the stump beside his. "What are you doing out here so early?"

If he told her the truth, would she think he was posturing? He decided to try. "I was praying."

She frowned. "It can't be Sunday again. We haven't been gone so long."

"Who says you only pray on a Sunday?"

She opened her mouth, then closed it and cocked her head as if considering the matter from a different angle. "I suppose you could pray on other days. We say grace over meals, after all."

He nodded toward the barn. "Your mother never prayed with you before bed when you were little?"

"I suppose she did, when I was very young. But when she married her second husband, that stopped. I was never sure why. Did your mother pray with you?"

"She did, until I went to Seattle for college. I grew out of practice for a while, but being out here, it comes naturally. How can you look at that and not turn to praise?" He gestured toward the south.

She swirled and gasped. Rainier sat, as proud and upright as Mrs. Winston, her white skirts trimmed by the green of fir at the hem.

"Just a few more days, Cora," he murmured. "And you'll be standing at the top with a view most glorious. Tell me you won't pray in thanks then."

12

Sitting on the stump, the air cool and the fire glowing, Cora was warmer than when she'd woken wrapped in a wool blanket in the hay. The man beside her had something to do with that. This was what she'd been missing. Sitting, talking, sharing. She and Mimi did that often. With him it was deeper and richer. Another time, she would have tried to analyze why. Now, for once in her life, she just wanted to sit and breathe.

And what an intriguing concept, that he prayed even when it wasn't Sunday and not in any sort of gathering. She'd seen a book in his hands as she'd approached. The Bible perhaps? She'd never known a man other than a minister who consulted that book on a regular basis. Perhaps she should give it a try.

"What were you reading?" she asked.

He pulled the book back into his lap. "Psalms."

His deep voice held a surprising hesitancy. She could not understand why.

"And what do you like about Psalms?" she asked.

His hand smoothed the leather, worn and curling over the edge of the pages. The spine was cracked, as if he'd opened the book too many times or with great passion. "There's a cadence to them, a story. They mean more than the mere words on the page."

Cora cupped her chin with her hand and rested her elbow on her knee. "Fascinating. Which is your favorite?"

He regarded her. "Why do you want to know?"

Cora dropped her arm and straightened. "Friends show interest in each other's activities."

He nodded. "You're being polite. One of those rules of society."

She frowned. "I'm sure it isn't just a rule. It's what people do."

"And that makes it a rule." He rose, tucking the book under his arm. "And because I remember the rules too, I'll beg your pardon and excuse myself to see what's for breakfast."

He strode for the house, where smoke was beginning to rise from the chimney.

Impossible man! Just when she thought they were becoming attuned, he broke the harmony. Was he determined to be nothing more than a guide?

With a shake of her head, she went to see how her mother was faring.

———— H H ————

Sally made cornmeal mush with honey for breakfast. Cora thought her mother might refuse the simple fare, but she smiled her thanks as Sally handed her the bowl. Despite her fears, her mother had slept through the night, and she and Cora had taken turns combing and pinning up each other's hair and brushing off their riding habits.

"Just because we're journeying through the wilderness doesn't mean we cannot look our best," her mother had insisted.

She was just as gracious when they took their leave of Henry, Sally, and their family that morning. "Thank you for hosting us."

"It is a pleasure," Henry assured her.

Sally pressed a long-toothed wooden comb into Cora's hands. "The Boston men leave something on the summit to show they were there. Leave this. It will say a lady has been there."

Cora fingered the polished cedar, carved with a leaping salmon. "I'll do it. Thank you. I hope when women are given the vote, all women will have that right."

Sally nodded. "All men as well."

"Agreed," Cora said.

The entire family waved them out of the yard, and the children ran as far as the fence would allow.

Nathan followed the hillside back to where they'd descended, then led them up a slow rise into Eatonville. Clapboard and log buildings clung to either side of the main street, wagons and horses moving among them.

"A hotel, Mr. Hardee," her mother declared, glancing around. "And a second! Why could we not have stayed in those?"

"Because they are overpriced and overbooked," Nathan informed her, gaze on the dusty road curving through the town. "You didn't like the possibility of sharing your bed with mice, I heard. You'd like less sharing it with a logger or miner."

She snapped her mouth shut, but her glare could have set his hair on fire.

Besides the two hotels, Cora spotted a general store, blacksmith, post office, and feed stable. She made sure to wave at anyone she passed. When her story appeared in the newspapers, they'd remember they'd seen her and think about what she represented.

On the other side of the little town, a wooden bridge spanned the Mashel River. The horses and mules clattered across. Almost immediately, another ridge rose, thick with fir, cedar, and hemlock. The way was rough enough that they went single file. Cora ended up behind Waldo, with her mother and Winston right after and Nathan bringing up the rear. She could only conclude he preferred his solitary place.

She would have liked nothing better than to urge Blaze to the top, but soon all the horses slowed. Then even the sure-footed mules balked. From the back of the line came a deep squeak that did indeed sound like a duck. Quack protesting, perhaps?

"Halt!" Nathan called, and Cora reined in Blaze. Waldo stopped Bud and Sparky. Glancing back, she saw that Winston and her mother had followed suit.

"Dismount," Nathan ordered. "We'll walk the rest of the way to the top."

"I do not recall joining the infantry," her mother complained, but she allowed Winston to hand her down.

Cora slid out of the sidesaddle and took Blaze's reins in hand. Up they went, the air scented with rich fir and dry cedar. She thought her mother might comment, but she was soon breathing so heavily she did not seem disposed to speak.

Winston was worse. When Cora looked back again, her stepfather's face was gray, his breath came in rasps, and he stumbled.

"Could we rest?" she called to Nathan.

"Not until we reach the top," he called back. "It's not safe."

On they struggled up the long and twisting road. The rattle of stones behind her warned that Winston continued to stumble. He would never allow her to support him. He had that much pride, at least. She was wracking her brain for a way to stage a rescue when she heard Nathan's voice directly behind her.

"I want your advice on the next stage, sir," he said. Glancing behind, she saw that he had brushed so close to her stepfather on the narrow trail, his horse trailing behind, that Winston had to put a hand on his arm. "If you'd be so good as to listen to my plan, I'd appreciate it."

Cora met Nathan's gaze, and he gave her a nod. Once more feeling warmed, she faced front again.

Winston made it to the top of the hill, Nathan at his side, rambling on about timetables and chimneys and lake trout, of all things.

They came out into a high valley, where a creek bubbled down a stony draw. Nathan called a halt to rest the horses and mules, who lowered their heads to the water gratefully. Cora dismounted and splashed water on her hands and her face.

"I can't see the mountain," she said as Nathan squatted beside her.

"Nor will you until we reach my cabin," he told her, large hands scooping up the clear, cool water. "The foothills are closing in."

She saw what he meant when they started down a short while later. The forest on either side of the road was so close and so thick that light struggled to penetrate. Nathan moved up to ride beside her through the gloom. Small things scurried away from their approach, ferns rustling with their passage. A droning buzz sounded by her ear a moment before she felt a prick. She swatted her neck.

"Mosquitoes," Nathan said. "Keep moving, and speak little."

"Another excuse not to converse with me?" Cora accused, waving a cluster away from Blaze's head.

"No," he said. "An excuse not to get bitten." He slapped his cheek.

"Is there nothing to be done about this scourge?" her mother complained. Cora glanced back in time to see her mother strike herself on the side of the nose. Cora quickly faced front again.

"Waldo," Nathan barked. "Pick up the pace."

"Hyack!" Waldo called, and Bud and Sparky broke into a trot.

Her mother found more to complain about when they rode through Elbe later that morning. They had been paralleling the Nisqually River for some time, the gray waters visible through the trees. Now the way opened up to show weathered board buildings clustered around a bridge south. The silty waters of the river rushed by faster than the men lounging in front of the log post office.

"Two more hotels, Mr. Winston," her mother fumed, even as Cora waved to those fellows too.

This time, Nathan did not respond.

Instead of taking the bridge, he led them on a road through the little hamlet. Cora pulled her compass out from the pocket in her riding habit. Due east now.

Toward the mountain.

The road veered away from the river, until it was only a murmur in the distance. The way was flatter in the valley, and they could ride two abreast again. But the going was rougher. In places, stumps stuck up like guardians, a reminder that the forest had been breached only recently.

Unfortunately, as the day warmed, Winston's face turned from gray to red, and he mopped his forehead under his broad-brimmed hat more times than Cora could like.

Nathan called a halt when the river came into view once more, and they all dismounted to sit on fallen trees in a small clearing. Beyond them, the twists and braids of the boiling river showed boulders and bone-white logs lodged against the banks. If the Nisqually was this fast and chaotic in August, what power it must have in the spring!

Waldo handed around tin cups of water. Winston guzzled his. Her mother sipped, but she finished her cup in a remarkably short time.

Nathan had his booted foot up on a stump. "At this pace we should reach my cabin by late afternoon. We'll pass Ashford's on the way. They host guests, but I didn't make arrangements to stay."

Her mother narrowed her eyes at him.

As if he'd seen the look, Winston put a hand on her arm. "We will have a lovely hotel at Longmire's Springs tomorrow night, dearest."

She nodded, relaxing.

"I wouldn't call Longmire's hotel lovely," Nathan cautioned. "It's far rougher than the hotel at Lake Park. But the company is good, and many enjoy the springs."

Now her mother turned her glare on Winston.

Cora moved closer to Nathan. "I'm concerned about my pack, Mr. Hardee. Would you take a look at it?"

He dropped his foot to follow her to where the horses and mules were resting under the shade of some trees at the edge of the clearing. Already, their heads were down as they cropped the bright grass.

"Can we slow the pace?" she murmured as his large hands moved over the pack, checking buckle and strap.

"A little," he said. "I can see they're both tiring."

She laid a hand on his arm. "Thank you."

He turned to face her fully. What had been so open for a moment this morning was now tightly closed. "It's a temporary measure. You must see it. Winston is struggling. He may not be able to make it to the summit. You'll have to decide whether you're willing to go alone."

He left the troublesome thought hanging in the air as he turned to call to the others. "Time to go. Mount up for now. We may have to walk the horses later."

Cora took hold of Blaze's reins, mind whirling. Nathan had lived in society. He must know the choice he'd given her. If she didn't make the climb, she failed, and so did Mimi's gambit to promote suffrage. Just as bad, Cora would have to honor her promise to her mother and marry Cash Kincaid or some other wealthy, powerful man.

But if she climbed alone, spent two nights on the mountain with only Nathan and Waldo as company, she would lose her reputation. What sort of statement did that make for women's rights? Even if she decided to marry at some point, there would be whispers about her character. Was it fair to ask a husband to endure them?

The climb had seemed attainable before. Was she doomed now, whatever choice she made?

———— ‡‡ ‡‡ ————

They passed Ashford's late that afternoon. The sturdy plank-sided home, nestled among the trees, with ivy growing up around the doorframe, always looked welcoming to Nathan. Mrs. Winston sniffed as they rode by, and he wasn't sure if it was because of the house or the fact that he had refused to allow her to stop there.

As it was, they reached his cabin later than he would have liked, but earlier than he'd feared after the banker's poor showing today.

He'd hated pointing at the obvious, but Cora had to know what she was facing. Better that she decide to turn back now than that she risk her stepfather's, and her own, health and safety later.

Yet the thought of having her turn back sat like a rock in his stomach. No matter how hard he tried to keep a distance, she danced closer. And he wanted to dance with her.

Honoré, Bud, and the mules picked up their paces as they left the main road. They knew they were heading home. But Nathan's shoulders felt as tight as a violin string, and he caught himself glancing at Cora, who rode beside him. She was as upright and easy in the saddle as she'd been when they'd left Lake Park yesterday. When she smiled at the log cabin just ahead, he was certain the sun brightened.

It seemed he wanted her to like his home.

And why shouldn't she like it? It was a vast improvement to the single-room cabin Waldo and his family had lived in before Nathan arrived. The wide front porch bordered a two-bedroom space with a loft above and a root cellar below. The back porch looked out over the clear waters of Celestine Lake, and the creek that flowed from it sang along the eastern edge of his property on its way to meet the Nisqually. He had a pump that tapped groundwater, at least when the mechanism wasn't frozen in winter, and a good shake roof that sloughed off snow and fir needles alike.

He and Waldo had peeled every log, planed each plank. Mud from the lake bottom mixed with clay from the Nisqually River chinked any crack. Their guide work had paid for the lumber used in the interior walls. He'd brought the panes of glass in the front and back windows from Tacoma in barrels of molasses and washed each one before caulking it in place. He had gathered every stone in the fireplace and chimney from the Nisqually and built them into a hearth that was as beautiful as it was functional.

He had a right to be proud. So did Waldo.

"Here we are, folks, home, sweet home," Waldo called as Nathan led Quack toward the barn they had also built. The planed wood structure tucked in among the trees wasn't as tall or long as Henry's, but it had room for their horses and mules, with a few stalls left over for visitors. Cora and her family would be the first.

The first of many?

He shook the odd thought away as he followed Waldo to the barn.

Mrs. Winston reined in her horse and waited for someone to assist her down. "I suppose this will have to do."

"There's room enough for all," Waldo assured her, swinging down. "Remove your saddles and tack, and wipe down your horses. I'll feed and water them." He set about unstrapping the packs from the mules.

Winston must have learned to tend his own horse at some point, for he went straight to work. Nathan already knew Cora had the matter in hand. Her horse was in the stall next to his. Once again, he caught himself watching as she began. How quickly those hands moved over her horse, gentle and supportive. She murmured too, the words low and warm. What would it be like to hear such warmth directed his way?

"Mr. Hardee."

That voice was neither low nor warm. He threw his saddle up over the stall wall and looked to Cora's mother, who was standing in the aisle.

"Some assistance, if you please," she said, as if he had been tardy to school.

In the end, he had to see to her horse, then his, before helping Waldo with the mules. Cora and Winston were finishing brushing down their horses. When Nathan took the first load of supplies to the house, he found Mrs. Winston sitting on one of the two cane-bottomed chairs he and Waldo had brought up from the city. She was gazing around the long main room of the cabin with narrowed eyes. He began putting cans on the shelf in the area he and Waldo used for a kitchen and workroom.

"I would not have expected to find bone china out here," she ventured. "Have you a wife, Mr. Hardee?"

"No, ma'am," he told her, wondering why Waldo thought they needed six cans of stewed beef when they could always hunt or fish. "Those belonged to Mr. Vance's late wife. I take it she had them from her mother. They brought them west when they moved here from Illinois."

"She had exceptional taste," she said, eyeing the scarlet and teal pattern on the creamy white dishes. "English, unless I miss my guess. A touch of civility in the wilderness. A reminder of happier times."

"They're dishes," Nathan told her, setting the last can in place. "They serve a purpose."

"Of course," she said, but she did not sound the least convinced.

Waldo came through the rear door, arms full of wood. "Could get cold tonight," he said, going to stack it near the hearth. "You ready for another load?"

"Right behind you," Nathan promised. Nodding to Mrs. Winston, he followed Waldo out the door. Cora and Winston passed them for the house.

"She looked impressed," Waldo said as they reached the barn.

Nathan snorted. "With our dishes."

"Not her." Waldo opened a pack and pulled out a sack of dried beans. "Our Cora. She liked what she saw when she rode up. That's good."

Very good. No, what was he thinking? "How Coraline Baxter feels about our house makes no difference to me." He heaved up a sack of flour.

Waldo grinned at him. "Liar."

They made several trips before they could rejoin their guests. Cora, too, regarded Waldo's dishes before wandering around the cabin. Besides the two chairs that now held Winston and his wife, they had two more ladder-backed chairs on either side of a turned-leg table covered with a red gingham tablecloth that had also belonged to Waldo's wife. Copper pots and pans and a porcelain-dipped strainer hung from walls around the worktable near the back of the room. Two doors on the other side of the hearth led to the bedrooms, where Cora and her family would be sleeping tonight.

"There's a lake behind the house," she said as if she'd been the first to discover it.

"Filled with bull trout as long as your arm," Waldo bragged.

"And mosquitoes nearly as big," Nathan warned. "Best if you all stay in the cabin."

She didn't answer, gaze out the window. "Are you expecting more company, Mr. Hardee?"

Nathan glanced to Waldo, who shook his head.

"No," Nathan said. "Why?"

She turned from the window. "Because there's a group of men heading this way. One of them is on a stretcher."

13

They came around the cabin, and Nathan and Waldo met them on the front porch. Cora's mother and Winston peered out the window as if afraid to venture any closer lest they contract some dread disease. With a shake of her head, Cora went to see if she could assist. She had studied mathematics in college, but her efforts at lawn tennis and riding had acquainted her with the use of bandages at least.

"Never was so glad to see your mules go by the crossing," the older man was saying. They all wore flannel shirts with no collars, dark stains here and there and everything speckled with white crumbles she recognized as sawdust. Suspenders held up denim trousers with pant legs folded to reveal thick black boots. What she could see of their hair under battered, round-crowned hats was rough cut, as if someone had taken a saw to it.

"I'll get the bag," Waldo said before bustling back into the cabin.

Nathan crouched beside the canvas stretcher, which the other men had set on the porch. "What happened?"

"Widow-maker," the man on the stretcher wheezed out, face pasty white under his thatch of brown hair. "From a nearby tree. Missed my head but hit my shoulder and knocked me off the springboard. Think something broke."

"You should have heard him yelp," the youngest, whiskers not even evident, said.

"When did this happen?" Nathan asked, hands gentle on the fellow's misshapen shoulder.

The man grimaced nonetheless. "Day before yesterday."

Nathan rocked back on his heels. "Did you try ice? Heat?"

"Didn't have any ice," the redhead among them volunteered.

"Leastwise, none we could get easily," the fourth, another with brown hair, added.

"And the wool we soaked in boiled water was too heavy," the youth explained. "He said it hurt too much."

"What I have to do now is going to hurt more," Nathan told them as Waldo reappeared with a black leather satchel. Doctor Thomlinson in Tacoma had one. She'd seen it when he'd come to treat her mother for some complaint. Who'd left a doctor's bag out here? One of Nathan's clients, perhaps?

He nodded to the men. "Hold him still."

"No, wait!" the injured man protested. "I'll be fine. Don't you touch me!"

Nathan's face was grim as the others lay hold of the man's legs and good arm. The fellow's fear reached for her, set nerves tingling.

"Mr. Hardee?" she asked. "Nathan, are you sure this is wise?"

He cast her a quick glance. "If you want to help, Miss

Baxter, open that bag and unfold the sling you'll find near the top."

She should, but she couldn't tear her eyes off him. He took hold of the man's injured arm and began to rotate it up and out.

"On the count of three," he said. "One."

"Don't you do it," the injured man ordered.

"Two."

"I'm not kidding, Hardee. I'll come for you in the night."

"Three."

He shoved it up above the man's head. There was a rending pop, and the man on the stretcher screamed. Cora stumbled back into the cabin.

Her mother met her at the door. "What is he doing? Mr. Winston, have you entrusted us to a murderer?"

"Not a murderer," Cora managed, trying to still her heaving stomach. "He seems to be treating the fellow from sheer strength." She shuddered, then squared her shoulders. "It will be fine, Mother. Forgive me for frightening you."

Taking calming breaths, she stepped back outside. The other men had released their friend and now stood watching as Nathan ran his hands over the fellow's torso and legs. Waldo was watching too, arms crossed over his chest, so she knelt and opened the bag.

As Nathan had said, a square of fabric lay on top. Underneath sat several rolls of linen, neatly packed, the ends tucked in to keep them tight. Below, she spotted more medical items: forceps, a stethoscope, and dark glass bottles that must hold ointments and medicines.

"Besides the dislocation," Nathan told the injured man, "it looks like you bruised your ribs and sprained your ankle.

Keep the ankle up on a chair for the next few days. Once I put that arm in a sling, don't use it for at least a week. I'll give you a bandage for your ribs. Only apply it at night. It's better if you sleep sitting up."

Cora offered him the sling, and he nodded in thanks before turning to the injured man. "Do I need to worry about closing my eyes tonight?"

He colored. "No. Sorry about that. I'm glad for your help."

"Well, maybe not glad," the redhead joked. "Not the way you whined like a kicked pup."

The injured man made a face. "Well, I'll have you know it hurt like a . . ." He glanced at Cora. "Beg pardon, ma'am. My ma taught me not to cuss in front of a lady."

"She probably taught you not to cuss at all," Cora replied. "But I imagine pain can make a fellow forget propriety. Is there anything further I can do to assist, Mr. Hardee? Perhaps some water for your patient and his stalwart companions?"

His friends all straightened and grinned at her, showing more than one gap between teeth.

"That's very kind of you, Miss Baxter," Nathan said. "Waldo, why don't you show her the pump? There's a pitcher and cups near the table. These boys get tin."

They laughed as if they understood why. Waldo motioned Cora ahead of him into the house.

"What is happening?" her mother demanded as they came through the cabin.

"Nathan's just tending to an injury," Waldo said as he led Cora toward the table. "Happens all the time. He's the doctor in these parts." He took down a crystal pitcher and nodded to Cora. "The pump's outside the back door, but I'll fetch the water. You get the cups."

"Coraline," her mother said as the older man headed for the pump. "What are you doing?"

"Practicing the hospitality you always espouse, Mother," Cora said as she scanned the cupboard. Four tin cups were stacked next to eight ruby-colored crystal goblets. Apparently, these men didn't warrant such beauties.

"While I applaud Christian charity as much as the next person," her mother said as Waldo returned with water dripping down the sides of the pitcher, "you must remember your reputation."

The comment only reminded her of Nathan's warning earlier. Cora made herself smile. "You can see me through the window. Surely that is chaperone enough."

The fellow on the stretcher was sitting up, arm in a sling, when she and Waldo came out bearing the pitcher of water and the cups. Cora distributed them around, and Waldo poured the clear water.

"Much obliged," the redhead said.

"Old Nathan never mentioned his sweetheart was so pretty," the youngest ventured.

"Or that he had a sweetheart at all," the third complained with a look to Nathan.

Nathan stood at last, dwarfing them. "Miss Baxter is not my sweetheart. I'm guiding her and her father up Mount Rainier."

The youngest spit out his water in a gasp. They all stared at her. Waldo tutted.

"Now, that's not funny," the injured man declared. "Man's got no call dragging a little thing like her up the mountain."

His friends nodded.

"You can stay with us, miss," the oldest offered. "We'll protect you."

"Very kind of you," Cora said. "But you mistake Mr. Hardee. I'm the one dragging him and my stepfather up to the summit. I mean to prove any woman can do it. And if women can climb mountains, surely they have the same right to vote as a man."

The redhead whistled.

"Makes sense to me," the injured man told her. "I'd go with you, if I wasn't stove in."

"I'd go with you anywhere," the youngest vowed, "even if I was stove in."

"That's enough," Nathan said. He bent and pulled out one of the bandages, then dropped it into the injured man's lap. "Finish your drinks and take Albertson to camp. I'll check on him when I return from guiding Miss Baxter."

They tossed back the water, then handed her the cups with shy smiles. Waldo watched as if counting each cup. Finally, they hefted the stretcher and carted their friend off. He waved to her with his good hand as they rounded the cabin. "Votes for women!"

Cora grinned. If only all men could be persuaded so easily.

"I'll take those," Waldo said, reaching for the cups and jumbling them together. He started for the door.

"Waldo says this happens often," she told Nathan, lifting the bag to return to the cabin.

"Often enough," he admitted, turning toward the door. "Felling trees, sawing lumber, even clearing a field to farm can injure a man. And folks could come down sick from spoiled food or tainted water."

"Waldo also said you were their physician," she marveled.

He paused on the porch. "Waldo talks too much."

She lifted the bag as evidence. "You do seem to be equipped."

He sighed. "I studied medicine at the university and apprenticed to Doctor Thomlinson in Tacoma. When my father died, Thomlinson feared his patients wouldn't trust a man with my background. I thought about going elsewhere, but I didn't have the heart for it then. So, I may be close to a doctor, but I'll never practice in Tacoma."

Anger pulsed through Cora as she lowered the bag. "How shortsighted of Doctor Thomlinson. Your tragedy might make it easier for you to understand others so affected. I am very displeased with the fellow and will look to take my patronage elsewhere."

He cocked his head. "On my word? Thomlinson is regarded as one of the best physicians in the area."

"He cannot be the best if he so cruelly cuts off an associate. And of course I accept your word on such matters, Nathan. I see the care you take of others, Winston, me. You have proven yourself a man of character."

He nodded. "Very well, Cora. I'll take your word as well. But you can decide what you think about my character after you're safely back from the summit."

————— ⊩⊣ —————

They had spent a few days together, and she thought she knew him. She trusted too easily. That cool demeanor masked a warm heart. Her mother hadn't been willing to do more than watch the lumbermen, as if they were specimens of mollusk dotting the shores of Puget Sound. Cora had been willing to assist, to converse, to persuade.

To treat everyone as if they had worth.

Now he followed her back inside the cabin and took the bag from her. After all this time, the leather handle conformed to his fingers. His first doctor's bag. His father had given it to him. The brass plate with his initials had popped off over the years; the satin lining had torn at the bottom. Helping his neighbors and clients wasn't exactly what he'd been expecting to do. But he couldn't mind.

When he returned from the bedroom, Cora continued to eye him as if she hadn't seen him before. Waldo was already at the worktable, peeling some of the potatoes they'd brought in. As if she thought she'd be served immediately, Mrs. Winston waited at the dining table, hands folded in her lap, back straight, her husband across from her, brow seamed in worry as he watched her.

He perked up as Nathan headed to add a log to the fire. "That was well done, my boy. I'm sure your neighbors are grateful."

"They work hard at the lumber camp," Nathan allowed as flames wrapped around the dry wood. "The venture started about a year ago. I'm not sure how this downturn in the economy will affect them."

Winston sighed. "It's affecting us all."

His wife sighed as well, but at the dreary forecast or their choice of conversation, he wasn't sure.

Cora followed him out the rear door as he went for another load of wood. She stood on the grass, gazing at the lake. "It's beautiful here."

He paused to look too. Trees clustered around the lake, so close their reflection made the still waters look dusky green. In fall, he knew, the aspens on the other side would turn a brilliant yellow and the vine maples below them crimson. The lone madrone, its reddish bark peeling to reveal the golden brown beneath, reached branches out like hands offering a blessing. His claim was a shelter, like an oasis in the desert, a lighthouse in the storm.

But its beauty was nothing to that of the woman gazing out at it with wide blue eyes.

"It's a good claim," he said, stacking wood into the crook of his arm.

She took an audible breath, as if she could sense the peace. Nathan led her back inside.

Waldo had the potatoes in the frying pan with bacon grease. He'd also skinned and filleted a couple trout and had them in another pan.

"Petrosky left us a brace," he reported when Nathan raised a brow in surprise. Then Waldo turned to Cora. "Have pity on an old man, Miss Baxter. I bet you could whip these fish into shape in no time."

"I don't know how I gave you that impression." She went to join him by the worktable and peered around his arm at the flaky fillets. "I've never cooked a meal in my life."

"We have a fine cook at our home," her mother put in.

Nathan dropped the wood beside the hearth. "I'll lend a hand."

"Good." Waldo offered Cora the pan with the potatoes and brought Nathan the pan with the fish. "You two cook. I'll just set the table."

The old codger. He'd planned this—Nathan and Cora working side by side, as if they hadn't spent the last two days together. Nathan shook his head, but he crouched beside the hearth.

"You'll have to correct me on the finer points," she said, the fire bringing a flush to her skin as she bent closer.

"Just hold the pan steady and listen for the sizzle," he

advised. "That will tell you when it's time to turn them over or remove them from the heat."

Just listen. Easy to say. Having her so close made it nearly impossible to listen or concentrate. He tried to focus on the fish as the fat began to sizzle. The fillets weren't thick. Shouldn't take too long to cook. He gave the pan a twist and the fish flipped as neatly as if they'd jumped right out of the brook.

"I don't dare try that with the potatoes," she admitted.

At least her gaze was focused on the pearly nubs, the edges starting to turn gold. His gaze kept wandering to her. Why look at trout when two pink lips were inches away? Soft pink lips that could curl up so sweetly, whisper words of encouragement.

"Should they be doing that?" she asked, and he jerked his gaze back to the trout in time to save them from burning to a crisp.

Together, they managed a passable meal, but it was no doubt the day's exertions that made Mrs. Winston and the banker clean their plates. Of course, neither offered to pitch in on the cleanup afterward, clearly assuming that was his and Waldo's job. Once again, Cora helped, as Waldo washed, Nathan dried, and she set the dishes back where they belonged. Funny how he'd never noticed the cramped space. Yet every time he moved, he seemed to connect with Cora. His arm brushed her shoulder as he reached for a clean pan. His fingers caressed hers as he handed her one of the crystal glasses to replace. Relief and disappointment fought when he hung up the towel and went to settle the cabin for the night.

"A host generally provides some sort of entertainment in

the evening," Mrs. Winston said as he moved to close the shutters over the front windows. What, did she think he was a traveling player as well?

"Sorry, ma'am," he said, turning for the fire. "I have no talents other than directing people about."

"He's being humble," Waldo said. "Why, he's a dab hand at a fiddle. Prettiest sounds you ever heard."

He shook his head as he straightened. "I gave up playing for others years ago."

Waldo frowned at him. It was only the truth. His mother had loved trotting him out to play at dinner parties. Her little prodigy. Now he played only for himself and his Lord. If Waldo listened, that was his choice.

Mrs. Winston sighed. "Pity, but only to be expected in these surroundings. It will have to be you, Coraline."

Cora placed the last ruby crystal goblet, Mrs. Vance's pride and joy, on the shelf as if she understood its importance. "Perhaps you could sing, Mother. I'm terribly tired."

"One should never be too tired to bring joy to others," her mother said. "Your voice is quite lovely. I'm sure everyone would enjoy hearing it."

"I certainly would," Waldo told her.

Nathan knew the pressure all too well. How many times had he risen to meet it? The dutiful son, exceeding every expectation, sure he was destined for glory. Now he knew his glory was second and the only expectations he had to meet were those of his heavenly Father.

"You needn't feel obliged, Miss Baxter," he said. "You've earned your peace."

Her smile was soft. "Well, perhaps one song, for Waldo."

She came to stand by the hearth. The lingering glow

silhouetted her in red. Nathan sat on one of the cane-bottomed chairs while Waldo took the other.

She smiled all around, clasped her hands in front of her, and raised her head, the display of perfect womanhood her family no doubt expected.

> In the gloaming, oh my darling
> When the lights are soft and low
> And the quiet shadows, falling,
> Softly come and softly go.
> When the trees are sobbing faintly
> With a gentle unknown woe
> Will you think of me and love me,
> As you did once, long ago.

This was no display. This was true. Her voice was pure and sweet. It called to something inside him. He was leaning forward before he realized it, watching every movement. The graceful sweep of a hand, the emotion crossing her pretty face.

> In the gloaming, oh my darling
> Think not bitterly of me
> Though I passed away in silence
> Left you lonely, set you free
> For my heart was tossed with longing
> What had been could never be
> It was best to leave you thus, dear,
> Best for you, and best for me.

Beside him, Waldo rose and stalked out the door. Cora swallowed the last of the words, face falling. "Oh, I'm sorry. I should have thought. His wife, his son . . ."

"It's all right," Nathan assured her, rising. "That was beautiful. Give him a moment, and I'm sure Waldo will tell you the same. Excuse me."

He followed his friend out the door, before his heart betrayed him too.

14

"That was nicely done, Coraline," her mother said as Cora stared after Nathan and Waldo. "Although I have heard that particular song a number of times. We must widen your repertoire when we return."

"Yes, Mother," Cora said, moving toward the door. "If you'll excuse me."

She slipped out onto the porch. In the dim light, she could just make out Waldo and Nathan at one end, voices a murmur. As if in sympathy, the small noises of the night had gone silent. She hurried closer.

"Please, Waldo," she said. "You must forgive me. I'd never do anything to hurt you."

The older man wiped at his cheeks. "No need to apologize. Best singing I've heard in a long while. Tell her, Nathan."

Nathan kept his gaze on his friend. "I've already told Miss Baxter it was lovely."

He'd done more than that. She was used to seeing admiration when she sang—from the men in the room, from friends, occasionally from her mother. The look Nathan had directed her way had been something more. In such a look, she could not doubt herself talented, lovely.

And cherished.

"Well, you could tell her again," Waldo insisted with a sniff. "You mustn't mind me, Miss Cora. You touched an old man's heart, that's all. I'll just go check to make sure the barn's closed proper." He hopped off the porch and loped away.

"Will he be all right?" Cora worried, watching him disappear into the darkness.

"Very likely. He gets melancholy on occasion, though it's rarer in recent years."

Cora nodded. "I'm sure you've been a great comfort to him. He looks on you as a son."

She could not make out his features in the darkness. "I suppose he does. He's been more of a father to me than mine ever was." He leaned closer, and the scent of woodsmoke drifted over her. "In case you haven't noticed, he's determined to play matchmaker. Ignore him."

Matchmaker? Something fluttered inside her as he straightened. A moth drawn to the flame and just as easily burned. She knew better.

"I will," she promised.

He drew in a breath of the cool night air. "Your mother and Winston will want to turn in. Let me show you the accommodations."

They returned to the cabin, and he directed her mother and Winston to the bedroom on the left. They must have been as tired as they looked, for neither protested sharing a bed even though they had their own suites at home.

Nathan then opened the door to the bedroom on the right. "And here's where you'll be sleeping. Good night, Cora."

He left her then, but not entirely. The room had a familiar scent, equal parts woodsmoke, soap, and sunshine. She managed to peel off her riding habit and loosen her stays, but she could not lie on the big bed without thinking that he must have slept there only a few days ago. When she closed her eyes, she saw the look of wonder on his face when she'd sung.

Her mother had introduced her to every wealthy bachelor within miles of Tacoma, and none had had this effect on her. She knew what her future held and had done all she could to construct it—independence, self-sufficiency. After seeing her mother's three marriages, she had never thought to enter into one herself.

Was her fascination with Nathan Hardee merely because he was so different from the men she'd known? It seemed more. Feelings she was not willing to name simmered inside. Was she willing to let them deepen? Wouldn't that threaten everything she'd planned?

She finally fell asleep and woke to birdsong outside the window, the trilling notes bright and joyful. She wrestled her stays back into place, then brushed out and donned her riding habit. It, too, smelled of woodsmoke. So did her hair as she combed it and pinned it up on the top of her head. With no mirror, she could only hope she didn't look a fright as she stepped out of the room.

Her gaze darted around, but there was no sign of Nathan. No sign of her mother and Winston either, and the door to the other bedroom was closed.

Waldo was stirring a big pot hanging from a cast-iron hook over the fire.

"Oatmeal in a bit," he told her. "Mighty pretty out by the lake just now. You should go look."

"I will," Cora said, passing him. "And thank you. I'll be back in a moment to set the table."

She stepped out the door and caught her breath. The eastern sky was a wash of pink echoed in the clear waters. Across from her, deer grazed, heads down and tawny bodies moving slowly. As she watched, a fish leaped out of the water and plunged back in, ripples spreading. The air was so cool and crisp it might have been early fall instead of summer.

Something moved under the shadows of the firs, and she focused on the figure seated on a fallen tree. As before, Nathan had risen early and gone off by himself to pray, it seemed.

Ministers prayed, sometimes in long, drawn-out recitations of all the ways God could grant favor. Winston prayed before meals at home, the same words each time and with no particular emphasis or urgency. What did Nathan pray about? Surely not for a blessing. He had all this, and he did not seem to long for more.

He must have finished, for he rose and started toward her, Bible in his large hands. Panic pricked her, and she backed up until she bumped into the door. What was wrong with her? He was no threat. He was a friend.

A friend who made her think about things she'd already forsaken.

"Good morning," he said, deep voice a warm rumble. "Sleep well?"

Better than she'd expected when she'd first lain down, but she didn't want to tell him where her thoughts had gone last night. "Fine. You?"

He stretched his shoulders. "Porch is a little hard, but I've had worse."

"Today, we reach Longmire's, if I remember correctly," she said, trying not to let her gaze linger on the breadth of those shoulders. "Will it be as long a ride as yesterday?"

"Not as far," he replied. "But we'll have to cross several fords. This time of year isn't too bad, especially since we haven't had a good downpour in a while. We should reach the springs by dinner."

They did, but it wasn't as easy as he'd made out.

With the supplies delivered to the cabin, they could leave the mules behind, and the packs on Honoré and Bud were smaller. A peeled stick poked out of Nathan's. Was he bringing firewood with him so as not to cut timber in the Forest Reserve surrounding the mountain? She'd also wondered how Sparky and Quack would get by in Nathan's absence, but Waldo told her Mr. Ashford would be coming back daily to check on them.

So, they all rode out, Nathan at the head of the cavalcade, and followed the main trail east through firs and fern, cedar and creek. The air was warming, bringing the dry scent of the forest. Just ahead, her mother talked with Winston of events when they returned, friends they should have over to dine. Waldo brought up the rear.

Cora let the noise of the discussion in front wash over her. It was enough to be riding through such glorious country, where anything seemed possible.

A few miles on, they passed a side road. Waldo drew Bud up alongside Blaze.

"Palisade Ranch," he remarked. "The Kernahans built it some years back. Nice folks."

"What do they do out here?" Cora asked.

"Farm, ranch," Waldo explained. "Takes a lot to clear

a field, but once cleared, it's fertile. You couldn't tell from inside our cabin, but beyond the barn we have a vegetable patch and a few acres of hay. Keeps us and the horses fed in the winter."

Must be nice, everything in your own control. Perhaps she ought to start her own bank and encourage the women of the city to invest. What wonders could they accomplish if they kept working together after securing the vote?

A little farther on, they made their first crossing, just downstream from a sawmill that whined with activity. The water splashed up to the horses' fetlocks.

"That wasn't so bad," Cora said when Nathan called a halt to rest on the other side.

"That's the shallowest crossing," he explained as Waldo once more handed around cups of water. "The next two will be more challenging, but I don't expect any problems."

Perhaps it was his insistence, perhaps her own confidence, but she didn't find the next crossing any more difficult. It was a broad, rocky cut through the forest, boulders and logs attesting to the fact that the milky river sometimes ran higher and with greater power.

"Tahoma Fork of the Nisqually," Nathan told them as they started across.

She felt the pull of the rushing water, which almost reached her skirts, but the horses made it safely to the other side, riders and packs intact.

At the third crossing a short while later, the river ran deeper, with rocky shores topped by tall, crumbling banks. The thunder of the rushing waters echoed down the gorge. Nathan called a halt and studied the crossing awhile before ordering everyone from the saddle.

"Lead the horses down the bank," he ordered. "You can remount at the base and ride across, but dismount on the other side and lead them back up. Follow me closely on the crossing. There are deeper pockets where a horse can flounder."

Not Blaze. Cora patted her gelding before sliding from the sidesaddle. Taking up the reins, she let the palomino find his way to the shore, a breeze fluttering the hem on the banner. Easy enough to locate a boulder where she could remount. She didn't even have to wait for Nathan's help.

Which was unaccountably disappointing.

He remounted and rode out into the roaring waters that splashed against his boots and brushed his horse's belly. Her mother and Winston followed, and Cora was glad to see them mimic Nathan's path and pace.

"Ready, Miss Cora?" Waldo called from behind her.

"Ready," Cora answered. Squaring her shoulders, she eased Blaze out into the silver-gray waters.

Slowly, carefully, she followed her mother and Winston, watching for a path only Nathan seemed to see. Twigs and leaves bobbed past, victims of the creek's fury closer to the mountain. A branch sailed closer. She turned Blaze's head a little to avoid it.

With a shudder, Blaze stumbled, struggled, canted.

And Cora was sliding, falling, tumbling into the icy waters.

———— {{ }} ————

"Nathan!"

Waldo's cry had him turning on the shore. Mrs. Winston and her husband were dismounting beside him to lead their horses up the bank. Cora's horse was righting itself in the middle of the stream, the bright banner floating away down the river.

Along with Cora.

He tossed his reins to the startled banker and took off down the riverbank at a run, leaping logs, sliding over boulders.

Please, Lord! Keep her safe!

He lost sight of her in the churn. The river was born of the Nisqually Glacier, from ice strong enough to turn boulders into powder. How much more could it grind down anyone caught in its grip? And the cold. The frigid waters could freeze limbs in a moment, hamper movement, steal breath and life.

There! Sunlight caught on pale hair. She was bobbing with the current but upright. For now. Between her heavy skirts and the rush of the water, she'd never regain her footing. How could he reach her?

Ahead, logs braced the canyon, wedged there when the river had been at its highest. He scrambled up onto them, dashed across the damp wood, boots slipping on the water-stripped sides. No, he would not fall. Too much depended on it.

Over the center of the river, he threw himself down to straddle the largest log and bent toward the water.

"Cora! Here!"

He wasn't sure she could hear him over the roar of the river, but she must have seen him, for her arms moved, pushing against the current. Then she heaved both hands free of the churning waters.

He caught one, clung to it though the tug of the current threatened to pull him over too. Leaning against the weight, he hauled her up until her belly lay on the log.

She was panting harder than her stepfather on a climb. He patted her back, thanksgiving surging through him. "How much did you swallow?"

She spit as if she could taste the glacial silt. "Not as much as you might expect." She managed to roll over and sit beside him. "Well. Tha-tha-that was an ad-ad-adventure."

He could not be so sanguine. He gathered her close, held her safe. His heart refused to slow its frantic pounding.

"Th-th-thank you, Nathan," she murmured. Then she leaned back. "Oh my. I ca-can't seem to st-stop my tee-teeth from ch-chattering."

Her skin was turning blue. Nathan gave her his hand to rise. "Careful. We need to get you to a fire. Can you walk?"

She took a step and nearly tumbled from the log. "Apparently not well."

He didn't trust carrying her, not until they were on the shore. He braced his hands on her hips and pivoted until she stood in front of him, her back to his chest.

"Put your feet on my boots," he told her.

It was a scramble, but she managed to do as he bid. The pressure was firm, but now her whole body shook. Keeping one arm about her, he walked her off the log, then handed her down to the rocks on the other side.

Waldo had almost reached them. "What can I do?" he called.

Nathan swept Cora up into his arms. Blue eyes widened in surprise. "Stay with the Winstons. Keep them moving. Bring Miss Baxter's horse. I'm riding for Longmire's. Meet us there."

He didn't wait for Waldo to agree before striding down the shore for Honoré.

"Is she all right?" her mother begged as they approached.

"She will be as long as we get her warm," Nathan said as he lifted Cora up onto the saddle. She swayed, but he swung up and behind her to anchor her in place with his arms.

"Go with Waldo," he told her mother. Then he put heels to Honoré.

James Longmire and his sons had built a road from Palisade Ranch to the springs, finishing it only that summer with the help of Henry and his sons. Nathan was thankful for it now. Still, not knowing what might be waiting around the next bend, he could do no more than a canter through the thick forest pressing on either side.

"Stay awake," he told Cora as the cold of her wet habit began to seep into him as well.

"I'll do-do-do my be-be-best," she promised as a shiver went through her.

He cradled her closer, offering her any warmth he possessed. As they came around the final bend and the straightaway to the springs, he gave Honoré her head.

Other horses were grazing in the wide clearing when he came tearing in a short while later. Nathan paid them no heed.

"Help!" he shouted as he reined in. "We need help!"

People came pouring out of the two-story cedar plank structure the Longmires used as a hotel on a rise above the meadow. The first to reach him was Elcaine, Longmire's oldest son, heavy black beard obscuring the lower half of his face and part of his chest.

Nathan handed Cora to him. "She was swept down Kautz Creek. We have to warm her."

"The hot springs," he said, supporting Cora as Nathan dropped from the saddle.

As one of Elcaine's boys took the reins, Nathan picked

her up once more and followed Elcaine to one of the mineral pools that dotted the clearing, steam fluttering on the breeze.

"B-b-but my clo-clo-clothes," Cora protested.

"Are already wet," Nathan reasoned. "A little more won't hurt." He let her slide down into the warm waters.

They reached to her chest.

"Lower," Nathan ordered. "Until all that's out is your head."

She frowned at him, but she slid down.

"Quite the entrance," Elcaine joked beside him.

"Miss Baxter was on her way to see you," Nathan explained, finding breath easier. "She hopes to climb the mountain."

"Welcome to you both," Elcaine proclaimed with a little bow. "I'm very sorry Kautz Creek wasn't accommodating. You ought to see about a bath too, Hardee."

"Later," Nathan growled. The breeze chilled his damp clothing, and the water was drying to ash-colored mud. All that mattered was Cora. Slowly, the blue of her skin faded, to be replaced by a healthy flush.

Elcaine turned to the others who were gathering. "All safe here. Let's give Miss Baxter some privacy. I'm sure she'd be happy to regale you with her adventure later." He shepherded the others toward the hotel.

One man refused to follow. Nathan felt him behind them, but he didn't turn until the fellow spoke.

"Not even on the mountain yet and already nearly a casualty," Cash Kincaid mused. "I came to see how Coraline would fare with you as her guide. This surpasses all my expectations."

15

By dinner, Cora was tucked deep under wool blankets and a patchwork quilt in one of the hotel rooms, heated rocks at the foot of the bed. Her plunge in the river had happened so fast, she'd had little time to fear. And just when panic had threatened, Nathan had been there, catching her, holding her, rescuing her. Just as he'd promised when he'd agreed to guide her. She'd told him she didn't need rescuing then. Now, she could only be thankful for him.

She was plenty warm, but her mother continued to hover.

"You might have been killed," she said, pacing the little room with its unpaneled walls and plank floor. "You might have been carried over some cataract, washed out to sea. This entire trip was ill advised. We will return home as soon as you have recovered."

Her stomach tightened, but she kept her smile in place. "And go back on my pledge to Mimi and the other suffragettes? Never."

Her mother paused in her pacing to tug the colorful quilt a little farther toward the right. "I know one of the reasons you're climbing is to thwart my plans for you. They aren't so onerous. Why, Mr. Kincaid came all this way to plead with you to abandon this foolish course of action. He, at least, is a gentleman."

Cora was fairly sure he'd come in hopes she'd fall into his arms for comfort from the challenges, but before she could say as much, her mother continued. "The very fact that he is here ahead of us should tell you something. There is obviously a quicker, easier route than the one Mr. Hardee insisted on taking."

"I doubt it was easier," Cora said. "But Mr. Hardee told us there was a faster way. He chose the one we took to give me and Winston time to acclimate ourselves to the change in elevation."

Her mother sniffed. "How convenient that the route also prolonged the number of days we must spend in his company, and, hence, his price."

"That is between him and Winston," Cora said. "And he has not increased the price to my knowledge even though we added another member to the party."

A knock sounded on the door a moment before Winston poked in his head. "How are we feeling? Better, I hope."

"I'm fine," Cora assured him. "No need to change our plans."

His face fell a moment before he mustered a smile. "Well, that is . . . good news."

Nathan looked more relieved when he came to check on her a short time later. Her mother insisted on staying for the exchange and tucked the covers higher around Cora's neck before consenting to allow him to enter.

"Do not stay long," she told him. "Coraline needs her rest."

He ventured closer to the bed. Damp hair curled around his neck. His green eyes looked darker, as if shadows clung to them, and, wonder of wonders, he was wearing a different set of clothing. The collarless white shirt made his skin look as brown as the trunk of a fir. Green suspenders held up gray wool trousers. She wanted to jump from the bed and hug his solid frame close, but of course her mother would never allow it.

"You saved my life," she said instead. "Thank you."

He ducked his head as if embarrassed by her praise. "You hired me to guide you, Miss Baxter. That includes catching you when you fall."

She hadn't enjoyed the thought of falling into Kincaid's arms, but she suddenly had a far more pleasing image of Nathan holding her close.

"I hope you were able to warm up as well," she said, face heating.

He shrugged. "A bath in the hot springs and some of Mrs. Longmire's huckleberry pie were all I needed. But I thought you might want a day to rest before starting the climb."

Her mother eyed him, brows up, as if certain this was another ploy to take more of their money.

"No," Cora said. "I'll be ready to go in the morning."

The weather had other ideas.

She saw it the moment she opened her eyes. Rain pattered against the windowpanes, drummed on the cedar roof. By the time she had dressed with her mother's assistance and they had ventured downstairs to the main room of the hotel, water was streaming from the eaves, and she could barely see across the clearing to the springs.

"The mountain is weeping for your injuries, my dear,"

Kincaid said, holding out a chair for her at the wide round dining table in the middle of the room.

"I'm not afraid of a little water," Cora said. She was tempted to sit on the opposite curve of the table, but her mother was watching, so she accepted the seat.

"You should be afraid," Nathan said, joining them. He was back in his usual outfit, though it did seem a little cleaner. Had he jumped into the hot springs fully clothed too?

"Why is that, sir?" her stepfather asked from across the table.

"Water makes the glaciers slicker and washes away trails," Nathan supplied. "When it falls as snow on the higher elevations, it can mask crevasses and make climbing harder. We're going nowhere until this has stopped for a while."

The black-bearded man who'd met her and Nathan yesterday rubbed his hands together where he stood by the rounded-stone hearth at the end of the room opposite the stairs. Her mother had told her he was their host, Elcaine Longmire.

"You are all welcome to stay as long as you like," he assured them now.

Cora puffed out a sigh.

Besides Cash Kincaid, three other men were in residence, camping in canvas tents beyond the fence that ringed the clearing. They made it through the storm to join the others in the hall. So did the tall, gaunt Mr. James Longmire, patriarch of the family and the one who had discovered the springs, and his more ample wife, Virinda. They had a summer cabin nearby.

"Exactly how many of these Longmires are there?" her mother asked her as two little boys in short pants chased each other past the stone hearth.

Elcaine, who was watching them, must have heard her. "Fewer than usual, ma'am. Most of my brothers are down in Yelm minding the farm. Besides my parents, there's my wife, Martha, and six of our children. That's Kane and Lafe dashing about. Len's out checking the horses. Susan and Mary are back in the kitchen helping their mother, and little Grover Cleveland is in the crib napping. I expect you'll have a chance to hold him later, if you'd like."

Her mother's smile was cooler than the rain. "How thoughtful."

It was a good thing the Longmires had their own cabins, for the hotel wasn't overly large. The main building held the kitchen and hall, with bedrooms upstairs. A more recent wing offered more bedrooms. The camping party, her party, and Cash Kincaid filled the large, round table for breakfast.

"Mr. Kincaid tells me you hope to climb the mountain," Mr. Garbury, the leader of the campers, said to Cora over a breakfast of oatmeal dotted with huckleberries and drizzled with honey. "What a noble ambition. Why, you must be the first woman to attempt it."

He was a short, slender man with blue eyes that tended to sparkle, as if he were impressed by his own wit. The widest thing about him was the bushy red beard that hung to the center of his flannel-clad chest.

"No, sir," Waldo put in from across the table. "Miss Fay Fuller reached the top three years ago. She was a schoolteacher in Yelm, but she writes for the Tacoma papers now. And Miss Edith Corbett made it in '91."

"So did my Susan," Elcaine said, bringing some sweet rolls to the table. "Still, it's something to do it, no matter who you are."

"But an arduous journey for so fair a flower of womanhood," Garbury waxed, gazing at Cora with oatmeal dripping from his spoon. His two friends elbowed each other and grinned.

Cora met his gaze straight on. "No more arduous than for any of the men who've climbed it. Men and women are capable of many things, Mr. Garbury—climbing a mountain, voting in elections. Where do you stand on the issue of women's suffrage?"

"Why, if you're for it, so am I, Miss Baxter," he assured her.

His friends regarded him as if he'd suddenly dived headfirst into a hot pool.

"All the Longmire ladies agree," Elcaine said, thumbs in his suspenders, as if his chest swelled with pride. "And if they get the vote soon enough, maybe they can help us convince the government to make the mountain a national park, like Yellowstone and Yosemite."

"Rainier could use the protection," Nathan said, seated between Winston and her mother. "Already we've had trouble with campers cutting down trees for firewood or limbs for sleeping boughs."

Elcaine nodded. "We had a group a few weeks back who set fire to a fir, just to watch it blaze up like a firework on the Fourth of July."

Cora stared at him. "That's horrible!"

"Unwise at the very least," her mother tempered. "Why, they might have set the whole forest ablaze and damaged farms and cropland."

"There will always be those who seek to profit from beauty," Kincaid said with a look to Cora.

Anger pushed her to her feet. "Mother, I must walk to keep my legs strong for the climb. Would you join me in a promenade?"

Her mother dabbed her mouth with her napkin before answering. "I fear our exertions have left me fatigued, dear. But I'm sure Mr. Kincaid would be delighted to accompany you."

He climbed to his feet and offered her his arm. No way to refuse him without embarrassing her mother. She put her hand on his arm, but she did not grant him a smile. Nathan eyed them as they set off.

They couldn't go far. The main room was only about a dozen feet square and dominated by the dining table in the middle and tall stone hearth on the end wall. The murmur of voices and drip of rain accompanied each step.

"You've proven your point, Cora," he said when they had reached the hearth and were out of earshot of most of the other guests. "Women are perfectly capable of fighting for what they believe. You don't need to climb a mountain."

Cora lifted her chin. "Your refrain is becoming tiresome, sir. I will climb Rainier, and women will win the right to vote. Perhaps then you will hire them for equitable pay."

He stopped and gazed down at her. His voice came out low and intimate. "If this is about hiring you for a position, I can think of a number of more pleasant ways you could earn money."

Cora stared at him. He wouldn't, he couldn't be suggesting what she thought. The very idea made her skin crawl. She removed her hand from his arm.

"I won't speak to you again, sir, until I return in triumph." Pivoting, she stalked back to her seat. It was all she could do to manage a pleasant face for the others at the table. She must not have succeeded, for Mr. Garbury regarded her as cautiously as if she'd suddenly aimed a rifle at him.

But Nathan nodded, as if he alone knew what she was truly up against.

And believed she could succeed.

It was the longest day he could remember, and not just because of the heavy skies and unrelenting rain. Every one of the unmarried men in the hotel, except Waldo, was attempting to capture Cora's attention. Garbury clung to her side, and his two friends followed with puppylike adoration. Young Len Longmire fell over himself to offer advice on climbing. Kincaid watched, clearly amused. Nathan had had to stifle a cheer when Cora had left the fellow standing alone by the hearth.

After breakfast, Elcaine offered to lead them in worship. Garbury and his friends joined in gladly. Kincaid sang the words of the popular hymns alongside Cora's mother and Winston, his voice a warm baritone. All the Longmires took part, from James with his stub of a beard, white now, to little Grover Cleveland, who let out a squeal as the last verse ended.

Cora stood next to Nathan. For protection from Kincaid and her mother, he was sure. But the fact that she had chosen to ally herself with Nathan kept his head high as Elcaine read from the Bible and then offered a prayer of thanks.

After services, the Longmires returned to their duties. Virinda, Martha, and the girls congregated in the kitchen, which included a large lean-to attached to the back of the hotel. James, Elcaine, and Len sat at one end of the big table, mending tack and refixing caulks into climbing shoes. Cora was so fascinated by the latter that she pulled up a chair to watch, peppering the guide with questions. Len's face turned a pleased pink over his sandy beard.

Susan, a young lady of nineteen, came out of the kitchen, bouncing her littlest brother on her hip. Like her mother and grandmother, she had light-brown hair and a figure many a lady might envy. She joined Nathan by the window.

"You don't think she can do it," she accused.

The baby blew a raspberry, then laughed.

Nathan grinned at his saucy little face. "I think she stands a better chance than most, present company excepted." He held out his hands. "Here. Let me have a word with this fine fellow."

She handed over her brother, then brushed down her flowered cotton shirtwaist.

Nathan tucked him close. Grover Cleveland Longmire regarded him solemnly, brown eyes thoughtful, like his grandfather's. Then he wiggled, face bunching.

"Ah, a man who prefers to keep moving," Nathan guessed. He strolled the baby around the room and back to the window, bouncing him in his arms. "Better?"

Grover babbled happily.

Cora abandoned Len to join them. "Isn't he a dear? May I?"

Nathan relinquished the baby into her arms. Once more, the little fellow sobered as he regarded her, but he must have liked what he saw, for he started chatting again.

"Is that so?" Cora asked as if she understood every word. "Why, I would never have guessed."

Grover nodded his head as if emphasizing his point.

"Well, I think it's marvelous," she assured him. She pulled him closer and rubbed her chin against his hair. Then she smiled at Nathan over the top. "He feels like swan's down."

His heart tumbled out of his chest and into her embrace.

The baby wiggled again with a squeak that sounded a great deal like Quack, and she pulled back. Then she glanced out the window and gasped.

Nathan whirled to see what threatened them now.

"It's snowing!" Cora exclaimed.

The three campers rushed over, and they all stared out at the feathery flakes drifting down.

"It will be a cold night tonight, gents," Garbury predicted, and his two friends shivered as if they could feel it even now.

"You can always stay here," Elcaine offered. "We've a few beds left in the north wing."

"It's already melting," Nathan felt compelled to point out. "See? It's not even reaching the ground."

That didn't stop Garbury from going to dicker with the hotel owner about price.

Susan took charge of her brother and carried him off, leaving Cora standing alone with Nathan.

"Tell me about the way ahead," she said.

At the table, Kincaid was attempting to teach poker to Mrs. Winston and the banker. Cora's mother, however, seemed more interested in what was happening by the window than the pasteboard cards she held. Even Kincaid excused himself to edge closer.

Nathan had to pull his thoughts together, tuck his heart back where it belonged. "Tomorrow, weather permitting, we'll take the trail up along the Nisqually," he told her. "Then we'll follow the Paradise River to Cushman Falls. From there, it's an easy climb up to Paradise Park and Camp of the Clouds."

"What picturesque names," Kincaid said, moving in beside Cora.

Nathan felt the change in her. Her breath caught, and she straightened. Her gaze narrowed on Nathan's face as if she would block out any other sight.

"And then?" she asked him as if Kincaid hadn't spoken.

"Then we climb to Camp Muir," Nathan said, "up the Cowlitz Cleaver, around a massive rock called Gibraltar, and onto the snowfields to the top."

"How easy you make it sound," Kincaid said. "Don't mislead her. I hear it's a long, hard climb, through ice and snow, over crevasses so deep you can't see the bottom, so wide they require a ladder to cross. What sort of gentleman encourages a lady to take such risks?"

"Indeed," her mother put in as if shouting amen to a wise preacher.

Nathan eyed him. "A gentleman who supports the achievements of others without wondering how he can line his pockets from their downfall?"

Kincaid flamed.

Garbury returned to them, eyes bright. "I certainly think your efforts should be applauded, Miss Baxter. I only wish I'd brought my climbing gear so I could go with you."

Cora sent Kincaid a quelling look, then put on a winsome smile. "You climb, Mr. Garbury? Any practices you think I should consider?"

As the camper flushed at her attentions and spouted nonsense, Kincaid eased around him until he was beside Nathan. His gaze was hard, his tone harder.

"I won't forget your part in this matter, Hardee. When she fails and marries me, I'll see you ruined."

"Too late," Nathan said. "You saw to that when you took my father's last dollar. I've nothing left for you to steal."

"We'll see about that," he said before turning and striding for the stairs.

16

The rain stopped that afternoon. The sun came out and set the trees and buildings to steaming as much as the hot springs. Cora couldn't wait to leave. The Longmires were welcoming, Mr. Garbury and his companions affable, but she was always aware of Cash Kincaid, murmuring with her mother, watching her for any sign of weakness.

"Why don't we start for Paradise Park now?" she asked Nathan.

He grimaced. "Too late in the day. But if you'd like to stretch your legs, we could walk around the springs."

Cora readily agreed, and her mother and Winston decided to join them. She hurried them out the door before Kincaid could offer as well.

The cool, clear air brushed her as she followed Nathan into the meadow. The Longmires had encircled the more prominent springs that dotted the area with rounded stones, making it look as if little chimneys poked out of the ground. Some of the springs were hot, puffing out fluffy clouds of steam as Cora passed. Others were cool and clear and deep, giving her a glimpse down into the earth. Nathan dipped up a cup for her to drink. The water was sweet and satisfying.

"Jim Longmire claims the springs have medicinal properties," he told her when she asked for a second helping. "I know I threw you into one of the warm pools when we arrived, but there's a bathhouse to the northwest and cedar bathing tubs available if you'd like."

"A gentleman does not discuss bathing with a lady," her mother commented to Winston.

Nathan inclined his head. "My apologies, ma'am. Just making sure your daughter is aware of the options. There will be no opportunity for . . . hot water the next few nights."

"I shall take that under advisement," her mother replied, turning toward the hotel.

As soon as she and Winston were on their way, Cora stopped Nathan on the plank path the Longmires had laid over marshy ground. "I saw Mr. Kincaid take you aside earlier. I'm glad you didn't let him convince you to give up the trip."

He raised a brow. "Me? I was under the impression he was bullying *you*."

Cora raised her chin. "I make it a habit not to allow myself to be bullied, sir."

He glanced to where her mother had stopped to peer down into one of the hot pools. "Only by your mother, it seems."

Heat pulsed up, warmer than the spring water. "She is my mother. I owe her a great deal, the least of which is respect."

"Even if she forces you to climb a mountain to earn her respect?"

She drew in a breath to keep her temper from flaring. "She isn't forcing me up a mountain. I agreed to go to help the suffragette cause. If agreeing to my mother's stipulations as well is the price I must pay, so be it."

He was watching her again, green eyes shadowed. "Then you'll be ready to start for Paradise Park at first light tomorrow."

Cora raised her chin. "Yes, I will."

Well, not quite.

Cora was ready, but Martha Longmire insisted on cooking them a hearty breakfast of eggs brought up from the Kernahan ranch, pancakes, fresh-churned butter courtesy of the cow the Longmires kept, and huckleberry syrup. Her daughter Susan motioned Cora closer as breakfast was ending.

"We'll take care of your horses while you're gone," she reported. "Father says you don't have to pay the fifty-cent per person fee to use the trail he built to Paradise Park. He thinks that highly of you and Mr. Hardee."

"Please thank him for me," Cora said.

"There's something else. I didn't think to leave anything on the summit when I reached it two years ago. I'd be honored if you'd carry this for me, as another sign that the women of Washington remain undaunted." She held out a hooked bone needle.

Cora took it from her hand. "A crochet needle, isn't it? Our maid Darcy uses one to craft collars and such."

Susan nodded. "My brother Len carved my name in the shaft. You might say, it will show I made my mark."

"You certainly have," Cora agreed, clutching it close. "Any last words of wisdom?"

Susan grinned. "Don't let the gentlemen slow you down."

It wasn't the gentlemen but Cora's mother who attempted to hold her back. She cornered her as Cora was checking the thick canvas pack before giving up her room. Cora was just glad she hadn't donned Miss Fuller's bloomers yet and wore the other ensemble she'd brought with her besides her riding habit. This blue dress had sleeves that puffed out from her shoulders to her elbows, and a minimum of darker blue ruching at the high neck, down the bodice, and on the hem.

"Coraline, please, must you do this?" her mother begged, eyeing the pack as if certain it would leap up and strike her.

Cora straightened, exasperation making her tone sharp. "You set the stakes, Mother. Even if you backed down now and agreed I have no need to marry, I'd still make the attempt."

"To draw attention to these silly suffragettes," her mother retorted, eyes flashing. "They've already lost—twice in the courts and once on the ballot. Why keep fighting? And why fight Mr. Kincaid? You can see he is devoted. You must think of your future."

"Mother." She drew in a breath to steady herself. "You are asking me to exchange a few days of danger for a lifetime of regret."

"It is no less than was expected of me," her mother informed her. "How could you have attended that seminary if not for my second husband? The university if not for my third?"

Guilt wrapped steely arms around her, squeezed the breath from her body.

Her mother laid a hand on her arm, tears coming to her eyes. "Please, my darling, don't risk your life this way. Tell Mr. Kincaid you're sorry you've been cool to him. I'm certain he'll forgive you."

But she would never forgive herself.

"I can't, Mother," she said, shrugging off the touch and

bending her knees to lift the pack. "I should go. I'll see you when I return from the summit."

Her mother stepped aside and let her pass, then followed her down the stairs. Was this how the salmon in the bay felt when an eagle roosted nearby, watching their every move?

Winston stood with Nathan and Waldo beside the main door of the hotel. Each also carried a pack, though only Nathan looked as if it wasn't a burden. He gripped a long, pointed staff in one hand, the wood bleached white, though markings showed where it had been carved. So that had been the wood she'd seen sticking out of his horse's pack.

Clustered near the hearth, the Longmires, Mr. Garbury and his friends, and Cash Kincaid waited.

"Ready to go, dearest?" Winston asked.

"Absolutely," Cora said.

The sight of Cash Kincaid's smug face disappeared as the Longmires, Mr. Garbury, and the others surged forward, cheering. They followed her out the door, and the children ran ahead to wave them out of the clearing. It was a smaller send-off than she'd had in Tacoma or at Henry's, but it made her heart beat faster, her smile broaden. She could do this. She was going to do this.

As the cool shadows of the forest surrounded them, she wiggled her shoulders to settle the pack. Sunlight slanted in golden columns through the dusky firs, with glimpses of the Nisqually on their right, and striped-back chipmunks skittered across the trail to dive into the ferns. Somewhere a woodpecker sought lunch, the rata-tat-tat making them marching music.

As before, Nathan went first, with Winston behind him, then Cora, and then Waldo.

"You're doing great," Waldo assured her every once in a while. "You just follow Nathan. He'll see you through."

Nathan was visible over the top of Winston's derby. His gold-flecked hair was a bright spot among the fir boughs. As the trees opened up and he stopped, she came abreast of him. "How do you feel about crossing that?" he asked.

Ahead, the forest was split by a wide swath of white and gray. Boulders, some twice the size of her head, lay tossed about like balls. The river seemed far less angry than when she'd crossed it the other day. Here it was slow and wide and shallow as it threaded its way among the rocks.

Cora drew in a breath of the fir-scented air. "I'll be fine."

"Walk beside me," he ordered as if he doubted that.

She paced him across the break, hopping from rock to rock in places. Her hem was dark with water and speckled with mud by the time they reached the far bank, but she gave him a smile of triumph that he returned.

They followed the trail along a creek that bubbled down to the Nisqually, the way constantly climbing and the forest growing thicker. Here and there, a stump stuck up where the Longmires had had to fell a tree to clear the path.

After a while, she heard another sound, like a rushing wind, growing louder. Cool mist hung in the air, clung to her hands and face.

"Cushman Falls coming up," Nathan called back.

They broke from the trees at the top of a cliff. Across the gulf, a torrent poured from the mountain in clouds of foam to pool in the creek below. A rainbow arced across. Cora just stood and stared.

"We'll halt here," Nathan said, pulling an arm out of the straps of his pack as he moved upwind, where the mist did not reach. "Waldo, water. Mr. Winston, you should have the lunch Mrs. Longmire packed."

Her stepfather had acquitted himself well on the climb so far. Now he slung off the pack and drew in a deep breath that expanded his chest. Then he bent and began pulling out brown-paper-wrapped bundles and handing them around.

Martha had provided smoked venison, hard-rind cheese, and thick slices of bread. Not a bad meal washed down with the clear water from the springs.

"All up from here," Nathan announced.

Oh, joy.

And yet, it was rather pleasant. A breeze wound its way through the forest, setting the trees to rustling and cooling Cora's skin. Waldo whistled, and a bird answered in the distance.

"Delightful," Winston proclaimed, and she could not argue.

At one point, they had to clamber over a downed tree. Most of the smaller branches had broken off in the fall, but Nathan planted his staff and bent to pull first one and then another branch from the debris. He ran his hand down the sides to snap off smaller twigs, leaving a long stick at least an inch thick and taller than he was.

"Your alpenstock," he said, handing one of the sturdy poles to her and the other to Winston.

Cora held hers in a fist. "I've seen these before. Miss Fuller had one in her climbing picture. You're using one now."

"Many of the alpine climbers rely on them," he said. "An alpenstock can help you keep your balance on a slippery slope, anchor you in the snow, and break through ice."

190

"Then I thank you for the gift," Cora said, tightening her grip.

"Indeed," Winston said.

Her stepfather had said little after lunch, but Cora had heard him puffing ahead of her. As they continued up the hill, he leaned more and more on the alpenstock.

The sun was behind them as the trees began to thin. Nathan turned north, and the climb grew steeper. Now they were in an area recently burned, the charred remains of giant fir crowded by the aspen and grasses rising from the ashes. The sun beat down until she thought she must be steaming like one of Mr. Longmire's hot pools. She strained against the pack, puffing almost as much as Winston. Then the trees dropped away. Once more, she stopped and stared.

Verdant meadows stretched in every direction. In places, she could hardly see the grass, so thick were the wildflowers. White-throated lilies, blue anemones, and golden buttercups clustered next to the tall purple spikes and tufty crimson of flowers she could not name. On the edges, among stands of short alpine fir, nestled white rhododendrons. Nathan kept walking, as if the sight wasn't one to stun. She wandered after him, bending to let her fingers graze the silky petals. Why didn't he stop? She wanted to sit and soak it all in.

Finally he paused on a slight rise, and Winston sank down to sit, heedless of the grandeur he crushed, and heaved a sigh.

"It's magnificent," Cora said, gaze following the jagged snow-capped peaks of the range to the south.

"So is that," Nathan said with a nod to the north.

She turned and gasped. Tacoma—Rainier—the mountain loomed over them, so close she might have reached out to touch the blue-white ice.

"Can't we reach the top today?" she begged, feeling like a child wheedling for a sweet.

"Rainier is nearly fifteen thousand feet high," he said with a smile. "You've traveled more than five thousand feet above sea level already, but we have a good nine thousand left to go, and it's the most difficult. Best to rest now and head out in the morning. We won't reach the top until the day after tomorrow, weather and the good Lord permitting."

———— {{ }} ————

She looked disappointed, but Nathan couldn't relent. He wanted her to reach the top. Safely.

"May we camp here?" Winston asked.

He'd done better than Nathan had expected on the climb up to Paradise Park. They both had. Cora stood gazing around with the wonder he felt every time he reached the flowered meadows. He could understand her desire to keep going. But he couldn't let her take the risk. The summit might look as if it was right there for the taking, but they had a long way to go.

He nodded ahead, to where a creek tumbled down the valley. "Just a little farther. Take it slow. Waldo, walk with him. You'll be able to see us as we go."

"Glad to help," Waldo said. But he gave Nathan a big wink.

"What was that for?" Cora asked as they set out side by side.

"Waldo being clever," Nathan said, boots brushing the heavy-headed flowers. "In this case, not clever enough." He glanced her way. "You're walking well. No blisters? Aches?"

She moved her shoulders, then made a face. "The pack is

noticeable, but my feet are fine." She drew in a deep breath of the air, now tinged with the cool snows ahead. "Oh, Nathan, but it's lovely here. I'm surprised someone hasn't built a cabin, even before the area was made a protected forest."

"It's livable now," he cautioned, heading for a line of alpine fir. "But come September, the snow will start piling up, and by the end of November it could be thirty feet deep or more."

She blinked. "You're teasing."

"No, ma'am. Henry and his kin would vouch for me. So would the Longmires. They leave come fall. It would take a tall, strong building to withstand the winter, and you'd have to pack in enough food to last for six months."

"Well then I suppose I'll just have to enjoy it in the summer," she said. "What about your cabin? How deep does it get there?"

"A few feet. Deep enough the horses and mules have to stay in the barn and neither Waldo nor I can ride for supplies for a few months. Which is why we have to make several trips between now and October to stock up."

"And why you refused to leave anything behind when my mother requested space in the packs."

He snorted. "She didn't request. She ordered."

She cast him a glance. "A trait the two of you share."

He stopped at the edge of the trees, where charred wood and blackened rocks showed that others had camped recently. "When your mother orders you about, it's more often for her benefit, not yours. When I give you an order, it's for your benefit, not mine."

She nodded. "I see the difference. I still don't like being ordered about."

"I don't imagine you do," he allowed.

A shrill whistle Nathan knew all too well trilled higher on the mountain. She turned toward the sound. "We have company, it seems. Another camping party?"

Nathan started to shake his head, but a movement behind her caught his eye. Winston had veered away from Waldo and the trail and was starting across the meadow at a clip Nathan would have thought impossible for the older banker. Another whistle, closer now, only accelerated his pace.

The fool! He had no idea what he was rushing to meet.

"Stay here," Nathan told Cora.

She caught his arm as he passed. "Why? What's wrong? He's only going toward the other party."

"That's not a party," Nathan said, gently removing her hand. "It's a marmot, a fat, furry rat that can scramble up scree faster than any of us. There's a sheer drop just beyond those trees. Winston is following that whistle to his death."

Her eyes widened, but she stepped aside and let him go.

Waldo was already puffing in pursuit. Nathan met him just short of the timberline. "He got away from me," he said as Nathan brushed past.

"I'll fetch him back," Nathan said. "Take care of Cora." He pressed on.

Ahead, on the other side of the firs, he spotted a derby bobbing. "Winston!" he shouted. "Stop!"

The maddening whistle pierced the sunlight. What had gotten into the banker? "Winston!"

He caught up with Cora's stepfather at the edge of the trees, inches from where the ground dropped away. The banker was seated on a rock overlooking the cliff, pack at his side, mopping his brow.

"Trickster," he wheezed. "Did you hear him, Nathan, making fun of my slow progress with his jeering whistles? No doubt some young buck with no respect for his elders." He shook a fist at the towering mountain. "Well, I'll show you, sir! I will stand on the summit and whistle at *you!*"

"I admire your determination," Nathan said, bending to assist him in rising. "But I doubt anyone would make fun of a man who had already climbed this far. Unless I miss my guess, that sound you heard was a whistling marmot."

Winston frowned at him. "A what?"

"A whistling marmot—fat little beast that lives in these parts."

Winston peered at him. "I do believe you're making that up to appease me."

Nathan lifted his right hand. "On my honor. As far as I've seen, there's no one else in the valley but us right now. Pretty much anyone who comes this way stops at Longmire's. Elcaine or Len would have mentioned if they'd seen a party before ours."

The banker must have believed him at last, for he allowed Nathan to lead him back down the slope and over to where Waldo was setting up camp on a hill known as Alta Vista.

"No one else about, eh?" Winston said with a glance at the trampled dirt and the blackened wood of former campfires. He went to where Cora was erecting their tent.

"I put in a good word for you," Waldo murmured as Nathan came to work on their tent with him. "Told her all about your best qualities."

Nathan nearly dropped the short tent pole he'd picked up. "What qualities would those be?"

"Qualities ladies like. You're a good provider, loyal, kind, punctual."

"Oh, I'm sure she was impressed," Nathan drawled, shoving the pole deep into the ground.

"Of course she was," Waldo agreed. "She's clever, that one. She knows a man is worth more than the amount he has in the bank, otherwise she would have accepted Kincaid."

Nathan glanced to where Cora was helping Winston spread the canvas over the poles. "She's clever, all right. Clever enough to see through you and me."

Waldo shook his head. "You know what? I think you're scared of her."

"I am," Nathan said, returning to the work. "And I doubt climbing the mountain with her is going to make me feel differently."

17

Dusk crept across the valley. The sky turned azure, then a rosy pink that glowed in the snows above them. Cora sat on the ground before the fire, sipping tea. The warmth settled inside her along with other feelings less common: satisfaction, contentment.

Peace.

From high above them, something boomed as loud as a thunderclap.

Cora shuddered. "Not more rain!"

Winston, who was sitting on her left, legs stretched to the fire, glanced up. "But there doesn't appear to be a cloud in the sky."

"That noise wasn't thunder," Nathan said from her right, large hands cradling his own cup. "That was ice breaking off a glacier."

"Are we that close, then?" Cora asked.

He shook his head. "Miles. Gives you an idea of the power and size of them."

"It certainly does." She clung to the safety of her cup. Tomorrow, she'd stand on one of those glaciers. She shivered.

"Have some more stew, Miss Cora," Waldo said, taking up the tin plate she'd set aside and adding more venison stew to it. "Enjoy the hot meal. It's the best food we'll have for a while. The higher we climb, the less we can carry."

"Do I understand that water will be more difficult to boil as well?" Winston put in with one more glance to where the rose was fading into purple with the coming of night.

Waldo pursed his lips. "Well, yes and no. They say it boils at a lower temperature on the heights, but the air is so cold it can take longer just to reach that temperature."

"We won't be able to rely on the compass either," Nathan added. "Near the summit, it can be off by several degrees from sea level."

"Why is that?" Cora asked, fascinated.

"Some of the geologists say the iron in the mountain's basalt affects the reading."

Waldo leaned forward, brown eyes glittering in the firelight. "And others say it's because there's gold on the mountain."

Winston perked up. "Is that so?"

"That's just an old story," Nathan scoffed.

"Henry pays for his supplies with gold nuggets on occasion," Waldo protested. "He's getting them from somewhere."

"Likely from guests in his barn as payment for a good night's sleep," Nathan said. "I wish you'd stop repeating that story. The last thing we need is a stampede of prospectors thinking they'll strike it rich in the snow. There's plenty of wonders on this mountain. Gold isn't one of them."

"There may not be gold here," Winston mused, "but there could be silver or even iron. Once this Panic subsides, the nation will boom again. Steel will be needed."

"Then I'll hope for a national park sooner than later," Nathan said. "This land should be protected, not exploited for profit."

Winston wisely sipped his tea and said no more on the matter.

While Waldo was rinsing the dishes in the stream with the last of the light, Nathan drew his alpenstock closer and nodded to Cora and Winston to do the same.

"I'll give you my knife," he said, angling his staff so they could see the bottom. "Whittle the butt to a point like this. It will dig better into the ice."

His fingers covered most of the markings on his alpenstock, but Cora could make out a few words as he offered the knife to Winston with his free hand.

"What does it say?" she asked.

He pulled the staff closer. "It's a Bible quotation, from First Timothy, chapter 6. 'But godliness with contentment is great gain.'"

"Quite right," Winston said, chipping away at his staff. "And I believe the verse before it advises against following those who mistake worldly gain for godliness."

Cash Kincaid came to mind. So, sadly, did her mother.

The idea haunted her as she lay wrapped in her blanket in the tent with Winston that night. Her body was weary enough that it didn't protest the packed earth surface overly much, and she only started when a glacier boomed. What was making her more uncomfortable was the idea behind that verse. Her mother, her mother's friends, even Mimi sometimes, seemed to assume that if a man was wealthy and well-spoken, he must be of good character. Some, like Winston, certainly were. When she'd first met Cash Kincaid,

she'd been as blind, supposing him a paragon for his dona-
tion to the university and his willingness to talk to her about
business and industry. Now she knew he wanted something
else entirely, and all his good deeds had been no more than
a ruse to convince her to lower her guard.

Then there was the idea of making a profit from the mountain. She tried to imagine Longmire's Springs and Paradise
Park if men like Cash Kincaid and even Winston had their
way. The flowered alpine meadows would be given over to
cattle grazing. Rough-wood sluice boxes would clog the
chalky streams. Short-lived boomtowns would spring up
where stands of fir had once stood proud.

No, she could not wish that. Surely here, above the sights
and sounds of civilization, the air, land, and all they sustained
were meant to be free. On that thought, she fell asleep at last.

Waldo had the fire going when she ventured out of the
tent the next morning after Winston had woken. Knowing
they'd be starting their climb, she'd donned Miss Fuller's
flannel bloomers and put the heavy coat over her own blue
wool bodice. The bloomers only showed a few inches below
the hem, but they still felt odd against her legs. Winston immediately averted his gaze at the sight of her as she exited
the tent, as if she'd appeared in her corset and stockings.
Waldo didn't appear to notice.

And Nathan . . .

Was seated on the edge of the rise, looking toward the
east, for all the world as if he greeted the sunrise like an old
friend. More likely he was praying again. What could he
possibly ask for from God in all this wonder?

With a call of *shook-shook-shook*, the bluest bird she'd
ever seen landed on the nearest fir. It cocked its gray-crested

head and regarded her, blue feathers over its eyes raised like brows in question.

"Steller's jay," Waldo told her before shaking his cooking spoon at the bird. "Go on, you camp robber. You'll get nothing from me."

With another cackle, this one sounding rather derisive, the bird flew off.

Nathan rejoined them for a breakfast of oatmeal. He didn't comment on her bloomers either. Perhaps she needn't feel so conscious of them. It wasn't as if she was the only woman to try the practical pants. Ladies who were avid cyclists had been known to favor them.

"We can leave the tents and some of our belongings here," Nathan explained between mouthfuls. "We'll take only what we need for the two nights at Camp Muir and the climb to the summit itself. That will minimize the weight in the packs."

"Though we'll need to carry some kindling for the fire," Waldo put in. "There's no wood at the camp. It's above the timberline."

After breakfast, Nathan had them bring out their packs and inspected them. Cora couldn't help but be pleased when he approved her choices.

"And room for your coat," he noted. "You may not need it most of today, but you'll want it tonight and tomorrow."

She glanced up at the mountain, standing guard over the glories of Paradise. To think that tomorrow morning she would step onto the summit. A thrill zinged through her, faster than a hummingbird in flight. She was going to do it.

They set out for Camp Muir midmorning, heading up the hill directly behind Camp of the Clouds. As before, Nathan went first. Besides his pack, alpenstock, and canteen, he had a hatchet and knife strapped to his belt, and a coil of rope was lashed to the pack with twine. Winston followed, with Cora and Waldo at the back. The meadows accompanied them, as did the sound of the babbling brook. The air was cool, crisp, for all the sun was climbing. The bloomers made it surprisingly easy to walk up the gentle hills, even though she kept one hand on her alpenstock just in case.

"The lady who marries Nathan Hardee inherits all this," Waldo said.

Cora glanced quickly back at him, and he gave her a grin.

"He's made it plain this will soon be a national park," she said, facing front again. "I don't see how anyone inherits anything."

"Oh, we'll see a national park," Waldo agreed, "but he'll still be asked to lead parties to the summit. His wife could go as often as she liked."

Once more, something zinged. She hitched up her pack with her free hand. "I don't need to reach the summit more than once, Waldo."

He chuckled. "You say that now."

Of course she did. And she'd say it when she was finished. He couldn't understand all she had to return to—her position at the bank, her goal to see women vote, her friends, the society she'd been raised in. Climbing the mountain was an objective, like graduating from college. Once achieved, it would be time to move on.

The way became steeper even as the landscape changed. The flowers began to disappear, until only a few bold clumps of yellow and white dotted the grass. The grass, too, grew shorter, sparser. So did the trees, until they resembled the firs her mother had cut and brought into the house for Christmas.

They stopped at one point for lunch, and Waldo offered jerky and hardtack, which she washed down with water from the canteen hanging off her pack. He hadn't been joking, it seemed, about the food. Still, two days of jerky wasn't much of a sacrifice to reach the summit.

She was rather enjoying the brisk climb. Even Winston was weathering it well, for she'd heard no puffing from him, and his face at lunch was a healthy pink. But as they set off once more, she was always aware of the tall man at the front, head moving from side to side, watching for any difficulties and ready to protect.

His first challenge came from a herd of mountain goats.

Cora and the others had crested a short rise when she spotted them, a cluster of shaggy white against the rocky gray of the hillside. Their backs were humped, their faces were long, their ears stuck out either side, and their short black horns pointed almost accusingly at the sky. Winston must have noticed the herd too, for he drew up short. Waldo stopped beside her.

"See there?" he said, pointing to a bearded fellow standing off by himself looking for all the world as if he were glaring at them. "That's the lookout. He's keeping watch for any trouble."

Her gaze moved to Nathan, who had paused just ahead and appeared to be glaring back at the goat. The lookout took a step forward, daring him to move.

One of the youngsters bounded out of the herd, as if eager to make their acquaintance. A larger goat stormed after him and coerced him back in line. It seemed Cora wasn't the only one with a mother who liked things just so.

The lookout goat must have taken their measure; he scaled the hillside and led the others in a hasty retreat.

"Show's over," Nathan said. "Let's go."

And it seemed they were beating a hasty retreat as well.

They sighted the first snow a short while later. The air felt colder too. The hill was so steep now that Nathan had to guide them through a series of switchbacks to climb it. Her breaths came quicker, as if her lungs could not get enough. Worse, she could hear Winston taking great gulps in front of her. When he paused on one of the turns, she passed him to catch up to Nathan.

"Could we rest?" she called, reaching out to touch his shoulder.

He stopped and turned carefully, pack brushing the rocks of the upward side, sending them skittering down onto the path. "For a moment."

She turned as carefully. For the first time, she had a clear view of how high they'd climbed. Paradise Park was a colorful carpet far below, the snows of the mountains to the south at eye level.

"We're at about seven thousand feet," he said as if he'd seen her look. "About seven thousand more to go."

"And what of Winston?" she asked, nodding to where her stepfather was leaned over, hands braced on his knees, while Waldo stood close as if fearing he was about to plunge over the edge. "Is there nothing we can do to support him?"

"He has to make the climb himself," he said, voice as deep a rumble as the fall of glacier ice and as hard. "Have you decided what you're going to do if he can't?"

To have come so far, climbed so high, only to turn back because of some social stricture? It was not to be borne. "I have to reach the summit. I'll do what must be done. But I'd prefer Winston be beside me."

He nodded. "Rest awhile longer. I'll climb to the top of the ridge and check the way ahead. There's a slide area that could have been affected by the rain the other day. We may have to go back and detour around it."

More time, more climbing? That didn't bode well for her stepfather.

"We'll follow shortly," she said. She remained where she was until Nathan made the next turn on the hill, then hurried down to Winston and Waldo.

Her stepfather had removed his pack. She did likewise. It was the work of a moment to flip open the upper flap on his and pull out the blanket and food that were on top.

"Dearest?" he asked between pants. "What . . . are you . . . doing?"

"My pack isn't balanced well," she said, transferring the items to hers. "I'd like to even the load."

He seemed to accept that, though Waldo's narrowed gaze told her he suspected her true motives.

Her pack weighed on her shoulders and hips as they started up again, but at least Winston's breathing sounded less labored. She went first now, knowing Nathan must be just ahead. A short time later, they came out onto a flat stretch, with a hill on one side and a drop on the other. But instead of grass, rocks covered the slope. Unlike the rounded boulders of the riverbed, these were jagged, jumbled, as if the mountain had shrugged them off in a fit of pique.

Nathan was waiting just at the base of the slide. "There's been further fall. The way ahead is partially blocked. We can cross, but it will be slow. I'll help you over, one at a time. Winston first, then Waldo, then Cora."

Winston must have been more wearied than she'd thought,

for he did not so much as raise a brow at the use of her first name. Waldo, however, grinned.

"Very well," Cora agreed.

———— ‖‒‖ ————

She'd have to make a choice soon. Every step the banker took was one more than Nathan expected. At least crossing the slide required slow, careful movement. Winston's breath had evened out some by the time he and Nathan reached the other side. Then he pulled off his pack and sat heavily beside it.

"I'll just wait here, my boy," he told Nathan.

Almost afraid to let the fellow out of his sight, Nathan made himself turn and go back for Waldo.

"I watched you," his partner declared. "I know where to walk. Help Miss Baxter."

Surefooted as a mule, Waldo set out across the rocks.

Nathan reached for Cora. "Take my hand."

Her fingers slid into his palm, and he marveled at her trust. Cautiously, he directed her over this boulder and around that one. As if the mountain protested, pebbles bounced past their feet. He made himself focus on the rugged basalt in front of him, black and gray and rusty.

Above them came the now-familiar boom of a glacier breaking. A moment more, and another rumble rose, setting the rocks to shifting.

Fear lanced him. He seized her and hauled her over the next boulder to push her in front of him. "Run!"

She ran. Pack banging her back and boys' shoes slipping on the stones. The rumble grew to a roar. It swept closer, raising dust that fogged his view. He couldn't lose her. He surged forward, pushing on her pack and shoving her the last few feet to where the hillside opened up into one last grassy patch edged by alpine fir. Winston and Waldo rushed to help them. Cora stumbled into the shade, braced her free hand against the bark, and took deep draughts of the clear air. Behind them, the rumble quieted to a rattle. Drawing a breath as well, Nathan turned to look back the way they'd come and saw only a wall of basalt.

"Rockslide," he said. "I should have realized any loud noise would set it off. We won't be able to go back that way."

He turned again to find that Cora was shaking. He could see the movement in the pack on her back, the bobble of the alpenstock she clung to. A fright could do that. His heart was still pounding from the near miss.

"We'll find another way," Waldo assured everyone.

"Quite right," Winston agreed. He reached out a hand to pat Cora's shoulder. "There now, dearest. You're safe. And I can only thank Nathan for it. You, sir, are a hero."

Nathan shook his head, but Cora glanced his way, look stern as if she dared him to continue arguing. "Yes, he is."

The mountain rumbled in agreement.

Nathan urged them farther from the slide. "Careful. It wouldn't take much to bring more down."

As if to prove it, a pebble rolled down to land by her boot.

Nathan glanced around at them all. Waldo was as taut as a violin bow, Winston's face had gone white instead of red, and Cora still trembled.

"Are you certain you want to go on?" he asked. "It only gets harder from here."

Waldo looked to Winston, and the banker looked to Cora. Everyone knew what was at stake. This was her decision, and he would have to honor it, whatever she chose.

18

He'd warned her she might have to choose. She'd thought herself prepared. But panic shook her, as if the mountain were trembling anew.

When she'd fallen in the river, it had seemed only her life that had been at stake. Now she saw what else might be lost. What if Winston had been struck by a falling rock? What if Waldo fell over a cliff? What if Nathan was injured trying to protect them? How could she justify such a cost?

"I would not see any of you harmed because of me," she said. "I am willing to continue, but if you feel it too dangerous, I will understand."

Winston lay a hand on her arm. "Wherever you go, dearest, I go."

"I'm no turntail," Waldo assured her.

Nathan gazed down at her, green eyes as bright as the alpine grass in the sunlight. "I am at your service."

There was no denying that deep voice or the words spoken with such faith.

"Then we go on," she said.

Nathan nodded. "Catch your breath, and we'll set out."

A few minutes later, they were marching again. Cora tried to put the rockslide from her mind and focus on her surroundings. The little dark firs paralleled them for a few yards before halting, as if keeping their toes from the pocket of snow ahead. Nathan waded across. Winston followed. With Waldo at her back, Cora hesitated. The snow was deep enough to reach halfway up Nathan's shins, likely knee-deep for her. She reached for her skirts with her free hand, then remembered the bloomers. Stretching, she stepped into the hole left by his passing. Well, how nice. Because of Miss Fuller's bloomers, she could lengthen her steps more than any gown would have allowed. Using her alpenstock for balance, she followed Nathan and Winston across the white.

On the other side, a few more trees greeted them. Nathan paced them for a short while before they had to ford another finger of snow.

"They're like little rivers," Cora marveled, pausing to glance up and down the mountain.

"And they'll only grow wider," he predicted.

Winston sighed, breath puffing white in the chilling air.

Indeed, the next while was nothing but up onto rocky ridges and down into snow-filled valleys. With Nathan's assistance, she clambered onto the last ridge, which ran like the spine of some great beast toward the summit.

"How much longer?" she asked, trying to catch her breath.

Winston teetered on his feet, and even Waldo had to pause.

"Several more hours," Nathan told her. "Rest a moment, then we'll continue."

She sighed as she sat on one of the larger outcroppings, Winston and Waldo joining her with grateful smiles. Nathan stretched his shoulders, cracked his neck to one side. Energy radiated off him like a second sun. All too soon, he started out again, stalking along the spine at a pace that kept them moving.

They reached the end of the spine later in the afternoon. Ahead, all she could see was snow.

"Time to put in your spikes," Nathan said. "And put on the glasses."

They peeled off the packs. Cora felt as if some of her skin went with hers. Shrugging her weary shoulders, she drew in a deep breath. The air was colder now, the breeze coming straight down the snowfield like a blast of winter.

They all sat on the rocks. Waldo knew what to do, but Nathan showed her and Winston how to insert the steel caulks into the soles of their shoes, much as Len Longmire had done. Soon the bottoms of her feet resembled the back of a porcupine.

Nathan pulled a small jar out of his pack and unscrewed the lid. "Smear this on your nose, cheeks, and chin."

Cora peered down into the white creamy substance. "What is it?"

"Actor's paint. It will protect your skin from the sun."

"Actor's paint?" Winston asked, perking up. "Ingenious."

Cora made a face. "And I thought the bloomers were scandalous! Mother would have apoplexy if she knew I was putting on paint." She scooped up a fingerful and began covering her skin as he'd directed. Winston and Waldo followed suit. The stuff was the consistency of paste and smelled faintly metallic.

Next came a wool cap, pulled down over her hair, and leather gloves lined with wool. Finally, they put on the blue glasses.

"Everything looks odd," Cora said, blinking as she turned this way and that.

"The sky is purple, snow blue, and the rocks black," Winston agreed.

"But you can tell which is which," Nathan pointed out.

He was right. It was far easier to see the knobs of rock here and there, sticking up like islands in the sea of snow. And she didn't relish the idea of going blind, even for a short time.

Once more they set out, but crossing the snow was like walking over hardened ocean waves, up mounds and down into valleys. Nathan moved beside her now, safeguarding every step. Waldo did the same for Winston. The air seemed too thin, too sharp. She could not get enough. Their stops became frequent.

At one point, he put his hand on hers and planted her alpenstock into the snow. Then he nodded behind her. "Look."

Cautiously, she and Winston turned.

"More mountains!" she cried.

He pointed past her, arm around her body. "That's Mount St. Helens closest to us, Mount Adams behind her. And there, that pointier one in the distance—that's Mount Hood."

The grandeur was almost enough to forget his body was so close to hers. Breath seemed even more difficult. It must have been the altitude.

"Has anyone climbed them all?" Winston asked, voice awed.

"Not that I've heard," he said. "But they will. The desire is too great."

She felt it tugging too. To rise so high, to vanquish such beasts. The air would be rarified indeed.

As they started up again, her legs felt heavier with each

step, the pack a boulder on her back. She concentrated on keeping moving, keeping breathing. Beside her, Winston did the same. Cora glanced his way from time to time. His wrinkled face was whiter than the snow, and she could not like the way he clung to his alpenstock.

It seemed like forever before Nathan stopped again, this time pointing upward. "There's Camp Muir."

She squinted but only saw a ridge of rock ahead.

It seemed so close, but they kept climbing and climbing. The sun moved farther to the west, and they hadn't reached the ridge. It was flatter here, easier going for a while, but none of them seemed to be able to gasp in enough air for conversation. Nathan planted his feet in the snow, each stride determined.

The last half mile was the worst. They scrambled up and up, until all she could see was snow, endless snow. Her hand was stiff on the alpenstock, as if it had frozen in place. Her skin felt like sand under the paint. Her shoes were so crusted they looked like snowballs.

Nathan stomped his feet as they came out onto rock once more, and the snow fell off in clumps. Cora and the others copied him. Ice broke off the hems of her bloomers.

"Welcome to Camp Muir," he said.

Winston's cracked lips moved silently, as if in a prayer of thanks.

Cora glanced around at the jumble of rock. "This is Camp Muir?"

A narrow wedge of basalt slabs stretched across the snowfield, a slash of black against the white. In the distance, a towering mass of rock rose far too high. Was that the summit?

"This is Camp Muir," Nathan assured her, easing off his pack. "Named for the famous naturalist who reached the summit in 1888 and spent the night here. Waldo, look for the easiest spot to set up camp."

His partner wheeled away over the slabs, the only one with unlimited energy, it seemed.

Winston sank to the ground, and Cora settled beside him. The straps of her pack felt as if they'd embedded themselves in her shoulders. Pain stung as she tried to tug them free.

"Let me," Nathan said, reaching out.

She sucked in a breath as he lifted the weight away, and cold filled her lungs.

He frowned as he set it aside. "Your pack wasn't that heavy when I checked it in camp."

Winston frowned as well.

She shrugged her shoulders, willing them to relax. "I took a few things from Winston, to balance the load."

"So, you put yourself at risk for injury," Nathan said, voice hardening.

"Dearest," Winston chided. "I'm fine." He stopped to hack a cough.

Cora patted his back, but her gaze was on Nathan. "I wasn't the one dodging boulders on the rockslide. You put yourself at risk for me."

As if he didn't like the reminder, he grimaced and rubbed his left leg. "That's what you pay me for."

"That is most assuredly *not* what I pay you for, sir," she informed him. "I cannot like any of us taking undue risks."

"I'll remember that," he promised. He motioned to the island of rock. "You can see stretches where the basalt has been moved aside to leave pumice. There's sand under it, much softer than last night. That's where we'll spread the bedrolls. Waldo and I have kindling in our packs, enough for a small fire tonight and in the morning. We can stretch the tent canvas over the top of the rocks for a shelter. For the moment, we need more water."

She glanced around again. "There's a spring up here?"

"No," he said. "Take your cup and mine, and gather snow to melt. Stay where you can see me."

Winston tried to rise. "I'll help."

Nathan put a hand on his shoulder. "I need you here. I'd like to verify our location before the light fades, and you'll be the quickest to calculate the adjustment to the compass reading."

He knew exactly where they were. This was clearly another ruse to make things easier on her stepfather. Cora cast Nathan a grateful look before locating her compass and handing it to Winston.

Waldo came back to point them to their campsite, and they set to work. Nathan moved rocks while Waldo pulled the camping supplies from the backpacks, and Cora ventured out onto the upper snowfield. The snow was more folded here, as if great forces conspired to shove it down the mountain. The wind raced over the white, tugging at her as if determined to shove her down too. She crouched and scraped the cups against the ice, the movement surprisingly hard, until she had filled the cups with sparkling white.

Rising, she looked up, toward the summit, a hump above them. Still nearly five thousand feet to go, from what Nathan had said. Exhilaration vied with exhaustion. Oh, for more strength!

Could she borrow some? She glanced toward Nathan, who

was anchoring canvas on a pile of basalt. He always looked to a higher power. Maybe she could too.

She closed her eyes behind the blue glasses.

He talks to you, heavenly Father. No one I know talks to you, unless he's in holy orders. But if there is any place or time you want to hear from me, surely it's here and now. We're so close, yet I know the danger is close too. And I fear for Winston. Please, keep us all safe. Help me do what I came here to do.

Peace and surety rushed at her in a wave, nearly bowling her over. Oh, such joy. Her eyes were tearing, and not from the rising wind. Was this amazement, this assurance, her answer? Small wonder Nathan sought such comfort every morning.

"Cora!" he called. "Come back!"

She would, but she would come back changed.

———— {{ }} ————

Nathan beckoned her into the shelter he'd erected by stretching the canvas over the tallest rocks on either side of the pumiced pit. She came quickly, smile glowing. Prolonged time on the mountain tended to do that to a person. This seemed something more.

"Everything all right?" he asked.

"Everything is wonderful," she said. She crouched to climb inside the shelter with Winston and Waldo, then handed Nathan his cup. "This looks cozy."

He gripped the tin cup. Already the warmth of his gloved hands was making a puddle of water at the bottom. Waldo had scooped ice for himself and Winston, and both men were taking sips.

"We still have to lay out the bedding, kindle a fire, and

eat dinner before the sun goes down," Nathan pointed out. "That's about two hours from now."

"We are at your disposal, my boy," Winston said, voice sounding faint.

Cora sipped some water from her cup, then nodded. "Just tell me what to do."

Nathan couldn't like the banker's color, but moving might help him warm up. He set Winston to arranging the bedding so that the banker and Cora would sleep with their heads pointing west and he and Waldo would sleep with their heads pointing east. Waldo worked on the fire and food. Cora pitched in wherever she was needed. Nathan couldn't remember a more willing worker on any of his trips. All his other clients had expected him to do most of the labor—setting up and taking down camp, preparing meals such as they were. Cora did what he asked, no questions.

As the sun started heading for the horizon, they gathered around a sputtering fire. Winston hunkered in a blanket, but Waldo rubbed his hands together. "Why don't we ski down the glacier on the way back?"

Cora eyed the snowfield, which was turning rosy with the setting sun. "Is that possible?"

"No," Nathan said with a look to his partner. "At least, not safely. We've had more than one climber end up in a crevasse attempting it."

Waldo humphed.

Cora turned her gaze back to the fire, which was fluttering in the cold, and shivered as if the cutting wind had run its icy finger down her spine.

Winston shivered as well as he tipped back his cup. He handed it to Waldo. "I believe I'll turn in."

"Right behind you," Waldo promised. He secured the cup and wandered off around the nearest outcropping.

Cora showed no interest in retreating to the warmth of her blankets. "How did you and Waldo become partners?" she asked Nathan.

He smiled, remembering. "When my father died, I just wanted to get as far away as possible as fast as possible. I was out near Henry's when I ran across Waldo. He'd come to Tacoma on a supply run and started back right after a storm had passed. A tree fell, hitting him and his horse. We couldn't save the horse, but together Waldo and I reached the cabin he had then, and I stayed to make sure he healed. He insisted on paying me back with room and board. We've been friends since."

"What made him locate out so far?" she asked, pausing to sip the melted snow. "The lake is beautiful, but surely there are closer places to homestead, like near Lake Park."

"A lot of those homesteads were taken before he arrived," Nathan said. "And I think he liked the independence out near the mountain. He'd built a one-room cabin, but he had grand plans for the place, until his wife and son died of influenza, before I came along. That took the wind out of his sails."

"That would take the wind out of anyone's sails," she said. "I've lost my father and my first stepfather, neither of whom I particularly liked, and I still struggled through the changes. Imagine the pain of losing someone you cared about."

"I don't have to imagine," he said.

Immediately, she set down her cup, eyes widening. "Oh, Nathan. Forgive me. I didn't mean to imply you didn't care about your father. It was different with mine. I barely remember him, and the loss of my mother's second husband saddened only those to whom he owed money."

He tucked away the pain as he picked up his alpenstock and gave the coals a stir. "My mother's second and third husbands were no prizes either. At least the last left her sufficient funds that she doesn't need to rush to find number four."

Unless this Panic threatened her too. He hadn't considered that until now. When he returned to Tacoma with Cora he should try once more to see his mother, mend bridges, ensure she was cared for.

He gave the fire another stir, separating coals, which began to wink out in the cold just as Waldo returned.

"We should get some sleep," Nathan said to Cora. "Take your trowel. Pick a spot. I'll look the other way."

He thought her color deepened where it wasn't covered by paint, but she ventured out along the rocks to do as he bid. When she returned, he levered himself up to do the same. Even though he returned quickly, the fire had become an ashy pile, a thin line of smoke following the breeze to the west.

He eased himself down into the sheltered trough beside Waldo. She'd already burrowed under her blankets next to her stepfather. Nathan tried to settle, but his legs protested. His back as well. The wind picked up, snapping the canvas, whistling across the icy wastes. Somewhere nearby, ice fell with a crash that echoed.

Cora's feet bumped his as she shifted. He thought he caught the faint scent of roses, even after two days on the trail.

Perhaps it was that scent that pushed his mind to wandering into waking dreams. He could see other climbs with

Cora at his side, leading women who also longed to reach the heights. With her on the trip, those ladies would feel safe in having him as their guide. He could expand the cabin, build others, turn the property into a haven for those seeking the thrill and peace of the mountain. And he'd make rooms that could be filled with children to love and nurture.

He blew out a breath. Fantasy, every bit of it. Eugene had warned him what would happen if he admired Cora overly much. She'd already refused other proposals. What did he have to offer a wife? He had no social standing, no wealth, and no grand ambition. However many rooms he added, his home would still be a log cabin beyond the reach of civilization. Cora had graduated college, could balance the books at banks and check the capital of corporations. She had dreams of giving every woman in Washington the vote. Why would she settle for life on a mountain?

For life with him?

19

Cold woke Cora. It was dark, but she rolled over and sat up. Her cap brushed the stiff canvas above her, and something crackled. Ice breaking?

Beside her, Winston did not so much as stir, yet it seemed to her the bedding across from them was empty.

"Nathan?" she called.

"Here." A darker shadow moved where the fire had been last night. "Bring your alpenstock. It's time to go."

She scrambled out of the blankets so quickly her head swam. Or maybe it was the knowledge that she was about to reach the top that made her so dizzy.

Waldo was crouched beside the remains of the fire, blowing on a few winking sparks. The light was enough to give her a glimpse of his rugged face.

"What about Winston?" she asked.

"Waldo and I talked," Nathan told her, deep voice a rumble. "Winston isn't going to make it to the summit."

Cora stiffened. "Is he worse this morning?"

"I told you you'd only worry her," Waldo scolded, rising as flames cut into the kindling. He turned to Cora. "His breathing's rough, and I was having trouble waking him earlier. But I'll take care of him. You go on to the summit with Nathan."

"Let me talk to him," Cora said. Before either man could argue, she ducked under the canvas and felt her way to her stepfather's side.

Winston must have woken, for he put his hand over hers as she pressed it against his chest.

"Good . . . morning, dearest," he wheezed. "Is it . . . time to go?"

She had never heard him sound so weak. "Nathan and I will be leaving shortly, but we think it best if you rest here with Waldo."

"Rest? Nonsense. Not when my daughter . . . is about . . . to triumph." He sat up and sucked in an audible breath, then started coughing.

"Winston!" Cora cried.

He waved her off, then flopped back onto his bedding. "I'll be fine, dearest. But . . . perhaps you were right. I'd only . . . slow you down. Go with Nathan. I have complete faith in him."

So did she. Cora bent and kissed Winston's cheek. "We'll come back for you soon."

She thought he nodded. She slipped out of the shelter to find Nathan pacing.

"We'll go together, then," she said.

"Good. We'll leave most of the bedding and food here. I was hoping to return to Camp Muir to sleep tonight, but Winston will rest easier if we descend. We need to try for Paradise Park."

"Is that why we're up so early?" she asked, looking to the east, where the sky was the faintest of gold.

"You have to pass Gibraltar," Waldo answered.

"Once the sun is up, rocks and ice start falling," Nathan explained. "If we don't get past the formation, both directions, before the melt, we run the risk of being struck."

She shuddered. "It's not going to be easy, is it."

His voice was grim. "No, but you can do it. You've more than proved that, Cora."

"That's right," Waldo cheered.

She drew in as much air as she could, until her chest expanded in the long coat. "Thank you both."

They ate more of the jerky and washed it down with water from the canteen. The snow had frozen solid in the night, making it hard to scrape off chunks.

When they'd finished, Nathan pulled a blanket out of the shelter while Waldo began melting ice over the fire to make tea for Winston.

"We're not planning to spend the night in the crater as some have done," Nathan said, tucking jerky and hardtack into a corner of the blanket and rolling it into a sausage shape. "But it doesn't hurt to be prepared, just in case." He draped the roll from one shoulder to the opposite hip and tied it off with one of the strands of twine that had lashed his rope to his pack. But when he set about making a second roll, she stopped him and scrambled back into the shelter for her pack. Winston didn't stir.

"Add these," she said, handing Nathan Sally's comb and Susan's needle. "Put them where I can pull them out easily."

The dawn had brightened the sky enough that she could see his frown. "And you need these on the summit because . . . ?"

"Because friends want others to know a lady has been there," she said. "And so do I."

He nodded and wove them into the roll. As he draped it around her, for a moment she stood in his embrace. She tried not to notice the woodsy scent and the warmth radiating off him.

"They're here," he said as he tied off the bottom, "near the twine. They shouldn't fall out, but you can reach them when the time is right." He stepped back and eyed her. "Paint, glasses, and alpenstock. I'll add my hatchet, canteen, and the rope. Then we'll head out."

Her hands trembled as she reached for the jar of white paint he'd left. Nearly there. Just a while longer. Waldo gave her two thumbs up.

A short time later, she and Nathan set off across the rocks.

The wind tugged at her as they reached the end of their little island. A few yards clambering over ice brought them to a cliff that dropped away into mist. Cora stepped back and bumped into Nathan, who steadied her, both hands on her shoulders.

"We're starting up the Cowlitz Cleaver," he explained. "That's the Nisqually Glacier below us. We'll be fine so long as we stay on the route."

A route only he could see as they pressed forward once more.

The craggy rock formation called Gibraltar grew in front of them, until she could see nothing else. The way narrowed to a thin ledge between the rugged gray stone and the fall to the glacier.

"Give me your hand," Nathan said, and once more she slid her fingers into his keeping.

They edged along. The sun had risen but not high enough to reach the shadows here. Her glasses weren't much help, but she didn't dare remove them. Their tint made the white paint on his nose and cheeks glow blue.

Slowly, the cliff below and the one at her back shortened, and more light trickled into the space. More wind too. It nipped at her face, until she felt her lips cracking.

Nathan stopped and nodded to the way ahead. "We can't climb that."

She stared at the wall of ice, made bluer by her shaded glasses. For a moment, she thought he meant to give up, and she nearly sagged to the ground. But he pulled the hatchet off his belt and began to beat at the ice at about knee level. When he'd broken off a ledge, he stepped up on it and began hacking out another.

"Stairs!" Cora realized.

"Follow me," he called back, "but stay at least two steps behind, just in case."

She didn't want to know what he feared.

It was slow going—hack, crack, move. Hack, crack, move. But gradually, the rock beside them fell away, until they stood at the top.

Nathan called a halt then. He was breathing hard, and his face was reddening where the paint had chipped off.

"Just a few minutes," he cautioned, offering her the canteen. The water from Paradise Park had frozen inside, but a trickle remained to wash her throat.

Breath was even more difficult as they continued to climb over the billowing fields. Small wonder Nathan had feared Winston wouldn't make it. At least the snow was harder packed. Her feet barely made a dent. It was as if the mountain wanted no trace of strangers on her slopes.

From time to time he detoured around a massive crack

in the snowfield, the famed crevasses of the mountain lying gaping like jagged-toothed maws. Finally, she and Nathan reached one that stretched so far in each direction she could not see the end.

He uncoiled the rope and then looped one end around her waist and tied it. "If I fall," he told her, "plant your alpenstock and pull this rope off."

"Why?" she asked, but he was striding forward to where a ledge of snow arched over the crack. He eased out onto it, tapping here with his alpenstock, stopping there, walking on a bridge that should not be strong enough to hold him. He played out the rope as he went, then hopped down on the other side to brace his feet and his staff in the snow.

"It should hold you," he called. "Come across. I'll catch you if you fall."

Cora craned her neck to see into the crevasse. Swirls of blue ice, like the spires of a crystal fairy palace, descended into darkness. She could not see the bottom. Already, snow fell from the bridge, as if his crossing had loosened it.

"Are you sure?" she called. "Is there no other way?"

"None that will let us reach the summit quickly. Come on."

Swallowing, she stepped out onto the thin sheet of ice. More snow fell away on either side. Surely she shouldn't plant her alpenstock. Wouldn't that just break the bridge further? Her stomach clenched.

"Come on, Cora," he urged. "I won't let anything happen to you."

She sucked in a breath of the icy air and plunged forward. Right into his arms.

He caught her close, held her a moment. "Well done. Just a little farther now."

She wished she could believe that. It took all she had to disengage from him, untie the rope, and continue.

The wind was dying as they clambered up the snow. Every few feet, he stopped to let her catch her breath. So hard. But she'd come so far. Must push on.

She was so focused on climbing that she nearly bumped into him when he stopped. She glanced up to ask him why and realized there was nowhere else to climb. On either side, black basalt thrust into the air, like whales cresting the surface. The rocks ran in a gigantic arc over a bowl of ice and snow, where steam puffed from vents to freeze into ice caves.

They had reached the summit.

Amazement, joy, exhilaration overwhelmed in waves higher than the snow.

"We did it," she whispered, trembling.

"You did it," he said, voice warm with pride. "Whatever happens, no one can take that away from you."

She pulled down her glasses and turned in a circle. White tufts of clouds lay like sheep in the valleys below. Rivers wound silver through hills on their way to the blue waters of Puget Sound. To the south, St. Helens, Adams, and Hood waited. There to the north, that peak. Baker?

Thank you, Lord, for all this, for allowing me to see, to feel. It truly is a view most glorious.

Tears stung her eyes, freezing on her painted cheeks in the icy breeze. There was someone else she had to credit.

"Thank you, Nathan," she murmured. "I wouldn't have made it without you."

In answer, he bent his head and kissed her.

Cora stiffened in surprise, but she didn't step away. The

kiss was perfect, as pure as the air she breathed and as magnificent as the view.

He straightened to gaze down at her, ice glistening on his beard. "You deserve every praise. Remember that."

Now she could only look at him in wonder. How extraordinary. She'd always been pretty and clever, and, while compliments were pleasant, she'd known they were caused more by circumstances than accomplishments. This kiss, his words, were more.

"Oh!" She dug in the blanket roll and pulled out the comb. The crochet needle was harder to grasp with her gloves, and she nearly dropped it in the snow.

"Here," he said, and she pulled her glasses back on as he led her toward a pile of basalt to the west. In the lee of the rocks, protected from the gales that could sweep the mighty peak, she tucked in the precious items.

"There," she said. "That proves it."

Something flashed in the light. She peered closer. "Someone's wired a mirror to these rocks."

She glanced up to see Nathan smile. "Mr. Van Trump. I couldn't find it the last time I was up. We'll have to let him know it's still here. You should mention it when you speak to the reporters. That will help prove you reached the top. Now, let's go." He turned from the rocks.

She glanced around once more, memorizing every angle, each vista. There, a slight rise in the mountain even now. She seemed to recall Mr. Van Trump mentioning two parts to the summit. Surely she should try for the other portion too.

"Must we?" she asked. "There's so much more here."

When she looked back at him, his smile was sad. "For safety's sake, yes. We need to leave now."

Following him from the summit was the hardest part of the journey yet.

———— {{·}} ————

She was amazing. The view from the top never failed to humble him, but standing at her side, seeing the same awe and joy on her face, had made the accomplishment sweeter still. He hadn't been able to stop himself from kissing her. If she asked for an explanation, he'd put it down to the thrill of the climb.

Even if he suspected there was far more to it than that.

The way back should have been quicker, being all downhill, but the sun was warming the snow, making it softer, harder to traverse. Melted ice ran sparkling in little streams down the slope. He had to watch every step and keep an eye out for crevasses hidden by blowing snow. Worse, the snow bridge they'd used to cross the biggest crevasse had thinned to a veneer he didn't dare take Cora over. Instead, he tied the rope around her waist and his once more.

"Watch me," he said, stomach knotting as tightly as the rope. "And remember, if you fall, I'll pull you up."

She nodded. Behind the tinted glasses, her eyes were impossibly blue, impossibly wide.

Nathan backed away from the crevasse, then sprinted toward it. A foot from the edge, he planted his alpenstock and pushed off, yanking his alpenstock up and along with him. Over the yawning crack he flew, catching a glimpse of darkness far below. He skidded on the wet snow as he landed, but he dug in his staff and brought himself to a stop.

Drawing a breath that speared icy air into his chest, he turned and steadied himself. "Come to me, Cora."

She backed up, two steps, three, then lunged for the hole. His heart leaped with her jump. She landed on the very edge, and one shoe slipped back. She careened, tilting, crying out.

Falling.

Nathan surged toward her, pulling on the rope, and she plunged forward instead, onto her chest in the snow.

He reached her side as she raised her head. Snow clung to her eyebrows and the tip of her nose. He had to fight the urge to kiss it off.

Whispering a prayer of thanks, he bent and helped her to her feet.

"All right?" he asked.

She brushed snow off her long coat. "Yes, but I think you should have warned me that to climb a mountain I needed to know how to fly."

Relief pushed laughter past his lips. "I'll remember that the next time I take a lady to the summit."

She glanced back the way they had come, face lined by yearning. He understood. One of the reasons he agreed to act as guide was the excuse to reach the heights again and stand for a moment at the top of the world.

"Ready?" he asked.

"Ready," she said. Then she gathered herself, and they continued their descent.

Gibraltar proved the next challenge. Nathan had to ease his way around the towering formation. Rocks sifted down from above, falling with a whistle like a cannonball, and once ice crashed in front of him. He grabbed Cora, sheltered her with his body. The need to protect her had never been stronger.

"Thank you," she said as he released her. "And those words do not seem adequate for what you've done for me."

And for all he was feeling. He made himself lead her on.

They had reached the top of the Cowlitz Cleaver when he spotted the other figures at the foot.

Cora must have seen them too. "Winston is up!"

That made their steps all the easier.

About five hundred feet above Camp Muir, Waldo and her stepfather were waiting. Their grins could have lit the night.

"You did it, dearest!" the banker exclaimed, enfolding her in a hug. "We saw you on the summit. So tiny, but so clear against the snow. I've never been prouder."

She smiled as she pulled back. "And you sound much better."

"A little tea and a little rest were all I needed."

Beyond him, Waldo shook his head at Nathan. Right. Still best to get the banker to lower altitude and warmer temperatures as soon as possible.

"Do you want to go to the summit yourself?" Cora asked. "We could stay another night."

Winston glanced at Nathan, and something crossed his face. The fellow knew his limits. "No, dearest. I feel fortunate to have made it this far. I'm just glad you had Nathan beside you."

Which meant he'd done his job. He had to remind himself of that. This was just a job. She'd return to society now, take her rightful place at its head, trumpeting the cause of women's rights. All too soon, it would be time to say goodbye.

"That's settled, then," Nathan said. "We need to break camp and return to Paradise Park before sunset."

"What about the rockslide?" Cora asked as they turned for Camp Muir.

"There's more than one route down the mountain," Waldo

said. "Maybe we can find one that shortens the time to Paradise Park some."

"We can hope," Nathan said. "Either way, we have one more night in Paradise, then Cora can tell the world she climbed a mountain."

20

Climbing down was not as easy as she had expected. Nathan had been right about the snow. What had been firm and icy this morning now had a layer of melting slush on top. It sucked at their shoes, made each step a chore. And the packs didn't seem nearly as light as they should. Even after his rest, Winston was soon puffing, breath a white cloud in the air. Cora's legs were like lead.

But she'd done it. That knowledge alone sustained her. Having reached the heights, she couldn't rest until she could see the feat reported. Oh, what Mimi could make of it as they argued for the vote! As if to celebrate with her, a golden butterfly danced by above the snow.

Nathan was quiet, pointing them to more reliable routes, breaking trail where needed. But even he seemed to be slowing.

"Perhaps a rest?" she called.

"When we hit rock," he called back.

It seemed an inordinately long time before they hit rock. Waldo alone seemed undeterred by the descent. As they came across a long stretch of snow, he darted to one side. "You all are too slow," he declared, and he took a run before planting his feet to slide on the icy wastes. He shot past Cora, Winston, and Nathan, flying down the hillside.

"Remember to plant your alpenstock!" Nathan shouted after him.

Winston watched him go, face sagged in longing. "Wouldn't that be something to move so quickly."

"I can't recommend it," Nathan cautioned. "It's called glissading, and only the most experienced climbers try it. There, he's had to stop for that outcropping of basalt. He might just as soon have smacked into it."

Winston's look was resigned.

Cora wasn't quite so ready to give up. "You said it was possible to ski down the glacier, Nathan. Waldo's waiting. Why not try? We'd be sure to reach Paradise Park before dark."

Nathan eyed her, then snapped a nod.

He had her and Winston line up parallel with him on the slope, showed them how to bend their knees and lean forward just the slightest, push off with their alpenstock, then dig in the staff to slow their movement. After a few short runs, he gave them his approval.

"I'll go first," he said. "That way I can come back up if there's trouble."

"Race you to the bottom," Cora said, pushing off.

The icy wind whipped past, tugging at her blue glasses, her cap, and her coat. She was flying, soaring, a falcon diving for its prey. She was freedom, joy, and exhilaration.

Nathan came into view beside her. He shot her a grin before passing. She leaned farther forward, but he beat her to the rock, dragging his staff the last few feet to slow himself.

She managed the same feat and jerked to a stop just short of the basalt. Easy to bask in his admiration. Then his smile melted into a frown, and she turned to look up the slope.

Winston was struggling, leaning left, right, and then one foot came free of the ground entirely. His alpenstock waved in the air.

"Stay here," Nathan told her. "Waldo, with me. We have to catch him."

They both sprang back up the slope.

Winston careened toward them, and Cora held her breath. Nathan and Waldo veered to intercept him. Nathan caught one arm, Waldo the other, and all three of them slid backward toward the rock.

She couldn't simply wait and watch. She stepped out onto the snow, planted her feet and her alpenstock, lowered her head, and stood firm.

Winston slid right into her, but she stayed upright, and so did he.

"Sorry, dearest," he said, breath puffing in the air. "That wasn't as easy as you all made it appear."

"From now on," Nathan said with a look to Waldo, "we walk down."

Waldo had the good sense to look abashed.

They had to descend through snow for another half hour before they reached the next outcropping of basalt. Cora collapsed on a slab and eased off her pack, then stowed her blue glasses. The world didn't look much brighter without their shade. Mist was rolling into the valleys, making it seem as if they stood on the banks of a sea. She gladly accepted the cup of water Waldo handed her. At least as the day warmed, the ice in the canteen melted.

"We should be able to move faster on the next leg," Nathan said, gaze on the way ahead, which disappeared into the bank of clouds. "Without having to glissade. What do you think of that path for our way down, Waldo?"

Cora looked to where a narrower rut led off toward the south.

"Might do," Waldo allowed, capping the canteen. "I seem to recall Len Longmire mentioning one that ran down the backside of Alta Vista to Camp of the Clouds."

She could have slept where she sat. "A few minutes rest would be appreciated."

Nathan turned from the view. "A few minutes only. We need to remove the caulks from our shoes, after all. But we don't want to be caught on the hill after dark."

His words hung like Winston's breath in the chill air as they descended. The mist closed around them, leaving drops glittering on her gloves, her alpenstock. She could barely make out Nathan at the head of their column. She'd take a couple of steps on the uneven ground, pause and orient herself, then look down to go forward again. Her neck started to ache with the movement. Ahead of her, Winston shambled along as if unable to lift his feet from the ground.

"Only a little farther," Waldo encouraged behind her. "And you might want to go a little faster. We don't want to lose Nathan."

Nathan must have heard his friend, for he slowed his steps.

Gradually, the sun burned through the mist. Trees appeared ahead. But the light was dipping toward the west, until it caught in the branches of the alpine firs. When they reached the meadows, wildflowers nodded drowsy heads, and she knew it couldn't be long now. Everyone's pace picked up then.

"Mules heading for the barn," Waldo said with a chuckle.

She didn't mind the comparison in the least. Below, she could see the peak of the tent they'd left behind. Almost there.

Dusk blanketed the meadows when they reached camp at last. Waldo chased some chipmunks out of the tent, but otherwise nothing had been disturbed. Winston crumpled beside the firepit, face gray. Cora flung off her pack and dropped beside him. "We made it."

"And just in time," Waldo said with a nod to where the sun was hiding in the forest. "I'll get a fire going."

"I'll put up the other tent," Nathan said, removing his pack as well.

He had to be as weary as she was. Cora managed to regain her feet. "Let me assist."

He didn't protest as she joined him.

"Tired?" he asked, unfolding the canvas.

"Bone tired," she said. Then she smiled at him. "But you know, I climbed a mountain."

His smile warmed her more than the fire Waldo had kindled.

She was still smiling when he served up beef soup and tinned apples a short time later. The hot, salty soup seeped into her as the four of them hunkered around the glow. Sighs echoed. She'd taken a moment to wash off the last of the actor's paint, and her skin felt free again. Even Winston recovered a little to beam around at them all.

"We can't sleep too late tomorrow," Nathan warned as if he feared they would nod off where they sat. "We need to return to Longmire and retrieve Mrs. Winston, then make the cabin by dark."

Waldo grinned, teeth flashing in the firelight. "Can't wait to see Mrs. Winston's face when she hears our Cora made it all the way to the top."

Once more Cora traded smiles with Nathan.

"I'm sure Cora's mother will be pleased to have us return safely," Winston said. "Will you accompany us all the way to Tacoma, Nathan, my boy?"

Cora started, soup sloshing in her cup. That's right—his work was done. He had no further role in her life. That felt wrong, as if she'd put too much in her pack and was suddenly overbalanced.

He glanced her way, face lined by light. Was she mad to see the same sorrow she felt at their coming parting?

"I finish what I start," he said. "I'll get you all back to Tacoma."

"We could stock up on supplies too," Waldo reminded him.

All at once she was so heavy she could scarcely sit upright. She managed to stand, then held out a hand to prevent the men from rising as well. "I'll turn in now. Thank you, gentlemen, for everything."

"I'll join you shortly, dearest," Winston promised.

She stumbled to the tent.

What was wrong with her? She slumped on the blanket, fumbled with the laces on her climbing shoes, and managed to pull the things off her aching feet. She'd known Nathan would only be in her life a short time. He hadn't pledged undying devotion. She'd never sought his attentions. He had helped her achieve her greatest triumph. Nothing said he had to stay at her side forever.

And truly, were her feelings worthy of forever? For all she knew, they had been born of proximity and a shared goal.

Would they last longer than a day or two now that the goal was won?

She had never felt more tired, but sleep refused to come as she lay bundled in her blanket. She heard Winston enter the tent and crawl into his bedding, then the rumble as he started to snore. Even that couldn't eclipse her thoughts. She ached, but it was deeper than her muscles. It was as if she'd never made it to the top, as if she'd lost something precious.

———— {{ }} ————

Nathan drew in a deep breath as he pulled the blanket around him. His body commanded sleep, but he couldn't stop thinking about Cora on the summit, glowing with purpose, achievement, and joy. And then there was the kiss, so sweet, so rich.

Whatever he thought, whatever he felt, it would all end once they reached Tacoma.

From the other tent, a snore rattled the night. Next to him, Waldo moved and rustled his bedding. Nathan wasn't surprised when he spoke, just at what he wondered.

"So, did you ask her to marry you yet?"

"No," Nathan said.

Waldo huffed. "Why not? She's beholden to you, has warm feelings right about now. I've no doubt she'd say yes."

If only he had such faith. "Get some sleep, Waldo."

Grumbling, Waldo shifted away from him.

But thoughts of Cora filled Nathan's mind until he finally drifted off to sleep. It seemed fitting that she was the first person he saw when he exited the tent the next morning, leaving Waldo still dreaming.

The sun was veering toward the top of Rainier, and birds

welcomed it in chorus. She stood on a boulder, head up, eyes closed, light bathing her. As he watched, she lifted her hands to the sky.

His heart rose. Worship was all too easy here. Even now, thanksgiving filled him, and he stood for a moment, murmuring his gratitude for safety, for prosperity.

For her.

She climbed off the rock and came toward him. She'd removed the bloomer suit and was back in the blue dress with all its little tucks. Her hair hung down around her shoulders like a silken cloud, and for the first time since meeting her, he wasn't sure where to look, what to say. He grabbed a pot and went to fetch water from the stream.

He returned to find her wading through the wildflowers, arms down and fingers splayed, as if she would gather them all close. Oh, how strong the urge to follow, to hold her, to kiss her. He made himself crouch beside the rocks and start the fire.

"It's so beautiful here," she said as she joined him. "I want to bottle it and carry it home with me."

"Most folks seem to feel that way about the mountain," he said. "They take flowers to press into books, rocks from the streams for their curio cabinets. Better for the mountain if they just take memories."

"I certainly will." Her gaze went toward the peak above them. "When you pulled me from the river, pushed me out of a rockslide, drew me over a bridge of snow, taught me to fly down the mountain. When we reached the top, together."

When he'd kissed her? Well, perhaps he was the only one who dwelled on that. "I'm glad." He might have said more, but her stepfather tumbled out of their tent then, and the work began.

They moved about the tasks, a team now—cooking oats for breakfast, striking the tents, balancing the packs. They'd eaten enough, used enough fuel, that the things were lighter now. Cora carried her alpenstock like a trophy as they made their way across the valley for the forested path to Longmire's.

They followed the same order—him first, on the lookout for potential difficulties; Winston behind, where Nathan could keep an ear on the older man's breathing; then Cora and Waldo at the back. He'd had little trouble with the order before. Now all his senses seemed trained on her.

When she stopped to watch a jay take flight through the trees and sunlight anointed her cheek.

How the mist from Cushman Falls sparkled in her hair like diamonds.

The way she hurried to assist her stepfather over a tree that crossed their path, hands gentle, look kind. Oh, for such a look directed at him.

What was he thinking! He had to get ahold of himself.

They came out at Longmire's meadow midmorning. Another group had arrived, their presence evident in the tents set up near one of the springs, the horses grazing on the marshy grass. A half dozen women were lounging in front, some with fans to swat at mosquitoes. All movement stopped when they must have spotted Cora.

Martha Longmire greeted them as they came into the hotel. "Miss Cora and Mr. Winston! Mrs. Winston will be so glad to hear you've returned." She nodded to her daughter Mary, who scrambled off to deliver the news. "Triumphant, I hope." Her dark eyes brightened.

"Triumphant, indeed," Cora assured her. "And I left Susan's crochet needle to prove it."

She beamed. "A shame Len isn't around at the moment to hear it. He's off with Mr. Kincaid to see the Nisqually ice caves. I expect them back shortly."

"Coraline, Winston." Cora's mother glided up to them, then stopped a few feet away and wrinkled her nose. "My, but your travails are apparent. Mrs. Longmire, might we see to a room and a bath for my husband and daughter?"

"But dearest, don't you want to hear of our adventures?" Winston asked as Mrs. Longmire whispered to her daughter, who had returned with Mrs. Winston.

"Certainly," her mother told him. "As soon as you are presentable."

"We don't have time for that," Nathan put in before Martha could send her daughter running once more. "I hadn't intended to spend the night. We'll make our cabin before dark if we leave now."

"Ah," Martha said. "Well, we'll be sad to see you go, but you know you're always welcome back."

Mrs. Winston inclined her regal head before turning to Nathan. "I thought you might insist on departing, sir. While you were gone, I had Mr. Longmire send word to the Ashfords. We will be staying with them this evening. Mr. Kincaid will escort us to Tacoma. So, you are no longer required, Mr. Hardee. Mr. Winston will send you what we owe. Good day."

21

The steam rising from Rainier's crater was nothing to the heat surging up inside Cora. How dare her mother order Nathan about! As if they thought the same, Waldo was glaring at her mother and Winston was turning red.

Nathan merely gazed down at her mother, face stoic. "My agreement is with your daughter, Mrs. Winston. She's the only one who can discharge me."

She thought Winston might argue, but he nodded. Cora drew in a breath. "I would very much like your escort to Tacoma, Mr. Hardee. You saved my life on the mountain when you rescued me from the rockslide, not to mention the fall in the river earlier. And I believe you were planning to visit your mother as well."

"I was," Nathan agreed. "I'll see you home, then, Miss Baxter."

Winston nodded again. Her mother shifted on her feet as if she had grown uncomfortable. Good. She needed to remember who Nathan was and what he had done.

As if he suspected what Cora was doing, Nathan arched his brows, but he said nothing more on the matter.

Her mother turned to the innkeeper. "Mrs. Longmire, if you would be so kind as to have my horse saddled. It appears I will be leaving as soon as Mr. Kincaid returns. Coraline, will you assist me in changing into my riding habit?"

Cora knew how to accept a win graciously. "Certainly, Mother." Leaving her pack and alpenstock in the main room of the hotel, she followed her mother upstairs as Nathan enquired about having the other horses saddled.

She thought she might have to gather her mother's things as well, but most were already in her horse's pack, sitting in one corner of the room. She also thought she might have to endure a scold, but her mother was uncharacteristically tight-lipped as Cora assisted her out of her fine wool gown and into her riding habit. As the heavy folds passed her face, her mother wrinkled her nose once more.

"We'll have to burn this when we get home," she said as she started fastening the jet buttons on the bodice. "And we'll burn everything you wore on this trip. I don't see how any of it can be saved."

"A good brushing and some air should do wonders," Cora said, folding the gown. "Besides, what I wore to climb belongs to Miss Fuller."

Her mother looked up to frown at her. "What do you mean? What did you wear?"

Oh dear. Well, if admitting what she'd worn would save Miss Fuller's suit from being burned before Cora could rescue the outfit from Lily, then so be it.

"A pair of bloomers and a long coat," she said, bending to put the gown in the pack.

She glanced up to find her mother staring at her, face paling. "Coraline, you didn't!"

Cora straightened. "I did. It was the only way to be safe, Mother. I certainly couldn't have crossed the crevasses, climbed some of the rocks, or waded through snow in skirts."

"Then perhaps you should not have been doing any of those things." She sucked in a breath is if trying to still her temper. "Please tell me no one saw you."

"Only Mr. Hardee, Mr. Vance, and Winston." She cinched the pack shut.

Her mother nodded. "Good. Mr. Winston will say nothing of the matter, and the other two are of no import. Still, I cannot like the way you allow Mr. Hardee to influence you." She started for the door as if assuming someone would follow with her belongings. "It was one thing when you had to rely on his instruction to make this climb. I see no need for further association now."

"So you've made abundantly clear," Cora replied, hefting the pack. "I like him, Mother. He stands by his principles. He helps those in need. You should have seen the deference to which he held Winston."

"And well he should," her mother said with a sniff as she opened the door. "Winston is a prosperous banker, a pillar of the community, and worthy of respect. And, if I may point out, he is paying Mr. Hardee's fee."

"Those men who came to his cabin didn't pay him for treating their friend," she reminded her mother as they stepped out into the hallway. "He did what he could for them nonetheless."

She sniffed again. "Perhaps he does have a generous nature. I am still not convinced he is a fit associate for a young lady of your considerable accomplishments."

"He attended college, I attended college," Cora countered

as they started for the stairs. "He's making his own way in the world, and so am I."

Her mother tsked. "Because of Winston's kindness. You cannot repay that kindness by turning your back on everything I taught you."

Perhaps not, though she had to admit the urge was greater than ever before.

And never more so than when they reached the bottom of the stairs and found Cash Kincaid waiting in the main room of the hotel.

He was dressed in clothes she now recognized would have little use out here—tailored black trousers that would make it hard to climb and which already showed the gray splattering of mud; a satin waistcoat of a muted gold that would likely never endure a good washing; and a silk tie that had crumpled from his exertions. Martha, who was wiping down the dining table, cast him a glance and shook her head. Her husband, Elcaine, stayed near the hearth, but his black beard looked even more bristly than usual.

"Mrs. Winston and Miss Baxter," Kincaid said with a bow. "A vision as always."

"You are too kind, Mr. Kincaid," her mother said.

"No indeed," he assured her. "Why, your daughter appears so refreshed, I might never have guessed she'd been to the summit and back."

"Then look closer, sir," Cora told him before her mother could answer. "I have the chapped lips to prove it."

Her mother tsked again, but he made a show of looking her up and down. "You seem perfection to me. It is as if you merely strolled to Paradise Park, camped a few days, and returned."

Such flattery. Did he think she'd believe him sincere?

"Alas, if only it was as easy as a stroll," she said, setting down the pack. "Winston nearly lost his breath. Mr. Hardee saved us all from a rockslide. I'm not sure how we made it safely to the summit to stand beside Mr. Van Trump's mirror. The mountain is far more treacherous than I expected. But then, I am becoming accustomed to dealing with treachery."

Her mother and Kincaid were saved a response by the opening of the door to the meadow. Nathan came in. He must have dipped his head in the springs, for his hair was wet and dripping against his collar. His gaze went straight to Cora, as if there were no others in the room. "Ready to leave?"

"Ah, Hardee," Kincaid greeted him before she could answer. "Miss Baxter was just telling me how she made it to the summit. A shame I wasn't there to see it. I might have been able to verify the fact for the papers."

As if she needed his word.

Nathan cast him a quick glance. "Not everyone has what it takes to reach the top."

Kincaid's face darkened. "Or remain in society after a setback."

For a moment they stood, gaze to gaze, frown to frown. Heat rolled from them. Even her mother took a step back.

Elcaine Longmire pushed off the hearth and strolled closer. "Is there a problem, gentlemen?"

"No," Nathan said.

Time to keep moving. Cora turned to Nathan. "You asked me a question, Mr. Hardee, and I regret that I could not answer until now. I am quite ready to leave. I can't wait to reach Tacoma and tell everyone the good news."

———— ‖ ‖ ————

That smile was all triumph.

Nathan bent his head closer to hers. "You're never going to let Kincaid forget what you did, are you."

"Not in the slightest," she murmured back. "Nor any fellow who needs proof about a woman's abilities. Give me a moment to say goodbye to Martha and Susan, then I'll join you."

"Allow me to escort you to your mount, dear lady," Kincaid said, sweeping Mrs. Winston a bow.

She inclined her head with a queenly look and suffered herself to go with him and Winston to where Len waited with the horses.

Nathan took out Mrs. Winston's pack and secured it to her horse. She didn't so much as acknowledge him. When he returned to the hotel for Cora, he found her and Susan searching the main room.

"What are you looking for?" he asked them.

Susan paused, but Cora continued casting about, face tight. "My alpenstock. I don't see it on Blaze. It was right by my pack."

"It's out there," Nathan promised her. "I strapped it to the other side of your horse. I thought you might want it."

She stopped and drew in a breath. "Thank you. I do. And thank you, Susan, for looking."

"Any time," Susan told her with a smile. "Safe travels back, and watch those crossings!"

They finally made it out the door, and Nathan assisted Cora in mounting. Kincaid's eyes narrowed as if he begrudged Nathan the honor. Maybe that was why the businessman insisted on taking the lead, as if determined to show he had pride of place.

"So delighted you could journey with us this time, Mr. Kincaid," Mrs. Winston said beside him as they followed the path down the river.

Nathan almost regretted riding behind the pair, but he'd wanted to accompany Cora. She rolled her eyes at her mother's praise now, as Winston and Waldo brought up the rear.

"The pleasure is mine, ma'am," Kincaid assured Mrs. Winston. "Though I might suggest a change in route. I understand some of the places you stayed were a bit rustic."

She cast a glance back at Nathan before answering. "Yes, they were. I took the liberty of securing rooms with the Ashfords tonight."

"Are they good people?" Cora whispered to Nathan.

"The best," he told her.

Kincaid appeared to agree, though Nathan had never heard of him staying in the area before. "Ah, you will find Mr. Ashford and his charming wife a delight," he was saying to Mrs. Winston. "The husband originates from England, so you know there's breeding there."

As if every Englishman was a duke. Nathan smothered a snort. Cora rolled her eyes again.

"How pleasant," Mrs. Winston said. "And have you any suggestions for the next night?"

"The Pioneer Hotel in Eatonville," he answered readily. "It's finer than the hovel at Longmire's. Larger too. And then back home through Lake Park to retrieve your carriage."

"Jim and Elcaine might have something to say about calling their hotel a hovel," Nathan murmured.

"Martha too," Cora agreed.

"That sounds divine," her mother said to Kincaid. She glanced back. "You see, Coraline? There's no need to inconvenience Mr. Hardee. Mr. Kincaid has a sensible plan to return us home."

"It's no inconvenience," Nathan said as Cora looked to him. "Though I'll stay at my place near Ashford's tonight and Henry's while you're at the Pioneer Hotel."

"My, but you've embraced this rough life, Hardee," Kincaid tossed back over his shoulder. "I can only hope it will continue to offer you comfort."

"More than I had imagined, Mr. Kincaid," Cora put in.

Nathan was only glad her mother and Kincaid grew silent for a while then.

Winston had also been largely quiet during the ride. Waldo kept commenting—on the weather, on the journey, even on the bank—but Winston made only polite replies. Cora must have noticed too, for she glanced back. So did Nathan.

"Everything all right?" she asked.

"Fine, dearest," Winston said, his face a reasonable shade of pink over his white mustache, his breath easy. "Just a great deal on my mind."

And it seemed he wanted to share it with Nathan, for when they stopped to rest the horses before starting the river crossings, the banker drew away from his wife and Kincaid and beckoned Nathan closer.

"I haven't had an opportunity to express my heartfelt thanks for all you've done for us, my boy," he said, eyes dipping down at the corners, as he led Nathan farther from the others in the little clearing. "Even discounting your gallantry at Camp Muir, don't think I didn't notice the number of times you or

Mr. Vance had to come to my aid. You are gentlemen of the highest order, and so I shall tell any who ask."

Nathan glanced to where Kincaid was laughing over something Mrs. Winston had said. "Except perhaps Cash Kincaid."

"Ah, best to go carefully there," Winston admitted. "I will rest easier when I know he no longer pursues Coraline."

Nathan frowned. "Your wife's ultimatum was satisfied once Cora reached the summit. She can't force Cora to marry him."

Winston stroked his mustache with one finger. "True, but she won't give up without a fight. And I begin to fear what that may mean for Coraline. Kincaid's aim from the beginning has been to possess her, through marriage, if he must."

The icy wind at the summit was nothing to the cold that pushed through him now. "Can't you protect her?"

"With all my being," Winston vowed. "But that may not be enough. You see how her mother has fixated on him. He's taken her measure and Coraline's. He knows that if Mrs. Winston pressures her sufficiently, she may give in."

She might at that. It was her only weakness, that Nathan could see. Her devotion to her mother led her to say and do things she might not have otherwise.

The banker took a step closer. "My advice may not be enough to turn the tide. Which is why I must ask: Have you ever considered taking up your place in society again?"

Nathan stared at him. "No. I haven't missed it."

Winston peered at him. "Truly? How extraordinary. You must know you'd be welcomed back."

Eugene had said the same. "That I doubt. And it wouldn't

matter. I'm a better man out here. I wouldn't trade that for anything."

Winston cocked his head. "Even for the opportunity to marry Coraline?"

Why did his heart reach for those words like a drowning man a rope? Nathan took a step back. "You can't mean that. Even if Cora were willing, her mother would never allow it."

Winston straightened. "She might. My wife loves Coraline and wants the best for her."

"That I believe, but I won't believe she'll ever see me as the best."

Winston put a hand on his arm. "But I begin to believe, my boy. These are challenging times. Coraline will weather them because she is who she is, but I prefer that she have someone at her side she can trust, who has her best interests at heart. You have more than proven yourself that person. And I can see you care for her. If I'm not mistaken, she cares about you too."

He could not know what he offered, or the price he asked. "And so I must rejoin society, take a chance that it will not corrupt me, for her sake."

Winston's eyes were bright in the sunlight. "I can offer you a job at the bank. Associate director. The title alone will give you entrée into the finest circles. The salary wouldn't be as much as I'd like until we come out of these turbulent times, but you and Coraline could live with us until then."

Nathan tried not to shudder at the idea of living with Cora's mother. "I know nothing about banking."

"But you know people, my boy, and that's half the battle. Coraline mentioned the incident with the men outside the church. Together, you and I might be able to find a way to help those who are struggling, perhaps connect them with the right position. We'll know who is planning to invest in new lines of business, after all." He patted Nathan's arm. "Think on it. We have all the journey to Tacoma for you to give me your answer."

22

Cora had been sad to say goodbye to Longmire's Springs. Oh, to live so close to the mountain with family surrounding her. Now, that would be paradise indeed.

"You're welcome back any time," Susan had told her while they were searching for her alpenstock. "You never explored the ice caves on the Nisqually Glacier or hiked to the other waterfalls. And there are still a few smaller mountains that could use naming for their climbers. Coraline Peak sounds pretty."

"I'll keep that in mind," Cora had said with a smile.

The ride along the river had been uneventful, even if she had had to listen to Kincaid continue to drown her mother in butter sauce. Really, couldn't she see it was all an act? Apparently not, for she glanced back at Cora every time he said something particularly flowery, as if to point out how well-spoken he was.

At least Nathan understood. He'd shake his head at every platitude, and when Kincaid called her mother the wisest woman he'd ever met, Nathan had snorted. That had earned him a look from her mother. He didn't seem to care.

She wasn't sure what had changed after they'd stopped to rest the horses. He said nothing as they continued through the forest, and he didn't respond to any of the silly things being said ahead of them. Indeed, his face wore a frown, and his gaze seemed to be off in the middle distance.

"Penny for your thoughts?" she asked.

He started, then cast her a brief smile. "Sorry. Just thinking about the future."

"Oh?" she encouraged.

"Nothing worth elaborating on," he told her. "At least, not yet."

That would have been a perfectly maddening statement, if she hadn't become aware of the roar ahead. Her muscles tightened. They were approaching Kautz Creek.

"Rein in," Nathan called well shy of the bank. Kincaid obeyed along with the others. Nathan dismounted and strode to the bank. Offering her reins to Winston, Cora slid down and went to join him. Then she swallowed at the sight that met her eyes.

The same rain that had weakened the rockslide had swelled the waters and pushed mud and debris before it until the river roiled down the channel like a hydra intent on prey. How high was it? Up to her horse's belly? Up to hers?

Nathan eyed the churning flow as if making the same calculation. Then he turned to Cora. "Are you willing to cross that?"

What choice did she have? She could run back to Longmire's Springs—oh, such a tempting thought—but the sooner she reached Tacoma, the sooner Mimi could capitalize on Cora's efforts.

She'd climbed a mountain. Surely she could manage this. "You lead," she said. "I'll follow."

He took her hand, held it a moment as if in promise, then nodded.

"Bring up the rear, Kincaid," Nathan told him as he and Cora moved back to the others. "Watch for any trouble."

"You seem to forget I'm not a member of your party," Kincaid said. "I'll see you on the other side." He urged his horse to the bank and clambered down. A moment more, and Cora could see him splashing into the water.

"I'll go last," Waldo volunteered.

Nathan held up a hand to keep them all back. "Wait until he reaches the other side."

Kincaid pushed his horse, heels digging into the beast's flanks. For a brief moment, they were swimming, the current pushing them downstream. Then they must have found a shallower spot, for the horse regained its footing. He reached the other side safely and climbed the bank to the top.

Nathan went next, easing his horse into the river, then urging her faster. He kept more upstream than Kincaid had. Cora followed suit. Blaze balked but finally consented to enter the river, plunging after Honoré. This time, Cora refused to look left or right, or allow Blaze to step away from Nathan's path. He'd found a more level route, for she never had to make Blaze swim. A few moments later, and they came out on the other side. Blaze shook himself, and Cora drew in a deep breath of the moist air.

"Well done," Nathan said, and she nodded. They waited for the others to reach them.

As soon as her mother had come up to join Kincaid, he continued on his way.

"Funny fellow, that Kincaid," Waldo said as he rode up

onto the bank. "Sometimes I think he favors you, Miss Cora. Other times he acts like you don't exist."

"That's all it is, an act," Cora told him. "Mr. Kincaid cares for no one but himself."

For some reason, that made Nathan go quieter still.

He called another halt when they had navigated the other two crossings. As if Kincaid felt they were wasting his time, he rode ahead. Her mother seemed eager to follow, but she consented to stay with Winston. Waldo handed around cups of water.

Nathan motioned for Cora to join him by the horses. His trousers were caked with mud from the river, and speckles dotted his coat as well. Some had even splashed up onto his cheek and into his hair. She had to grab her skirts to keep from reaching up to wipe it away.

Of course, her riding habit wasn't in much better shape.

"Aren't we a pair?" she said, spreading her stiffening skirts.

"We made it across with no accidents," he said. "That's all that matters."

"Was there a reason you called me over here?" she asked when he fell silent again.

He brushed mud off his horse's side, but he didn't meet her gaze. "I wanted to talk to you about tonight. With your mother and stepfather at Ashford's, you'll want to stay with them."

"I don't *want* to," she clarified. "But I'll have to, for propriety's sake."

He nodded. "Understood. I'll see you there and stay until I know they have room for you all. Then I'll return in the morning and escort you to Eatonville."

"And spend the night at Henry's," Cora remembered. "When you see Sally, please tell her where I left her comb."

His smile lifted. "I'll do that."

Cora glanced to where Waldo was chatting with her mother and Winston. "I wish I could do it myself. I don't like these arrangements. I don't trust Kincaid. He's up to something. I'm sure of it."

"He wouldn't be Cash Kincaid if he wasn't up to something," he acknowledged. "Just stay close to your stepfather or the Ashfords, and you should be safe."

Safe? Cora frowned as she glanced back at him. "Do you know something about Mr. Kincaid's intentions that I don't?"

His gaze went down the trail as if he could see the businessman ahead of them. "I've met enough men like him to be wary. Watch out for yourself, Cora."

"I will," she promised.

He hesitated, then shifted so that he blocked her view of the others and them of her. His gaze brushed hers at last, softly. His voice was as soft. "Your stepfather offered me a job, at the bank."

Her heart leaped, like a deer bounding over a log, but she made her voice come out level. "Is that what you want?"

He blew out a breath. "I never thought so. But it might have certain . . . benefits."

"Like what?"

"Like the chance to court you properly."

She forced herself not to react. "And you want to court me?"

He nodded slowly. "I believe I do."

All at once, she was on the summit again, the world at her feet and glory in sight.

"I might not mind," she said.

His grin pulled her closer. "You're right. We are a pair."

The look faded. "I don't suppose you could see yourself living out here."

Her doubts rushed her, like storm clouds surrounding the mountain. "I don't know, Nathan. I worked hard to graduate college and begin work as an accountant. There's not much call for those skills in Longmire's Springs."

"If not the Longmires, then a sawmill or a mining camp might need one," he insisted.

And how likely would they be to hire her? The Longmires, maybe, but it was doubtful they'd need an accountant often enough to pay a salary. The others would likely find an excuse not to hire a woman.

"I don't know," she repeated. "But I promise you, I'll think on the matter."

She did little else as they rode down into the Succotash Valley. Nathan as a banker? Hard to imagine. Oh, he'd certainly have the proper skepticism to review a person's portfolio before extending credit or granting a loan. Winston too easily believed the stories brought to him. She had to be constantly on her guard.

But Nathan would dominate everyone else at the bank, from sheer size if nothing else. And she could not make herself believe he would be happy in so narrow an existence. How could an office at a bank satisfy when he'd been to Paradise? That he would even consider such a change, just to be near her, said he had strong feelings.

And that thought set her heart to soaring once more.

They passed the fork to Nathan's cabin, then he veered sharper right, closer to the hills. The short path led through firs and cedars, and white and yellow wildflowers raised heads in the cleared spots as if yearning for more of the sun.

"The Ashfords have room for twenty guests," he explained to Cora, who was riding beside him at the head of the column now, her mother and Winston right behind. "But it's a popular place to stay, so I'm glad your mother thought to secure rooms ahead of time."

"I still don't understand why you didn't take us here on the way in," her mother complained. "A hotel is always preferable to rougher accommodations."

"It's not really a hotel," he said. "This is the Ashfords' property. The house has a few rooms, but many folks bed down in the barn, just like we did at Henry's. I thought you'd rather have a bed at my cabin, and free."

"I'm certain Mrs. Ashford will insist on a bed for us," her mother said.

"Though I appreciate you thinking of my wallet, my boy," Winston put in. "Still, we must consider our ladies' comfort. A hotel is always a wiser choice."

It wasn't for Cora. Already she missed a cabin by a shining lake, where fish jumped and sunrise came softly to shine on a man determined to pray. A man willing to give all that up, for her.

———— H H ————

Walter Ashford and his wife were as welcoming as always. Nathan wasn't surprised. The planed wood house with its cedar shake roof had made room for many a visitor since the family had arrived in the area five years ago, and now made room for Kincaid, who had arrived before them. Mrs. Ashford assured Mrs. Winston of a bed, with clean sheets and a thick down-filled comforter, though she seemed mystified as to why Cora's mother would want to retire to it immediately.

"Some ladies have a refinement of spirit we can only envy," Kincaid explained as Winston followed his wife and their hostess.

"I'll take care of the horses," Cora said without looking at him. "We'll see you in the morning, Nathan."

She'd used his first name on purpose. He was sure of it, just as sure as the scowl on Kincaid's face said he didn't like it.

It wasn't easy riding away. Something kept urging him back, warning him not to leave Cora's side. Why? It was only one night. Winston understood the danger Kincaid posed. And Mrs. Ashford wasn't one to countenance nonsense. Cora would be safe.

Would he?

Every time he thought about leaving the cabin, taking the job Winston had offered, his heart shriveled a little. It didn't matter that he had been born to that life. He'd thrived inside it for years. He might still be part of it if not for his father's death.

Yet now he saw it for what it was—shallow, hollow, and meaningless. Oh, some men worked hard and took pride in what they accomplished. Look at Eugene and Winston. Some made fortunes and supported others in doing the same. Bankers were uniquely poised to give people a leg up. They kept businesses afloat, encouraged growth and prosperity. Nothing wrong with that. It just wasn't any dream he'd had.

Then again, it had been a long time since he'd let himself dream of anything.

And what great deeds had he done here? He and Waldo took care of themselves and had a little left to help others. He'd been content with that. Happy.

Now happiness had another name. Cora.

"You're going to have to fight for her," Waldo said as they rode into the yard.

Nathan cast him a glance but decided not to take the bait. He dismounted to open the gate into the field, where the mules were grazing.

"You can't deny it," Waldo insisted as he rode past him. "A lady like that—smart, pretty, educated, rich—every man in Tacoma will be looking to stake his claim."

Nathan grabbed the reins as Honoré trotted into the grass, then set about removing the tack. "Cora Baxter isn't a mineral claim, Waldo. She has a future and plans of her own."

"And that's good," Waldo said, dismounting as well. "She'll encourage you to have plans too, push you forward, so you can become the man you were meant to be."

That's what he feared. The man his father and mother had meant him to be was not the man he wanted to become. He pulled off the saddle, and Honoré headed deeper into the field, chestnut sides gleaming as she whickered a greeting to Sparky and Quack.

Waldo followed him to the barn with his own saddle. "I saw the two of you, heads together. Did you propose marriage? What did she say? Does she like the idea?"

Nathan paused as he remembered that soft look in her eyes. "She said she wouldn't mind a courtship."

"Woo-wee!" Waldo threw his saddle over the sidewall so hard the wood shook. "I knew it! I knew she favored you."

"She has some feelings," Nathan acknowledged, still marveling at the very idea. "But that doesn't mean a marriage is the right choice for us." He heaved his saddle up on the side-wall and turned to face his friend. "Look at me, Waldo. What do I have to offer a woman like Coraline Baxter?"

Waldo snatched up a handful of straw and threw it at him. Nathan waved to keep it from hitting his cheek.

"If you don't know the answer to that question," Waldo declared, pointing a finger at him, "then you don't deserve her."

Frustration bit. "I know my worth. I have a claim along the mountain road. We make enough to get by."

"And then some," Waldo put in.

"And then some. But everything we own combined wouldn't fill the first floor of her stepfather's house. I can't give her silk dresses, carriages, tickets to the theatre."

"Who says?" Waldo argued. "You found a way to get us to the theatre to hear that fancy fiddle player. And who says she wants any of that? Besides, you missed quite a few credits in your favor."

Nathan eyed him. "Like what?"

Waldo held up a finger. "You have respect, for one—from the boys at the mill, the fellows up at the mining camp, Ashford and Longmire and Henry and any gentleman or government agent you led safely through the area. There's none who would disagree."

"Kincaid?" Nathan suggested. "My mother. Her mother."

Waldo spit. "None of them count to our Cora. You're honest. You're clean. You don't smoke or drink."

"Oh, I'm such a paragon," Nathan drawled.

"You are," Waldo said. "The only person who can't see it is you. There are things far more important than the amount of money you have in the bank or the acres of land you hold. Maybe if your father had realized that, he wouldn't have left you."

Every muscle tightened. Even in his face, it seemed, for Waldo dropped his finger and took a step toward him, eyes widening.

"I'm sorry, Nathan. That wasn't fair. But it wasn't a lie either. You left Tacoma because you thought you'd lost everything that mattered. Now you think you have nothing to offer Cora. You're wrong. You found what matters, what really matters. That's something to offer anyone—friend, sweetheart, wife, or children. I just hope you realize it before it's too late for you, for her, and for the grandchildren I can't wait to spoil."

"You're incorrigible, you know that," Nathan said with a shake of his head.

"Not sure what that means and don't care," Waldo retorted. "Deep down, you know I'm right." He grabbed the brush and comb and stalked from the barn.

"You're the one who's wrong, old man," Nathan shot after him. Deep down, he doubted.

But there was One he never doubted. He waited only until the horses were brushed, fed, and watered before going for his violin.

Waldo must have been worried about him still, for he brought one of the cane-bottomed chairs out behind the cabin as if to keep an eye on him. Nathan turned his back on his partner. The smooth wood of the violin warmed in his hand as he tucked it under his chin. He'd left his original instrument in Tacoma and purchased this later secondhand. That didn't make it any less precious to him. The bow conformed to his fingers and slid softly along the strings.

Music flowed, across the grass, across the lake. It filled the clearing. It filled Nathan too. Incense rising. A pleasant sound for the King's ears.

Here is where you made me whole, Father. Here I can feel you, praise you. Why am I tempted to leave?

As if on its own, the bow moved faster, furiously. Music danced, raced, roared in his blood.

Do I need a temple, a cathedral? Can you not praise me anywhere?

"Yes, Lord, I can. Thy will be done."

The music slowed, like a quiet stream, and peace flowed through him.

He knew what he must do.

And Waldo wasn't going to like it.

23

Cora wanted to dislike Mrs. Ashford simply because her mother approved of her. But she couldn't. The piled-up brown hair, the wide brown eyes, and the neat printed cotton shirtwaist and dark wool skirt were only part of the picture. It soon became apparent Mrs. Ashford had opinions of her own and wasn't opposed to sharing them.

"We may be small now," her husband said in his polished British accent over a dinner of venison steaks and mashed potatoes as they all sat at the large table in the family's dining room, "but better days lie ahead."

His estate seemed to prove as much. The Ashfords might live in the wilderness, but their home didn't look all that much different from her mother's. The parlor had comfortable horsehair furnishings, and the dining room boasted a maple sideboard filled with fine china. The bedroom where Cora would be sleeping had a four-poster bed with carved posts and landscape paintings on the walls.

"What do you expect, sir?" Winston asked, digging into the fluffy potatoes. "Lumber? Farming?"

"Indeed, I'd love to know how you plan to invest," Kincaid put in from his place at her mother's elbow.

Ashford shook his blond head, thick mustache curling up with his smile. "There are many industries to consider. We have coal deposits to the north, timber on the hillsides, visitors flocking in to see the mountain. There are plans to make Mount Tacoma into a national park."

"There is a certain grandeur to the place," her mother allowed.

"So, you use Tacoma over Rainier for the name of the mountain," Cora ventured. "May I ask why?"

"Really, Coraline." Her mother turned to Mr. Ashford. "You must excuse her, sir, for bringing up such a difficult subject."

"The name is hotly contested in the city," Kincaid added, as if Cora had been somehow ignorant of the fact.

She kept her smile in place and waited for her host's answer.

"In this house as well," Mr. Ashford said with a smile to his wife at the other end of the table.

She tossed her dark head. "I prefer Rainier. Mr. Ashford favors Tacoma."

"Easier to attract tourists," he admitted to Cora. "They already know they're taking the Northern Pacific to Tacoma. Why confuse them with another name?"

"Because that is the name the Board of Geographic Names approved," his wife said, frowning at her oldest daughter, who had been reaching for the serving spoon for the potatoes.

"For now," her husband agreed. "In the meantime, we've platted the town of Ashford and applied for a post office."

He grabbed the spoon and served both his daughter and his son a hefty dollop. "When the application is granted, Mrs. Ashford will be the first postmistress."

Her mother's brows rose just the slightest, but Cora turned to the lady. "So, you will be serving the community, Mrs. Ashford, as well as managing this establishment. I find that admirable."

Her hostess returned her smile. "If you want something done, do it yourself. That's what I always say. Now, if we could just convince these gentlemen to do the right thing and give us the vote."

Her husband leveled the spoon at her. "On that we agree."

Cora grinned at them both.

"Your china pattern is lovely, Mrs. Ashford," Cora's mother said. "Is it English?"

Mrs. Ashford was gracious enough to allow the change of subject. She did not, however, show any sign of leaving the men to their discussions as the meal ended. Cora's mother finally rose with a pointed look to Cora.

She stood as well, and Winston, Kincaid, and Mr. Ashford popped to their feet. But she couldn't make herself follow her mother from the room. The convention seemed so stilted and confining. She wanted to breathe again.

"Thank you for a lovely dinner and even lovelier conversation," Cora said. "I'd just like to see if the moon's risen before retiring." She swept past her mother and headed for the front door.

Once outside, she drew in a breath of the cool air. Trees clustered close enough to the house that she couldn't see much of the sky. Somewhere nearby, a creek chuckled. And in the distance—was that the sound of a violin?

She strained to catch the song, but the melody eluded her. Waldo had said Nathan played. Was that him? The notes were slow and humble. She wanted to pluck them from the air, hold them close. Her cheeks felt cold, and it was a moment before she realized she was crying. She wiped away the tears with her hand.

The music grew more determined, slicing through the night, as if he had made some important decision. Then the notes softened, faded. She tried to catch the last of them, but the music was gone.

She stayed out until she had no more excuse, then returned to the house, thinking.

She should have slept well, as tired as she was. It was the first bed she'd seen in days. But the sheets masked a firm slab of a mattress that didn't seem all that much softer than the pumice sand at Camp Muir, and she fell asleep thinking about the view from the summit, with Nathan at her side.

———— ⊬ ⊬ ————

She was in the barn, saddling Blaze, as soon as she could after breakfast the next morning. In the yard, mist gathered on the ferns, clung like silver plating to the firs. Each breath felt cool and moist.

"Hyack, now! Sparky! Quack! Keep moving!"

The reins fell from her fingers at Waldo's call, and she snatched them up and led Blaze out of the barn. The old pioneer had the two mules tethered behind him. Quack's piebald ears wiggled as if he were waving to her.

Waldo doffed his cap. "Good morning, Miss Cora."

Disappointment fell colder than the mist. "Isn't Nathan coming with us?"

Waldo cocked a smile. "'Course he is. Couldn't keep him away. He's out yonder, talking to Walter. Sorry we didn't come earlier. Nathan wanted to check on that lumberman with the bum shoulder. Did you have a good night?"

"Good enough," Cora allowed, drawing a breath.

A sound behind her made her turn. Nathan was coming around the house, leading Honoré. The misty air had set his hair to curling. It was all she could do not to run to him.

"Ready to go, I see," he said. "And your mother? Winston?"

He didn't ask after Kincaid. She only wished the fellow was that easy to dismiss.

"I'll fetch them," Waldo said, swinging down. He handed Nathan his reins and stumped for the house.

"More of his matchmaking?" Cora asked.

Nathan watched his friend disappear behind the ivy-shaded door. "Very likely. But I don't mind."

Her pulse kicked up. "Neither do I. I heard violin music last night. Was that you?"

He stilled. "Yes. I didn't realize the sound carried so far."

"It wasn't an imposition," Cora hurried to assure him. "It was beautiful."

He inclined his head. "Thank you. My mother insisted I learn as a boy. She even found a music tutor in Tacoma when we moved here."

"I had a voice master for a while too," Cora admitted. "He was always going on about my vowels and dropping my s's." He frowned, so she clarified, "So you don't end up sounding like a snake."

His brow cleared, and he leaned closer. "You could never sound like a snake."

"Sssso you're cccccertain?" she rasped out with a grin.

He grinned back. "Absolutely certain."

His lips were inches away. Just a little closer . . .

"Thank you, Mrs. Ashford, for your kind hospitality," her mother said as she, Winston, Waldo, and their hostess came out of the house.

Nathan straightened, and Cora tried not to look disappointed.

Mr. Ashford brought the other horses from the barn just as Kincaid exited the house, pulling on his tan leather gloves. His fine clothing looked even more battered than it had yesterday. He turned from the sight of Nathan standing next to Cora and went to assist her mother in mounting. Winston allowed him the honor, but his eyes were narrowed under his derby.

Once more, Nathan put his hands on Cora's waist and lifted her to the sidesaddle. For a moment, he lingered, gazing at her, and the light in his green eyes said anything was possible. Then he released her to go mount his own horse.

Cora gathered her wits and turned to their hostess. "Thank you so much for your hospitality, Mrs. Ashford. I won't forget it."

"You're welcome back any time," she assured her. "We could use a few more ladies willing to speak their minds and dirty their hands to see the job done."

"Shall we, Mr. Hardee?" her mother called, as if Nathan had been the one to delay things. He turned Honoré and led them all from the yard.

Cora had planned to ride beside him on the road to Eatonville, but Cash Kincaid lodged himself next to her the moment they reached the road through the Succotash Valley.

"You seem to enjoy Mrs. Ashford's company, Cora," he noted as they followed the Nisqually toward Elbe, the forested hills clinging to their right.

"She is clearly a woman of vision," Cora said. "I admire that."

"You admire that she wants to give women the vote," he clarified.

She kept her gaze on the dusty track ahead. "Of course. Giving women the vote is an action that stems from respect, Mr. Kincaid, something you seem to find difficult, as you have again used my first name without my permission."

He inclined his head. "My apologies. I thought we were becoming friends."

"No," Cora said. "We are not. I doubt we could be unless you change your stance on suffrage and amend your business practices."

He chuckled. "You may persuade me on suffrage yet. But my business practices? What could possibly offend there?"

"Paying wages lower than others for the same work, cheating your rivals out of business, ruining your opponents," she suggested.

"You've been listening to the representatives of the worker organizations," he said. "They are quick to point out supposed wrongs. But then, the man rich enough to issue salaries is seldom admired by those receiving the salaries."

Not true. Many worker organizations in the city seemed sure that any wealthy owner must be exploiting the laborers, but she knew a number of gentlemen who provided good housing and decent pay for the men in their companies.

"Perhaps you should consider why your workers are particularly unhappy," she said. "Wages? Working conditions?

The opportunity to advance through hard work rather than favoritism? And you could be fairer in your dealings with other businesses too—the ones that sell to you and the ones to whom you sell."

"I'll do that," he promised. "And if I make changes, guided by your example?"

Cora frowned at him. That furrowed brow, those earnest eyes, said he was serious. "I'm not sure I could believe you'd change for me."

He put one hand on his heart. "Then I will have to prove to you I am a true gentleman. Perhaps, once we reach Tacoma, you will be persuaded to change your mind as well."

Cora offered no promises. She made sure to align her horse next to Nathan's after they had stopped to eat and rest at Elbe.

"Is he bothering you?" Nathan asked with a nod to where Kincaid was once more at the front of the column, this time with her mother at his side and Winston right behind. They were deeper in the forest now, following the edge of a hill, with occasional meadows opening up on their right.

"I know how to swat flies," Cora said.

Nathan chuckled, a much warmer sound than Kincaid had made. "And here I thought you had staff to swat flies for you."

Cora tossed her head. "I long ago realized I must rely on my own resources, sir."

"I learned the same lesson," he said. "Keep the good Lord at your side and your head down, and all will come out right in the end."

Cora eyed him. "Your head down, Nathan? Avoiding conflicts?"

He shrugged. "Isn't that what the Bible advises? Turn the other cheek? If they ask for a mile, give them two?"

"Yes," she allowed, "but I also recall the Lord taking a whip to sellers in the temple to right a great injustice. It seems there are times we must act. Women will not be given their due unless we speak up."

He was quiet a moment, gaze on the twisting turns of the road as it ascended ahead. "I gave up on taking action years ago. It was easier, safer, if I put aside dreams. If I didn't allow myself to want anything, I had nothing that could be taken away."

The pain reached for her. She wanted to touch him, to hold him. She couldn't from her sidesaddle.

"That's a narrow way to live," she said. "I don't see how it brings satisfaction."

"I thought it brought peace," he said, shadows from the trees crossing his face. "Now, I wonder. Meeting you, climbing the mountain with you, made me see things differently."

He glanced her way. "You make me want, Cora."

Heat pulsed up her. "What do you want, Nathan?"

"You and me, together. A home. A family."

That yearning in his eyes made her want too.

He glanced around, then pointed to the meadow below the road. The sun had broken through the mist and glowed on wildflowers, sparkled in the stream winding down the center of the grasses.

"Can't you see it? A log cabin big enough for a husband, wife, and children. Waldo playing grandfather. Planted fields to feed the family, the horses. A cow for butter. And visitors. Henry, the Ashfords, the Longmires, they've all opened their homes to travelers, but the demand for services will only increase, particularly once Rainier is named a national park. We could provide a similar service. Guide folks up the mountain, give them room and board while they tour the area, help them see the beauty and appreciate the need to protect it for generations to come."

The vision rose up, strong and pure, until she could have reached out and embraced it. "A grand goal, to be sure."

He returned his gaze to hers as if from a great distance. "One you could share?"

The image popped like a soap bubble in the sun, and all she could see was the rocky road ahead. "Perhaps."

"We both have choices to make, then," he murmured.

They certainly did. And those choices would not be easy, for either of them.

———— ⑂ ⑂ ————

They reached the Pioneer Hotel late in the afternoon. Mrs. Winston didn't look pleased with the two-story clapboard building, but she agreed to stay the night since Kincaid recommended it. Nathan had to ride away and leave Cora behind. Each time it seemed harder.

"What do you think about building cabins around the lake?" Nathan asked Waldo as they turned west for Henry's. "Host visitors like the Longmires do."

"I think we'd have to hire a cook," Waldo mused, giving the mules a tug to keep them from stopping to crop the lush meadow grass. Quack gave a squawk of protest. "Though maybe our Cora would want to learn to cook."

Nathan shifted on the saddle. "She could learn any skill, but I'm not sure she'd want to spend her day cooking and cleaning."

"Maybe one of the Longmire young'uns, then," Waldo suggested. "Or one of Henry's grandchildren."

"Rein in a minute," Nathan said, slowing Honoré.

Waldo stopped Bud and gave the mules their heads. Quack waded happily into the grass.

"What's wrong?" Waldo asked. "Hoof pick up a stone?"

"Nothing like that. We need to talk, and I'd rather do it here than in front of the audience we'll have at Henry's."

Waldo scratched an ear. "You still mad about last night? I stand by what I said. You're a fine fellow when you're not stewing in your own juices."

"Stewing!" Nathan swallowed the rest of the words that threatened to burst out. "I don't stew, Waldo."

"You look to be simmering pretty good right now," his partner pointed out.

Nathan drew in a breath and let it out slowly.

"I need to tell you something," he explained. "Winston offered me a job at his bank. Associate director."

Waldo goggled. Then he shook himself. "You told him no, of course."

Nathan shook his head. "He gave me until Tacoma to think about it."

"But you're not even thinking about it," Waldo insisted. When Nathan said nothing, he peered closer, then reared back. "You are! You said you'd never go back. You washed your hands of the lot of them."

"I did," Nathan agreed. "I thought I'd done the right thing."

Waldo nodded. "And that you did. Who needs all that posturing, the positioning? You're a better man out here—you said so yourself."

Nathan met his gaze straight on. "But I'm not the man I'm meant to be. *You* said *that*. I ran away, Waldo—from the pain, the loss, the disappointment. Maybe, to be the man God wants me to be, I have to go back, face all that and grow beyond it."

"But you'll come home," Waldo persisted, eyes pleading. "You won't let it pull you under again."

"I won't let it pull me under," Nathan agreed. "I have a stronger rope now—God, you. But I don't know where home is at the moment."

Waldo yanked off his hat and smacked it against his thigh. Bud shied, and Quack let out a startled squeak.

"If that don't beat all," Waldo declared once he had his horse under control again and his hat back on his grizzled head. "I encourage you to give me grandchildren, and you take away my partner instead."

"I'm not gone yet," Nathan told him. "And I may never be. But I have to do this, Waldo. I have to know I've made the right choice. For all our sakes."

24

Nathan thought the matter settled, but Waldo wasn't ready to admit defeat. As soon as they reached Henry's and had let the horses and mules out to pasture, his friend tried to enlist their host's support.

"Tell him, Henry," Waldo urged as the three men sat around the fire in the yard before dinner. Henry's sons and grandchildren were at their own homes for the day. "A man can live better out here than cooped up in a city."

With the day fading into twilight, the sky turning purple, and a soft breeze whispering through the firs, it would have been all too easy to agree.

"Some like the city," Henry, ever the diplomat, allowed. "Big houses. Big buildings. Trains and ships that will carry you far. But my heart is here." He smiled as Sally came toward them bearing a cast-iron kettle. Nathan had told her first thing about how Cora had set her comb on the peak, and Sally had grinned with pride.

"I heard you talking," she said now as she nestled the kettle into the coals. "You have it the wrong way. Nathan Hardee honors Miss Baxter by joining with her family. They have only one child in her. Now they will have two. It is a blessing."

Henry nodded as if the matter were settled. "So says my wife."

Waldo humphed.

He tried once more after he and Nathan had climbed to the hayloft later to sleep.

"Nice night tonight," he ventured.

The stars over the valley had been glorious. "Good night to sleep," Nathan agreed.

"I hear smoke from the houses and sawmills in Tacoma can blot out the sky sometimes."

Nathan shook his head as he lay on his bedroll. "Rain clouds and tall trees can do that out here."

"Lots of folks out of work, unhappy," Waldo persisted. "Could lead to mischief."

"Get some sleep, Waldo," Nathan said.

His partner's grumble was louder than the rustle of the hay as he turned away.

Nathan could only marvel at the certainty that flowed through him. He had chosen the right path. Now he had to see it through to the end.

⸻ ‖‒‖ ⸻

Cora was awake before anyone else and waiting outside the hotel when Nathan and Waldo rode up the next morning. A breeze blew tendrils of her hair past her eyes, but they couldn't disguise the smile on Nathan's face.

"Ready?" he asked.

"Always," she answered. "But we'll have to wait for Mother, Winston, and Mr. Kincaid."

He swung down from the saddle. "Maybe we should hurry them along. It's a hard ride from here to Tacoma."

"From here to Lake Park," she reminded him as he looped his horse's reins over the hitching post. "We have to fetch the carriage before we can return home."

Waldo landed on the ground in a puff of dust. "Makes no never mind. It's still a long day. You go hurry them folks along, Nathan. I'll just keep our Miss Cora company."

Their "Miss Cora." She couldn't help her grin as Waldo hitched Bud as well. Sparky waited patiently, and Quack glanced around, ears up with interest.

Nathan narrowed his eyes at his partner a moment, then turned to climb the steps to the boardwalk in front of the hotel. Waldo watched until the door shut behind him before venturing closer to Cora.

"Nathan tells me you two intend to court."

A tingle shot through her. "We've discussed it."

Waldo snorted. "Too much discussion, not enough action, if you ask me."

Cora raised a brow. "I don't recall asking you, sir."

He held up his hands so fast Quack brayed a protest. "Now, don't go getting up on your high horse. I'm on your side. I want to see Nathan settled, with young'uns running around. It's where you'll settle that concerns me. Would you give up all this"—he waved a hand around—"for city life?"

Quack plunked down on his rear as if planning to sit a spell. Across the street, three men staggered out of the saloon. "And stay out!" the proprietor shouted after them.

Cora regarded Waldo.

He dropped his hand. "Well, all right, this right here isn't all that grand at the moment. But it's a fine town, a growing area. You've seen Paradise, Miss Cora. You've been to the summit."

"Which is why I know I can't live there, Waldo," Cora explained. "I worked hard to graduate from college and secure a position. I know what my future holds."

Waldo peered closer, eyes bright. "Do you? And are you sure it's what the good Lord intended?"

"Do not spout that nonsense about women being meant to be only wives and mothers," Cora warned him. "Those are fine callings, noble even. Some of us are called in other ways."

"So long as you know it's a true calling," he insisted, leaning back. "Nathan, he was called to help folks—doctoring, guiding."

"And what were you called to do?" Cora asked, curious.

He puffed out his chest. "I was called to see Nathan happy. You make him happy—happier than I've ever seen him. I just can't believe leaving the mountain will keep him happy."

Her whole body felt tight suddenly. "I suppose we'll both find out shortly."

The door opened, and Winston and Kincaid emerged. Waldo stepped away from her as her mother and Nathan followed. The men went for the horses while Waldo checked Bud and the mules.

"Good morning, Mother," Cora said.

Her mother inclined her head. "Good morning, dear. One more day of this tedium, and then we'll be home."

She waited for the anticipation, the excitement. None came. Very likely, she was merely tired.

But as she and her mother waited for the horses to be brought around, Waldo's words came back to her. Her calling. She hadn't really thought about her work that way. It was an opportunity for independence, to live beholden to no one who might disappoint her or abandon her. She felt called to fight for the vote, but, once won, permanently this time, what then? Was there something greater, something more important, she should be doing with her life?

Her mother was gazing out at the town, nose wrinkled as if she could not like what she saw. Cora closed her eyes.

Dear Lord, is there more you want of me? Will you give me wisdom to know the right choice for my future? Show me the way forward, for I'm not sure I see it correctly.

She didn't know what to expect, but no heavenly voice thundered an answer. Instead, her tensions melted away like puddles in the sun, and, opening her eyes, she smiled at the strength coursing through her. All would be well.

As if her mother noticed the change in her, she frowned at Cora.

Cora couldn't care. There was much to be said for talking with the One who held all the answers.

They made Lake Park by supper. Waldo insisted on stopping to eat, and even Mrs. Winston appeared grateful for the meal. Nathan's partner was planning to stay the night there before moving on to Shem's tomorrow.

Nathan was more concerned about Cora. He had ridden beside her, crowding Kincaid out when necessary, as much of the way as the road allowed. They'd talked of friends, her work at the bank, her efforts to secure the vote, his violin, anything except their future. He wasn't sure whether to be relieved or disappointed when she left Blaze to rest at the Lake Park livery stable and climbed into the carriage with her mother and Winston for the last leg into the city. One of the lads from the stable agreed to drive for them.

"Surely we require no further escort, Mr. Winston," her mother said as the banker handed her into the coach.

Waiting her turn, Cora looked to Nathan.

"I started from your front door," he said. "That's where I finish."

She nodded, smile pleased.

"And I would not abandon you so close to your home, my dear," Kincaid assured her.

Her smile vanished.

He and Kincaid rode ahead of the coach.

"Outriders for the queen," Kincaid mused. "Quite the honor once."

Nathan refused to comment.

Kincaid tsked. "You still blame me for your father's poor choices it seems."

"Not his choices," Nathan said. "Yours. You didn't have to call in the debt when he was already reeling."

"He wasn't the only one in trouble when the Japanese tea fleet went to San Francisco instead of Tacoma. I had deals to bolster too."

Nathan eyed him in the twilight. He sat confidently, reins held lightly, face calm. Could he truly not see the damage he'd done?

"And it never dawned on you to team up, support each other?" he challenged.

"No," Kincaid said. "We often competed for the same work. I only loaned him money when I knew I'd gain the greater profit than pursuing the work myself. Now you and I are apparently competing for the hand of the fair Coraline."

Nathan shook his head. "We're not competing, Kincaid. She'll never have you."

"Perhaps not today," he allowed. "Not flush from her triumph on the mountain. But it's only a matter of time before she realizes she was meant for more than a cabin by the creek."

The urge to tell him about Winston's offer tugged. How satisfying to see that smug smile fade. Few would sneer at Nathan with the title of associate director of the Puget Sound Bank of Commerce after his name and Coraline Baxter on his arm.

The thought knifed his chest, and he caught his breath.

"Might have a stone," he managed, before turning his horse aside and letting Kincaid ride on. He caught a quick glance of Cora's face in the window as the carriage rumbled past as well.

Nathan raked his hand back through his hair. What was he thinking? Not even in the city yet, and he was dreaming of posturing. Strutting about, showing off Cora's admiration of him, was a sure way to lose that admiration. Unlike Kincaid, he wasn't courting her because she was the most sought-after woman in Tacoma.

He was courting her because his life wouldn't be right without her in it.

Might as well admit it. He was falling in love, deeply, finally. And he was willing to pay any price if it meant her happiness. But turning himself into his father, or, worse, Kincaid, was no way to make Cora happy.

Lord, help me be your man. That's the only way to happiness, for me and for Cora.

He drew in a breath and urged Honoré after the coach. He'd promised Cora he would accompany her home, and he would keep that promise.

———— {{ }} ————

It was dark when the coach pulled into the porte cochère. Winston handed Cora and her mother down. The young man from the livery stable was gazing around, eyes wide, as if he'd entered another realm. Darcy must have gone for Charlie, for he came hurrying around the house, and Lily stood in the doorway waiting for them.

"I'll call on you tomorrow, Miss Baxter," Kincaid said from his horse, doffing his hat.

"We look forward to it," her mother said, eyeing Cora as if defying her to disagree.

Winston turned to Nathan instead as Kincaid rode off. "I cannot thank you enough, my boy. You were as good as your word. All the way to the top of Tacoma and back. Who would have thought it possible?"

"Cora," Nathan said. "She knew. It was a pleasure serving you both."

She pulled away from her mother and hurried to his side, reaching out to cling to the worn leather of his stirrup. "But you're staying in town. We'll see you again." She nearly winced. Was that desperation in her voice?

He leaned down to cover her hand with his own, gaze soft.

"Waldo and I will be in town for at least a couple of days to gather supplies," he assured her.

"And to give me an answer to my offer of employment, I hope," Winston suggested.

He released Cora. "That too. I'll call on you both soon."

All she could do was nod as he turned his horse and rode into the night.

Her mother didn't speak until they had entered the house. Lily took Winston's derby.

"Tell Charlie to take good care of the stick on my pack," Cora said to the maid. "And see if someone can send a word to Miss Carruthers tonight to let her know I've returned successful."

Lily nodded.

"It was beyond generous of you to offer Mr. Hardee employment, Mr. Winston," her mother was saying, "and I'm certain he must be grateful, but is it wise to continue an association?"

Cora bristled as Lily hurried off, but Winston patted her mother's shoulder. "He's a fine man, dearest. Whichever path he takes, he will go far."

"Perhaps you're right," her mother said. "Very likely he will refuse you in any event. He seems to enjoy his mountain retreat." She turned to Cora. "Coraline, I know you must be tired, but be sure to bathe and wash your hair before going to bed. I don't want to have to burn the sheets too."

"Yes, Mother," Cora said dutifully. Weariness fell like a rock off Gibraltar. She could almost hear the whistle. She moved to her stepfather's side and pressed a kiss to his cheek. "Thank you, Winston, for everything. I couldn't have done it without you."

His eyes twinkled. "I think we both know that isn't true, but thank you, nonetheless. I couldn't be prouder to call you daughter."

"And I to call you father," Cora assured him.

His cheeks were turning pink as he followed her mother. The stairs felt narrow as Cora climbed behind them, the walls too cluttered with patterns and paintings. Her room seemed overly fussy as well. And it took Lily quite a while to fill the bathing tub. Unlike at Longmire's Springs, which had hot water waiting, their cook had to heat the water on the stove, and Lily had to carry it upstairs for the tub. Her mother and father—yes, she would call him that—would be bathing too. While she waited, Cora sat on the window seat in her dressing gown and gazed out at the moonlight.

She'd never thought the house particularly noisy, but now she was aware of voices down the corridor, the clack of Lily's shoes as she crossed the wood floor. Outside, from near the tideflats, came the horn of a Northern Pacific engine, mournful and long. Carriages trundled by on C Street.

And the smells. Lemon—must be the polish Darcy used on the wood. Lavender—her mother's sachet. Something smokey. Had her mother already burned her clothes?

It was all normal, all commonplace. But it seemed odd, as if she'd suddenly outgrown a favorite gown.

That was it. She was bigger, stronger, than when she'd left. This life no longer fit. In fact, it felt entirely too tight.

Was this why Nathan hesitated to return to society? He'd certainly grown from the young man who had walked away after his father's death. Was he willing to allow himself to be confined once more?

Or had she grown sufficiently to shake off the shackles herself?

———— ⚹ ⚹ ————

Eugene's houseman left Nathan standing on the porch when he knocked that night. He couldn't blame the older fellow. Not only didn't Nathan look like someone with whom Eugene would associate, but he'd arrived after dark and with a favor to beg. Eugene could well order the servant to tell Nathan to return in the morning.

Instead, his friend came to the door, banyan wrapped around his widening frame, and ushered him into the house.

"Nathan! What a pleasant surprise. I didn't expect to see you back in town for some time." His eyes were as wide and penetrating as an owl's. "Did she do it? Did she climb the mountain?"

"She did," Nathan assured him with a smile. "It should be in the papers soon."

Eugene rubbed his hands together. "Well, that calls for a celebration. Come, let me introduce you to my wife."

Nathan glanced down at his clothes. "You sure? I don't look like good company."

"Nonsense." Eugene clapped him on the shoulder, and dust puffed out. "Amelia will be delighted to meet you. This way."

He led Nathan into a parlor. Fine wood furnishings, pretty paintings, a carpet from the Orient, if he didn't miss his guess. Eugene was doing all right for himself. The petite brunette sitting on the sofa by the fire looked up with a pleasant smile, hands pressed into her printed cotton skirts.

Eugene moved up to her and put a hand on her shoulder. "Darling, this is my old friend, Nathan Hardee. He guided Miss Baxter as she climbed Mount Tacoma."

"Mount Rainier," his wife said with a laugh. "That is the one area on which we disagree, Mr. Hardee. Please, sit down. Would you like refreshment?"

"I'm fine, ma'am, but thank you." Nathan glanced around for a safe place to sit that wouldn't risk dirtying the Thackerys' fine furnishings. He settled for pulling a hardback chair closer to the couple on the sofa.

"Nathan tells me she did it," Eugene reported to his wife.

"Oh, wonderful news," she exclaimed. "I knew we were right in asking her to represent the Tacoma Women's Suffrage Association."

"Indeed," Eugene said. "So, tell us why you've come to see us now, Nathan. It wasn't just to bring us the news."

"No," Nathan admitted. "Last time I was in town, you asked me to contact you if I ever needed anything."

She glanced between him and her husband. "Would you like me to leave the room?"

Eugene looked to Nathan, brows up.

Nathan shook his head. "No, ma'am. This affects you as much as your husband, now that I think on it. I've been offered a job at the Puget Sound Bank of Commerce, and I'm debating whether to accept."

"Congratulations," Eugene said, though the words held doubt. "I didn't realize you were considering returning."

"I wasn't," Nathan said. "Until I grew to know Coraline Baxter. That's why I need your help. I'd like advice on how to pass for the sort of gentleman who courts a woman like Cora."

Eugene's eyes widened.

His wife frowned. "But Mr. Hardee, how can you court Miss Baxter? She's going to marry Mr. Kincaid. The announcement was in the paper today."

25

Cora was up and waiting when Lily came in to start the fire the next morning.

"Will you want your blue silk for church today, miss?" the maid asked, moving to the wardrobe.

"I suppose I will," Cora said. "And you'll find Miss Fuller's bloomer suit near the top of my pack. We must make sure it is returned to her safely."

"Yes, miss." She removed the dress from the wardrobe, then hugged it to her chest a moment. "Are you really going to marry Cash Kincaid?"

Cora tossed her head. "Of course not. I don't care what Mother says."

Lily lowered the dress. "It wasn't Mrs. Winston that told me. It was in the paper. Charlie showed us."

Cold, icier than the mountain wind, stabbed her. "Then show me," Cora demanded.

Lily dropped the dress on the bed and ran.

Cora paced her room, cold quickly replaced with the heat of anger. This had to be Kincaid's doing. Did he think she'd capitulate to save herself embarrassment? Even being called a jilt was better than marrying him.

She was still fuming when Lily brought her the paper with trembling fingers. Sure enough, the announcement featured prominently on the society page.

"And he's even set the date for September twentieth and booked the Tacoma Hotel for the reception. The rat!" Cora lowered the paper to look at Lily. "Has my mother seen this?"

"No, miss," Lily said warily, as if she expected Cora to burst into flames any moment. "Darcy was going to set out the paper for Mr. Winston at breakfast this morning, but I took it first. The mistress asked not to be disturbed this morning. Too much traipsing about."

Cora pivoted. "Help me dress. I must speak to my father."

She found him as he was finishing a breakfast of eggs, tea, and toast. Cora dropped the paper beside his plate.

"Good morning, dearest," he said with a welcoming smile that faded as he took in her face. "What's happened?"

"Mr. Kincaid announced our engagement while we were gone," she told him. "He must have sent the information to the paper before he left."

"What's this?" He quickly scanned the page she'd left open, skin turning redder by the moment. "Oh, the affrontery! I have a mind to bring him up on charges."

Cora dropped into the chair next to his. "On what? I doubt a judge would see this as slander. But nothing says I must honor that announcement."

"Of course not," he assured her. "But I will understand if you prefer to stay home from church today."

Cora shook her head. "No. I have much to be thankful

for, and I was looking forward to worshipping. I won't let him push me into a corner."

Unfortunately, Kincaid found a way to do just that.

Winston had gone to check on her mother and Cora was forcing herself to eat some breakfast when Darcy brought word she had visitors.

"Miss Carruthers and a Mr. Fenton from the *Ledger*," their maid confided.

A reporter? Of course—Mimi would want Cora's climb publicized as soon as possible. She must have been persuasive indeed to convince the reporter to call so early on a Sunday morning.

Cora rose. "I'll see them."

Darcy had put Mimi and Mr. Fenton in the formal parlor. The reporter was tall and slender, with a thatch of black hair as disheveled as his plaid coat and trousers. Had Mimi ousted the poor man from bed?

"Darling," her friend heralded, coming forward in a swish of mint-colored taffeta to take Cora's hands. "Congratulations! A veritable triumph. Mr. Fenton would like to hear all about it. I promised him an exclusive, for a few days at least."

Mr. Fenton whipped a small notebook and stub of a pencil from his coat pocket. "Yes, Miss Baxter. I understand you climbed on the mountain."

"I didn't climb *on* the mountain," Cora corrected him. "I reached the summit, where I left mementoes for Mrs. Sally Harris and Miss Susan Longmire. Like me, they are ardent supporters of equal rights for women."

He frowned as he jotted in his notebook. "Equal rights to climb?"

"To climb, to work at a profession, to vote," Cora explained.

"Some men have the misguided notion that women must be protected like children and cannot be expected to take part in civil discourse. I just climbed a mountain. I am proof that those notions are wrong."

"And how does your fiancé, Mr. Kincaid, feel about the matter?" he asked, gaze on his notebook. "I take it he helped you climb?"

"You are mistaken, sir," Cora told him, hanging onto her fraying temper with difficulty. "Mr. Kincaid was not with me, and he is not—"

"Usually late for appointments," Kincaid said from the parlor doorway, an apologetic-looking Darcy at his side. "I didn't realize you intended to start the interview so early, Coraline."

Her mother's porcelain figurines had never been in such jeopardy, for Cora was highly tempted to hurl them at his head.

"Mr. Kincaid," Mimi put in swiftly, "Cora was just telling Mr. Fenton about her success at the summit. I'm sure you're more than happy to wait in the family parlor until we've finished."

He inclined his head. "Of course. I expect the story will tell how my Cora reached the top and struck a blow for women everywhere."

"Then you support women's suffrage?" the reporter asked as Kincaid began to back from the door.

Kincaid met Cora's gaze. "I support my Cora in everything she does."

It was all Cora could do to focus on the reporter and answer the rest of his questions.

"Well done," Mimi said as Mr. Fenton saw himself out.

"Though I must say, I was surprised by your engagement. I thought you loathed the fellow."

"I do," Cora told her. "The announcement surprised me too. Come with me, and let's find out what he's up to."

Mimi's dark brows rose, but she followed Cora from the room. Even the sound of their skirts against the hardwood floor sounded militant. Cora marched into the family parlor, only to draw up short at the sight of two men who rose to their feet at her entrance.

"Sorry, miss," Darcy said, face white and puckered. "I didn't want to interrupt your interview. Mr. Hardee came to call."

---------- ❙❙-❙❙ ----------

Nathan had to stop himself from begging an explanation. His stomach hadn't unknotted since Amelia had told him about the engagement. He'd had to read the announcement twice before it had sunk in.

"No," he'd said, shoving the paper back at a worried-looking Eugene. "Cora didn't agree to this. She wouldn't."

Eugene and Amelia had regarded him sadly.

He'd come this morning to learn the truth, only to find a smug Kincaid ahead of him.

"Come to wish me happy?" the businessman had jibed.

Nathan had plunked himself down on the sofa, travel-dirty trousers and all. "Not until I hear it from Cora."

Now she took another step into the room, her gaze meeting his. "Nathan, you must know I didn't approve of the announcement."

"But you agreed to have it printed," Kincaid said, "for which I will be forever grateful."

She rounded on him. "I did no such thing. I knew nothing about it until I saw it in the paper this morning. How could you be so underhanded?"

Nathan had to stifle a cheer as Kincaid's insufferable smile melted into a frown. "What are you talking about? I never placed that announcement. When my butler showed it to me, I assumed it was your way of telling me you agreed to my suit."

Cora glared at him. "Why should I believe you?"

"Because I have no wish to appear the fool," he said, voice hardening in a way guaranteed to raise Nathan's hackles. "My business associates and my friends will all have read that notice. How will it look if you refuse me now?"

"I don't care," she said, and Nathan wanted to kiss her for it. "I won't marry you."

Kincaid closed the distance between them, and Nathan moved to protect Cora. Kincaid narrowed his eyes at him before turning to her.

"Think, Coraline. You saw how that reporter reacted when he questioned me. My support could help further your cause."

Miss Carruthers, who had been hovering in the doorway, took a step into the room, chin up. "No cause is worth marrying without love."

To Nathan's surprise, Cora bit her lip a moment before responding. "No cause is worth marrying without love," she agreed, "but Mr. Kincaid has a point, Mimi. If I refute the announcement, it's sure to drum up a scandal. I wasn't worried about how it might affect me, but what of you? That could eclipse every bit of publicity about the climb."

Though Nathan knew she was right, he wanted to argue. What, was he about to lose her because of social posturing? His hands fisted at his sides.

Miss Carruthers tossed her head. "I couldn't care less. I will not have you trapped by this lout."

"Perhaps this lout has a solution," Kincaid put in smoothly. "Allow the announcement to stand for a week or two, enough time for your climb to win the acclaim you'd hoped. Who knows? I might be able to convince you to change your mind about marrying me."

"You won't," Cora said, aligning herself closer to Nathan. "I'll give you until Thursday. The story should be printed in the paper by then and sent for distribution on the Eastern circuits. It will be a few days more before a retraction can be printed here. Will that suffice, Mimi?"

"More than generous," her friend said with a dark look to Kincaid. "Now, church services will be starting shortly. I'm sure you wouldn't want to be late, Mr. Kincaid."

"Of course not," he said with a smile that told Nathan he thought he'd won. "I was hoping you would accompany me, Cora."

"That shouldn't be necessary," she said. "We've usually attended different churches. No one should remark on it if we do the same this week."

His face tightened, but he stepped back. "Then I'll call on you soon." He strode from the room as if fearing one of them might argue with him.

Cora put a hand on Nathan's arm, the touch soft. "I'm so sorry you had to see that announcement, Nathan. I'm sure it gave you pause."

His muscles were thawing at last. "Scared me out of three

years of growth, as Waldo would say. But I knew it couldn't be true."

"That sure of me, were you?" she said, mouth hinting of a smile.

"That sure of how you felt about Kincaid. I know you want to publicize this climb, but I don't like that you have to pretend you're engaged to him."

She sighed. "Neither do I."

Mimi glanced between the two of them. "Is there more to this story? I feel as if I've walked into the theatre on the second act."

Cora blushed. "Nathan and I have agreed to a courtship."

Just hearing her say it made him stand taller.

Mimi squealed, then clapped both hands to her mouth and glanced toward the parlor door. "Does your mother know?" she whispered around her fingers.

"Not exactly," Cora admitted. "But Father is aware of the plan. He's offered Nathan a position at the bank."

"Well." Mimi looked him up and down, and Nathan didn't so much as flinch. She grinned. "This is going to be fun."

26

Whispers blew like a driving wind through the church as Cora and her father walked to a pew that morning, and everyone seemed to be staring. Cora didn't know whether it was because they'd heard she'd climbed a mountain or because they thought she was engaged. She was only sorry Nathan wasn't beside her. Mimi had convinced him he shouldn't be seen with Cora so soon after the announcement. He'd agreed, but Cora had seen the frustration simmering in his green eyes. She could only be grateful that, once more, he was putting his own wishes aside for her.

She kept her head high, her eyes forward, throughout the service. How much richer, fuller the hymns seemed now that she knew she could speak to her Creator whenever, wherever she felt led. The songs sprang from her lips as if leaping for joy. Her new fervor must have sounded in her voice, for her father kept glancing at her, wonder on his lined face.

He managed to extract her from the service without having to answer any of the questions she'd feared and return her home, where they found her mother had risen at last. Gowned in silk moire of a delicate shade of blue, she was seated in the formal parlor.

"I'm glad you're feeling better, dearest," Winston said, going to lay a hand on her shoulder. "But are we expecting company?"

She smiled at him. "Certainly, even on a Sunday. Many will want to congratulate Cora on her engagement, however much it surprised everyone."

She must have seen the announcement, after all. "I'm not engaged, Mother," Cora told her. "Mr. Kincaid claims he didn't send that announcement to the paper, but it's clear he's trying to trap me. I've agreed to go along with it until Thursday, so the publicity Mimi planned won't be overshadowed. But I won't be marrying him."

Her mother paled. "Then you'll expose us to scandal."

"For a short time, dearest," Cora's father said, giving his wife's shoulder a pat. "I'm sure we agree that's better than Cora being forced to wed someone she abhors."

Cora was spared her mother's response by a knock at the front door. A gaggle of her mother's friends flew into the parlor, cooing their delight. While her mother sent Darcy for tea and sandwiches, the ladies surrounded Cora and peppered her with questions.

Was she delighted to be marrying Mr. Kincaid?

What was she putting in her trousseau?

Where were they spending their honeymoon?

Had she really reached the summit?

She redirected most questions, but they only seemed to doubt her response on the last point. It didn't matter how many times she assured them she'd climbed to the top. They still regarded her with puzzled frowns and pursed lips. She wished Nathan was there to confirm the fact.

Well, she just wished Nathan was there.

The last group of ladies pressed her mother about upcoming social engagements. Cora's mind wandered with her gaze. Sunlight sparkled through the windowpanes. It was a lovely summer's day. Why was she inside? Would the mountain be out? Or had Rainier veiled herself again now that Cora had left? It was rather gratifying to think the grand lady might miss her.

"Cora?"

She blinked and focused on one of her mother's friends, whose head was cocked as if she waited for an answer to a question Cora hadn't heard.

"I fear Coraline is still fatigued from her exertions," her mother put in smoothly. "Mrs. Reynolds asked what you were going to wear tomorrow night."

Cora glanced between them. "Tomorrow night?"

"To Mrs. Underland's ball," her mother's friend clarified, hands pressed to her pink taffeta skirts.

"Oh, I probably won't attend," Cora said.

Mrs. Reynolds reared back. "What?"

"She simply miscalculated the days," her mother said. "Far too common when traveling, I fear. We will be there, Martha. Mr. Kincaid is accompanying us."

"Oh," Mrs. Reynolds said, regarding Cora with a brow up as if concerned about her health. "How nice. I will see you there, then."

They exchanged a few more pleasantries before her mother's friends took their leave.

"You must attend this ball, Coraline," her mother insisted

as soon as the women had gone. "You agreed when the invitation came weeks ago, before all this nonsense about climbing Rainier. You cannot refuse now. You'll leave Mrs. Underland at odd numbers."

And wouldn't that be a terrible shame. "If I attend, Mother, I'll only have to pretend this engagement is real," Cora pointed out.

"It isn't only about this engagement," her mother said. "You must think of your reputation. Some will notice that you have been gallivanting all over creation, associating with those of low repute."

Cora raised her chin. "Mr. Hardee is highly respected."

"Among those with whom he associates," her mother said grudgingly. "Among those renowned in the city, perhaps not. You do not want a reputation for wildness, Coraline. Every eligible suitor will look elsewhere. And if you insist on working, who would hire you if something should happen to Mr. Winston?"

Only the last gave her pause. Any admiration she might have gained from climbing the mountain could easily turn to ridicule, which would hardly help Mimi and the other suffragettes. Even working for Winston, she needed a solid reputation. Some men were already threatened by her accomplishments. How much more when it became widely known she'd climbed Rainier?

But to hide her light under a bushel? No, that was too much to ask.

"Very well, Mother," she said. "I'll go, if only to hold my head high and show any rumors for lies. But I will not dance attendance on Cash Kincaid."

Her mother sighed. "Must you be so unreasonable?"

"I'm sorry if I offend you," Cora said. "Now, please excuse me. I must see about returning Miss Fuller's things. If Mr. Hardee should call, send word."

Her mother eyed her. Cora tried not to cringe at the look.

"And tell Lily I am no longer home to any other callers," she continued doggedly, "especially my supposed fiancé, Mr. Kincaid."

———— ⊣⊢ ————

Cora did not see Cash Kincaid until the next day, when he came to accompany them to the ball. In the meantime, she had hoped to return to work at the bank, but her mother had insisted that she stay home to manage the callers. They had so many, Cook had exhausted their supply of tea, and Darcy seemed as out of breath as Winston after answering knocks at the door.

Nathan hadn't called. His was the only face she would have been glad to see, besides Mimi's, of course.

Now Cora stood under the porte cochère, her cream-colored skirts belling about her. When she'd chosen the satin with its huge puffed sleeves and fine net collar gathered in a white rose at her bosom, she'd thought it particularly pretty. Applique of the same material in large circles like bubbles speckled the skirt from the hem to the waist, as if she'd risen from a churning sea. Now that she had risen, from a churning river no less, the dress seemed a little overdone.

Cash Kincaid didn't seem to think so.

"You look particularly fine this evening, Cora," he said as he handed her up into the lacquered coach. Mrs. Underland's house was less than a block down C Street, but of course he insisted on taking them in his carriage. "As do you,

Mrs. Winston. Why, you and Coraline might pass for sisters instead of mother and daughter."

"Keep this up, and she'll catch on to you," Cora said as he took the seat beside her.

"What Coraline means is that you mustn't flatter us so, Mr. Kincaid," her mother amended from her seat beside her husband across the carriage. "You'll turn our heads."

"I predict you will both turn heads tonight," he said gallantly.

"Nicely put, sir," Cora's father agreed. "Was any man ever so fortunate in wife and daughter?"

"You are too sweet, Mr. Winston," her mother told him with a smile.

Mimi came to her rescue as soon as Cora, her mother and father, and Kincaid had finished the receiving line and entered the ballroom. Mrs. Underland, the wife of one of the Northern Pacific executives, prided herself on originality. Accordingly, the white walls of the cavernous room had been draped with swags of blue satin, until it appeared they walked through the ocean. Cora's gown was perfectly suited, after all.

So was Mimi's. A sunny-day blue, the dress had shoulders and skirts adorned with clusters of darker blue ribbons holding sprays of lavender.

"Mr. Kincaid," her friend said brightly, offering him her hand. "I'm so glad to locate you."

Kincaid inclined his head over her hand. "Miss Carruthers. Always a pleasure. Did you have a particular need of me?"

Mimi fluttered her sable lashes to effect. "Why yes. A gentleman was looking for you. Something about your largest mill. I believe he's over by the refreshment tables."

Kincaid glanced to where long tables, draped in white, held every manner of delicacy. He must have seen someone he knew but did not particularly like, for he paled. "Excuse me, my dear. I'll return shortly."

As soon as he'd moved away, Cora grabbed Mimi's hand and drew her in the opposite direction, until they were largely hidden by the crowd. "Thank you, but I fear my reprieve won't last long. I've been just this side of rude, and still he hovers."

"Perhaps you're too much of a challenge," Mimi suggested. "Flatter his consequence and look besotted. He might lose interest."

Cora made a face. "Not before I gag. No, I simply must refuse to dance, with him or anyone else."

"A shame your Mr. Hardee could not attend," Mimi said.

Would Nathan feel at ease in such company? Likely he would have to attend these events if he took the job at the bank. "Perhaps I can plead weariness," Cora said.

"Well, you did climb a mountain," Mimi pointed out. "If anyone has an excuse to rest, it's you." She glanced around. "I must determine which man I want to persuade to our side first and put the idea in his mind to ask me to dance. Oh!"

Cora turned to see who her friend had spotted and nearly lost her footing.

Amelia Thackery and her husband, Eugene, had just entered the ballroom, and with them was Nathan. Very likely Cora was the only person besides them who recognized him. Oh, that height could not be disguised, but now those shoulders were encased in a black coat with satin lapels. His black waistcoat sparkled with silver threads, and his dusty pants had been replaced by sleek black trousers. And his hair! It lay neatly against the side of his face, and his beard was gone, leaving paler skin below the tan of his cheeks. She might have decided not to dance, but her stomach seemed to have other ideas, for it set up a polka.

"Who is that?" Mimi hissed. "I must make his acquaintance and convince him to partner me."

"You've already met him, though he certainly doesn't look like what you remember," Cora said. "And I fear you won't get a dance. He'll be far too busy dancing with me."

———— ⊦⊦ ⊦⊦ ————

Nathan shifted from foot to foot, scanning the ballroom. All of Tacoma's finest in one room, silks and satins and fine wool wherever he looked. Jewels glittered in the light from the crystal chandelier. Once he'd thought he fit here. Now, even a haircut and fancy new clothes didn't make him feel welcome.

Amelia had supervised the metamorphosis. Though Nathan had agreed to lay low until Cora had officially called off the engagement, he couldn't help worrying about her. He didn't believe Kincaid's claim to innocence for a moment. If the fellow had placed an announcement in the paper, what else might he do to trap Cora into marriage? There had to be some way to remain close if she needed him.

Amelia had been determined to help. "You must give Mr. Kincaid a run for the money by being seen with her," she insisted when Nathan and Waldo had dined with her and Eugene Sunday evening. "That way, when she refuses him, people will understand she had a better offer."

Nathan snorted. "No one will see me as a better choice than Kincaid."

"You might be surprised," Eugene said as Waldo nodded.

"I took the liberty of asking Mrs. Underland to extend you an invitation to her ball tomorrow night," Amelia said. "Miss Baxter will be attending."

Waldo elbowed him where he sat beside Nathan at the table. "You should go. Our Cora will need you."

They all watched him eagerly.

"I don't look like the sort of fellow who attends balls," Nathan reminded them.

"Leave that to me," Amelia said.

She'd had Nathan at the barber first thing Monday morning, the tailor right after. Only that fellow had lamented the rush.

"No time to sew anything new," he'd said. "And good luck finding ready-made for a fellow his size."

Amelia had sighed as she gave her fringed parasol a twirl. "I am so disappointed, Mr. Brimhall. I have extolled your virtues to all my friends and their husbands, and now I find you cannot rise to the occasion. I suppose I will simply have to take my business elsewhere and encourage them to do the same."

Amelia must have had a great number of friends, for the fellow had found a way to procure a coat, waistcoat, and trousers for Nathan.

"You can borrow one of Eugene's shirts," Amelia had told him as he carried the boxes from the shop. "It will be tucked in, so no one need know it's a little short."

Waldo had whistled when Nathan had rejoined him at Shem's tavern, where they were staying. "Look at you," he said, strolling around him until Nathan felt his cheeks growing warm. "Our Cora will be pleased."

Now he supposed the number of looks being directed his way could be considered gratifying.

"Smile," Amelia encouraged him. "You are enjoying yourself in such distinguished company, are you not?"

Nathan smiled at her. "In your and Eugene's company, certainly. He's a very fortunate fellow."

"And don't think I don't know it," Eugene said with a grin as he threaded his wife's arm through his own.

"Oh, look," she said. "Here comes Miss Baxter."

Nathan's heart slammed into his rib cage, forcing him to stand taller. Cora was bearing down on him, her friend Miss Carruthers at her side. He had only a moment to take in her curves in the creamy satin gown that seemed to be covered with . . . bubbles?

"Mrs. Thackery, Mr. Thackery," she said with a warm smile. "So nice to see you again. I didn't realize you were acquainted with Mr. Hardee."

"Nathan and I knew each other at the university," Eugene explained. "And it's very good to see you and Miss Carruthers again."

"How is your father, Miss Carruthers?" Amelia asked solicitously. "I understand he's been feeling poorly."

As Miss Carruthers moved to speak with her and her husband, Cora closed the distance to Nathan's side. "What are you doing here?"

"I've been asking myself the same question," he answered. "I suppose I'm trying society on for size, seeing how it fits."

"And how does it fit?" she asked.

He shrugged his shoulders and felt the coat protest. "A little tight."

"I know the feeling." Before he could question her, she put

a hand on his arm. "Here comes Kincaid. I have no desire to pretend I enjoy his company. Are you willing to run away with me?"

"Wherever you lead," Nathan vowed.

"Then follow me, and we will find something better to do."

He didn't resist as she tugged him toward a set of double doors at the side of the ballroom.

27

Cora towed Nathan out the doors and onto a flagstone terrace. Even though this was the second home Mrs. Underland had had constructed in the city, she'd had time to grow lawns, shrubs, and trees. Now the moon gilded the lush growth in silver as Cora led Nathan away from the house along paths that wound through the greenery.

The sounds of the ball faded behind her, until all she could hear were the strains of the music. She took a deep breath of the lavender-scented air and felt her shoulders come down. "There. That's better."

"Much," he agreed, strolling beside her. "But won't your admirers miss you?"

"I've had entirely too many admirers the last two days," she assured him. "Everyone came to gawk at the woman who climbed Rainier and agreed to marry Cash Kincaid."

"They'll find other curiosities to amuse them," he predicted as the horn of a railway engine split the night. "I hear a farmer in Puyallup has a two-headed calf."

Cora swatted his arm. "I'm not that much of an oddity, sir."

He glanced her way, eyes shadowed with the night. "But you are. Only a handful of people have reached the summit. That puts you in a rare class."

"And I still thought I could get on with my plans." Cora stopped on the edge of the lawn, moonlight glittering on the waves of Puget Sound below. "How? Now I know there's so much more than this."

"And this does not suffice?" he asked.

Was that hope in his voice? It tugged at her too.

"No," she said. "This seems utterly frivolous."

In the distance, in another life, she heard a waltz starting. Once, she would have had her pick of partners. Now she only wanted to be here, with him.

"You asked me why I came to the ball tonight," Nathan said softly. "I'd be pleased to dance with the loveliest lady in attendance." He bowed. "May I, Miss Baxter?"

Cora smiled. "I'd be delighted, sir." She took his hands and stepped onto the lawn and into his embrace.

He led her through the steps. One, two, three. One, two, three. His arms held her; his gaze flashed green, warm and appreciative. Her skirts swished across the grass, but she was certain she floated on air.

Then he slowed, stopped, and her heart pounded far faster than the movement of the dance had required. Lowering his head, he brushed his lips against hers.

This. This was what she'd missed. As exhilarating as the climb, as amazing as the view. Together, they were magnificent.

He raised his head and looked toward the house. She heard it then too, the crunch of a foot on gravel. Cora tensed, but Mimi appeared around a shrub. Nathan stepped back from

Cora. The cool breeze from the water raised gooseflesh on her bare arms above her gloves.

"It's a lovely night for a stroll," Mimi announced, glancing up at the moon as if she could feel its pull. "If anyone asks, do assure them I have been out in the garden the entire time."

Nathan frowned, but Cora understood. She put a hand on her friend's arm. "Thank you. Is my mother looking for me?"

"Not yet," Mimi said, dropping her gaze to meet Cora's. "But Mr. Kincaid is prowling around as if he means to dismantle the entire house to find you. I did try suggesting that he dance with me instead. He refused with his usual gallantry." She huffed.

Cora glanced to Nathan. "I suppose we should return."

He inclined his head, then offered each of them an arm. "Ladies?"

Mimi latched on right away. "Why, thank you, Mr. Hardee. I understand you are considering moving back into the city. Have you decided on a house yet?"

A house? On his other side, Cora looked up at him in surprise.

His smile remained pleasant as he led them toward the house. "Not yet. I'm still trying to determine my best course."

Mimi glanced around him to Cora. "Well, Cora and I would be glad to have you return to good society. Wouldn't we, Cora?"

Cora made herself smile. "Certainly, sir. If that's what you want."

But was it what she wanted?

Nathan held the door to allow Cora and her friend to enter the ballroom. The glittering chandelier sent rainbows over them as they moved across the parquet floor. After the cool night air, the room felt too warm, and too many scents fought for supremacy—the rose and gardenia of the ladies' perfume, the mint and bay rum of the gentlemen's cologne, the fruity punch and the sugary cakes on the refreshment table. Another time, he would simply have made his regrets and left.

But he knew what he wanted, and remaining in society might be the only way to win Cora, especially if her mother continued to pressure her about Kincaid.

Cora belonged here. Already people were moving closer, ladies to chat, men to implore her to dance. Her mother sailed up, a heavyset fellow with fierce whiskers at her side.

"There you are, Coraline. I vow you are so popular at these events I simply cannot keep track of you." She smiled at the older man. "You must meet Mr. Fischer. He is a staunch supporter of civic causes, and he is considering running for governor."

He beamed at Mrs. Winston before turning his gaze to Cora. "A pleasure, Miss Baxter. Your mother has been telling me all about you. A noted equestrian, I hear."

That was the sum of her mother's boasting, that Cora rode well? What of her graduation from college, her work at the bank, her support of women's suffrage, her climb up the mountain?

Cora inclined her head, pale hair flashing in the light. "I enjoy a good ride as well as the next lady, sir. But a gubernatorial candidate. My friend Miss Carruthers is particularly interested in politics."

Mimi assumed a charming smile as well. "Indeed I am, sir. You must tell me all about your plans. Advances in education? More jobs for our hard workers? Votes for women?"

He laughed, a booming sound that had several glancing their way. "Well, certainly not the last. It has been well proven scientifically that women's brains should not be strained by having to choose a candidate."

Both Cora's and Mimi's smiles froze on their faces.

"I've never heard of such studies," Mimi said. "Why, I can't imagine how I ever chose between the gentlemen asking for a dance. I might have been chatting with a fool and not known it."

"Even now," Cora added.

Her mother's face tightened, but Fischer remained blissfully ignorant. "Now, then, that's what we gentlemen are for, to protect our fine ladies."

"But who will protect the country from you?" Mimi asked sweetly.

"Ah, there's Winston," Cora's mother sang out. "You must meet my husband, Mr. Fischer. He's the director of the Puget Sound Bank of Commerce."

With a polite nod all around, Fischer allowed himself to be led away.

"That's one I won't bother to convince," Mimi muttered, watching them go. "I hope she doesn't see him as a suitor for you after you cry off from Mr. Kincaid."

"She sees advantage only," Cora said with a sigh. "And a daughter married to the governor of Washington State."

Miss Carruthers turned to Nathan. "Do you have any political ambitions, Mr. Hardee?"

"None whatsoever," Nathan promised her.

She waved her hand before her pretty mouth as if overcome by the warmth of the room. "A shame. Apparently, intelligence is quite an asset in that field. You could go far."

Nathan chuckled. "I like you, Miss Carruthers. You can share my campfire any time."

She dropped her hand. "I may take you up on that offer. Now, look sharp. Another villain is about to descend on us."

Kincaid bore down on them. Cora stepped closer to Nathan. He had to fight the urge to put his arm about her. That statement could not be made in public.

Yet.

"Coraline," Kincaid said. "Miss Carruthers. I was hoping for a dance."

"Delighted," Mimi said, stepping forward.

He hesitated a moment, but Cora narrowed her eyes at him, as if daring him to dismiss her friend. With a tight smile, he led Mimi out onto the floor.

"He's allowing himself to be trapped by all this," Nathan said. "He's trying to play by the rules."

"Aren't we all," Cora said. "Perhaps you should ask me to dance again, Mr. Hardee."

"You sure about that?" he asked.

"Why, certainly. A lady dances with whomever requests her hand. I'm sure you just offered."

"You took the words from my mouth." Nathan held out his arm.

It was a polka this time, so he didn't have the opportunity to hold her as closely as if it were a waltz, which was probably good given that everyone thought she was engaged to Kincaid. Still, she moved with an easy grace, spinning through the steps like sunlight rippling on water. As soon as the dance ended, a bevy of belles surrounded her, talking and laughing, and the gentlemen flocked to join them.

Nathan slipped back out of the fray. This was her time. Let her shine.

"Miss Baxter is much sought after," Amelia said when she ventured to his side a short time later as he stood by the back wall. He caught sight of Eugene at the refreshment table.

"With good reason," Nathan answered. He turned to her. "Would you care to dance?"

She fanned her face with one hand. "No, but thank you for asking. Now I may refuse the next gentleman with impunity."

Nathan laughed. "Happy to be your excuse."

Along with a glass of punch for his wife, Eugene brought back several gentlemen he knew from the Union Club. Soon, Nathan was in the middle of discussions of finance, legalities, the price of silver, and the downturn in the economy.

"If you ask me, the more charity we give out, the less these fellows are inclined to work," one of the men complained, gloved hand gripping his cup of ruby-red punch. "Let them go hungry for a time, and they'll be more reasonable."

"Never knew hunger to make a man reasonable," Nathan said.

"Forgive me, gentlemen, but I should get my sweetheart home," Eugene put in quickly. "Nathan, won't you join us?"

Nathan inclined his head, and they moved with Amelia away from the group.

"I wasn't *that* tired," Amelia told her husband.

"Sorry," Eugene said with a commiserating look. "But I thought it best to escape while we could."

"I take it some opinions aren't welcome now," Nathan said.

"Were they ever?" Eugene asked. He shook his head. "Mr.

Fischer may want to be governor, but everything in society is politics of a sort. Best to keep one's head down."

Funny. He'd said the same to Cora. Now the sentiment rang hollow, wrong.

Cowardly.

"You go ahead," Nathan told them. "I'd like to say good night to Miss Baxter and her family. And thank you, for everything."

Amelia gave him an encouraging smile before she and Eugene went to bid their hostess farewell.

Cora met him partway around the room. "This is far more tedious than I remembered. Are you ready to flee?"

"I've been ready for hours," he said. "But you haven't sat out a dance."

"And my feet are letting me know it."

He raised a brow. "You climbed a mountain in shoes that weren't designed for your feet. I won't believe dancing tires you."

"The mountain doesn't tread on your toes," she informed him. "And you haven't. Another dance?"

"Asking for trouble," he told her. "Your mother is headed this way as it is, with Kincaid beside her."

She slumped. "Will it never end?"

"I could probably cause a diversion," Nathan offered. "I could ask your mother to dance."

She shuddered as if imagining it. "No. I know my duty." As he watched, her body straightened, grew more poised. The smile on her face was polite and polished. By the time her mother and Kincaid reached her and Nathan, she was another person entirely.

"Mr. Kincaid feels it is time to leave, Coraline," her mother said. "He has requested that his carriage be brought around. Mr. Hardee."

"Ma'am," Nathan acknowledged with a nod.

Kincaid's look was cool. He knew he had the upper hand.

Cora obviously wasn't ready to concede. "Very well, Mother," she said. "*Nathan*, I do hope you'll call tomorrow."

"I'd be delighted, *Cora*," he said, trying not to spoil her performance with a grin.

He had seen planed cedar less stiff than Mrs. Winston, basalt softer than the glint in Kincaid's eyes. Cora's mother didn't so much as glance his way as she turned and allowed Kincaid to walk her and Cora to bid their hostess good night.

------------ {{ }} ------------

Shem's Dockside Saloon was more crowded than Nathan had expected when he returned from the ball. Laughter echoed out onto the wharves. Smoke clogged the air, looking like a fog had descended from the mountain. By the time he crossed the room to Waldo's side, he became aware of something heavier.

The looks stabbing in his direction.

"Did she like it?" Waldo demanded as he sat at the table across from his partner. "The hair, the fancy coat?"

The kiss?

Nathan leaned back in the chair. "She was willing to associate with me."

"And dance? Oh, I bet she makes a fine partner."

"She was as light as the first snowflake," Nathan assured him. The memory of her in his arms made anything less than a smile impossible.

Waldo slapped the table and set the tin cup there to rattling against the wood. "You see! You don't have to take that job at the bank. She likes you."

"A bank, is it now?" Another man brushed up to their table, two more at his back. His red hair was a flame in the smoky saloon. "And why would a fine banker need to come drink with the likes of us?"

"Banker!" Waldo sputtered. "Don't you know who this is?"

Nathan held up a hand. "It's all right, Waldo. Plenty of reasons not to trust banks and bankers these days. Why don't you gentlemen go back to your table?"

"Why don't you take your fancy clothes right out the door?" the ringleader demanded. "You have some gall coming here, flaunting your money, when my daughters are going without dinner."

Nathan pushed back the chair and stood. Waldo's face lit with glee, but the redhead in front of him looked up into his eyes and narrowed his own.

"If your daughters are hungry," Nathan said, "why are you here drinking?"

The man took a step back and raised both fists. His friends gave him room, but one was rolling up his sleeves, and the other peeled off his coat. Waldo rose as well. A dozen more climbed to their feet. Chairs fell with a crash that echoed in the sudden silence.

The leader spit on the floor in front of Nathan's feet. "You're no better than any of them in their fancy houses along the cliff. The railroad, Kincaid Industries—none of you knows how to pay a man what he's worth."

Yells of agreement erupted like gunshots around them.

"If you have a grievance with your employer," Nathan said, "take it to the law."

"The law won't listen to the likes of us," someone complained.

"Men like that, they make the law," another put in.

Agreement rumbled through the building. Shem dove behind his bar, likely going for the shotgun he kept for times like this. Best to stop things now, before someone got hurt.

Nathan glanced around at the reddened faces, the clenched fists. Were these the sort of men Cora's stepfather had hoped to help? It sounded as if they needed jobs.

"You want fair pay for fair work?" Nathan asked. "Come to the Puget Sound Bank of Commerce tomorrow afternoon, and we will help you find a position."

Arms fell, mouths gaped. Waldo grinned.

"Who are you, then?" Redhead demanded.

"This here is Nathan Hardee," Waldo declared, pushing in front of him. "He knows Mr. Winston, the bank director. We all just climbed Rainier together."

The ringleader squinted up at Nathan. "That so?"

"It is," Nathan said. "Stephen Winston is a good man. We'll do all we can to help you."

With grumbles, they began to shuffle back to their seats. Redhead went last, with one more defiant look to Nathan. Shem poked his head over the scarred wood of the bar and gave Nathan a thumbs-up as he laid the shotgun aside.

"You really think Winston can help them?" Waldo asked, watching them.

"He told me he wanted to," Nathan said. "I guess it's time to find out whether he meant it."

28

Kincaid escorted Cora and her family to the door.

"I wonder," he said to her mother. "I know the hour is late, but might I have a word with your lovely daughter?"

What now? Cora searched his face but saw nothing to indicate his purpose.

Her mother must have thought she knew, for she smiled. "Of course, Mr. Kincaid. Mr. Winston and I will wait in the family parlor for the good news."

Her father's brow puckered, but he nodded permission as well.

Cora followed Kincaid to the formal parlor instead, turning on the lamp as she did so.

"You needn't waste your time," she told him. "I won't change my mind about crying off."

He shook his head as he sat on the sofa. "Coraline, how did we end up at such cross purposes? You admired me once."

"That was before I knew you well," Cora replied.

"But I fear you don't know me at all." He sighed. "Please, sit down. I'll only take a few minutes. I promise."

She was tempted to refuse and make for her room, but her mother would never let her hear the end of it. She went to sit as far away from him as the room would allow.

"Thank you," he said. "It has become clear to me that you hold Nathan Hardee in the highest esteem. Perfectly natural, given that he led you up the mountain. And then there is his rise out of adversity. I wanted you to know he isn't the only man to conquer an unpleasant past."

Cora frowned. "So, you have forsaken society to make your own way?"

"No. I learned to master it." He braced his elbows on his knees and leaned forward. "Some here look down on me for my humble beginnings—the middle son in a large Irish family. Make no mistake—I have worked for every penny I now possess. I believe you value hard work."

Cora nodded. "I do. But it is one thing to better yourself, and another to better yourself by destroying others. The first is commendable. The last is despicable."

"I will admit I have not always considered the consequences to others in my business decisions. I can do better. Just as you needed Hardee's help to climb the mountain, so I need a guide to reach my business goals."

Cora cocked her head. "Are you offering me a position, Mr. Kincaid?"

He straightened. "More. I want you at my side, Coraline. With you as my wife, no door would be closed to us. We could attract additional capital, use it to improve working conditions, expand operations, and hire men who so desperately need work. With my money and influence in the business community, think how we could advocate for suffrage."

She felt not the least temptation. "You put a great deal of faith in my association."

"And you put too little. I see the respect to which you are held, to which your entire family is held. I want that for me and the family I intend to build."

"If it is respect you crave," Cora said, "then appoint a board of directors, men and women admired in the area. Surely that would be just as effective as marrying me."

His eyes glittered in the lamplight. "Ah, but I want to marry you. When I struck out on my own, I promised myself I would never settle for second best again. You, Coraline, are the best."

She tired of the game. She rose, and he stood.

"Thank you for the informative discussion, Mr. Kincaid. I'll be sure to let you know when I've sent the retraction to the paper."

He inclined his head. "Until then, I hope you'll consider my proposal. I'll bid your mother and Winston good night."

Cora watched him out the door, then hurried to her room before her mother could take her to task.

That didn't stop her mother from following.

"I understand you and Mr. Kincaid have yet to settle your differences," she said when she cornered Cora while Lily was assisting her in undressing for bed. "I will allow there must be a certain amount of reticence on the lady's part. We cannot let them think we are easily won."

"I'm not posturing, Mother," Cora said as she tugged down on the soft folds of the nightgown Lily had draped about her. "I don't want to marry Mr. Kincaid."

"Lily," her mother said, "I'll finish here. Go see to my night things."

Very likely Lily had set them out hours ago, but the maid bobbed a curtsy, threw Cora a pitying look, and scampered from the room.

Her mother went to sit on the turned-back covers on the bed and patted the space beside her. Cora joined her. The bed was high enough her bare feet swung off the floor. That only made her feel more like a child.

"You do not want to marry Mr. Kincaid," her mother repeated. "Or any other gentleman I have brought to your attention. Am I right in supposing you would entertain a proposal from Mr. Hardee?"

Why bother denying what appeared to be obvious even to her mother? "Yes," Cora admitted. "I would."

Her mother's shoulders sagged. "Oh, my dear. That isn't wise."

"Why?" Cora asked. "He's a fine man, Mother. I don't understand why you can't see that."

Her mother's mouth took on that pinched look that usually preceded a scold. "I can see the attraction, Coraline. But I want to know you are somewhere safe, provided for."

Cora waved a hand. "Is anywhere truly safe in this Panic?"

Her mother's look was prim. "Here, we have friends and resources. I saw no banks on the road to the mountain. Here, the marshal will come when called. Can you say the same for Mr. Hardee's cabin? What if the men at that lumber camp revolted? What if there was a forest fire? Who would protect you then?"

"Is it inconceivable that I might protect myself?" Cora challenged. "That Nathan and I might protect each other? That the two of us together might be stronger than we are apart?"

Her mother rose. "If that is the case, you have found something rare indeed. Just be very, very sure before you throw away everything I labored to provide for you."

———————— {{ }} ————————

Nathan called at the Winston house the next morning at an hour Mrs. Winston would likely find improper. He was just glad she wasn't up yet when the maid led him to the breakfast room at the back of the house. It was possible he might have passed muster in the other coat the tailor had found for him and tan trousers. He wasn't sure about the derby, which sat oddly on his newly cut hair, but he had to remove it inside anyway.

"Good morning, Nathan," Winston greeted him, plaid coat dapper. "I see even in town you're an early riser. Our Coraline rises with the sun these days too." He aimed a fond smile at her.

Cora lifted her teacup in salute, green taffeta sleeve rustling. "And finds remarkably little to do." She turned to Nathan. "Good morning. What are your plans for the day?"

"I thought I'd see how a bank is run," Nathan said, taking the chair beside her.

"Excellent," she said, eyes sparkling. "I'd be happy to show you around."

"And I need to confirm that I can honor a promise I made last night." He went on to explain the confrontation in the tavern. Cora's frown grew, until he told them about his offer to the men.

"There must be some way we can help," she said. "What do you suggest, Father?"

The banker beamed at her, and Nathan realized it was the

first time he'd heard her call him by that title. Then Winston gave his white mustache a tug. "Many of my depositors and those to whom we have extended loans need a worker here or there, even in these difficult times. I'm sure introductions can be made. The gentlemen will still need to prove their merit, but those with good character should go far."

Nathan's shoulders relaxed for the first time since he'd made the promise. "Good. Just tell me how I can assist."

"I will, my boy." Winston rubbed his hands together. "This will be a fine day. I'm certain of it."

And it was. Nathan wasn't sure why that surprised him so much. He'd visited banks before with his father, though the Puget Sound Bank of Commerce seemed brighter than he remembered. Perhaps it was the brass decorating so many surfaces, from the front door to the gilding on the cashier's cages. But he thought it had more to do with Cora's presence.

"We have the usual stands for making deposits and withdrawals," she explained as she led him about the carpeted space. "The doors there on the right accommodate offices for the directors and accountants. And, of course, we have a vault in the back to store the deposits. It is the finest German steel, and only Winston and the associate directors have the combination."

So, he'd have the combination to the vault if he accepted the offer of employment. Winston was offering trust indeed.

"How many associate directors are there?" he asked as she led him toward one of the offices.

"We have two at present. If you accept my father's offer, you will be the third." She cast him a quick glance before focusing on opening the door.

Inside was a neat, wood-paneled office with desk, filing

cabinet, chair, and green-shaded lamp. Papers sat in piles, as if awaiting marching orders, and all guarded by an ornate brass clock that ticked off the minutes.

"This is my office," she said, taking a seat behind the desk. She glanced at the papers on the blotter in front of her. "I see a few proposals came in while I was gone. I'll review them, determine the risk to the bank, the potential credit or loss, and the length of time the money would be tied up. Then I'll make a recommendation to Winston and the associate directors as to whether we should accept the proposal as it was written, suggest changes, or refuse."

Nathan sat in the chair across from her. It was a little hard and a little tight, but perhaps that was the intention. Those who came begging would be reminded not to overstay their welcome. "How many do you recommend for funding?"

"It depends. I don't have a quota I must meet. It's all about the risk and the reward."

"So, you'll take a larger risk for the potential of a larger reward," he said.

"Of course. That's how businesses grow."

"Lives too," he said.

Her cheeks pinked. "I suppose that's true." She glanced out the door, and her brows went up. "Are these your gentlemen?"

Nathan turned. A group of men had entered the bank, and he recognized the redheaded leader as well as at least one other from the crowd last night.

"Excuse me," he said, rising. "I'll be back shortly."

Winston had already come out of his office to meet them. "Gentlemen, welcome. I propose we have a discussion, one at a time, and I'll see where you might best be placed. Will that satisfy?"

Redhead pulled up his trousers and nodded to one of the men, a sandy-haired fellow with a crooked nose. "I suppose that's all right. You first, Prentice. You have the most to feed."

The lanky fellow peeled himself away from the group and followed Winston to his office. Nathan stayed in the lobby to keep an eye on the others.

More arrived throughout the afternoon, though fewer than he'd expected. What kept the rest away? Pride? Distrust? Doubt? They had missed an opportunity. Winston met with each that had come, ascertained their skills and interests, then gave them one of his calling cards. Some he directed to another business in town. Others he asked to come back in a week or so to see if additional positions had opened.

"And if you have any difficulty," he told them, "have the business owner call me or drop in. I'll be happy to be of assistance."

"They grow three inches between the time they walk in the door and the time they leave," Nathan marveled to Cora, watching Winston escort the last man to the door.

"That's what hope does," Cora said. "That's really why most of our clients come to the bank. To deposit money for a hopeful future. To borrow money to give themselves and others hope."

"Hope," Nathan echoed, gaze coming back to her. "And what do you hope for, Cora?"

Once more pink rose in her cheeks. "In truth, I'm not sure anymore. I tell myself this is where I belong. This is the goal I set for myself."

"Like climbing the mountain."

She nodded. "And now that I've achieved it, I wonder whether there's more. More to life, more to me."

His mouth felt dry. "I find myself wondering the same things."

She cocked her head. "Then you've decided to stay in town?"

The idea made his skin itch as if he hadn't washed his clothes in too long. What was wrong with him? She was worth any effort.

The glass on the front door flashed as the next patron entered. Cora straightened. Kincaid strolled up to them and tipped his hat to her.

"Come to jilt me before I jilt you?" she asked with a ready smile.

"I would rather humble myself in private," he assured her. "As I did last night."

Trying to sow dissent again. Did he never tire of it?

"Yes, our conversation after the ball was quite interesting," Cora said. "Have you come for suggestions about who to appoint to your board of directors? Nathan may have advice in that area."

Kincaid stared at her. So did Nathan. The businessman recovered first.

"Intriguing idea. Join me for coffee at the Union Club, Hardee, so we can discuss it further. You won't be a member, but my invitation will see you through the door."

He had little interest in spending any more time with Kincaid, much less recommending others to work with him, but perhaps he could encourage the fellow to release Cora from this engagement with the least amount of fuss.

"Very well," he said. "If you'll excuse us, Cora."

She nodded, but he felt her gaze on him all the way out of the bank.

"Despite having no chance, you continue to pursue Coraline, I see," Kincaid ventured as they started up the hill to C Street. A breeze blew in from the Sound, bringing with it a touch of brine. "Given that you acted as her guide up the mountain, I assume she sees you as a brother."

"You assume nothing of the kind," Nathan said, "or we wouldn't be having this conversation."

Kincaid sighed. "You've allowed your time in the wilderness to roughen you, Hardee. Society is about subtleties, sophistication."

"Give me honesty and plain speaking any day," Nathan countered as they reached the club.

Kincaid didn't speak to him directly again until they had been seated at a table overlooking Commencement Bay, with black coffee steaming in fine china before them and cream and sugar in silver containers waiting on the white damask tablecloth.

"So, you prefer it plain," he said. "Very well. I have no interest in your opinion on a board of directors. How much money will it take for you to return to your squalor and leave Coraline Baxter alone?"

Nathan shook his head. "There's not enough money in the world."

"Ah." Kincaid made a show of stirring cream into his cup. "I feared as much. She won't have you. She and I are in the middle of a complicated dance, but it's only a matter of time before she follows my lead."

Nathan grinned. "You still don't know her, do you."

Kincaid's face tightened, then he barked a laugh. "Apparently better than you. You cannot accept that Coraline is used to the finer things in life. You can't offer her those things. I can."

The words plunged a knife into his dreams, but he said nothing.

Kincaid toyed with his cup, but his gaze lingered on Nathan's face. "Or is prestige not the issue with you? How sad. You truly think you're pursuing Coraline because you love her." He leaned forward. "If you loved her, you wouldn't think for a moment about subjecting her to the dangers of living in the wild, miles from those who care about her."

Once more the knife struck, this time even more closely. "And you offer her safety?"

Kincaid shrugged. "I offer more than safety. I offer civilization—the theatre, shopping, friends and acquaintances. Surely you see the advantages."

He did, to his everlasting sorrow. He knew the limitations of his life.

He knew the benefits as well.

Clean air, clear water.

Quiet nights lulled to sleep by the murmur of the creek, mornings heralded by birdsong.

The satisfaction of accomplishment, of achievement.

Friends and acquaintances who welcomed him for who he was, not the family he'd been born into.

Or married into.

Nathan pushed back his chair and stood. "I suppose we'll have to leave it to Cora, then. She's always known what she wanted. I doubt this time will be any different."

Even if his heart yearned for her to say she wanted him most of all.

29

Nathan did not return to the bank that afternoon. Cora told herself not to be disappointed. He wasn't used to the quiet work, the hushed surroundings, the walls on all sides. He would accustom himself to it.

Even if she could not quite re-accustom herself to it.

Kincaid reappeared midafternoon. She saw him cross the lobby through the open door of her office. She raised her head, but he did not approach her, going straight to her father's office instead. They remained behind closed doors for a full quarter hour by the brass clock on her desk. Oh, to overhear that conversation! As the door opened and the pair started toward her office, she busied herself with reviewing the proposal before her.

"Coraline," her father said as they paused in the doorway, "Mr. Kincaid has requested that I give you leave for the remainder of the afternoon. He has some matters he'd like to discuss in private." He scowled to the businessman. Interesting. Whatever Kincaid wanted to talk about, her father didn't approve.

"I can't imagine Mr. Kincaid could have anything he must say to me that could not be said in the bank," Cora replied brightly.

Kincaid took a step into her office and lowered his voice. "I'd like to conclude our engagement, Miss Baxter. Surely you can spare a few moments for that."

Was he going to release her before her Thursday deadline? She glanced at her father.

"Go only if you feel comfortable, dearest," he urged.

She rose. "Perhaps Mr. Kincaid would be so good as to walk me home. I must meet with the Tacoma Women's Suffrage Association tonight in any event."

He bowed. "I'd be honored."

She fetched her hat, and they set off.

He clasped his hands behind him as they started up the hill for C Street. He seemed to be deep in thought. A ploy to get her to ask about his thoughts? She refused to gratify him.

They reached the top of the hill and turned onto C Street by the Union Club before he roused himself to speak. "Sorry for taking you away from your work."

Cora cast him a glance. His head was down, his gaze on the rough wood of the sidewalk.

"A great deal piled up while I was away," she acknowledged. "But I'll sort through it soon enough. How was your meeting with Mr. Hardee? He did not come back to the bank."

He chuckled as they passed the Union Club. "I must apologize there as well. I fear I frightened him off with my questions."

Cora shook her head. "Oh, I doubt Mr. Hardee was frightened of anything you would have to say. Why would you need to question him in the first place?"

"Merely attempting to protect you," he assured her. "He may have been one of us years ago, but I cannot like the company he keeps now."

"Eugene Thackery and his wife are delightful," Cora argued as they moved into the residential area, the big houses stretching away on either side of the street. "And I quite enjoyed Mrs. Ashford's company. I sensed a kindred spirit."

"A shame she must limit her contributions to society, being so far out in the wild," he commiserated.

"I am persuaded she will make her influence felt, no matter the size of her sphere," Cora said. Her parents' home was coming up on the right, its stately shape visible among the trees her mother had had planted. "You might as well say it, Mr. Kincaid. Our so-called engagement is over."

"I have a different proposal," he said as they climbed the steps to the door. He moved forward to hold it open for her. Cora led him to the formal parlor. Darcy, who had been dusting there, ducked her head and clutched her rag close.

"Will you let my mother know we have company?" Cora asked her.

She bobbed a curtsy and cast Kincaid a glance out of the corner of her eye. "Yes, miss." She hurried from the room.

"I'm not interested in a different proposal," Cora said as she spread her skirts to sit on the chair by the window. "I believe I've made that abundantly clear."

"Ah, but I would be remiss if I did not take advantage of the opportunity." He went down on one knee in front of her. "Coraline, I have thought hard on our conversation last night, and I know I can be the man you want. Please, honor our engagement and marry me."

Cora shook her head. "I'm glad you've reconsidered your business practices, sir, but I will not marry you. I wish you would accept that."

He took her hands. "How can I when I now know anything else could mean your family's ruin?"

She pulled out of his grip. "Our ruin? What are you talking about?"

"That announcement in the paper," he pressed. "You blamed me, but it was your mother. She tried to trap me."

Anger pushed her to her feet. "That's a lie! My mother would never risk censure."

His eyes gleamed as he rose. "I have it from Winston himself. How do you think her friends, or better yet, her rivals will react when they learn of her cunning?"

He had to be spinning more lies, trying to catch her like a spider in its web. Cora clamped her mouth shut, but he shook his head.

"Ah, Coraline, can you not see the truth? She is so determined to marry you off that she would do anything. Given your beauty and accomplishments, some may wonder why she must go to such lengths."

"Why indeed," Cora flung back at him. "You seem ready to take me no matter how tarnished."

He drew in an audible breath through his nose. "I tire of your games. I have been patient. I no longer have that luxury. This Panic has affected my businesses more than I care to let on in polite society. A Seattle bank has offered the funds I need to keep my businesses operating, if I can prove myself respectable. The evaluator was very pleased to see the announcement of our engagement."

How ironic. No doubt a proposal evaluator like her,

looking at profit, loss, risk, benefit, debit and credit. And she was the dominant feature in the credit column.

"I'm sorry," she said. "I won't marry you."

"You will," he growled. "You stand in the way of everything I planned."

"This financial mess is of your own making," Cora insisted. "I won't be party to it."

His color flamed. "Stupid girl. You have no idea how the world really works. I've done my best to conform to your mother's rules. No more. You should be thankful I'm willing to accept you after what she did. Marry me, and I'll allow you, your mother, and your stepfather to keep your places in society. Refuse, and you'll all pay."

Fear nibbled at the edges of the anger sustaining her. No! She could not give in! She would not let him win. She could accept whatever censure might come.

But her mother? Oh, she would not survive such a fall.

"You promised," she said, frustrated to hear her voice crack. "I will cry off."

He raised a brow. "And have me declare you and your mother nothing but conniving tarts, in public?"

"Better shamed in public than married to you," Cora retorted.

His fist flew. It caught her on the cheek, rattled her teeth, and her knees buckled. She grabbed the back of the chair to keep from hitting the floor.

"That was your fault," he said, towering over her. "Perhaps now you'll see what's good for you. My financial troubles are only a momentary setback. I offer you a future of wealth. You offer the respectability that's been denied me. It's a fair trade. You will marry me, and you will be an obedient wife, or I can promise it will not go well for those you love."

"That's quite enough, Mr. Kincaid."

He turned at the sound of her mother's voice, and Cora stared. Her mother stood in the doorway, a pistol gripped in both hands.

"You will step away from my daughter and leave this house," she continued in her cool, crisp voice. "You are no longer welcome under my roof."

He eyed her, and Cora could almost hear his mind calculating. Did her mother mean it? Did she know how to use the weapon? Could he take it from her?

As if she heard the same thoughts, her mother pointed the weapon at his chest. "It's been a while since I used one of these, and I am understandably upset by your treatment of my daughter. I doubt I could shoot to kill, but in my agitation, I might aim for your arm and hit your stomach. I understand stomach wounds are a particularly foul way to die."

Kincaid washed white. "Your servant, madam."

Her mother backed into the hall to give him room to leave, and Cora went to join her. She must have sent for reinforcements, for Oscar and Charlie came barreling through the kitchen door then, Cook behind them armed with a rolling pin, Darcy with a fireplace poker, and Lily with one of Cora's long hatpins.

"I would have been a good husband to you," he said to Cora.

"No, Mr. Kincaid," Cora said, jaw throbbing. "You're incapable of being a good husband. If I see you again, it will be in court on charges of assault." She made sure he was down the steps before shutting the door behind him.

Her mother lowered the pistol and sagged. "Lock the door."

Cora did so, then hurried to her side. "Oh, Mother, you were wonderful."

"Never knew you had it in you, missus," Darcy marveled.

Her mother handed Oscar the gun. "Put this away before I hurt someone."

"Yes, ma'am," he said. Then he saluted her. So did Charlie. Oscar led him and the others for the kitchen.

Cora linked arms with her mother and felt a tremor run through her.

"Do you really know how to shoot?" she asked as she walked her to the family parlor.

Her mother nodded. "My second husband would on occasion become violent after imbibing overmuch. Protection, for you and for myself, seemed wise. Our gardener at the time showed me what to do."

Her face fell as she collapsed onto her chair. "Oh, Coraline, please forgive me for ever suggesting that man might make you a good husband. I thought you were merely being headstrong to refuse him. I didn't see how you could possibly climb that mountain, so I arranged for the announcement to be placed in the paper. I thought it would run the day after we returned, when things were settled, but you came down a day earlier than expected and you'd done it. There was no time to retract the announcement."

"You should have told me," Cora said, hand coming up to rub her sore cheek. "But you couldn't have known Mr. Kincaid was this awful. I misjudged him myself. I thought pride would force him to accept my refusal. He'll tell everyone the story about that announcement. I'm afraid we must prepare ourselves for a scandal."

———— {{ }} ————

Once again, Nathan stood looking up at the grand house on Tacoma Avenue. He had no expectation of a welcome. Why was he here?

My grace is sufficient for thee: for my strength is made perfect in weakness.

"Well, Lord," he said aloud, "you'll find plenty of room to be strong here."

He made himself climb to the door. This time, an older manservant answered his knock.

"Nathan Hardee," he told the fellow. "Here to see his mother."

The man's snowy brows shot up, then he must have remembered himself, for he inclined his head. "If you would be so good as to wait in the entryway, sir, I will endeavor to see if madam is home."

She was home. The servant would have said if she was out. Asking whether a lady was home was a polite way of saying that Nathan's welcome wasn't a given. He already knew that.

And so he stood in the entryway, rocking from his toes to his heels and back on the parquet floor, trying not to notice the massive portrait that covered the right wall, showing a stern-faced man with his hand possessively on his lovely wife's shoulder. And no children in sight.

The clatter of heels on hardwood made him turn. His mother stopped in the corridor to stare at him, hand to her lace-covered throat. Every golden hair was in place, every inch of her amethyst-colored skirts was pressed and proper.

"Nathan," she murmured. "I thought I'd refused you enough that you'd never return."

337

He couldn't tell whether she thought his return now was a good thing or a bad thing. But she was talking to him, and for that he was thankful.

"I was in town," he said. "Supply run."

She took in the fine coat and trousers. "I see."

The words hung in the air, like a wall between them.

"I've been offered a job at the Puget Sound Bank of Commerce," he blurted out. "I'm not sure I want to take it."

She moved closer, then opened the door on his left. "Come into the parlor. Let's talk."

Feeling numb, he followed.

It looked very much like the family parlor in Cora's mother's house: overstuffed furniture draped with lace-edged doilies, polished wood occasional tables crowded with ornate boxes and porcelain statues. It seemed his mother had amassed a great deal since he'd last seen her.

She sat on the camelback sofa that was covered in a flowered pattern and nodded to the spot next to her. "Please, join me. It's been an age."

"At your request." He couldn't help the reminder, but he sat beside her, feeling as if he'd dropped onto one of the flowered meadows at Paradise Park.

She made a face. "I know, Nathan, and I must apologize. After your father died, my world fell apart. And I lashed out. I thought I'd found a better way, a more stable existence."

He glanced around at the rich furnishings again. "It seems you have."

"It is gilding only," she murmured. "The substance is missing. It's taken me years to understand that. Please, forgive me."

Sorrow trembled in her voice. Forgiveness was surprisingly easy. Trust, however, was harder.

"You did what you thought you must to survive," he told her. "I see that. That's what I did too. But are you well now? I know too many people who have been hurt by this Panic."

She nodded. "My last husband left me well off, with solid investments that should see me through. I've found friends in my church to sustain me. And you? You made a life for yourself? You have friends, a family?"

Cora's face sprang to mind.

"I have friends," he allowed. "Land out in the Succotash Valley, a cabin, a barn."

She frowned. "Then how did you win an offer with the Bank of Commerce?"

"Mr. Winston, the bank director, and his daughter, Coraline Baxter, needed a guide to climb Mount Rainier."

She pressed a hand to her chest. "You must have done an exceptionally good job to be offered a position as cashier."

"Associate director," he corrected her.

She blinked, then her brows came down. "They want something from you. You mustn't compromise your integrity, Nathan. You know where that can lead."

"I," Nathan said, "am not my father."

She cringed and looked away. "No, of course not. But your face just now, when you spoke of your land and your cabin. You love them. And you're obviously good at this guide business to find a way for Miss Baxter to reach the summit."

Nathan chuckled. "If I hadn't been along, she'd have found a way to do it herself."

"Perhaps," his mother said. "But you think you would be happy returning to society now?"

"I don't know," Nathan admitted. "That's one of the reasons I'm considering refusing."

"And the others?" she asked.

He should not confide in her. This change in her attitude was too unexpected. Yet she genuinely seemed to care about the decision, about him. She'd once been his biggest supporter. Shouldn't he try to find a way to bridge the chasm between them?

"I'm in love with Cora," he said.

Her smile was sad. "So are a great many men, I hear, or at least in love with what she represents—beauty, wealth, power. Small wonder Mr. Kincaid proposed. Or are you merely hoping to steal his bride the way he robbed your father of hope?"

Nathan stiffened. "It's not that. You didn't see her on the mountain. She was focused and fearless. She knew what she wanted, but she was prepared to give it all up if it meant protecting her stepfather. When she smiles, the world is a better place."

"I see she made quite an impression," his mother said. "And does Miss Baxter feel the same way about you, despite her engagement?"

A shame he could not tell her the truth about Cora's engagement, but he'd promised to keep it quiet. Nathan leaned back against the sofa. "I don't know how Cora feels. Sometimes I think she does. Other times I wonder how she could."

She raised her chin. "Nonsense. Any girl would be fortunate to marry my son."

Now that sounded like the mother he remembered.

"Hence the interest in the bank position," he said. "Coraline Baxter can't marry a mountain man. She can marry the associate director of a bank."

She cocked her head. "If Coraline Baxter cannot marry

a man with a cabin in the Succotash Valley and the skills to climb a mountain, then perhaps that man has no business marrying her."

Nathan shook his head. "Spoken like my mother."

She reached out and took his hands. "Then allow me to be your mother and share with you what I've learned from this tragedy with your father. We can too easily focus on the wrong circumstances. He wanted position, standing, and so did I. I blame myself for not encouraging him to put more important things first. Faith. Family. It's taken me years to reach that point. Here, I'll show you." She released him to go to a hutch along one wall, bending to open the doors at the base. Lifting out the instrument, she brought it to him.

"My violin," Nathan marveled, taking it from her hands. Not a speck of dust marred the gold of the wood, as if she'd tended it, waiting for him to come claim it.

"I never forgot," she murmured. "Don't make the same mistake we did, Nathan. Choose a profession that provides satisfaction, and surround yourself with people who honor that choice. Anything else leads to sorrow."

Her words, her care of the violin, touched something inside him. "Thank you, Mother. Whatever I decide, I hope you and I can remain family."

Her silver-gray eyes swam with tears. "Oh, I'd like that very much. And your Cora too."

His Cora. He could only hope.

30

Cora winced as her mother laid a cold compress on her face where she stretched out on her bed. Her teeth ached, and the hand mirror Lily brought her showed the purple spreading across her cheek.

"You cannot go out in public like this," her mother said, stepping back to eye her. "People will talk."

"Let them," Cora said, handing the mirror back to her maid. "If we're to be part of a scandal, I'd be delighted to tell them exactly how I came to sport this bruise. I'll start with Mimi and the other suffragettes tonight."

"That will be all, Lily," her mother said, and the maid curtsied before leaving.

"Don't cause a stir, Cora," her mother said in the quiet that followed. "Perhaps this will all blow over, without Mr. Kincaid resorting to blackmail. I only heard the end of his horrid conversation with you, but that's what he implied. He intends to ruin your reputation by ruining mine."

Now her stomach ached as much as her teeth. "Yes, Mother. But we will survive. We must."

"But if Mr. Kincaid tells the story," her mother said, eyes shadowed, "I'll never find a good match for you."

"Perhaps," Cora said, "we can dispense with finding a good match."

Her mother's lips trembled. "You mustn't give up, darling. He may not be believed. Not everyone appreciates his finer qualities."

"After today, Mother, I think we can agree that Mr. Kincaid has no finer qualities."

"Yes, you're right."

The concession was said so softly, Cora had to remove the compress and turn to look at her mother to make sure she'd heard correctly. "Did we just agree on something?"

"I'm sure I don't know why that would surprise you," her mother said with her usual sniff. "You were always clever. It was only a matter of time before you saw things my way."

Cora started laughing, then winced again as her face protested.

Her mother rose, smile hinting. "Now, then, Coraline, you have been through a great deal. You should rest. I'll send Charlie to let Mimi know you won't be attending the meeting tonight. Lily can bring you some chamomile."

She ought to protest, but she was as tired as when she'd climbed the mountain. As her mother left, Cora rolled onto her back, replaced the compress, and closed her eyes. Rest, her mother said. That was the expectation of society—that she faint, recline, while others dealt with the difficulties that had laid her low. Why couldn't she convince even her mother that she would never be that person? Would Mrs. Ashford go into a decline if she faced penury? Would Susan Longmire refuse to rise if a flood threatened? Fay Fuller certainly hadn't shrunk from climbing a mountain.

So why was she shrinking even for a moment from the idea of accepting Nathan's proposal, should he offer?

Nathan was fresh air, blowing away the doubt and worry.

Nathan was truth, strength. He'd showed her a better way to worship, to find faith again.

Nathan was her alpenstock. She could lean on him, knowing he'd be there to help and encourage.

Yes, she would have to give up everything she'd been raised to embrace, but wasn't he worth the sacrifice?

Sacrifice?

She sat up so suddenly the compress fell into the lap of her gown. Why hadn't she seen it before? She'd been as bad as her mother—focusing on the trappings of wealth, determined to use them to gain independence, for herself and other women. An independent woman would always be odd in the sort of society her mother favored. She'd be whispered about behind painted fans, gossiped about over tea in bone china cups. She would be made to feel out of place, an aberration, so as to maintain that very society.

In her own way, she was as trapped as the women who married men like Cash Kincaid to keep up appearances. An independent woman would never be valued for who she was, what she'd accomplished, perhaps for a while even *after* they'd won the vote.

But she would be accepted, even applauded, in Nathan's world.

He'd said society no longer fit, and she'd felt the same. Now she knew why.

Lily eased into the room then, as if expecting to find Cora

in a swoon. She started when she saw her sitting up, and the tea sloshed in the cup.

Cora rose to take it from her hand. "Thank you, Lily. I need you to bring me the city directory and my father's travel desk. I'll have you deliver notes for appointments tomorrow. I have a future to secure, for myself, my mother and father, and anyone who relies on Cash Kincaid. And I don't mind causing a stir to do it."

Cora was out of the house the next morning before her mother rose. She breakfasted with her father first.

"Your poor face, dearest," he said as he regarded her over his coffee. "Your mother told me what happened. I've half a mind to accost Kincaid myself, but I fear this is at least partly my fault."

Cora set down her cup. Chewing didn't hurt as much this morning as it had last night, but she had no intention of sampling the ham on the sideboard. "I will never agree you had any part in Kincaid's schemes."

"His schemes, no." He pleated the napkin beside his plate, gaze dropping. "But I couldn't hide the truth from him, and I shouldn't have hidden it from you. I heard the story from your mother Sunday evening. I simply didn't want you to be angry with her. Can you forgive me?"

"Father." When he looked up, she smiled. "Of course I forgive you. I've forgiven Mother as well. But I need you both to understand that I must make my own choices about my future."

He peered closer. "You are still considering Nathan, are you not? I find him in all ways a good man."

"So do I," Cora assured him, rising. She came around the table and pressed a kiss to his cheek. "I've a number of errands to run today. I will only come into the bank for a moment."

He waved a hand. "Whatever you need, dearest."

She returned home just before dinner, thoroughly pleased. She had never considered showing her previous assessment of Cash Kincaid's business practices to anyone else. How gratifying that others found it as persuasive as she had.

Darcy met her at the door, as if she'd been keeping watch.

"Mr. Hardee is here," she murmured as she took Cora's hat and gloves. "He's with your mother in the formal parlor, and neither looks too happy about it, if you don't mind my saying."

"I'll see to it," Cora promised, and Darcy hurried away as if she didn't want to be near enough to scold.

Cora smoothed down her blue-striped skirts. She'd dressed to impress for her meetings with the worker organizations, but she didn't mind the tailored shirtwaist or the lace at her cuffs and throat. She looked every inch a lady who knew her own mind. Only her heart seemed to protest, for it was pounding faster than her steps as she strolled into the room.

Her mother was in her favorite chair, skirts held close. Nathan, once more in his mountain clothes, was again relegated to a chair by the window, where he might not dirty anything important.

He rose at the sight of her. "Cora." His eyes widened as his gaze touched her face, and he took a step forward. "Are you all right? What happened?"

"An accident," her mother answered calmly. "I advised her to rest, but young ladies these days are so determined to prove themselves competent."

"You needn't posture, Mother," Cora said, going to join him. "By tomorrow, everyone in Tacoma will know the depths to which Mr. Kincaid can sink."

Her mother frowned as if she wondered about Cora's meaning, but Nathan's fingers grazed Cora's cheek, cool against the heat of the bruise. "He did this? He won't live the night."

She caught his fingers. "No! I am honored you wish to protect me, but I have this in hand. And I will not have you stoop to his level."

He studied her a moment longer before nodding. "As you wish."

She squeezed his fingers before turning. "Mother, I intend to say some very pointed and personal things to Nathan. You are welcome to stay, but I will understand if you prefer to leave. And under no circumstances may you interrupt, explain away my words, or argue against them."

Her mother brushed off her skirts. "This is how you speak to me?"

"Sadly, yes," Cora said. "I love you, Mother, but I must do what I know to be right."

She waited for the protest, the scold, the guilt that would wrap around her and squeeze her purpose from her heart. Instead, her mother rose and glided from the room without another word.

Well! Cora hid her smile of triumph, squared her shoulders, and faced Nathan. He was regarding her with a half smile.

"You look like you did the day we first met," he said. "A plan in mind and determined to achieve it. Should I be afraid?"

Her mouth was dry. "Perhaps. This plan is even more important than climbing Rainier. I have a proposal for you."

He cocked his head. "I'm listening."

She drew in a breath. "I want to marry you, but I'm aware I'm not made to be the sort of wife many men prefer. I can't cook or sew beyond embroidery, but you know I'm not afraid of hard work or learning new skills. I will not grovel or humble myself before you. If you're wrong, I'll tell you. If I compliment you, it will be because you earned it. We'll live by the lake, build the accommodations you wanted, help others climb the mountain. I won't miss Tacoma. I have no interest in maintaining appearances or in trying to pretend I enjoy society. I will, of course, work with Mrs. Ashford to drum up support for women's rights." She stuck out her hand. "What do you say?"

"No," he said.

Cora blinked, hand falling. "No? But I thought . . ."

He opened his arms and pulled her closer. "I love you, Cora, and nothing would make me happier than to be your husband. But not under those terms. Allow me to make you a counterproposal."

———— {{ }} ————

She gazed up at him. Her eyes were as bright as a sunny morning and warmed him nearly as much. But she could not like his refusal. Would she refuse him in turn? He held his breath.

"I'm listening," she said.

He allowed himself to relax a little. "I'm not what your mother would expect for you in a husband either."

She rolled her eyes. "I've had quite enough of that sort, I promise you."

"Still, you should be warned. I've grown a bit set in my ways. I tend to order people about. Like you, I have strong opinions, and I'm not shy about stating them."

A smile tugged at her pretty lips. "Do tell."

His smile was building as well. "But I understand what you bring to a marriage—strength, determination, and drive. You light up every room you enter. You give me confidence to try."

A slight frown marked her brow. "Then why refuse me?"

He gave her a squeeze. "Because you see things I've never considered, opportunities and threats. Maybe that's why you saw so clearly what I'd even hidden from myself. When my father died, I ran away. I came out of the experience a better man, but I abandoned my friends and family all the same. I don't want you to make the same mistake."

"I'm not running away," she protested. "I'm running toward something—you, our future together."

"I see that, but you're still leaving people you love behind— your mother and Winston. Miss Carruthers. You're leaving work you enjoy. So, here's what I propose. Marry me, come live in the shadow of the mountain with me, allow me to love and honor you all the days of my life. Spring through fall, we will stay at the cabin, build our retreat, and show others the joy of God's creation."

She nodded as if considering it. "And the rest of the year?"

"When the snow starts to fly, we'll move into town and assist Winston at the bank. We'll see them other times of the year, of course. Until there's a closer store, we'll still need to make a supply run every month."

He gazed down at the woman who had become as important to him as breath. "So, what do you say, Cora? Will you marry me?"

"Yes."

Surprise made his hands fall. "That easy?"

She wrapped her arms about his waist as if to keep him close. "I review proposals, remember? I can see the merits in this one. Besides, I love you too."

He had to kiss her then. All the fire, all the promise, all the joy rushed through him. This, this was real and true. This was right.

This was love.

31

Cora clung to him, joy stealing speech and thought. She'd wondered whether such feelings could last. These were true and sure. They would only grow with time. Here, with him, was where she was meant to be. This was her calling.

From out in the hall came the sound of the door, then hurried footsteps. "Coraline, Mrs. Winston! Oh, you must hear."

Cora separated from Nathan as her father bustled into the parlor, hat askew and mustache spiking. If he noticed them still standing scandalously close, he didn't show it.

"You will not believe it," he declared, pacing about the room. "*I* scarcely believe it. Where is your mother? She must hear this."

"Calm yourself, Mr. Winston," her mother said, moving into the room in a whisper of silk. "What could possibly warrant such emotion?"

Had her mother been in the room a few moments earlier, she would have seen a rather thorough display of emotion. Cora exchanged smiles with Nathan and knew he was thinking the same.

"Kincaid's workers are in revolt," her father announced,

chest heaving so much the silver buttons on his paisley waist-coat glittered. "Protests have broken out all over the city, and the suffragettes are marching in front of his largest mill. Stories will appear in special editions of the newspapers by tomorrow."

Cora's smile must have been glowing, for her mother frowned at her. "Coraline, did you have something to do with this?"

"Mr. Kincaid had already made a bad name for himself with his employees," Cora said. "I merely gave them the information they needed to make a case for themselves. And the Tacoma Women's Suffrage Association was glad to help, especially after they learned how this bruise came to be."

Her mother's mouth tightened, but her father rubbed his hands together. "Excellent work, dearest. Those men deserve fair pay." His smile took in Nathan. "Oh, hello, my boy. Come to call on Cora?"

Nathan's gaze was all for her. "As often as I can."

Cora took his hand and gave it a squeeze before facing her parents. "And I have news as well. Nathan and I are going to be wed."

Her father clapped his hands. "Marvelous news! All my congratulations! Then you'll be taking the position at the bank, my boy?"

"Not exactly," Nathan said. "Cora and I have big plans."

"If you'd both sit down," Cora said, "we'll explain them to you."

It took some time. Her mother had doubts, and her father had questions, but by the time Darcy poked her head in to ask if Mr. Hardee was staying for dinner, everything had been settled.

"Give us a quarter hour," her mother instructed the maid, "and then you may serve." She turned to her husband. "Mr. Winston, you will want to change."

He popped to his feet. "Excellent thought. I'll just be a moment." He paused to peck Cora on the cheek. "Congratulations again, dearest. I think you've made a very good choice."

As he trotted from the room, her mother looked to Cora. "I must apologize, to you both."

Cora blinked. As usual, her mother continued without her response.

"I was certain, Mr. Hardee, that you were not the man for my daughter. I will concede that my view may have been too narrow. Coraline has always known her own mind, and I concur with Mr. Winston. She has made a good choice this time."

Cora laced her fingers with Nathan's. "The only choice for me."

"Indeed." Her mother rose to come offer her hands. Cora released Nathan to take them, and her mother drew her to her feet as well. "I hope you know I only ever wanted the best for you."

Cora pulled her into a hug. "I know, Mother. However much we disagreed, I always knew you loved me." She disengaged and looked to Nathan, who stood to join them.

"I hope you can understand my decision now," Cora continued to her mother. "This life was too constraining. With Nathan, I feel as if I can finally fly."

Tears gathered in her mother's eyes. "Oh, I'm so glad."

"I will do everything I can to see your daughter happy, always," Nathan promised, deep voice rough with emotion.

Her mother suffered his hug, then sniffed. "Now, that is entirely enough of such sentimentality. You must tell me more about this retreat, Mr. Hardee. I can advise you on the sort of assembly rooms you will require." She sailed for the dining room as if expecting them to follow.

Nathan shook his head. "Do you think she will ever call me Nathan?"

"Doubtful," Cora said. "She still calls my father Mr. Winston. Just don't let her bully you into building assembly rooms."

"I don't bully easily," he said, standing taller.

Cora laughed. "That's true enough." She sobered. "Speaking of bullies, do you think this workers' rebellion will be enough to quell Cash Kincaid?"

They didn't learn the answer until they attended services on Sunday.

In between, her life became a flurry of activity. She and Nathan rode out to Shem's Dockside Saloon to tell Waldo. The old pioneer hugged her, then pulled back, eyes shining with his tears. "Always wanted a daughter."

Then she made sure her mother sent a correct announcement to the paper about who Cora was going to marry. It ran in the Thursday edition, along with the story of her climb, but it was still the talk of the town when she went to the bank that day.

"Never liked the fellow," one of the businessmen who was requesting a loan told Cora when he came to discuss changes in the proposal with her. "Good for you for finding a better groom."

Mimi said the same when she stopped by the bank on Friday morning.

"These banker's hours are entirely inconvenient," she declared before plopping down on the chair in front of Cora's desk in a flurry of linen and lace. "I wanted to rush right over and congratulate you and your mountain man the moment I saw the announcement, then I realized you'd be working. You've no idea how hard I had to work to convince Mother to let me visit you here. She seems to think you're doing something more subversive than supporting suffrage." She wiggled her black brows.

Cora nodded toward the lobby. "I see she insisted you bring your brother as escort."

Mimi twisted, and they both looked out the open door at the young man conversing with Cora's father.

"It appears Peter is growing into his long legs," Cora commented.

"Like a thoroughbred," Mimi agreed, and they both giggled.

As Mimi's gaze came back to her, she frowned. "That bruise still shows, I see."

Cora touched the spot, which was already greening. Lily had insisted on covering it with face powder, which had only turned it yellow. "A little, but it's fading."

"Unlike the zeal of our suffragette sisters," Mimi told her. "Between your climb and the revolt against Kincaid Industries, each one of our ladies is thoroughly revived. I'm planning a march on Olympia to catch the attention of the state government."

"Well done," Cora said, lowering her hand. "There's something else you might want to factor into your plans. I'd like you to be my wedding attendant."

Mimi squealed, hopped to her feet, and rushed around the

desk to hug her. Over her shoulder, Cora saw several people glance their way with upraised brows.

"That's what we like to see at the Puget Sound Bank of Commerce," her father told them all, beaming. "Happy patrons."

Her mother wasn't nearly so happy about the arrangement.

"Really, Coraline," she said Friday evening over dinner, "you cannot simply marry and ride off. It will take me at least a month to make all the arrangements—the proper flowers for the church, invitations printed and mailed, and your gown chosen, created, and fitted."

"I don't need any of that, Mother," Cora told her. "You and Father, Nathan's mother, Waldo, the Thackerys, the ladies of the Tacoma Women's Suffrage Association and their husbands, and Mimi and her family are all I planned to invite, and we can simply let them know the time and place to arrive. Mimi can wear any of her ball gowns, and so can I. It isn't as if I'll be needing them in the wilderness."

Her mother sniffed. "Nonsense. My daughter must be married in style."

But Cora held her ground. So did Nathan.

"I leave for the mountain tomorrow after services," he explained to her mother and father over dinner on Saturday. "I'll be back with Waldo in two weeks for more supplies. We'll be married then."

Her mother's mouth was a tight line, but she nodded.

Cora had also met Nathan's mother. She hadn't been sure how to react knowing his mother had refused to see him all those years, but the society hostess's welcome was warmer than her mother's and she obviously regretted past mistakes. Cora could only hope for better times ahead.

Once more, whispers blew through the church when they entered for services on Sunday, and any number of people stopped them afterward to congratulate them on their upcoming wedding. While Cora's mother and father talked with the minister, Mimi took her arm and drew her and Nathan aside.

"If you're done basking in the adulation, I have other news you'll want to hear." She peered up at both of them. "Mr. Kincaid has left town. Permanently."

Cora started. "You mean he ran away!"

"Crawled away, more like," her friend said, shaking out her lavender skirts as if she would shake him off as well. "Rumor has it he hopped a boxcar East to escape his creditors."

"And his businesses?" Nathan asked, frown evident.

"Will be sold for pennies on the dollar, most likely," Cora said. "He implied only a loan would save them. I hope the new owners will negotiate with the worker organizations for fair wages."

"Yes, yes," Mimi said with a wave of her hand. "But I must know, Cora. When is the wedding? What will you wear? What do you want me to wear?"

Cora smiled at her. "Wear whatever makes you happy, and I will do the same."

Nathan caught her arm close. "And to answer your other question, Miss Carruthers, the wedding is in two weeks."

Mimi's cry of delight turned all heads in their direction, and it was some time before Cora and Nathan could extricate themselves from another round of well-wishes.

Leaving her parents to take the carriage, they walked home down C Street, past the tall, elegant homes and the gardens that helped proclaim their status. Carriages rattled by, carrying their occupants to and from church services. Other gentlemen and ladies strolled the wooden sidewalk.

"Sure you won't miss all this?" he asked her.

The wail of the train horn seemed to fade when she looked in his eyes. Green, like the forest where she'd be living. Warm, like the glow inside her.

"I'm sure," Cora said. "This was never home. You are home, Nathan. With you, I can be who I was meant to be."

He cradled her hand. "When I'm with you, I'm on the summit again, and the view is glorious."

"A view of forever," Cora agreed. "Let's see where it takes us next."

Dear Reader,

Thank you for choosing Cora and Nathan's story. When I visited Mount Rainier National Park a few years ago, I purchased a postcard showing Fay Fuller as she was depicted after her historic climb, and I knew I had to write about a lady like her.

Mount Rainier is very special to me. I grew up near it and live in its shadow today. My father loved that mountain. He took us camping or hiking up on it nearly every weekend. He always helped me find the perfect alpenstock, though we always left it on the mountain so as not to take away from nature. I've been to Indian Henry's Hunting Ground, the area of the mountain Henry favored for hunting mountain goat and picking berries. I've hiked Rampart Ridge, visited Narada Falls (Cushman Falls in Cora's day), and wandered through fields of wildflowers. My father liked to brag that I hiked all the way to the ice caves (now gone) above Paradise when I was only six! There are pictures of me up on his shoulders during the hike, so I'm pretty sure I didn't make it all the way on my own.

Cora did, though. So did Fay Fuller, Edith Corbett, and Susan Longmire in the early 1890s. Like the Long-mires and the Ashfords, they are historical figures, as is

Henry So-To-Lick. Today, he is known as Indian Henry, but the first guidebook to Mount Tacoma, published in August 1893, around the time that Cora makes her climb, notes him as Henry, so that's what I called him in the story. I also could not verify that Fay Fuller was in Tacoma in August 1893. She left to cover the Chicago World's Fair in July, but it appears she was home in September, when she was elected poet of the Washington State Press Association. All the attitudes and descriptions of these historical figures are as accurate as I could make them, but their words are my own. I also tried to use place names in vogue at the time. I grew up knowing Longmire and Paradise. Cora and Nathan would have known Longmire's Hot Springs, Medical Springs, or Soda Springs, and Paradise Park.

I could not identify a Tacoma-based suffragette group in my research, but the movement in Washington State was demoralized in 1893 after three attempts (two successful) to give women the vote. Small wonder Mimi and Cora hoped to reignite interest with a historic climb. Washington State granted women the right to vote in 1910, ten years before the nation.

When it comes to climbing, I have nothing but respect for those who scale the mountain to the summit. Today, it takes months of training, sophisticated equipment, and knowledgeable guides to reach the heights. But historical records show that many climbers summited Rainier with none of those things. Even the ropes that link climbers safely together were rarely used, being deemed a danger to the other climbers. Len Longmire, mentioned in the book, once reached the crater in his shirtsleeves and suffered no ill effects!

When I first proposed this book to my editor, the incomparable Rachel McRae, I couldn't wait to research all the history that surrounds me. The Tacoma Public Library has the Northwest Room, with copies of original materials. More materials beckon from the Washington State History Research Center. Because of the pandemic, I wasn't able to visit either of those places, so I am indebted to Google Books and the many historical tomes I was able to purchase to flesh out Cora's life and times. It was from those books that I learned about the controversy over Rainier's name, a controversy that even resulted in public fisticuffs on occasion.

From the shadow of the mountain,

Regina Scott

Regina Scott started writing novels in the third grade. Thankfully for literature as we know it, she didn't sell her first novel until she learned a bit more about writing. Since her first book was published, her stories have traveled the globe, with translations in many languages including Dutch, German, Italian, and Portuguese. She now has more than fifty published works of warm, witty romance.

She credits her late father with instilling in her a love for the wilderness and our national parks. She has toured the Grand Canyon, Yellowstone, Crater Lake, Yosemite, the Olympics, and the Redwoods and currently lives forty-five minutes from the gates of Mount Rainier with her husband of thirty years.

Regina Scott has dressed as a Regency dandy, driven four-in-hand, learned to fence, and sailed on a tall ship, all in the name of research, of course. Learn more about her at www .reginascott.com.

Don't Miss Book 1 in the

AMERICAN WONDERS
★ COLLECTION ★

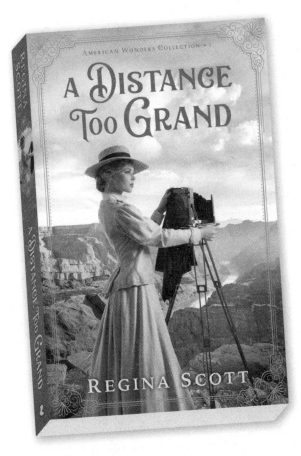

When a spunky photographer wrangles her way onto an 1871
survey crew of the Grand Canyon, she thinks nothing can stand in
her way. But her mind changes when she finds out she'll be working
alongside the one man she doesn't want to fall in love with.

R Revell
a division of Baker Publishing Group
www.RevellBooks.com

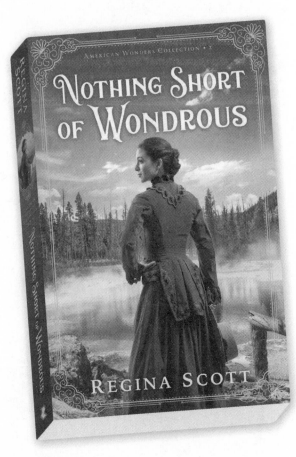

Connect with
Award-Winning Author

Regina Scott

www.reginascott.com

authorreginascott